In the center of the room, Ereshkigal strode into the pool of bl~~ood~~

Kane watched her ~~...~~ th the surface as she ~~...~~ il of feathers ruffled ~~...~~ away. A trail of bloo~~d...~~ floor already, like str~~...~~

Kane stepped onto the first of the springy, leaf-like steps descending toward the pool, and something struck him from behind. Suddenly, Kane found himself falling, tumbling end over end down the staircase.

He rolled as he reached the bottom, bringing the Sin Eater up as one of Ereshkigal's Terror Priests leapt from the topmost stair. His torso seemed freakishly long and his limbs stretched impossibly out at his sides like the wings of some bird of prey.

The man was throwing something. Kane saw it flash in the air even as he rolled.

Kane fired.

Across the room, Ereshkigal was still standing in the pool. Blood lapped at her slender hips. She smiled as she fixed Kane with her stare. Her lips moved and she began to speak the words of the chant designed to deliver the equation to the human body—the equation that could kill a man.

Other titles in this series:

Shadow Scourge

Hell Rising

Doom Dynasty

Tigers of Heaven

Purgatory Road

Sargasso Plunder

Tomb of Time

Prodigal Chalice

Devil in the Moon

Dragoneye

Far Empire

Equinox Zero

Talon and Fang

Sea of Plague

Awakening

Mad God's Wrath

Sun Lord

Mask of the Sphinx

Uluru Destiny

Evil Abyss

Children of the Serpent

Successors

Cerberus Storm

Refuge

Rim of the World

Lords of the Deep

Hydra's Ring

Closing the Cosmic Eye

Skull Throne

Satan's Seed

Dark Goddess

Grailstone Gambit

Ghostwalk

Pantheon of Vengeance

Death Cry

Serpent's Tooth

Shadow Box

Janus Trap

Warlord of the Pit

Reality Echo

Infinity Breach

Oblivion Stone

Distortion Offensive

Cradle of Destiny

Scarlet Dream

Truth Engine

Infestation Cubed

Planet Hate

Dragon City

God War

Genesis Sinister

Savage Dawn

Sorrow Space

Immortal Twilight

Cosmic Rift

Wings of Death

Necropolis

Shadow Born

Judgment Plague

Terminal White

James Axler
Outlanders®

HELL'S MAW

A GOLD EAGLE BOOK FROM
WORLDWIDE®

TORONTO • NEW YORK • LONDON
AMSTERDAM • PARIS • SYDNEY • HAMBURG
STOCKHOLM • ATHENS • TOKYO • MILAN
MADRID • WARSAW • BUDAPEST • AUCKLAND

Recycling programs
for this product may
not exist in your area.

First edition May 2015

ISBN-13: 978-0-373-63886-4

Hell's Maw

Copyright © 2015 by Worldwide Library

Special thanks to Rik Hoskin for his contribution to this work.

It is easy to go down into Hell; night and day, the gates of dark Death stand wide; but to climb back again, to retrace one's steps to the upper air—there's the rub, the task.

—Virgil

The Road to Outlands—
From Secret Government Files to the Future

Almost two hundred years after the global holocaust, Kane, a former Magistrate of Cobaltville, often thought the world had been lucky to survive at all after a nuclear device detonated in the Russian embassy in Washington, DC. The aftermath—forever known as skydark—reshaped continents and turned civilization into ashes.

Nearly depopulated, America became the Deathlands—poisoned by radiation, home to chaos and mutated life forms. Feudal rule reappeared in the form of baronies, while remote outposts clung to a brutish existence.

What eventually helped shape this wasteland were the redoubts, the secret preholocaust military installations with stores of weapons, and the home of gateways, the locational matter-transfer facilities. Some of the redoubts hid clues that had once fed wild theories of government cover-ups and alien visitations.

Rearmed from redoubt stockpiles, the barons consolidated their power and reclaimed technology for the villes. Their power, supported by some invisible authority, extended beyond their fortified walls to what was now called the Outlands. It was here that the rootstock of humanity survived, living with hellzones and chemical storms, hounded by Magistrates.

In the villes, rigid laws were enforced—to atone for the sins of the past and prepare the way for a better future. That was the barons' public credo and their right-to-rule.

Kane, along with friend and fellow Magistrate Grant, had upheld that claim until a fateful Outlands expedition. A displaced piece of technology…a question to a keeper of the archives…a vague clue about alien masters—and their world shifted radically. Suddenly, Brigid Baptiste, the archivist, faced summary execution, and Grant a quick termination. For Kane there was forgiveness if he pledged his unquestioning allegiance to Baron Cobalt and his unknown masters and abandoned his friends.

But that allegiance would make him support a mysterious and alien power and deny loyalty and friends. Then what else was there?

Kane had been brought up solely to serve the ville. Brigid's only link with her family was her mother's red-gold hair, green eyes and supple form. Grant's clues to his lineage were his ebony skin and powerful physique. But Domi, she of the white hair, was an Outlander pressed into sexual servitude in Cobaltville. She at least knew her roots and was a reminder to the exiles that the outcasts belonged in the human family.

Parents, friends, community—the very rootedness of humanity was denied. With no continuity, there was no forward momentum to the future. And that was the crux—when Kane began to wonder if there was a future.

For Kane, it wouldn't do. So the only way was out—way, way out.

After their escape, they found shelter at the forgotten Cerberus redoubt headed by Lakesh, a scientist, Cobaltville's head archivist, and secret opponent of the barons.

With their past turned into a lie, their future threatened, only one thing was left to give meaning to the outcasts. The hunger for freedom, the will to resist the hostile influences. And perhaps, by opposing, end them.

Prologue

The room was too warm, too dark, and the dry smell of burning dust clung to it possessively.

The small space was made smaller by the drapes that had been hung from the walls and over the doors, patterned in the dark colors of blood and red wine intermingled with the purples and blacks and deepest blues of bruises on human flesh.

The room had no windows. It was located in an underground bunker, a single room in a facility that had once been called Redoubt Mike and had served the US military back in the twentieth century, two hundred years earlier. That name had been cast aside by history now, blown away on the nuclear wind that had reshaped the world and its people.

Where once there had been fluorescent lighting functioning on automated circuits, now there were candles, three dozen of them scattered across every cluttered surface and dotted across the floor like seeds broadcast from a farmer's hand.

The room was cluttered by an odd selection of mismatched objects, feathers and bones, driftwood and skulls, jars of dried spices and plant roots vying for space along the walls, everything lit by the flicker of candle flames.

Everything here looks worn-out and tired, Nathalie thought as she pushed a hanging scarlet drape aside and strode through the doorway. She was a slim, dark-skinned

woman in her twenties, six feet tall with long, bare legs
that seemed to flow almost like liquid in the flickering
light of the candles. She wore a calfskin jacket that jutted
tightly across her breasts, leopard-print shorts and long,
black boots that laced up at the back, the corset-like lac-
ing running all the way up to the top of the boots where
they sat just below her knees. The knife sheathed at her
hip was as long as a man's forearm and broadened along
its length to become wider at its tip. Her hair was an afro
of tight black ringlets, encircling her head like some shadowy halo. She wore dyed feathers hanging from her ears,
and these seemed to twist and flutter as she entered the
room, brushing against the tops of her shoulders. Her face
was fixed in a solemn expression that gave nothing away,
insouciant mouth unreadable.

A canvas bag hung from her shoulder on a thick strap,
colored a dirty olive green but within which had been
weaved threads of blue and yellow and silver. The silver
threads glistened as they caught the light from the flickering flames.

Nathalie strode across the room toward the figure waiting in its center, admiring the ragged collection of junk
with disdain. It was appropriate, she thought, the worn-
out junk that cluttered this underground lair. Its tired and
broken nature was in sympathy with the tired and broken
nature of the man who presided over it, king of the flea
pit, who sat in his chair at the midpoint of all the trash.

"Welcome to the *djévo*," the man pronounced in a rich
basso voice. "Enter freely." His name was Papa Hurbon
and his was a large frame with the richly dark skin of
an octoroon. His corpulence was barely contained in the
straining short-sleeved shirt he wore, and he had a bul-
let-shaped head that widened from his pointy crown to a
bucket-like mouth. When he opened that wide maw, he
showed a line of fat teeth, with two missing in the lower

jaw and a golden replacement for his upper left canine. His head was shaved and beads of sweat glistened there. Both of his ears were pierced a dozen times or more, with a line of gold studs running from lobe to shell-like helix, golden hoops depending from the midpoints, and what seemed to be two petrified three-inch-long fetuses hanging from the lobes.

Hurbon sat in a wheelchair, a blanket cinched across his lower half where his waist met his legs, or more accurately, where his waist should have met his legs, for he had none. The blanket was black and patterned with skull designs that seemed to swirl like mist. Despite his disability, Papa Hurbon remained a charismatic figure, commanding all attention in the room.

Two other figures waited at the rear of the room, where a mirror had been hung, as tall and wide as the doorway on the opposing wall through which Nathalie had entered, and painted with an oily black sheen that peeked through the heavy drape that partially hid it. The figures were both tall, muscular men, so similar in fact that they might have been twins. They, too, had shaven heads, and they wore dark pants with no shoes or shirts, bare chests of defined muscles gleaming with sweat. The heat of the room was almost unbearable.

Two long strides brought Nathalie before Papa Hurbon, and she kneeled down in deference to him, casting her eyes downward. "Thank you for your 'ospitality," she said in a soft voice that was barely a whisper.

Hurbon reached down and placed his hand against the side of Nathalie's face, tilting it—not gently—up until she looked at him. "How wen' your quest, sweet child?"

"It went well, my beacon," Nathalie said, the timid hint of a hopeful smile crossing her wide lips. "I visited the site of the dragon's death as instructed."

Papa Hurbon nodded thoughtfully, his smile broad and bright in the shimmering flicker of the candles. "Good."

Hurbon had heard of the dragon that had appeared on the banks of the Euphrates River in the territory known as Iraq some months ago. The dragon was not alive—instead it was a bone structure, as if the gigantic creature had died there and its carcass had been left to rot. Some had mistaken it for a city, such was its grand size, and this dragon city had played host to a fierce war between two would-be gods from the sky along with their respective armies of indoctrinated humans and fearsome lizard-like soldiers. Papa Hurbon did not know who the victors were, only that the battle had ceased almost as abruptly as it had started, and that the skeletal dragon had been abandoned and left to rot, forgotten by the gods who made it.

Papa Hurbon knew a lot about gods—he was a houngan, a vodun priest, and he followed the dark path of the Bizango. He had witnessed gods appear once before from the sky and he had heard tell that the dragon was their symbol, their home. When he had heard about the dragon city that had appeared in the Middle East, he had immediately dispatched his servant Nathalie to acquire a part of the leviathan for him. There was power in the parts of the body, power in desiccated and petrified things, and there was definitely power in the things that the gods had shaped.

"And what did you bring me, child?" Hurbon asked.

Nathalie shifted her weight just slightly until the bag she carried dropped before her, still hanging on its canvas strap. She unzipped it and pulled the mouth of the bag open. Papa Hurbon leaned closer to see what lay within under the flickering light of the candles. At first glance it looked like a drugs stash, for the bag contained layer upon layer of small plastic bags filled with white powder. Hurbon reached into the larger bag and drew out a bag, lifting it close to his face to examine its contents more closely. There were thicker flecks and chips scattered among the white powder, each of them the yellow-white of cream.

"Dragon's teeth," Nathalie explained as Hurbon studied the package, his brow furrowed.

"Dragon's teeth?" Hurbon repeated, turning the bag to one side so that the powdery contents slid to one side of the larger flakes.

"I met certain people there," Nathalie explained, "in the shadow o' the dragon city. Merchants. They trade in exotic t'ings, parts o' the dragon who died. You said you wanted the teeth, Papa."

Hurbon nodded, the smile materializing once more on his face. "Bring me my mortar and pestle, girl," he instructed. "The smallest ones, for the most delicate mixtures."

Nodding once, Nathalie rose from the floor, her tall, lithe frame moving like liquid. Hurbon watched her depart from the room, peering up from under, still holding the bag full of dragon remains.

The girl had joined his société after its near-destruction at the hands of the insane bitch goddess Ezili Coeur Noir. Nathalie was youthful, smart and able, capable of individual action and trustworthy enough not to betray him. She was loyal to Hurbon and the vodun sect he represented and would serve and service him however he asked.

NATHALIE PUSHED THE scarlet curtain aside and strode out into the corridor beyond. She knew the corridors of the old redoubt well. Like the *djévo*, the corridor was lit by candles that lined the floor, flickering in the passing breeze as Nathalie walked past them. There were jars and bottles resting on the floor behind the candles, curios stored and pickled for safekeeping, each one with a purpose in the dark Bizango rituals which Papa Hurbon practiced. Papa

Hurbon had taken over the abandoned military installation shortly after the whole complex had been flooded, and there were still areas that remained waterlogged, more like swimming pools now than the once regimented rooms that they had been.

Hurbon had another lodge located close by in the Louisiana countryside where he encouraged newcomers and old faithfuls to come worship in these harrowing times of destruction and confusion. The world had blown out two hundred years ago in the year 2001, when a nuclear exchange had escalated into a full-blown war in the space of just a few minutes, destroying Western civilization and setting back the course of history by generations. Only now, in the first decade of the twenty-third century, had the world finally moved beyond that awful legacy, and there was still so much of the old United States of America that remained unmapped, scarred by radiation, hostile to humankind. The survivors had flourished in nine grand villes, which dominated the landscape, their eerie otherworldly rulers—the barons—carving up the old United States into their own private territories. But it seemed that that golden age of safety and security had passed. The ruling barons had departed from their golden-towered cities, evolving into their true forms as Annunaki, lizard-like gods from outer space who had been worshipped many millennia ago in Mesopotamia and Babylon.

But the Annunaki had died, ripped apart by their own mistrust and bickering, turning on one another until there was nothing left of them but their legacy. That had been almost two years ago. In the aftermath, their villes had struggled to remain safe. Some had crumbled under attacks, others had been rebuilt as new cities that worshipped new gods, and some had simply closed the gates and knuckled down, worrying only about their own and leaving anyone outside the high walls to fend for themselves.

Papa Hurbon's temple fell under the terrain of Beausoleil, a ville that had chosen to close ranks and reject any outlanders. Outsiders felt afraid, scared that their lands and their possessions would be taken. There were even stories that their children were being abducted for the rich ville dwellers, handed over to childless couples, or worse, roasted and eaten as delicacies. The people were scared, so they flocked to Papa Hurbon, whose fearsome charisma and powerful ways steeped in ancient ritual offered the promise of security and perhaps salvation.

Nathalie was just one of the people who had joined Hurbon's société in the past few months since he had re-emerged after sacrificing both of his legs to his deranged goddess. When asked, Hurbon told her that the sacrifice had been worth it, and that it had granted him more power than any man had ever known before. She suspected that he was right.

There was a room of the redoubt, beyond the vehicle garage whose floor was now hidden beneath an expanse of stagnant water where green clouds lurked and flies buzzed, that contained a thick-walled chamber within it. Inside the chamber, through a tiny pane of six-inch-thick glass, something incorporeal could be seen, swirling as if caught in a hurricane, its component parts unable to cling on to a form. The feeling of dread that emanated from the chamber was palpable. Nathalie had looked inside the chamber on several occasions, peering through the thick, reinforced glass of the rust-lined door. Within, she had seen a face, lit momentarily as if spied in a flash of lightning, then gone again as if it had never been.

Papa Hurbon had told her that the face belonged to his precious Ezili, an ancient *loa* who had taken earthly form from the Annunaki goddess called Lilitu. He told her that she was his now, that she served him where he had once served her.

Hurbon held surgery in his lodge, but he had turned the redoubt into the société's temple, where the faithful came to bask in and add to his power. Hurbon took the responsibility easily, but then he had broad shoulders and a steady stream of young women who were only too eager to present themselves to the vodun priest.

Nathalie moved down the concrete-walled corridor, gloomy in the insufficient illumination of the candles, and stepped into the side chamber where Hurbon kept his mixing equipment. Hurbon could get it, of course, but he preferred to send others to do his bidding now—he had spent so long just striving to survive on his own he basked in the luxury of having a congregation once more.

Nathalie reached for the mortar and pestle, one of a dozen lined up by size along a dusty shelf that also contained aged items of jewelry and the skulls of a dozen different rodents and primates. The mortar was made from the curved bones of a monkey's hand, the pestle the carved bone of a human finger.

ONCE NATHALIE HAD departed the room, Hurbon unsealed the bag of white dust and spread a little across his left hand. He sniffed it, taking in its aroma. It was redolent of obscure spices and incense, and the smell made Hurbon smile wider than before.

"The smell o' the dragon," he muttered, before reaching into the bag for one of the larger shards of white. The shard was a little bigger than Hurbon's thumbnail, and it looked porous, tiny indentations running all the way across its surface. Brushing the dust back into the open bag, Hurbon took the shard and tapped it against his teeth. It felt rock-hard, and even though he had used the lightest of pressure the feel of the tooth bit was such that it made Hurbon's teeth sing, as though they might shatter. Then Hurbon placed the shard against his tongue and licked it, feeling its rough sides and sharp edges. He winced as the sharpest edge cut a tiny incision across his tongue, and he drew the fleck of tooth away with a start.

"How the hell did they cut this thing?" Hurbon muttered. Neither man in the room answered him, nor were they supposed to—they just stared vacantly into the middle distance, not reacting to anything that occurred before them.

Sucking on his tongue where it had been cut, Hurbon reached beneath the blanket that hid his missing limbs. He had a bag beneath there, an old leather pouch, its brown surface scuffed, frayed threads showing at its edges. The pouch was large enough for Hurbon to get both hands in, and it had a strap by which it could be carried, like a woman's purse.

Hurbon slipped the shard of dragon tooth into the pouch where it could reside beside other items that he found useful. Also in the leather pouch were a fith fath—what the ignorant nonbelievers called a voodoo doll—a chicken's foot and a knotted material pouch of black-and-red powder. There were other bags within the larger bag that Nathalie had brought, and as houngan of the société, it was his prerogative to take a share of any spoils that came through the doors of the redoubt-turned-temple.

His men would say nothing. They were there to guard him and he had removed from them the awkward inconvenience of independent thought.

Hurbon looked up as he heard Nathalie pad back into the *djévo* room. In a loose sense, the room was mirrored, each decoration reflected in an ornament of similar size and shape on the other side of the room, a femur for a knife, a crystal ball for a skull and the black mirror in place of the door. It was important to keep the *djévo* in balance at all times, Hurbon knew, if one was to tap the powers beyond the barriè to the spirit world.

However, it was not the voodoo deities—the *loa*—whom he planned to contact this day. No, Papa Hurbon planned to reach out for the other faces in the darkness, and the dragon's teeth were the vital ingredient he required to do just that.

"Are the teeth acceptable?" Nathalie asked as she handed Hurbon the mortar and pestle.

Hurbon nodded. "They are genuine, we hope" was all he said. Then he took another package of bone dust from the open bag that Nathalie had brought and tipped a small portion of its contents into the mortar where it rested on his lap.

"What is it you hope to achieve, Papa?" Nathalie asked as Papa Hurbon worked the powdery dust around in the bowl.

"Child, there is a story which comes from the Greece of ancient times," Hurbon explained as he mixed rat's blood with the splinters of tooth, "which tells of the Spartoí, the children of Ares. The Spartoí were powerful soldiers grown from the sown teeth of a dragon, walking dead things that fought with a great warrior called Jason. You see, the Greeks understood the power of the dragon's teeth in conjuring warriors into this world from beyond the grave."

"So your plan is to bring great warriors to life?" Nathalie questioned.

"No, not warriors, my sweet cherry," Hurbon said with a flash of his fiendish smile. "Gods. The Annunaki who came to Earth brought with them a whole new comprehension of technology, utilizing organic materials in the way so-called civilized man uses steel and silicon. In this sense, the Annunaki are closer to the old ways of the path, the voodoo ways—you see?"

Nathalie nodded, awed.

"Their ways and ours are so much alike," Hurbon continued. "Each fleck of tooth contains a genetic story, each shard a history just waiting to be unleashed."

Hurbon pressed down hard with the pestle, and Nathalie heard something snap inside the tiny mortar bowl. "The trouble with the Annunaki is—*they thought too small.*

"I will sow the seeds of the dragon across the globe," Hurbon told the woman, "and unto each shall come a new understanding and a new reckoning. The children of the dragon shall walk the Earth once again, and when they are done, my child—when they are done, why, what a glorious day that shall be."

Hurbon stirred the bowl once more, mashing together the shards and the rat's blood into a grisly paste.

Chapter 1

Seven months later, Zaragoza, Spain

Located in northern Spain, the city of Zaragoza was alive with color. The large city housed half a million people, and its narrow streets and alleyways were brought to life with music and the sounds of the citizens. Parts of the city had been destroyed and rebuilt over the years, but the oldest landmarks, like the Basilica of Our Lady of the Pillar—a huge, palace-like cathedral dedicated to Christian faith— and the Aljafería Palace, had somehow survived, repurposed, to revel in their second phoenix lives.

Above those ancient towering spires, the sky was turning a rich shade of red as the sun set, painting everything with its pinkish glow and turning the Ebro, the river that bisected the city, into a shimmering orange line.

Two figures were hurrying across the Puente de Piedra, a man and a woman. She seemed eager to cross the bridge of lions, while he was clearly more reluctant.

"Come on, Grant-san," the young woman urged, tugging at the man's hand, "I have no desire to be late." Her name was Shizuka and she was the leader of the Tigers of Heaven, the ruling group of New Edo in the Western Isles of the Pacific. A formidable warrior, Shizuka was a petite woman of Asian extraction, with golden skin and dark eyes with a pleasing upward slant, lips like cherry blossoms and fine dark hair.

Shizuka wore an elegant evening dress in midnight blue. The dress sat high across her neck, leaving her arms bare and reaching to midway down her legs, cinched tightly across her hips and legs to accentuate her figure. The figure beneath was slim and athletic, taut muscles moving in slick motion as she trotted across the bridge on three-inch heels.

The man beside her could not be more at odds with Shizuka's lithe and petite frame. In his midthirties, Grant was a hulking figure of a man, six-foot-four inches tall, all corded muscle without an ounce of fat. His skin was a rich mahogany, his head shaved, and he sported a gunslinger's mustache. He wore a well-cut suit with blazer jacket in a shimmering gray-silk weave. Beneath the jacket he wore a wine-dark shirt and a black bow tie that, despite his best efforts not to, he could not help adjusting as they hurried across the bridge that crossed the River Ebro. Grant was an ex-Magistrate, an enforcer of baronial law, from the US settlement of Cobaltville. In recent years he had traded that role for a position with the Cerberus organization, a group dedicated to the safety of humankind, defending it from alien threats and other terrors that had been caused by extraterrestrial intervention or as fallout from the alien barons' schemes to rule the world.

"Why should we hurry, Shizuka?" Grant asked. His voice was a rumble like distant thunder, but there was a tenderness there that spoke of his feelings for his breath-takingly beautiful companion. "This is our chance to relax. So slow down, enjoy the sights. A place this beautiful needs time to be admired."

Grant had been with Shizuka for several years, though they had seemed to have little time to relax and enjoy one another's company in all the time that they had been to-gether. This visit here to Zaragoza was Grant's attempt to change that, a moment's quiet in the ongoing battle against alien incursion.

Shizuka had to admit that it was hard to argue with her lover's point. She slowed down, admiring the view from the bridge as they approached the west bank. The city of Zaragoza had suffered a little at the hands of the nuclear devastation that had racked the Western hemisphere, but much of the city had survived, and what had not had been sympathetically rebuilt over the two centuries since that awful nuclear exchange. There was a palpable sense of age to the place, that tranquil beauty that only old buildings—and old stone—exhibited. The Puente de Piedra was an ancient stone bridge that crossed the Ebro in the center of the city. Two decorative bronze lions had been placed atop pillars at either end of the bridge—four in all—guarding the crossing and the travelers who used it. Making the crossing to the west side, one could see the towering, ornate turrets of the Basilica of Our Lady of the Pillar to the right, a beautiful palace that looked something like an upturned table with its exquisite carved legs thrust up into the sky. To the left stood the rich redbrick building that housed artifacts from the Roman era, and towering behind this was the ornate spire of La Seo Cathedral, its white brickwork recolored in a luminous strawberry red as the sun set behind it. Trees lined the wide avenue that ran alongside the riverbank, obscuring the towering gray-brown structures of ornate design that looked out across the water. Wheeled wags hurried to and fro, transporting locals and visitors to destinations amid the city's bustling nightlife.

"You continue to surprise me, Grant-san," Shizuka said as she took in the magnificent view.

"This is why we came here," Grant said, indicating the panorama that stretched out all around them. "The clean air, the sunlight on the water—I like to believe it's all been put here just for us."

"Oh, Grant," Shizuka whispered, turning back to him and gazing longingly into his eyes. "I forget how you can make me melt within."

For a moment Grant looked regretful. "Easy to forget," he admitted. "I don't make enough time for 'us' sometimes…"

Before he could say anything further, Shizuka placed her index finger against Grant's lips. "Because you are too busy saving people's lives, my brave hero," she reminded him, "and there can be no shame in taking that choice. A weaker man than you would turn his back on his obligations."

"Especially when there's a hottie waiting at home for him," Grant said, a broad smile appearing across his face as he admired his lover. But the smile faltered when he saw Shizuka's flawless brow furrow in uncertainty. "All right, all right," Grant said, holding his hands up as if in surrender, "so maybe I shouldn't have called you a hottie. You're a capable, vibrant woman who…who knows what she wants and…and…"

"Go on," Shizuka encouraged, an air of challenge in her voice.

"And…intelligent, beautiful and wise," Grant finished, an uncertain note of hope in his tone.

Shizuka crossed her arms over her chest and nodded. "*Hai*. Quite true," she agreed. "However, that was not what caused me to question your statement, Grant-san, because I am a hottie. Rather, when have you ever known this hottie to stay at home waiting for her man?"

Grant looked suitably chastised. "You have a point."

Shizuka raised Grant's left arm then and twirled beneath it until she was wrapped in his grip, ready to walk beside him across the bridge. "We both have busy lives,

Grant-san," she reminded him. "You with Cerberus, me with my obligations to the Tigers of Heaven. There is no shame in our choices, nor in shouldering the responsibilities we have both been tasked to endure. However, today is not about that. This night, this week—it is all for us, with no buzzing Commtacts or pleading advisers."

"I never had an adviser," Grant stated as they strode arm in arm across the vast stone bridge.

"And I have never had a Commtact," Shizuka replied, whip-fast.

The Commtact to which Shizuka referred was a remarkable tool that Grant and his fellow Cerberus operatives relied upon for global communications. It was a small radio device that was embedded beneath the skin of all Cerberus field personnel, including Grant. The subdermal devices were top-of-the-line units, the designs for which had been discovered among the artifacts in Redoubt Yankee several years before by the Cerberus rebels.

Commtacts featured sensor circuitry incorporating an analog-to-digital voice encoder that was embedded in a subject's mastoid bone. As well as radio communications, the Commtacts could function as a translation device, operating in real time. Once the pintels made contact, transmissions were funneled directly to the user's auditory canals through the skull casing, vibrating the ear canal to create sound. This facility had the additional perk of being able to pick up and enhance any subvocalization made by the user, which meant that it was unnecessary to speak aloud to utilize the transmission function.

Broadcasts from the unit were patched through the Keyhole communications satellite, or Comsat, and then relayed to the Cerberus redoubt headquarters in Montana. Thanks to the nature of the vibration system used by the Commtact, if a user went completely deaf they would still, in theory, be able to hear, in a fashion, courtesy of the Commtact device.

"Anyway, you promised me a romantic evening of dinner and dancing," Shizuka reminded Grant.

"The evening's barely begun," Grant told her, pulling the modern-day samurai a little closer as they walked past the lion-topped columns at the end of the bridge.

The pair had arrived just a few hours before, booking into a grand, family-run hotel after traveling via interphaser. Based on an alien design, the interphaser could tap quantum pathways and move people through space to specific locations instantaneously. The technology was limited by certain esoteric factors, the full gamut of which had yet to be cataloged, but what was known was that the interphaser was reliant on an ancient web of powerful, hidden lines called parallax points that stretched across the globe and beyond. This network followed old ley lines and formed a powerful technology so far beyond ancient human comprehension as to appear magical. Though fixed, the interphaser's destination points were often located in temples, graveyards or similar sites of religious significance. These sites had frequently emerged around the interphaser's use, ancient man sensing the incredible power that was being tapped for such instantaneous travel. Cerberus personnel's access to an operational interphaser had taken many months of trial and error to achieve.

This time, the quantum jump had brought Grant and Shizuka close to an ancient church, more ruin than building now, located in the middle of a dusty, overgrown graveyard on the east bank, their arrival unseen. From there, the couple had made their way to the luxurious rooms in which they would be staying. The rooms were typically Spanish, painted in light colors to reflect the heat and sparsely decorated to leave them uncluttered. The bed featured a brass frame shined to look like gold in the fierce sunlight that blasted through the open window of the balcony, and a complimentary bottle of wine had been left cooling in an ice bucket for their arrival. At reception, Grant had deftly navigated the questions about how their trip had been and when they had arrived; the interphaser was a method of travel exclusive to the Cerberus organization and not something he wanted to advertise.

The midday heat of the Spanish sun was enough to knock both of them out, however, so instead of exploring the city Grant and Shizuka had spent a restful few hours just catching up with each other, tracing the familiar curves of one another's bodies before indulging in a late-afternoon swim in the hotel's pool. Now, at a little before 8:00 p.m., the pair made their way toward their destination, a small café that became a restaurant when the sun set.

As the chill of the approaching night began to make itself felt, Grant and Shizuka strolled past a Roman theater, a series of stepped levels organized around a semicircle where ancient actors had once performed. Now it was a little tribute to those long-forgotten days, where only the occasional play might still be performed for a specific celebration or anniversary.

The sky had turned a pleasing shade of indigo when they found the restaurant, Shizuka still aggrieved that they were late. The owner—a large-bellied, red-faced man with a graying mustache and ragged, curly hair—did not mind their tardiness. It seemed that that was very much the culture of this city. "Time," he told them in ebullient Spanish, "is whatever you make it, and you may make of that what you will."

Inside, the restaurant was softly lit with candlelit tables and floor-length windows that were open along a side that faced into an alleyway to allow a through breeze to keep the place cool. As they were shown to their table, Grant squeezed Shizuka's hand, and she looked up at him. He said nothing, but his look seemed to say, *Look at this place. Look at all the wonderful things out here for us to enjoy.* It was a world away from the one they knew.

And so they ate, unaware of what was occurring barely a block away.

AFTER FOOD CAME DANCING. Grant jokingly tried to swear off, claiming he was too full of paella to move, but Shizuka shot him a look that could leave no doubt as to why she was the ultimate authority in New Edo.

"You will dance and you will enjoy it," she said.

"I will dance and *you* will enjoy it," Grant corrected with a mischievous, boyish grin.

They made their way down the alleyway that ran beside the restaurant, passing parked vehicles and other couples enjoying the city's nightlife. Spain was a country of night people, the heat of the day too fierce to enjoy. Now the burning heat had turned to a refreshing night breeze, and Shizuka rubbed her bare arms as they crossed a junction and made their way toward the grand hotel that was their destination.

From outside, the grand, four-story building was awash with lights, its windows burning brightly in the darkness.

"There's a dance hall inside," Grant explained. "I hear it can be quite an experience."

Shizuka smiled as she looked up at her taller companion, her face alive with delight.

Even from here, a dozen yards from the steps that led to the open front doors, they could hear the strains of a band, acoustic guitars rushing through some local number at furious speed, maracas click-clacking to keep time as the tune hurtled toward its finale, a blur of tumbling notes and riffs.

Grant and Shizuka hurried up the steps, a spring in Shizuka's step as she led her lover through the lobby toward the grand ballroom, which dominated the hotel's ground floor. Grant stopped momentarily to tip the doorman before dashing after Shizuka as she reached for the double doors into the ballroom itself, the strains of a flamenco emanating loudly from within.

Grant reached for Shizuka, wrapping one muscular arm around her and pulling her close as she pulled one door open. "I love you," he said as he brought Shizuka's face close to his own.

"I love you, too, my bravest one," Shizuka told him before kissing him on the lips.

Then the pair turned back to the doors that were swinging open where Shizuka had pulled their handles. The hurtling notes of the furious flamenco became suddenly louder, twin guitars racing through notes as if trying to outpace one another, the maracas chattering like an insect swarm, a woman's voice melodically reciting in a foreign tongue. But what lay beyond was enough to stop the two warriors in their tracks.

The ballroom was vast with an ornate ceiling and richly decorated walls, each carving lit by a flickering candle or the low, shaded light of a bulb. To one corner, the band was playing, four men in dinner jackets and a female singer with luxurious, dark hair tied up tight to her head with a flower clipped there and wearing a wispy dress the rich red of rose petals.

But no one was dancing. Instead, perhaps a dozen couples, dressed in their most beautiful clothes—the women's dresses cut to accentuate their curves, the men's suits cut to hide their own—were hanging from the ceiling in rows, each couple lined up together, two dozen nooses wrapped around two dozen necks, their feet swaying a few feet above the perfectly sprung wooden floor.

Grant and Shizuka stared at the scene in absolute horror. And suddenly a city of half a million people felt very, very empty.

Chapter 2

Grant could tell the twenty-four bodies hanging from the rafters of the ballroom were freshly deceased. He had experienced death from close up many times in his action-filled life and felt no need to shy away from it.

Beside him, Grant heard Shizuka gasp. She, too, had seen death, had dealt it at the tip of her katana sword. But this—this was something unexpected, something exceptional.

A forest of taut necks and sagging bodies hung before them, feet still twitching, tongues lolling out from faces that were strained red with pain, eyes open in accusation.

Grant took a step forward, then turned to the quintet who continued to play their whirling, racing music. "Can you all stop playing?" he shouted to them, striding across the room through the swaying human stalactites.

The band continued for several bars before its players finally brought the music to an abrupt stop. The woman singer in her rose-red dress seemed poised to say something, or perhaps to sing, and looked aggrieved as she watched Grant stalk across the room toward her.

"What happened here?" Grant demanded. "Why did they do this? *When* did they do this? Did you see?"

The singer stared at Grant, a flash of challenge in her dark eyes. Challenge and confusion, as if he had intruded on her dreams.

"You understand me?" Grant asked. *"¿Lo entiendes?"*

he repeated the question in Spanish as his Commtact help-fully translated in his ear.

"Grant—look!" Shizuka called from where she remained at the front of the room close to the open doors.

Grant turned to her, then spun, following where she was pointing. A pair of double doors stood at the far end of the room, identical to the ones through which Grant and Shizuka had entered. There, through the open doors, three figures were moving swiftly down a hotel corridor, away from the scene. It could be nothing, Grant knew, but he wasn't one to pass up a lead. Years of Magistrate training had taught him to investigate everything.

Grant ran, sprinting through the room toward the far set of doors. As he ran he called back to Shizuka, "Wait here and get the hotel people on this," he said. "See if you can help any of these people—if they can still be helped."

With that, Grant was gone, leaving Shizuka standing in a room full of swaying bodies, the band watching her with what seemed to be almost feral looks.

GRANT SPRINTED THROUGH the open doors and out into the corridor. The corridor was underlit, and it was decorated in luscious, dark colors with a small side table and two chairs resting against a wall. Grant glanced behind him as he chased after the rapidly disappearing figures and realized that the corridor turned in a right angle back there to wrap around the ballroom, and presumably back to the hotel reception. It probably functioned primarily as a service corridor, which staff used by way of shortcut between the kitchens and the public parts of the hotel.

A bellhop in a white jacket was just rounding the corner holding a tray of empty glasses, and his face became alarmed as he spotted Grant appear through the doors to the ballroom.

"¡Hey!" the bellhop shouted in Spanish as he spotted Grant.

Grant ignored him, scrambling along the corridor toward the retreating figures. There were three of them—two men led by a woman. The men had coffee-colored skin and were muscular and bare chested. They wore dark pants and boots. One of them seemed to have tattoos across his back, painted there in dark patches like beetles running across his skin. Two steps ahead of them, a curvaceous woman was stepping toward another door on six-inch heels. Grant saw the dazzle of the streetlight that was situated just outside when she pushed against it—and realized that it led out into the street. Glanced in the half-light of the service corridor, the woman appeared to be dressed for carnival, with a towering headdress swaying high over her head, and a plume of white feathers attached to her butt, swinging back and forth like a pendulum with every movement of her legs.

"Hey—wait up!" Grant called, scrambling along the corridor after the figures. He did not know if they had had anything to do with the scene in the ballroom, but he could only rule that out if he spoke to them.

The bare-chested men halted to let the woman slip out through the door before them. As they did so, they both turned back at Grant's call, and he saw them more clearly in the artificial light streaming in from the street. They had shaved heads and grimly fixed expressions. And, strangely, from this distance it appeared that their eyes were blank, white orbs, like hard-boiled eggs without their shells.

"Stop!" Grant ordered, using the same tone of voice he had employed in his days giving orders as a Magistrate.

The two men ignored Grant and stepped out through the doorway. Why shouldn't they—he had no authority here.

But Grant was determined. He dashed down the corridor and through the door before it could slam closed behind the disappearing party, shoving it open again as he stepped through.

He was in a back alley, six feet in width—just wide enough for a land wag. There were garbage cans out here and the alleyway stretched off around the edge of the hotel building, a streetlight blazing right into Grant's face. Grant turned left and right and spotted the three figures as they trotted off down the alleyway and slipped into another side passage, the woman's tail of white feathers bouncing up and down with every step.

Grant followed, chasing the strangely dressed trio as they disappeared from view. As he turned the corner into a narrower alleyway, he had a flash of premonition—the old instincts from his Magistrate days kicking in. He dipped his head, tucking it into his shoulders. As he did so, something came hurtling at him from the narrow alley between the tall buildings, whizzing just over his ducked head before impacting against the far wall in a shower of sparks as metal met brick.

Grant lurched aside, his right arm darting ahead to slap against the opposite wall as he sped after his quarry. It was at times like this that Grant regretted not coming armed. Behind him, he heard something metallic drop against the paving slabs with a low tinker like a falling paint tin lid—it was whatever had been tossed at him.

Up ahead, the trio turned again, and this time Grant saw as one of the men—the one with those eerie tattoos—plucked something small, circular and shiny from his waistband before drawing his arm back, ready to throw it. The object was roughly the size of a compact disc, and it hurtled toward Grant at incredible speed.

Grant stepped to the side, pressing himself against the wall as the silvery disc zipped by. In that moment he had a clear view of the woman where a streetlamp illuminated her, but only for an instant. She was stunning—olive-skinned with an oval face framed by long dark hair that cascaded to midway down her spine. Her skintight dress, the colour of a purple bruise, hugged every line of her lithe body like liquid before fraying at the hips into torn strips that fluttered all the way down to her ankles. Behind this, a cascade of white feathers fluttered at her rear like a peacock's fan. But it was her headgear that was most impressive—rising almost eighteen inches above her head. The piece was designed like twin horns, entwining one another in a complex web of twists and turns. Grant had the sudden feeling that the stag-like horns were somehow made from bone.

In the microsecond it took Grant to register all of this, the second dark-skinned man worked the door to a building on the alleyway, and suddenly the three figures disappeared inside.

Grant gave chase again, reaching the door a fraction of a second after it had closed. It was a fire door, he realized then, completely smooth with no provision given to opening it from this side. Which raised the question of just how the hell these people had managed to open it.

But that was only one of the many questions racing through Grant's mind at that instant. Grant hammered against the door for a few seconds, but no one responded. He looked around him, taking in the narrow alleyway as if for the first time. Three- and four-story buildings stood to either side of him, dark windows peering out onto the narrow passage, a sliver of indigo sky visible between them like an upturned river. Grant wondered where the doorway led, but there was no obvious entrance farther along the wall.

As he peered up and down the alleyway, Grant spotted something lying at the edge of the door. It was a feather, presumably from the woman's train. Leaning down, Grant picked it from the sill of the door, lifting it closer to study it. As he did so he felt its sharp edge cut him across his thumb, just like a paper cut, and he winced. The feather was eight inches long and almost two inches wide, goose white with a pale stem. But there was red at the edges of the feather, and as Grant held it, the red spread before his eyes. In a matter of seconds, the feather had turned from purest white to a dark, bloodred.

Grant studied the feather a moment longer before slipping it into the pocket of his jacket. He had lost the strange group by now, and he was woefully aware that he had left Shizuka alone in the hotel ballroom with the hanging bodies and the eerily playing band.

"Dammit," he cursed, turning back the way he had come. As he retraced his steps, Grant plucked up both of the metal discs that had been launched at him by the men. They were four inches across with sharp, jagged edges, a little like buzz saws. Studying them as he retraced his steps, Grant couldn't help but wonder what on Earth he and Shizuka had managed to walk into.

WHILE GRANT WAS chasing after the mysterious figures, back at the hotel, Shizuka rapidly enlisted several members of staff to assist in untying or cutting down the dancers who were hanging from the ceiling.

"Alert the authorities," Shizuka told a porter as he dragged a chair over from the wall to help her untie the first victim.

The porter looked mystified, and Shizuka repeated her request. "Authorities. Police."

"Policía," the porter repeated, nodding in understanding. He hurried off, and a few seconds later Shizuka could hear him having a hurried discussion with the hotel receptionist before he returned with more help.

It took four of them almost two minutes to get everyone

down from the ceiling, and Shizuka spent the whole of that time asking aloud for anyone to speak up if they could hear her while the receptionist translated the question in Spanish. Three of the hanging figures gurgled strained responses through the pressure of the nooses, and Shizuka ensured that they were the first she assisted down from their grisly positions.

The five-piece band remained dazed by what they saw here, Shizuka noticed, as if they had only just awoken— except in this case, the nightmare was all too real.

Despite her lack of Spanish skills, Shizuka managed to take charge and organize everyone, and it was not long before all of the previously hanging figures had been brought back down to the floor. A doctor who was staying at the hotel was found and called upon to check over the grisly scene. He was a portly man in his late forties who had been enjoying an after-dinner drink in the hotel bar, and he was efficient and calm as he looked over the ballroom's occupants. Over two-thirds of the figures were already dead; just seven had survived, and of those only two could speak.

The receptionist, a bottle blonde with dark roots showing, pretty and scarcely out of her teens by Shizuka's reckoning, spoke flawless English with only a trace of an accent, so while the doctor worked, Shizuka cornered her and asked her what had happened.

"I didn't know anything was wrong until Paolo called me," she admitted, referring to the young porter who had been the first to answer Shizuka's call.

"Didn't you hear anything?" Shizuka probed.

"No. Nothing," the girl replied, wide-eyed in astonishment. "I can't believe…" She stopped and crossed herself, unable to finish her sentence.

Shizuka looked back at the ballroom, eyeing the ceiling where the nooses had been attached to the open beams that ran crossways through the room. It was a curious affair, to say the least. As she pondered, Shizuka's eyes settled on the band, who were still waiting at one side of the room. They were talking among themselves and seemed distraught, faces ashen with the shock of what had occurred here. And yet, Shizuka recalled, they had been playing normally when she and Grant had happened upon the horrific scene, as if they were a part of it somehow.

Shizuka placed a hand on the receptionist's side and guided her across the room. "Come, I may need you to help me speak with them," she explained.

Bewildered by the almost-surreal scene around her, the receptionist plodded alongside Shizuka on her flat-soled pumps.

"Do any of you speak English?" Shizuka asked, addressing the band.

One of the guitarists nodded, as did the singer, while two of the others made "so-so" gestures with a shrug.

"You must have been here when all this was occurring," Shizuka said. "What did you see?"

"See?" the singer repeated. "It's…confused. We play as people arrive. They laugh, some dance. Then…"

"Then?" Shizuka urged.

"It's…*atropelladamente*," the singer said.

Shizuka looked from the singer to the other band members, some of whom were nodding. "I don't understand," she said.

The singer began rattling off something in fast-paced Spanish, her garbled words exhibiting the rat-a-tat rhythm of an old machine gun's fire. *"Un tobogán en espiral de altura sinuoso alrededor de una torre en una feria,"* she said. *"Una feria…*fairground."

Shizuka looked to the receptionist for help. "Fairground?" she prompted.

"Mónica says it was like seeing a twisting slide," the

receptionist translated thoughtfully. "Like the slide at the funfair."

"The helter-skelter." Shizuka realized after a moment.

"Si!" the singer agreed with a snap of her fingers. "But here, in my head. Inside."

The woman's bandmates seemed to agree, one of them translating for the drummer, whose grasp of English was very limited. Several of the men tapped their foreheads as if to show her. It was the point where many religions placed the third eye, Shizuka noticed.

At that moment, the authorities arrived, and the atmosphere in the room changed subtly. Shizuka felt it straightaway, the way that everyone suddenly became a suspect.

Two officers strode through the room, eyeing the sprawl of corpses and wounded scattered across the lavish surroundings. They were a man and a woman, both dressed smart-casual in charcoal-gray suits. The man was in his thirties, six feet tall with striking features and wavy dark hair slicked back from his forehead, a trace of stubble darkening his chin. He wore his jacket open, the pressed white collar of his shirt tightly clasped to his neck, a striped tie swaying before his broad chest. The woman was of a similar age, several inches shorter than the man, and her suit was looser, its baggy lines masking her taut, athletic figure. She wore a white T-shirt beneath the blazer, the bulge of a blaster almost hidden where it was holstered beneath her left arm. She had dark hair cascading past her shoulders in gentle waves and she wore a concerned expression that sat well on the sharp planes of her face, enhancing her flawless olive complexion.

The woman asked something in Spanish, addressing the room in general. The blonde receptionist answered, indicating Shizuka, and the two officers strode across the room toward her, while everyone else seemed to subtly rear back to give them room.

Shizuka looked mystified as the dark-haired woman babbled something in Spanish, then the hotel receptionist said something and the woman repeated her question in flawless, slightly accented English, "You found the people here? Like this?"

Shizuka nodded. "I did."

"I'm Pretor Cáscara," the woman explained, flashing her a badge, "and, my partner, Pretor Corcel. Are you able to answer some questions for me?"

Shizuka nodded again. "Of course." Then Shizuka explained who she was and that she had been visiting the hotel with her partner when they had, by chance, made their grisly discovery.

"And when was this, Senora Shizuka?" the man asked, speaking for the first time. He had a refined accent, as if he had learned English from the upper-class British of a bygone age.

"Ten minutes," Shizuka guessed. "Less maybe. I don't... It was very unexpected."

The woman touched Shizuka's bare arm gently. "We understand, you must have had quite the shock."

Shizuka took a slow, deliberate breath, gazing past the two officers to focus on the fallen bodies strewn about the room. She had seen worse than this, many times in fact—such was the cost of a life of adventure. But there was something poignant and hopeless about finding these people hanging here like this without warning or explanation. It sickened her, and for the first time since she and Grant had arrived, Shizuka had the chance to stop and realize that.

Pretor Cáscara raised her dark eyebrows, peering at Shizuka as she saw her tremor slightly. "Do you need to sit down?"

"Yes," Shizuka blurted, so sudden that the word caught her unawares. Even as she said it, Shizuka wavered in place as if she might fall. Shock, she realized at a disconnect, as if she was thinking about someone other than herself.

The woman called Cáscara took Shizuka by the arm and led her from the room, asking one of the hotel staff in Spanish to bring a glass of water as she escorted Shizuka into the hotel lobby.

PRETOR JUAN CORCEL was left alone with the doctor as the relevant authorities arrived to remove the bodies and take the survivors away to a nearby hospital. The hotel staff had departed the crime scene, waiting nearby. As he surveyed the room, pacing in a small circle on his Italian-made loafers, the doctor asked him a question.

"I bet you have never seen anything like this, eh, Pretor?" the doctor said in Spanish while several of the living where taken away on stretchers.

Corcel shook his head. "Sadly, that is not the case."

The doctor looked surprised. "You mean this has happened before?"

Pretor Corcel looked back at him with haunted eyes, saying nothing. "How many are alive?" he asked finally, gazing at the stretchers. Some of the sheets had been pulled over the heads to hide the faces.

"Seven," the doctor said.

"Yes," Pretor Corcel agreed distractedly, pacing across the room. He had seen this before; in fact this was only the latest in a spate of something that one might have called serial killings. But the details were vague, uncertain. He and his partner, Cáscara, urgently needed a break on this, before things became any worse. There had been sightings, two black men appearing close to the scenes sometimes, vague recollections of a woman, but that was all circumstantial, hearsay, like trying to grab ahold of something from a child's drawing. There had been tiny slivers of evidence—another Pretor had been killed using a razor-sharp disc that had been pushed into his belly somehow, shredding his gut apart; bloodred feathers scattered at two of the scenes. But it all felt disconnected, with no clear picture emerging.

Corcel huffed, shaking his head. *Who would do this, and why?*

It was then that Juan Corcel, Pretor of the Zaragoza Justice Department with a twelve-year unblemished record of service, had what he considered at that moment to be the greatest lucky break of his career. The twin doors leading out of the ballroom crashed open and one of the black men from the eyewitness reports came hurrying through, breathless from killing. He held one of the throwing disclike weapons in one hand, a bloody feather protruding from his jacket pocket.

In a flash, Corcel pulled his blaster—a compact Devorador de Pecados—from its hidden underarm holster and targeted the man in its sights, even as he stepped into the room. *"¡Congelar!"* he shouted.

GRANT HAD DASHED back to the hotel as quickly as he was able, concerned at leaving Shizuka alone amid the nightmare scene. He wished he had some way to remain in touch with her in those moments as he sprinted through the back alleys of this strange city, wished she had a Commtact like the Cerberus personnel. But she wasn't Cerberus, despite working with them on occasion.

It took a minute or two of backtracking before Grant reached the service door to the hotel, the same one he had rushed through in pursuit of the strange trio he had spotted close to the scene. His breathing was coming heavier now, the night air cold on his skin as the initial surge of adrenaline passed.

Grant trotted down the corridor, reciting a mantra in his head, praying that Shizuka was still alive.

The twin doors to the ballroom were closed, so Grant switched the sharpened disc to his left hand before reaching for the handle with his right. By now, the feather protruding from his pocket had become bloodred; not wet, but its whole color had changed.

Grant pulled at the door and stepped through, coming face-to-face with a handsome, dark-haired man in a loose-fitting suit. Before Grant could say a word, the man produced a compact blaster and jabbed it toward Grant's surprised face.

"¡Congelar!" the man hollered.

Grant's Commtact translated the bellowed word automatically: "Freeze!"

Chapter 3

One side effect of the fall of the baronies was that obtaining food had become a source of dispute once more, Kane reflected. Kane was a powerfully built man with broad shoulders and rangy limbs that lent something of the wolf to his appearance. His hair was dark and his steely blue-gray eyes seemed to emotionlessly observe everything with meticulous precision. There was something of the wolf to Kane's demeanor, too—he was a loner at heart, and a natural pack leader when the situation called for it.

Like Grant, Kane had once been a Magistrate for the Cobaltville barony in the west, where he had enforced the law of the ville. But he had stumbled upon the conspiracy behind the ville—that is, the intended subjugation of mankind—and had turned against the regime and found himself exiled along with his partner and fellow rebels. From that day on, Kane had become an active member of the Cerberus organization, dedicated to the protection of humankind, freeing humans from the shadowy shackles that had been used to oppress them and stunt their potential for hundreds of years.

Right now, Kane was sitting in the rear of a six-wheeler beside three dozen sacks of grain as it trundled along a dirt road in the province of Samariumville. The road was narrow and straight, flanked by the scarred earth of fields that had been abandoned and left fallow as legacy of the radioactive fallout from the nukecaust. Radiation levels fell year on year, but it remained an unwanted gift from the past that just kept on giving, spawning mutant crops and poisonous fruit that was of no use for consumption. Therein lay part of the problem that Kane and his team were tackling with their guarding of these transports— so much of the land was still too damaged to sustain life, even two centuries on, from the nuclear exchange that had slowed down Western civilization.

One of three, Kane's vehicle featured an open bed, the sacks secured with rope, leaving it easy-pickings for the scavengers and cutthroats who roamed the barony. The cloudy sky was dark and ominous, and only the occasional bird caw could be heard over the growl of wag engines.

It hadn't always been like this, Kane lamented as he eyed the overcast sky and its sheets of silver-gray ripples. Barely three years earlier, the baronies had been intact, their high walls and firm laws ensuring safety for their occupants and loaning a degree of safety to the provinces beyond. Local Magistrates had patrolled problem areas outside the ville walls, stemming the threat of outlanders and muties who might destabilize the local area or foster an uprising against the ruling baron. All of that had changed when the barons had received something Kane understood as a "genetic download," a kind of evolutionary trigger that drew their hidden DNA to the fore, revealing the ethereal hybrid barons to be merely chrysalis states for their true forms—the reptilian Annunaki. The Annunaki were an alien race from the distant planet Nibiru, who had once been worshipped on Earth as gods during the Mesopotamian era, over six thousand years ago. Hungry for power, the Annunaki had ultimately squabbled themselves into mutual self-destruction.

However, the power vacuum left by the disappearance of the barons had resulted in the villes having to find new ways to survive and remain stable. Some had installed new barons, imitating the old system as closely as they could. Others, such as Cobaltville, had covered up their baron's disappearance, relying instead on Magistrate rule to ensure their populace remained under strict control. Kane had even found a new experimental barony where the population had been reprogrammed to adhere to subliminal commands, losing all independent thought.

Kane didn't know how Samariumville was running its show, nor did he much care, just as long as its people were safe. What did matter, however, was that the local territory had become more treacherous as rival gangs vied to carve up the land beyond the ville walls for their own usage. Those gangs included slave traders, gunrunners and other lowlifes who were only too happy to exploit and abuse anyone, human or mutie, who fell into their clutches. And all those crooks and ne'er-do-wells needed feeding, which was how Kane and his partners found themselves guarding this three-wag convoy as it crossed the unpopulated terrain to the west of Boontown, close to what had once been the Louisiana/Mississippi border.

Kane was here, along with two of his partners from the Cerberus organization, at the behest of a local businesswoman called Ohio Blue. Blue was an independent trader who dealt in everything from purified water supplies to esoteric objets d'art. She was very much under the radar so far as the authorities went, meaning she was unable to turn to the local Magistrates while running missions like this one—mercy missions she called them, although Kane knew the woman well enough to take that with a pinch of salt. Ohio Blue was a rogue, what Kane would call a bottom-feeder, but she was well connected and, along with her wide-reaching organization, had provided support and safety for Cerberus during their direst hour. Kane considered that he owed her for that. So when she spoke to Cerberus about running into some transport problems on this route, he had volunteered to ride shotgun and help make sure she didn't lose any more men. Cerberus had access to resources that even the well-connected Ohio didn't, including footage from surveillance satellites and operational air support.

Kane had dressed in muted colors, a faded gray denim jacket and combat pants, along with his favored Magistrate boots, which had a little protective armor in their construction. Beneath his clothes, Kane wore something even more durable—a skintight shadow suit, made from a superstrong weave that could dull a blade attack and offer some protection from small-arms fire. The miraculous shadow suit had other qualities, too—it was a wholly independent environment, which regulated the wearer's body temperature, ensuring that they could survive in extremes of heat and cold and could also protect against radiation. In short, the shadow suit provided an almost undetectable layer of protection that was comparable to much more bulky forms of armor, only without compromising maneuverability.

Kane was not alone. One member of the Cerberus crew had been assigned to each of the three transport wags after a spate of attacks along this, the only route running from farms in the west to a litter of smaller, desperate communities in the south. What Ohio was getting out of the deal, Kane could only speculate, but he knew her well enough to know that the op would not be run from the goodness of her heart. Cold hard cash was in the equation somewhere, and if that didn't sit well with Kane's more philanthropic instincts, then he could console himself that the food was going to hungry people who needed it. Traders like Ohio Blue profited out of misery, but they served a need that otherwise went unfulfilled.

Kane's partners were located in the two other wags, while Kane took the foremost, wary of a frontal assault. The middle wag contained Brigid Baptiste, an ex-archivist from Cobaltville who, like Kane, had stumbled onto the conspiracy at the top of the ville and been swiftly exiled from its walls. Brigid and Kane had worked together for a long time, ever since that exile into the so-called hell beyond the ville walls. During that time, they had learned that they shared a mystic bond that traversed time and space. That bond named them *anam-charas*, or soul friends, and it put them closer than siblings or lovers, a deeper bond than mere flesh or chronological time could contain.

Guarding the rearmost wag was Domi. Domi was another exile from Cobaltville, although she had been born an outlander in the atomic wastes beyond its high walls. Unlike most of the Cerberus staff, which numbered almost forty housed in a refitted military redoubt in Montana, Domi had little in the way of a formal education. As such, she could come across as brash, even animal like in her desires and the methods that she considered acceptable in achieving those desires. Kane, however, trusted her implicitly. He figured that if she was wild with an uncontrollable streak, then it was better to have her at his side than at somebody else's.

The trio of wags trundled on across the stark landscape under the afternoon cloud cover. The wags were similar without matching. They were tired things, old designs patched together and brought back into service, a caking of mud and dirt and poor repaints loaning them the appearance of patchwork quilts as they bumped over the rough road. All three had flatbed rears, though the rearmost included a rail around the bed for added security. A two-man cab sat up front, where driver and shotgun traveled, scanning the long road for danger. Behind the cab of the front and rear vehicles, a makeshift gun turret had been installed, running a .50 gauge machine gun with belt ammo, while the middle wag had two smaller guns installed on tripods on the rear. The vehicles ran on alcofuel—"homebrew engines," the drivers called them, which gave some insight into where that fuel was coming from.

Crouched between sacks, Kane kept alert. Back in his Magistrate days he had been fabled for his point-man sense, a seemingly uncanny ability to sense danger before it happened. It was no supernatural ability, however—just the combination of his five senses making intuitive leaps at an almost Zen-like level.

The road seemed empty, abandoned even, like a lot of the back roads across the territory that had once been called the United States of America. So much had suffered in the nukecaust, and the population had been reduced to one-tenth of what it had been before the war. That left back roads like this abandoned and forgotten, and even now, two hundred years after the last bomb had been dropped, they remained overgrown and despoiled. There was an irony in that, Kane saw—that it was almost impossible to grow crops on the irradiated land and yet the old roads had become beds for wild grasses.

They were approaching a rise, the splutter of the wag engine loud as it tackled the incline. Kane thought back to how Ohio Blue had described the previous attacks on her freight convoys. "The wags were crippled and left to rot," she had said, "and my men had been singed by fire, their flesh burned away. Those who had survived had been incomprehensible, babbling about red and amber lights as though they had been attacked by a predark traffic signal."

He was armed, of course, even though that was not obvious from looking at him. Kane wore a Sin Eater, an automatic pistol, in a retractable holster hidden beneath his right sleeve. The Sin Eater's holster was activated by a specific flinch movement of Kane's wrist tendons, powering the weapon into his hand. The weapon itself was a compact hand blaster, roughly fourteen inches in length but able to fold in on itself for storage in the hidden holster. The Sin Eater was the official sidearm of the Magistrate Division, and his carrying it dated back to when Kane had still been a hard-contact Mag. The blaster was armed with 9 mm rounds and its trigger had no guard—the necessity had never been foreseen that any kind of safety features for the weapon would ever be required, for a Mag was judge, jury and executioner all in one man, and his judgment was considered to be infallible. Thus, if the user's index finger was crooked at the time the weapon reached his hand, the pistol would begin firing automatically. Kane had retained his weapon from his days in service at Cobaltville, and he felt most comfortable with the weapon in hand—its weight was a comfort to him, the way the weight of a wristwatch felt natural on a habitual wearer.

When it happened, it wasn't obvious. Kane's attention was drawn to a group of black-feathered birds who had been grazing on the scarred soil some way behind them when they suddenly took flight. The birds had moved when the wags approached, but they had returned to their meager feast almost as soon as the wags had passed. But now, a hundred yards down the road where nothing seemed to be passing, the birds took flight once more, circling in the air and issuing angry caws that could be heard even over the sound of the wag's engine. There was another sound, too, Kane realized. Low and deep, a bass note that vibrated the air and the ground beneath them as its pitch rose. The sound could barely be heard over the spluttering roar of wag engines, but it was there—a tuneless hum, the deep thrumming noise of something mechanical.

"Domi," Kane said, automatically activating the hidden Commtact that was located beneath his skin along the side of his head. "Pay attention to your six. I think there's something—"

His words trailed off as he spotted the wispy trail of gray smoke rising against the silver clouds where the birds had taken flight. Not from the road but to the side.

"You don't need to tell me how to do my job," Domi was complaining over their shared Commtact frequency. "I've stood guard over more than a sack of corn before now."

Kane tuned her out, watching the plume of smoke as it twisted in the breeze. It was not solid, it was little puffs of smoke being emitted at regular intervals—which probably meant it was an engine of some kind, Kane realized.

"Baptiste," Kane said, calling on the other member of his field team, "do you see smoke back there, on the road behind us?"

Brigid's familiar voice piped into Kane's ear a moment later. "Puff-puff-puff, pause…puff-puff-puff, pause," she began, copying the beat of the smoke. "Yes, I can see it all right."

Around him, the wag's engine growled as it struggled to ascend the hill, speed dropping with every foot it gained. The damn thing was overloaded, leaving them vulnerable on the incline—ripe for ambush. For a moment, Kane could see the whole of the road that they had traveled along stretched out behind him, a strip of grass and dirt and broken tarmac that ran in a perfectly straight line through the sparse fields. From this height, he could see the thing that was following them, too—not along the road but to one side of it, scrambling through the fields to his left where the crows had taken flight. It looked like a boxcar, the kind you would find on an old-style train, its dull metal finish almost perfectly camouflaged by the sky behind it. But this was no railroad train. The metal box swung high off the ground, depending from two pivoting legs that clambered over the uneven ground like a gigantic, grounded bird. Thirty feet high, it was moving at some speed, faster in fact than the three wags that Kane's crew were protecting.

Kane watched as the strange-looking machine continued forward, getting steadily closer to the back of the convoy.

"I see it," Domi said, her words echoing over their shared Commtacts.

"Me, too," Brigid chimed in.

It was at that moment that the strange vehicle unleashed the first of its heat bolts, searing red-amber energy cutting through the sky accompanied by a shriek of parting air.

"Traffic signal," Kane muttered. "Right."

The red-hot blast carved a path toward them like a slash of blood spraying through the air.

Chapter 4

"¡Congelar!" Pretor Corcel demanded, his pistol aimed unwaveringly at Grant where the Cerberus warrior was framed in the doorway to the ballroom.

Grant knew better than to argue with a man who had a gun. He raised his hands slowly, making sure not to make any sudden movements. "I'm freezing," he stated in English. "I'm freezing."

The doctor who had attended the nightmarish scene had been startled by Corcel's shout, and he looked up to see the strange man just entering the doorway.

The sharp-suited Pretor held in place, watching Grant carefully. "American?" he asked.

"Yeah," Grant replied. He saw that the bodies had been removed from the room. More worrying was the fact that Shizuka was nowhere to be seen. The man with the blaster was twelve feet away—probably too far to rush in an open space like this, Grant calculated, too risky anyway. For now at least, Grant would have to play along and hope he could find out just what the heck was happening.

Still holding the Devorador de Pecados pistol on Grant, Pretor Corcel's dark eyes flicked to the razor-sharp disc that his target held in his hand. "Drop the weapon," he instructed.

"Okay." Grant nodded. Then he lowered his left hand, moving it away from his body just slightly before dropping the razor disc. The disc struck the wooden floor with a hollow clang. "That ain't mine," Grant said, though he could hear how lame that must sound right now. As he dropped it, Grant studied the man whom he faced, eyeing his smart clothes and the weapon he held on him with professional surety. The man's blaster was black with sleek lines, compact but of a large bore—probably a 9 mm, Grant guessed. It reminded him of his own weapon of choice—the Sin Eater, side arm of the Magistrate Division.

Corcel ignored Grant's comment. "Now," he instructed, "hands up behind your head, you understand?"

"Yeah, I understand," Grant said, moving his hands as instructed until the fingers were laced together behind his head. He knew this move, had used it himself as a Magistrate and after that. It was the move of a professional, which meant his opponent had obviously had training in controlling people. "I think there's probably some mistake—"

"You keep quiet and you answer my questions only when asked," the sharp-suited man told him.

"Sure, you've got the gun," Grant confirmed.

Then Pretor Corcel gave instructions to the doctor to go find his partner and bring her here. He spoke in Spanish, though Grant's Commtact automatically translated the exchange in real time. The discussion gave little away, but Grant tried to piece together what he could. The man in the suit was addressed as "Pretor" by the other man, Grant heard, or Praetor, another word for *Judge* or *Magistrate*.

As the other man left the room, Grant addressed the figure in the dark suit. "You're a Mag, right?" he asked. "A Magistrate?"

Corcel studied him warily. "Yes—Pretor Corcel," he said. "You speak Spanish, then?"

"A little," Grant lied. "Only a few words."

Corcel nodded sullenly, waiting before Grant with the blaster aimed at him. Grant stood like that for almost two minutes until Corcel's partner came striding into the room in a suit similar to Corcel's.

"Pretor Cáscara," she introduced herself immediately, flashing an ID badge in Grant's direction, too fast to read.

Corcel rapidly explained the situation to his partner in swiftly spoken Spanish, and Grant began to understand what had happened. It seemed that Corcel had had reports of black men with shaven heads who were involved in a spate of murders, and that Grant fit the description. Cáscara stepped over to the sharp-edged disc that Grant had dropped, kneeling to examine it where it lay as the two officers spoke. Corcel explained that the suspect had been carrying the weapon when he had returned to the crime scene.

"Dumb mistake," Cáscara lamented in Spanish.

It would have been, Grant thought, *except that I picked this up from the people who actually did do this. I think.*

"You," Cáscara said to Grant in lightly accented English once she had been brought up to speed by her partner, "hands down, here, behind your back." She showed him, crossing her wrists together at the small of her back. "I'm going to cuff you. You try anything and Pretor Corcel will shoot you, okay? He's a good shot."

"Top of my graduating class," Corcel added, his pistol never wavering.

"Yeah, I get it," Grant said, lowering his hands as instructed. "You've got the wrong guy, you realize?"

"We'll figure that out back at the Sector Hall," Cáscara told him emotionlessly as she placed a pair of plastic handcuffs on Grant's wrists. Then she stepped away and produced a pair of latex gloves from a pocket of her jacket, which she slipped over her hands. Along with the gloves, she produced an evidence bag, into which she placed the metallic projectile that Grant had narrowly avoided.

"Had that thrown at me," Grant explained. "There's

another one of those out there somewhere. Couldn't see it, though."

The two Pretors did not respond to his comment.

Once the first evidence pack was sealed, Cáscara returned to Grant, who remained standing close to the open ballroom doors. She reached for the bloodred feather that poked from one hip pocket of his jacket.

"More of these out there, too?" Cáscara challenged him. It was hard to tell with her not being a native English speaker, but Grant thought that she was employing a sarcastic tone.

"Look," Grant said, "I had a partner here. A friend. We came here together—"

"We'll discuss that at the Sector Hall," Corcel cut him off.

"Sure, I just—" Grant began.

"Quiet now," Corcel said in a warning tone, gesturing vaguely with his blaster. "Don't make me shoot you."

"Okay," Grant said, "I just want to know what happened to her. If she's okay. Her name's Shizuka."

Pretor Cáscara looked up at that from where she had been labeling the evidence bags with a marker pen.

"Shizuka…?" Grant repeated hopefully.

Cáscara nodded firmly just the once. "She's here. We'll be bringing her in," she confirmed. Then she moved closer to Corcel and whispered something to him in Spanish. It was too quiet for Grant to hear, but he guessed he might have inadvertently just turned Shizuka into a suspect. At least she was still alive.

GRANT WAS TAKEN via secure wag past the bullfighting ring to the local Sector Hall of Justice, a grand building in the center of Zaragoza that housed the authorities. The building was four stories high and stretched the length of a block, with tinted glass in the windows and a basement

level housing the garage and firing range. The Pretors—
the local equivalent of Magistrates—were based here, and
they patrolled not only Zaragoza City but also the state
beyond, covering an eighty-mile radius that took them
well into the radiation-blighted lands to the south and east.

Once inside, Grant was swiftly processed by a uniformed Pretor—his uniform consisting of flexible armor
in black and red, the tailored jacket flaring at the bottom
so that it created something approaching a skirt across
the hips. The Pretor was armed with a boot knife and had
a holster—currently empty—at his hip. Grant could see
notches around the high neck of his uniform where a helmet would be secured while on patrol.

After he had been processed—a simple procedure of
taking holographs and prints—Grant was taken to a secure, white-walled interview room and left alone to wait.
The room featured harsh lighting and contained a single
table to which Grant's right wrist was cuffed on a short
chain, along with four chairs, two to either side of the table.
Grant waited almost forty minutes until Corcel, the officer
whom he had first met in the hotel ballroom, joined him.
Corcel's expression was unreadable as he greeted Grant,
pulling a chair across to him before reversing it to sit on,
his arms resting across its back.

"Your name?" Corcel asked without preamble.

"Grant."

"Grant…?"

"Just Grant," Grant confirmed. "Only name I ever
needed."

"And you are an American, we have already estab-
lished."

"That's right."

"Whereabouts from?"

"Originally Cobaltville. More recently, all over, but
still in that territory."

"I see. And your purpose for being here, in Zaragoza?"

"Vacation, with a friend."

Corcel checked something in the little A7 notebook he carried. "And that would be Shizuka, correct?"

Grant nodded.

"And what is your relationship to Shizuka?"

"Boyfriend/girlfriend," Grant said, eyes locking with Corcel's, an unspoken challenge there. "Is this going anywhere, Pretor Corcel?"

"Just establishing the facts. Do you know why you are here, Grant?"

"I got an inkling," Grant admitted, "but why don't you explain how you see it."

"You were discovered at the scene of a crime," Pretor Corcel stated, "the ballroom in the Gran Retiro. You match the description of one of our suspects, which is why you've been brought in for questioning. In addition to this, you had certain items about your person that we might expect to find on the perpetrator.

"Do you know what happened in the ballroom, Grant?"

Grant tilted his head to show he was uncertain. "When Shizuka and I arrived the place was full of hanging bodies—I didn't imagine that, right?"

Corcel nodded. "Go on."

"I guess there were twenty-two, twenty-four people hanging from the ceiling in nooses," Grant recalled. "Didn't know why."

"So you confirm you were at the scene prior to our engagement?" Corcel checked.

"Yeah. I saw someone I thought was suspicious—three people, all together—and so I followed them while trusting Shizuka to look after the   I dunno what you call them— victims, maybe?"

Corcel looked intrigued. "When you say you saw someone you thought was suspicious, what happened then?"

"I followed them through the service door and out into the back streets," Grant said, "but they threw something at me—the sharp disc-thing you saw—and escaped before I could catch up to them."

"I see," Corcel said, "and could you describe these people?"

Grant nodded. "Yeah, I got a good look at them and I have a good memory for faces, clothes."

"But you yourself had nothing to do with the bodies you saw?"

"No, sir," Grant confirmed.

Corcel watched Grant for a few seconds, searching for the truth among his words. Then Grant spoke up.

"You've had your chance," Grant said, "so let me now start answering the questions you should have asked, and we'll see if we can get somewhere on this—"

Pretor Corcel's eyebrows rose with surprise.

"Number one," Grant began, "I'm an ex-Magistrate what you'd call a Pretor. So I'm one of you."

"An *ex*-Magistrate…?" Corcel asked, placing emphasis on the first word.

"Cobaltville Mag Division, but I left," Grant elaborated. "Little disagreement, but not to do with the law."

Corcel gestured for him to explain.

"Turns out my boss was a snake—literally—so I found myself in an untenable position," Grant explained. "Me and Shizuka came here for a vacation—she's an important muckety-muck in New Edo, and I've got my own thing I wanted to get away from. My guess is that we should have been at that ballroom when all the hangings happened, but we were running late—ate later than we planned, didn't leave the restaurant until almost ten."

Pretor Corcel's eyes lit up at this. "Which restaurant was this?" he asked. "Do you think the staff there could confirm you were there when you said you were?"

"I'd hope so," Grant said. "Guy like me kind of stands out in your city." So did Shizuka, from what he could tell, Grant mentally added, recalling that he had seen no other people here of Asian descent.

Corcel nodded slowly, pondering the information that the hulking man had given him. It could be true, although it didn't confirm that the man calling himself Grant was not also the killer. He would need to take this one step at a time.

"So that's why I followed them," Grant finished. "Old instincts getting me involved when I didn't have an invite."

"I'll look into your story," Corcel told Grant, rising from his seat. "You're going to have to sit tight until then."

Grant nodded. Despite his frustration he could understand things from this local Magistrate's point of view. "Just tell me something," he said as Corcel strode across the room to the door. "Is Shizuka all right?"

Corcel stared at Grant, the professional hardness in his eyes softening for a moment. "She's a little shook up, but otherwise she seems to be fine. We have her here right now."

For questioning, Grant guessed. "Just make sure she's okay for me, all right?" he asked.

Corcel nodded. "I'll do that."

SHIZUKA, MEANWHILE, WAS in a room two flights above from where Grant was being held. She had been checked over by one of the Pretors' medical staff and now she sat with Pretor Cáscara on a comfortable couch, discussing what had happened in the hotel ballroom.

There was not much that Shizuka could say that she had not already told Cáscara, but she sketched out a rough timescale of the events and outlined the state of the room when they had entered and how she and Grant had discovered the bodies.

"You've had a traumatic few hours," Cáscara said sympathetically. "The clinician here wants to keep an eye on you, to make sure you don't go into shock. Do you think that would be okay?"

"I should speak to Grant," Shizuka said.

"I'll tell him you're here," Cáscara assured her. "He's fine."

Shizuka eyed the female Pretor warily. "Can I see him?" she asked.

"Soon, yes," Cáscara promised.

"When?"

"Soon."

Cáscara left Shizuka then, and the samurai woman was escorted to a safe room—a cell by another name. The room was comfortable and low-lit with white walls and a vase of flowers and a jug of water on a nightstand beside the single bed. It looked like a private hospital room. Shizuka was too tired to argue, but she remained alert for a long time, pacing the room and wondering about Grant.

In the corridor outside the room, Pretor Corcel met with his partner, Cáscara, to share information as they watched Shizuka pace back and forth through a one-way pane of glass.

"My guy says he's innocent," Corcel said in Spanish.

"That's always the first defense, Juan," Cáscara said dismissively.

"But there's more to it than that," Corcel continued. "He says he's—get this—an ex-Magistrate, US. He's retired from service, he's not shy about explaining that, and he happened to be out here on vacation."

Pretor Cáscara pushed one slender hand through the long bangs of her fringe. "So he's one of us. Do you believe him?"

Corcel looked thoughtful. "It's certainly an unusual tactic if he is lying," he concluded. "What about the woman, Liana? What does she say?"

Cáscara peered through the one-way glass before replying, watching as Shizuka tidied her hair in the mirror that lay on the obverse side of the glass. "She says she's the leader of the Tigers of Heaven from New Edo," she said.

Corcel let out a grim sigh. "Their stories match. Did she give you anything else?"

"The name of a restaurant she and the boyfriend were attending when the crime was committed," Cáscara stated.

"Yeah, I got that, too."

"What do you think? Are they for real?"

Corcel shrugged. "The man—Grant—is certainly built. And if his story is true, then he's been trained to kill. He could be our killer—he's physically capable."

"But why come back to the scene?" Cáscara wondered.

"To remove evidence maybe," Corcel proposed. "Something he left behind. Or…"

Cáscara raised a querulous eyebrow as her partner left the sentence unfinished. "Or…?" she prompted.

"Or maybe they really did just bungle into this mess, in which case we're no closer than we were before to finding out who's committing these showpiece murders and how, Liana," Corcel said grimly. "Except that my suspect claims he saw the killers—or, at least, some people he thinks were at the scene at the time of the 'performance.'"

Emiliana Cáscara shook her head heavily. "We already have over two hundred dead in less than three weeks, Juan," she said. "If this goes on—"

"It's unconscionable," Corcel agreed. "Let's check their story first, see if it gels with what the restaurant owner remembers. After that—well, we'll see."

Chapter 5

Crouched among the sacks of corn in the rearmost road wag, Domi watched with a growing sense of disbelief as the weird machine came trundling across the field toward her, and a fanlike aperture irised open on its front surface. An instant later, the aperture began to glow, before unleashing a beam of red-gold energy across the distance between itself and the convoy.

Domi didn't hesitate. She leaped up, scrambling across the rear bed of the wag even as the energy beam screamed toward her. It struck an instant later, clipping the port flank of the truck with a shriek, accompanied by a wall of burning hotness that seemed to wash across the wag in a wave.

As the wave struck, Domi dropped down behind a pile of grain sacks, sheltering behind them as the wall of heat caromed past overhead, rolling over the roof of the wag and leaving the sacks untouched.

Domi was a strange-looking woman, an albino with chalk-white skin and bone-white hair, red eyes the color of blood. She was petite and slender of frame with small, pert breasts and bird-thin limbs that she habitually kept on show, wearing only the bare minimum of clothing. For this mission, however, she wore a dark hoodie, its hood up to hide her face, and shorts, her pale legs darkened with a smearing of dirt for camouflage. She had kept her feet bare, preferring to feel the land beneath her than fuss with shoes or boots. Strapped to her ankle was a six-inch combat blade with a serrated edge. It was the same blade with which she had killed her slave master, Guana Teague, back in Cobaltville years before, and she carried it with her like a comfort blanket. Domi had another weapon, too, a Detonics Combat Master with a silver finish, which she wore holstered at her hip in a brown leather sheath.

The wag swerved under the force of the heat blast, one metal side liquefying in a moment until it resembled the remains of a wax candle, the cooling surface creating new patterns in a matter of moments. Behind her, Domi could hear the two men in the cab shout in shock as the heat ray rose the temperature within by a dozen degrees in those instants. One man cursed loudly as the surface he was touching became suddenly too hot to handle.

The wag bumped off the road for a half-dozen seconds, two wheels running along the uneven ground of the field to the right before the driver righted it.

As the wave of heat passed, Domi's Commtact blurted to life—Kane and Brigid both asking for a status update and whether she was okay.

"I'm fine," Domi growled between gritted teeth. Already she was unholstering her Detonics revolver, flipping off the safety as she watched the weird box on legs come striding across the abandoned landscape toward the convoy.

The towering box was moving closer, its long legs perfectly suited to traveling across the uneven ground of the surrounding fields, taking ten-foot strides toward Domi and the wag. As it closed in, Domi saw the secondary attachments running up both sides of the mysterious vehicle—twin railguns located on either side of the boxy cabin, belt-fed and situated in the gap between legs and box. The railguns were mounted on swivel balls, giving them a limited range of fire. But it was enough to cover everything in front of the weird, scaffold-like machine.

Domi took aim from behind the cover of the grain sacks, closing one eye and focusing on the aperture as it cycled again. The aperture looked flat when it was closed, interlocking metal shutters in a weblike pattern sealing off the hole. There was a flickering of brightness deep within where something was burning, Domi saw.

That was as much as Domi had time to process before the boxy construction fired again, sending another screaming blast of intense heat toward the wag like a man chucking a spear. Domi narrowed her eyes against the brightness and squeezed the trigger on her blaster, sending a 9 mm titanium-clad bullet toward the box-on-legs as the red-gold beam struck. The bullet was caught in the red wave and it disintegrated, melting down to liquid in less than a second.

Two wags ahead, Kane eyed the weird machine as it charged across the rough terrain toward the convoy. It had already blasted the rear wag, and Kane watched as the wag slewed off the road before returning to the track. He could see that it was losing ground—their attacker's plan was rudimentary, but that was how the classics worked.

Kane engaged his Commtact. "They're picking us off from behind," he shouted, "trying to split us up."

Brigid acknowledged Kane's observation with a "hmf" that seemed to say *"well, obviously."*

Kane shouted to his driver, "Take us back and circle before we lose the back man."

The driver—a blond-haired man of twenty with the puppy fat and bright white teeth of a teen—popped his head out of the cab and looked back. "I'll slow but I'm not stopping, Kane," he shouted over the roar of the straining engine. "We've lost too many people on this stretch of road already."

"Good enough," Kane spit, his eyes fixed on the mechanical colossus on the horizon.

As the driver spoke, his partner was clambering out of a roof hatch to operate the machine gun that was mounted just behind the cab. The man was slender with gangly limbs and a prominent Adam's apple, his shoulder-length hair decorated with twisted ribbons. Wedging himself behind the cab, the man swung the heavy gun around until it pointed to the rear. Then he squeezed the trigger. "I can't make the distance," he said with evident irritation as he watched the shots fall short.

Kane glanced at him, then back down the road. "Get behind it," he instructed to the driver, indicating with a circling motion of his hand. "Get behind it!"

With a shifting of grinding gears, the wag pulled up a slope to the side of the road and the driver began scanning for a clear route on which to comply with Kane's instructions. "You better not be getting us killed, Kane," the driver shouted as he fought with the steering wheel. "Ohio won't never forgive you if you do that."

"I'll do my best to avoid it," Kane shouted back as he watched the mechanical marvel stride closer to Domi's wag. It was still charging, blasting another red beam of light ahead of it. Between that and his wag was the other wag—the one that Brigid Baptiste was guarding.

Kane raced through the possibilities in his sharp mind, narrowing down his options. He was a veteran of combat, but at that moment, watching the heat beam carve another slice from the rearmost wag, he couldn't help feeling that they had brought a knife to a gunfight.

IN THE MIDDLE WAG, Brigid Baptiste had scrambled across the flatbed to operate the twin tripod guns located just behind the cab. She was a beautiful woman in her late twenties, dressed in a black, skintight cat suit—in fact a shadow suit like Kane's—over which she wore a quarter-length denim jacket and thigh-high leather boots with a TP-9 semiautomatic pistol holstered at her hip. She had long, luxuriant red-gold hair the color of sunset, green eyes like twin emeralds and the slender, perfectly defined figure of an athlete. She had a high brow that spoke of intelligence and full lips that promised passion, but in reality Brigid held both of those aspects and many more besides. An ex-archivist from Cobaltville, Brigid had become caught up in the same conspiracy that had seen Kane exiled and her removed from her post, a move that had landed her with the Cerberus organization. Brigid was well versed in hand-to-hand combat and a crack shot, but it was her eidetic—or photographic—memory that was her greatest asset, and the one that had got her into so much trouble back in her archivist days. Like Kane, Brigid was one of the high flyers of the Cerberus operation, and she had been instrumental in a number of their scientific advances. She had partnered Kane more times than either cared to count.

Brigid swung the guns around, watching as the lumbering, artificial behemoth came striding across the uneven terrain toward the rearmost road wag.

The boxy bulk of the unit was long and narrow, curved along its sides with the opening aperture located dead center, the twin railguns situated to the sides, slightly below the center—presumably geared for ground-based attacks rather than air assaults. There was a bank of windows above the heat-ray aperture through which Brigid could see several figures silhouetted. Beneath the cab was a cylinder running the length of the box, welded beneath it and bulging along its length in a series of metal rings. Brigid guessed that this housed whatever was generating the heat beam that their attackers were using to devastating effect. Two legs were positioned on either side of the cabin box, running higher than the box itself so that they pivoted above it as it walked, swinging the cab where it hung between them by thick lengths of chain. The whole thing had been left in raw metal, giving it a homemade appearance and blending perfectly with the overcast sky.

Brigid watched as the machine blasted again, counting the seconds between each fiery burst. Thirty seconds between blasts, she timed. *It's taking that long to achieve full power again. That's our window.*

She flicked the safety on the left-hand machine gun and pressed down the trigger, sending a stuttering burst of bullets at their fast-moving pursuer.

WRONG-FOOTED, DOMI dropped and started to roll across the bed of the rearmost wag as it began to glow red with heat. The wag careened off the road again, and this time the driver could not fight it. Suddenly they were cutting through open fields of ash and soil, a clutch of birds taking flight as they were disturbed.

The box on legs followed, stamping across the field in pursuit of the struggling wag. Bullets were hammering against its armored surface from the middle wag, but the distance was too great—too few were scoring hits, and none of those hits were making any difference.

Domi flipped herself back to her feet, snatching up her blaster where it had slipped out of her hand. Then the wag was bathed in that flickering red-amber light as their attacker launched another volley of heat at them.

The rear of the truck heated in a second, a faint glow of red appearing in the center of the drop-down gate at the back. Then, with a clap of bursting tires, the back of the truck sank down into the ground where the back wheels had melted under the assault. Domi was jerked left and right as the wag began to spin out of control, bumping over the uneven ground.

"We're losing it!" the driver yelped from up front.

Waves of dirt were kicked up as the wag continued forward for a few seconds, ripped from the ground by the ruined axles, before the wag came to a spinning halt.

Domi leaped over the glowing side of the wag as it came to a stop, landing on the churned soil with catlike grace.

Despite her youth, Domi was a seasoned veteran of combat and in peak physical fitness. She scrambled to the front of the wag as the box-on-legs began to power up its heat beam for another blast.

"Get out of there," Domi shouted, wrenching open the driver's door. "Get out of there before—"

Both driver and passenger—a man and a heavily tattooed woman—were slumped against the dashboard, blood on their faces and splattered against the windshield.

Domi reached for the driver, a dark-skinned man in a gray undershirt wearing a .44 in a chest rig. "Are you…?" she began, but her words died on her lips as she received no response from the man. He was alive but unconscious.

Before Domi had any more time to act, a stream of 15 mm bullets rattled against the side of the cab, churning up dirt and kicking against the wag's side like a kicking mule. It was her that they were targeting now, Domi realized as she ducked behind the front of the cab. No doubt these road pirates didn't want to ruin the crop that would be their haul.

CRIPPLE THE VEHICLE, disable the crew and then steal the goods—it was a pretty simple plan, Kane saw.

"We need to circle," Kane told Brigid over the Commtact. "Get behind these scavengers and take them off the board."

"Roger that," Brigid agreed. A moment later, Kane saw Brigid's wag bump off-road in preparation of making a circuit around their attacker. He only hoped that Domi was all right.

Brigid's and Kane's wags were both off the track now, splitting left and right to come around and challenge the mechanical assault vehicle. The wags bumped over the fallow fields, dropping down into potholes before rearing up again like scared stallions, their mounted guns blazing.

The wags were rugged, but they were not designed for this kind of treatment. Their cargo shifted and shook on their beds, and Kane's companion wailed in frustration as one of the guy ropes tore and three sacks of grain went tumbling over the side.

"Leave 'em," Kane instructed. "When we survive this, we can go back for them."

The gunner looked at Kane with raised eyebrows. "When?"

"Stay positive, boy," Kane told him. "No point losing the fight before you've entered it."

Bullets spit from the turret, finding their distance now as the wag closed in on the striding behemoth. In the opposite field, on the far side of the broken strip of road, Brigid was working one of the tripod guns while one of Ohio Blue's troops took the other, sending short bursts of bullets at the towering monstrosity trudging across the fields. Suddenly, the box-on-legs turned, slowing its stride as it brought its aperture to bear on Brigid's wag.

"Baptiste!" Kane shouted into his Commtact, unable to do anything else.

Chapter 6

Brigid had been counting off the seconds in her head. It had been twenty-five seconds since their mystery attacker had last fired that cataclysmic ray—and she knew she should have thirty before it could do so again.

As Kane's warning came, Brigid reached across to the other gunner, a woman in her forties with prematurely graying hair and the deeply tanned complexion of a Native American. "Get down!" Brigid instructed.

The gunner didn't stop to query the instruction; she just let go of the tripod gun and dropped to the deck behind it. Beside her, Brigid was doing the same.

Then the ray blasted, zapping a melting beam of incredible heat toward the wag, bathing it in boiling red light. Brigid turned her head away from the blast as it washed over the back plate of the six-wheeler. She could feel the warmth running down her right-hand side as the periphery of the beam lashed against her, her shadow suit compensating instantly. Beside her, the red-skinned woman fared less well, spitting a curse as the tassels of her jacket caught fire, then tamping the flames down with swift pats of her hand.

As soon as the beam faded, Brigid was back up to work the guns again. The wag was still moving, bumping across the uneven ground of the fallow field, and it took Brigid a few seconds to adjust her aim.

"Kane, it's taking them thirty seconds to power up that

heat ray," she said as she drew the tripod cannon around and squeezed the trigger. "That's how long you have to drop it."

"COPY THAT," KANE acknowledged as his own wag went caroming over the bumpy field. "Hey, Paul," he called to the driver while his partner worked the turret gun. "Get us closer!"

"Closer? You want closer?" the driver sounded outraged.

"Just do it!" Kane snarled back as he scrambled to the edge of the wag's flatbed. A moment later, as the wag sped past the towering machine, Kane leaped over the side, dropping into a tuck-and-roll as he stuck the soil. Above him, the boxy construct began firing with its secondary railguns, sending a swift burst of bullets in the direction of the scrambling wag that Kane had just disembarked, drilling 15 mm shells across the roof and side of the retreating wag. The bullets struck like hail, clattering across the metal and drilling through with a sound like clashing cymbals.

The wag swerved left and right behind him as Kane rose from the ground and began to sprint across the terrain toward their towering assailant. Kane was thirty feet away from it now, and this close it looked a lot like scaffolding with a box depending from the chains. The legs were part-built, all girders and tubing with great hinge joints running down the sides, two in each leg plus a whole network of smaller hinges at the ankles to better ensure stability across any terrain. The feet were wide, flat plates, each one seven feet across with a bobbled underside that could find purchase on the uneven surface of the ground.

As Kane ran, the heat beam screamed again, sending another red line at his retreating ride, carving it almost in two. The back end of Kane's wag tore partially away from the front and the whole wag collapsed in on itself, the wheels spinning uselessly as it sunk down in the middle. A moment later, the driver leaped from the cab, dropping the six feet to the ground where his cab had become raised. The gunner, meanwhile, lay sprawled against the turret, his flesh turned a ghastly red where the heat ray had struck him. He was dead.

Kane continued to run, knowing that he had thirty seconds to reach their enemy before it could fire another heat burst. As he ran, he powered the Sin Eater pistol into his right hand with a practiced flinch of his wrist tendons.

All around, bullets were whizzing through the air, the high mounted railguns firing down on the last of the moving wags while Brigid and her companion fired back from the twin tripods in the back of the rig. Domi, too, was shooting, using her Detonics to take potshots at the enemy's cab to distract them. From up there, it must have seemed that they were being attacked from all sides—the perfect distraction for what Kane had in mind.

Kane reached the underside of their monstrous attacker, dodging and weaving as more 15 mm bullets churned up the ground in his wake, the right-hand railgun swiveling on its mount to try to get a bead on him. Kane held down his trigger, sending a trail of 9 mm bullets at the closest foot of the walker, searching for a weak spot. The bullets pinged against the armor, ricocheting in all directions but barely scratching the metal.

"Damn," Kane muttered, easing his finger off the Sin Eater's trigger and scanning the underside of the towering vehicle for inspiration. There had to be a way to bring it down, had to be some way to crack that armor.

Dancing out of the way of the moving feet, Kane activated his Commtact once again. "Baptiste? What have you got for me? How do we bring this bastard down?"

Brigid worked the tripod gun as she responded to Kane. "Find some way to stop the heat beam," she said.

"Like how?" Kane replied, the note of desperation clear in his voice.

Brigid and her colleague were working the tripod guns mounted on the back of the wag in fits. The whole wag was warm from the effect of the heat beam, and the guns were threatening to overheat. The wag zigzagged across the field, bumping over ruts in the soil and tangled grass as a stream of bullets followed them from the high-mounted railguns, spitting sparks from the metal sides of the wag. One of the sacks of grain burst under the assault, spilling its contents in a cloud of yellow dust.

"Overheat it," Brigid said in a sudden moment of inspiration.

"Overheat it?" Kane repeated as he chased after the machine, which was striding after Brigid's wag. "How?"

"A weapon like that must throw out a lot of heat to operate," Brigid reasoned.

Kane's eyes roved across the metal surface of the walking weapon as Brigid spoke.

"If you can find the source and block it, you could—"

"Got it!" Kane said, spying a dark patch on the back of the dangling cab where wispy steam was emanating. He ran after the retreating vehicle, commanding his Sin Eater back into its hidden holster, and a moment later he leaped onto the swinging left leg as it hurtled past. Clinging there, Kane reached up, using the scaffold-like leg as a ladder, finding handholds and footholds as he ascended the swaying limb of the moving vehicle.

Bullets drummed against the cab above him as Kane scrambled up past the first knee joint, ten feet above the ground. Then he felt the whole vehicle vibrate and the heat beam fired again, cleaving the back from the remaining wag in an explosion of melted metal and tossed grain.

Kane clung tightly to the leg as it swung forward, then came down again, stomping on the edge of the wag where it was melting. Brigid and her companion leaped from the back of the wag as the colossus took another step, crushing the back end of the vehicle. It was obvious that its occupants did not mind losing a little of their spoils if it meant getting rid of the competition.

The cab turned as Brigid reached for the driver's door. The door was jammed where the metal had become buckled under the assault, and Kane watched helplessly for a moment as his red-haired colleague wrenched at the door. As she did so, the boxy cab of the walker whirred on its hydraulics, drawing around to line up the railguns on the people below.

"Hey, ugly!" The shout was harsh and it came from behind Kane and the walker.

Kane looked down, saw Domi standing there with her Detonics pistol held in a two-handed grip and aimed high at the cab of the walker. The pistol's silver finish glinted in the overcast light. The pistol bucked in her hands as Domi sent shot after shot into the side window of the boxy cab, firing over and over as the walking machine began to slowly react. The glass fractured, spiderwebbing in an instant but still holding in place.

Kane was close enough to the cab that he heard the voices coming from within. "Turn us around," a woman's voice bellowed. "Blast that pale-skinned bitch off the face of the Earth!"

Kane clung on to the leg as the cab swung around, but below Domi was already racing away, keeping up a circuit around her would-be killer as its pilots tried to affix her in their sights. It was a dangerous ploy, but it gave Brigid enough time to get the wounded driver out of her own wag, forcing the bent door open with six hard kicks of her heeled boot.

Kane did what little he could to help, reaching into a pocket of his jacket and priming the device he found there. It looked like a ball bearing, perfectly spherical with a silver finish, roughly two inches in diameter. There was a hidden seam running along the device's center, and it took Kane less than a breath to find it and twist it, setting the device to detonate. He dropped it then, not really able to throw it the way he would have preferred, and turned his face away as the sphere fell.

The device blew seven feet above the ground, just ahead of and between the walker's massive feet, unleashing a violent burst of light and sound as if a lightning bolt had struck the earth. The walker was unharmed but its occupants were momentarily dazzled.

The device was known as a flash-bang, and it was standard kit for all Cerberus field teams. It was not really a weapon so much as a tool, designed as a nonlethal part of their arsenal. Once detonated, the device exploded in an almighty flash of light and noise, similar to a grenade being set off. However, the flash-bang did no damage, and as such was used by the Cerberus personnel merely to confuse and disorient opponents.

Inside the walker's cab, confusion had taken hold. "What the hell wazzat?" a woman's voice howled from within.

"I can't see right, Ma," a male voice responded.

"Gimme that," the woman yelled. "Look where you're aiming."

The heat ray blasted again—but it was yards away from where Domi was scrambling across the dirt. The flash-bang had not done much, but it had disoriented the walker's crew enough to lose track of Domi—and that had kept her alive for another few seconds.

The nature of the battle had changed subtly, Kane realized as he reached across to grab the underside of the blocky cab. Initially, their attackers had hoped to cripple the vehicles and steal the goods, collateral damage be damned. Now it seemed that they were pissed—the fight back had caught them by surprise, used as they were to the wavering loyalties and easy pickings of the usual travelers on these roads.

Kane swung beneath the underside of the cab, his legs swinging freely as he grasped for purchase. Nearby, he could hear the whir of the heat ray as it cycled up for another blast. He was by the vent in an instant. It was located at the rear of the cab, two feet square, and this close it looked more like a gaping hole than anything technical, the kind of funnel outlet you might find on a cruise ship. He needed something to block it—but what? What could he use?

Brigid's voice drilled through Kane's Commtact as he clung there, looking into the blackness of the exhaust port. "Thirty seconds, Kane," she shouted. "It's going to—"

Her words were cut off as the heat ray screamed again, slapping against the ground.

Chapter 7

Domi leaped aside as the beam struck, rolling out of its path with just a couple of feet to spare. The wide beam tracked across the ground for three long seconds, leaving a trail of char-black soil in its wake. Domi felt her skin warm where she had gotten too close, and her exposed face and hand began to redden as she scrambled across the soil.

The exhaust vent hissed with a blast of steam as the heat ray fired, a sudden jet of hot mist blowing toward Kane's face even as he turned his head aside. It missed him by inches, tussling the hair on his head and flipping the collar of his jacket up against the side of his face.

The jacket, Kane thought as the heat ray winked off again, its scarlet glow ceased.

Kane clambered up the rear of the boxy cab, passing a two-foot-high metal door that must have acted as some kind of service hatch, he realized, before reaching the roof. He clung on, thirty feet above the ground, and shrugged out of his jacket, counting the seconds down in his head. All around, bullets were zipping through the air as each group fired on the other.

Once Kane had his jacket off, he reached down again, unnoticed, clambering back to the ventilation duct a few feet below.

"Baptiste," he demanded over the Commtact, "how long do I have?"

"Ten seconds," Brigid replied from where she was hiding behind the melted wag with the driver, blasting at the circling walker with her TP-9 pistol. The TP-9 was a bulky hand pistol with a covered targeting scope across the top, finished in molded, matte black. The grip was set just off center beneath the barrel, creating a lopsided square in the user's hand, their hand and wrist making the final side and corner.

Kane counted the seconds in his head while he bunched up the gray jacket and shoved it into the vent, pushing it down with his arm as far as he could. On *two*, he was done, and he drew his hand out just as the heat beam fired again, its scream like a bird of prey cawing right into his ear.

Trails of steam slipped around the edges of the gray denim, but most of the exhaust was trapped within. The ray generated incredible amounts of heat with each use, so much so that without the exhaust vent open, the underside of the cab began to glow pink as the beam continued its cruel assault.

DOWN ON THE GROUND, Domi was sprinting away from the towering mechanical beast, its heat beam cutting across the field behind her in a thick, red line. She kept running, sweat pouring from her skin, which had taken on a pinkish hue from her proximity to the heat.

"Come on, Kane," she muttered. "I can't keep this up forever."

KANE WATCHED AS steam continued to trail from the vent. He could barely see the jacket, he had pushed it in so deep, but he could see that it was turning darker, sodden with condensing water from the steam that was unable to escape.

Kane activated his Commtact again. "Baptiste, how long do they have before they can blast again?"

"Twenty…twenty-two seconds," Brigid estimated.

"Plenty of time," Kane muttered, easing himself from the cab and preparing to swing across to one scaffold-like leg as the vehicle swung around to smother the area with more bullets from its railguns. But as he reached down, a side door swung open on the metal box of the cab and a man's voice rang out.

"You're right, Umbra! There is someone up here!"

Kane cursed as a blaster followed up the shout, four bullets fired in quick succession at his swinging form where he dangled from the rear of the cab. There was a man in the doorway, just five feet tall but stocky as a prison door, with broad shoulders and muscular arms showing under the sleeves of his striped T-shirt. He held a Ruger MP9 in his hand, a compact and boxy little submachine gun with a clip that rammed up into the handle, giving the maximum balance in the minimum of space. The Ruger fired again, unleashing a stream of 19 mm parabellum bullets at Kane's swaying form.

Hanging on to the cab one-handed, Kane commanded his Sin Eater back into his right hand—its holster now visible where he had shed his jacket. The Sin Eater struck Kane's palm an instant later, even as a 19 mm slug from the MP9 skittered against the metal rung he was hanging on to, clipping against his skin so that his grip eased for a fraction of a second. Then Kane was falling, dropping backward from his handhold on the rear of the boxy cab, even as his right index finger squeezed down the trigger of the Sin Eater and sent retaliatory fire at his attacker. Kane's bullets struck the stocky man square in the center of his chest, and the man went stumbling back under their impact, screaming blue murder.

But Kane was falling now, plummeting down toward the ground between the two scaffold-like legs.

DOMI AND BRIGID stopped to watch as Kane fell. It was a high fall, thirty feet in total, and Kane was falling backward, down between those towering legs.

"Oh, Kane," Brigid muttered, while a rain of 15 mm bullets peppered the ground all around her.

KANE TWISTED IN the air as he fell, reaching for the nearest scaffold-like leg as he dropped the first fifteen feet. Above him, the stocky thug who had shot at him had dropped back inside the depending cab, his chest blooming with a red stain where Kane's bullets had ended his life, the unlatched metal door swinging back and forth.

Kane's left hand glanced against one scaffold-like leg but he was falling too fast—grabbing it was like trying to grab a bullet from the air. It was fifteen feet to the ground and he was falling fast now, the ground rushing up to meet him.

Kane shifted his body as best as he could, sending the Sin Eater back to its sheath and holding his arms and legs loosely out before him. He had to judge this just right, let his limbs absorb the impact without breaking anything. *Sounds easy,* Kane told himself sourly as the ground rushed toward him.

And then—*bang!* He struck the ground with more force than he could have prepared for, rolled automatically as his arms took the brunt of the impact, his breath forced out of his chest in a painful "woof!"

Above him, the cruel walking vehicle cycled around its heat blast again. It fired a moment later, sending another wide beam of red-hot heat at the smoldering wag where Brigid and her wounded driver were still crouched, setting fire to the retreating gunner.

BRIGID WATCHED AS the beam blazed toward her, unable to get out of its path. The beam slapped against the side of the wag that she had used as cover, pushing forward to sear the rear windows of the cab. But as she watched, the iris-like aperture at the front of the boxy walker started billowing thick black smoke where it was overheating, and a moment later the whole thing went up in a fireball, heat ray and cabin bursting into flame. Kane had done it—she only hoped he had managed to save himself.

ABOARD THE WALKING MACHINE, the woman called Umbra saw a sudden rush of flames writhe across the cracked windshield. The walking machine had been her late husband's dream. He had designed it to pick off unarmed transports traveling these forgotten roads, figuring out the nuances of clambering over the uneven ground in the most efficient way possible. He had died before the vehicle had been completed, so Umbra had named it Errol after him. The heat ray could be recharged thirty times before it needed to be restoked, and today was the first day in four years that she had ever come close to reaching that limit. Now Errol Number 2 was about to die on her, this one consumed by fire generated by its own heat ray.

Umbra, a stocky woman in her midforties, whose hair had a tendency toward "disarray" as a style, turned to Errol's driver—her own twenty-four-year-old son, albeit by a different coupling—and told him the bad news. "Time to evacuate, Junior."

Junior   dyed-red hair, gap-toothed smile, shirt and shorts—looked at his mother with furrowed brow as the flames played across the broken windshield. "You sure you don't wanna go down with the ship, Ma?"

"Going down with ships is for oldic time ship's captains and putzes," she chastised him as she reached for the metal handle of the side door, which had been swinging to and fro after Carlos had come stumbling back inside under the influence of the man's perfectly placed shot.

As she touched it, the door bit back, intense heat searing her hand and causing her to squeal in pain. The next thing she knew, Umbra was tumbling out the open door, plummeting to the ground thirty feet below, flames rushing up to meet her.

SPRAWLED ON THE GROUND, Kane watched as the towering death machine stumbled unsteadily, its boxy cab consumed with fire. Suddenly, a figure came dropping through the flames, on fire and falling like a dead weight. The figure struck the ground a moment later, a line of black smoke following it like the tail of a comet, scream echoing across the field.

"Damn," Kane spat, pushing himself up on aching limbs. He had been responsible for the inferno, but he couldn't just let its crew member die like that—not without at least trying to help. But even as he reached the screaming human torch that had once been Umbra, he knew already that he was too late.

AFTER THAT IT was just a mop-up operation.

The walker's driver had survived, but he was badly burned and had been shaken up to the point that he could hardly string a sentence together. The walker itself was nothing more than a burned-out shell.

Domi, Brigid and Kane had all survived, although they each sported a few scrapes and bruises from the adventure, and Kane's left shoulder complained a little when he tried to raise his arm above his head, causing him to wince.

The other members of the road crew didn't fare as well. The gunner who had worked with Brigid had been caught by the heat ray and was now nothing more than hanging, ash-black flesh on charred bones, and Kane's gunner had died instantly when his vehicle had split apart. The others had some cuts, but they had mostly survived intact.

Two-thirds of the cargo that the wags had been carrying had survived, although the wags were shot, meaning that Ohio Blue would need to source more transportation before the mercy op could be completed. "Grain keeps, my sweet prince," she told Kane when he spoke to her via radio comm. "At least we know the next journey through this pass will be less fraught. More important, when might I see you to thank you in person? My gratitude is overflowing, you know."

Kane passed on that offer. Blue had always been flirtatious with him, and her affection for him, whether or not it was reciprocated, gave Kane—and Cerberus—a useful contact in the darker underworld that existed outside the villes. For now he would keep Ohio at a safe distance, without actively discouraging her. "No point breaking a pretty woman's heart," he told Brigid as they gathered themselves up for the trip back home.

Brigid gave a bark of sarcastic laughter in response. "You couldn't break a woman's heart if you tried," she told him.

Kane had the good sense to look wounded rather than to argue. He could not face another fight today, not even a verbal one.

Ohio would be sending another vehicle shortly to salvage what she could and pick up her surviving team. While they waited, the trio of Cerberus warriors looked across the fields where the altercation had played out. Smoke billowed from the carcass of the walker vehicle, and trailed here and there from the wrecked wags and tracts of soil that had been caught up in the battle.

"Guess it's time to go home," Domi said as they retrieved their belongings, which included an operational interphaser, from the wrecked wags.

"Guess so," Kane agreed while Brigid calculated where the closest parallax point was through which they could teleport themselves home. "Baptiste, what's the news?"

Brigid peered up from her calculations and flashed him a tired smile. "It's a ten-mile walk to the nearest parallax point," she said. "And when I say ten, I'm trying to make it sound closer than it really is."

Kane sighed with resignation. "So," he said cheerily as the group began the long trek to their jump point, "does anyone want to guess how much more fun Grant's having than us on his vacation?"

Chapter 8

The Pretors obtained a register of who had been at the hotel at the time of the incident, but the records were inexact. There was a register for who had booked in, of course, but no definitive record of how many people had come to the dance. City fire regulations required only that a cap be placed on the number of people in a room, not that each was logged in or out.

Thus, it was assumed—*wrongly*—that the people found hanging at the scene had been the only ones who had died. However, there had been in fact three more deaths: a young couple honeymooning in the city, and an older woman who had returned here for the first time in a decade and had happened upon the "dance sinister" by chance when she had been searching for the hotel's restaurant.

All three had died, but their bodies were shuttled elsewhere, to let blood. Blood was needed. The why would come later.

Chapter 9

Grant had been left alone in the Pretor interview room where he was provided with water and allowed an escorted rest break before the lights were dimmed. The room was warm but not uncomfortably so, so Grant removed his jacket while he was uncuffed to use the restroom, and he hitched it over his shoulders for the rest of the night while he waited for Corcel to come back to him. He had no doubt that his story would check out, so he put that to the back of his mind and thought instead about the hanging bodies and the strange people he had seen in the alleyway behind the hotel.

It was impossible to guess at what he and Shizuka had stumbled upon. He had none of the facts, and reading between the lines he suspected that there was a lot that the local Magistrates—or Pretors—were not telling him right now. One thing seemed clear—they had seen this kind of activity before, presumably recently, and had eyewitnesses to at least one of the possible perpetrators, a man whose description matched Grant's to some degree. That could be one of the men he had seen, the bare-chested brutes who had thrown the lethal razor discs.

By three in the morning, Grant was pretty certain that he was not being observed. He was still sitting at the table, his head resting on his outstretched arm, eyes closed as if in sleep. He was alone in the room, but he could see there were cameras watching the interview room at all times.

He made an educated guess that those cameras were recording and monitoring the cell twenty-four hours a day and that someone was watching that feed—along with a number of others. But three in the morning was that time when even the most diligent of Mags gets bored and their attention starts to wander. Grant figured he could take a chance and maybe get a message out to Cerberus. Sitting there, Grant engaged his hidden Commtact and subvocalized a question.

"Cerberus, this is Grant," he hissed. "Have run into some trouble. Please respond."

There was a momentary pause before a Cerberus operator called Farrell answered. "Receiving you loud and clear," Farrell said. "What's the trouble?"

Grant gave a brief outline of what had occurred, of how he and Shizuka had walked into what appeared to be a mass murder scene and how he had subsequently been arrested for the crime.

"You need backup sent?" Farrell asked over the Commtact link, his words vibrating through Grant's skull casing.

"Not at this stage," Grant decided. "Is Kane there?" Kane had been Grant's partner in the Magistrates for years, before the two of them had become field agents for the Cerberus organization. They were a solid partnership, along with the third member of their trio—Brigid Baptiste—and were often considered inseparable by their fellow operatives.

"Kane is on-site," Farrell confirmed. "Just got back and probably sleeping off his last mission. You want me to hail him?"

"No, I can do that," Grant said thoughtfully. "Just speak to him when he's awake and tell him to stay ready. We may need him on this side of the pond."

"Roger that," Farrell confirmed. "Anything else?"

"Get Brigid and Lakesh and replay them the description I gave to you of the strangers I chased," Grant said. "Let me know if anything there rings a bell."

"Will do," Farrell agreed before signing off.

In the aftermath of the conversation, Grant tried his best to relax his mind and get some much-needed sleep.

MORNING CAME, AND with it the news that Cáscara had tracked down the restaurant owner as he opened up his café for the day. Emiliana Cáscara showed him her Pretor badge and explained whom she was looking for information about. The ruddy-cheeked owner nodded.

"Si, Si," he said as he poured her a black coffee from the machine. "Two Americans, didn't drink any wine. Typical Americans—ate fast, somewhere to rush off to."

Cáscara nodded thoughtfully as she stirred cream into her coffee. "Can you confirm what time they were here, and when they left?" she asked.

The café owner pondered this for a moment, then snapped his fingers in recollection. "They were here less than two hours and they arrived late," he explained. "Their table was booked for eight and the pretty lady was very apologetic about their lateness, but I assured her it did not matter to me and to enjoy themselves. They would have left a little before ten. This door," he added, pointing to the main doors of the café.

"Ten," Cáscara said thoughtfully. "That puts them... Yes, that works."

The café owner looked at her and smiled. "You want to stay for breakfast, Pretor?"

"Want to—yes," Cáscara told him as she stood up. "Going to—no."

"You're welcome back here anytime," the owner told her as the dark-haired Pretor left the café.

CÁSCARA RETURNED TO the Sector Hall of Justice for Zaragoza and passed her findings over to her partner, Juan Corcel.

"They're a strange couple," Corcel mused, "but the woman's story certainly checks out."

"You still think they had something to do with the deaths?" Cáscara probed.

Corcel shook his head slowly as he pondered her question. "No, but I do think there's more to these two than meets the eye. The woman's too graceful, too poised. And the man, Grant—he freely admitted to being an ex-Magistrate. I just couldn't get a lead on what it is he does now."

"Lot of work for ex-Mags," Cáscara mused. "You think he's a merc on business out here?"

"The pattern of deaths has been random," Corcel said, "but heaven help us if this is some prelude to a gang war or something of that nature."

Cáscara nodded solemnly. "So, I guess we release them, then?"

"Yes," Corcel agreed. "And let's hope our paths don't cross again."

A LITTLE PAPERWORK LATER, Grant and Shizuka were released from custody. Corcel explained to Grant that they were confiscating the items he had retrieved from the scene—the metal throwing disc and the bloodred feather—as evidence and that he would need to sign a waiver to the effect that he had been informed of this, and to make himself available for follow-up questioning if anything should arise.

"I know the procedure," Grant grumbled good-humoredly. "We're here for three days, staying at a hotel on the west bank called El Castillo."

Corcel nodded. "I know it."

"You have any problems, we will do what we can to help you," Grant promised.

Then Corcel and Cáscara escorted Grant and Shizuka downstairs, taking a gloomy staircase down to the first floor, and from there they went through a security door and out into the main foyer to the Sector Hall. The foyer was a grand space, with wooden walls and an eight-foot-high decorative shield of justice affixed to a wall behind the reception desk. A Pretor in black-and-red armor was poised behind the desk, discussing some infraction with a tired-looking man with scruffy hair and a knot in his shoelace. Other Pretors were just heading out to go on patrol, while civilians waited for their turn either to speak with the Desk Pretor or to be collected by someone within the building.

The four of them—Grant, Shizuka, Corcel and Cáscara—stood there facing one another as the noise and rush of activity burbled all around them like bubbles in a carbonated drink.

"I am sorry that we had to keep you overnight," Corcel said with genuine regret.

Grant shrugged. "Can't say that this was my first choice of cultural center to visit, but I kind of enjoyed seeing how you guys here run things," he said amiably.

Shizuka bowed at the waist as she faced Cáscara. "Thank you for the understanding and sympathy you showed me last night, Pretor," she said. "These are difficult times, but your behavior was faultless in the circumstances. I wish you swift success with your investigation."

"Thank you," Cáscara said with a smile.

Grant and Shizuka watched the two Pretors pace back through the security door that led to the staircase. It had been a lousy set of circumstances, but they had navigated it, and maybe even helped the investigation a little. Still, Grant could not help but wonder what it had all been about.

The pair turned to make their way through the busy

foyer and back to their hotel for a change of clothes. And then—

Pop!

It was like a lightbulb switching on in Grant's mind. One instant things in the foyer of the Sector Hall were entirely ordinary, the normal buzz of morning traffic as Pretors came and went about their business, shuffling paperwork and arming themselves for the streets. The next instant, Grant felt an eerie shiver, and it seemed as if the whole building had gone silent. It hadn't—that was just his instincts kicking in, years of experience as a hard-contact Magistrate alerting him to the sudden change in circumstances.

He turned, holding one protective arm up automatically before Shizuka where she walked beside him, scanning the foyer area. The Pretor at the desk had his head down, checking over a release form; two more Pretors, a man and a woman, dressed in the scarlet-and-black armor of the city, were just passing through the foyer on their way out to the street. A civilian waited in street clothes on a bench set against the wall before the desk, unshaven and with his dark hair in disarray, waiting to be seen. And Corcel and Cáscara were just leaving the foyer, returning upstairs to their desks, the door sealing behind them. But there was someone else, Grant spotted—a woman carrying a child's stroller through the double doors leading into the foyer, a scarf around her head, pulled low as if to hide her face. Grant sensed the nervousness in her posture, the way her eyes were darting anxiously left and right as she drew the stroller into the foyer. All this he took in in less than a second, honed instincts assessing everyone and everything as he locked in on the source of his concern—the woman.

Grant was moving straightaway, scrambling across the busy foyer toward the woman at a dead run as she pulled the nose of the stroller through the doors after her and let them swing closed again. Her eyes were fixed on the desk where the Pretor was engaged in a discussion, and Grant seemed to watch in slow motion as her hand reached beneath her flower-print skirt, a flash of bare leg showing before she pulled free the blaster that was holstered there.

"Corpses for my mistress!" she yelled in embittered Spanish, squeezing the trigger and unleashing the first bullet at the Desk Pretor.

Her eyes widened as Grant hurtled himself into her in a tackle, disrupting her aim as the blaster kicked in her hand, and shoving her toward the floor. She struck with a loud thump, and Grant was on top of her in an instant. He pushed her down by the face as he grabbed for the blaster with his free hand, trying to wrench it from her grip.

"Muerte!" she cursed as the blaster reeled off another shot—the bullet going wildly into the ceiling—before being yanked from her hand. "Death!" Her eyes were like pinpricks in their sockets, pupil and iris almost lost in the white abyss.

All around the foyer, people were reacting. Grant had disarmed the woman in two seconds flat. Grant was aware of voices asking what was going on, of blasters being drawn from holsters and people ducking behind convenient furniture as they tried to figure out what was happening and whether they were in the line of fire.

And then Grant realized that there was a second threat. The woman had brought in a baby cart before embarking on her killing spree, which made no sense—unless the cart contained something other than a child.

"The stroller!" Grant yelled as he held the woman down. "Somebody—"

The stroller blew up in a cacophony of sound and brilliance.

Chapter 10

The reinforced glass of the Sector Hall foyer shattered into a million tinkling pieces, spraying across the room in a sudden spread of gravel-like shards. The grand double doors of the building shook in their frame, one lower hinge buckling as the door tottered in place, another melting into a lump. The noise of the explosion continued to ring through the room for at least ten seconds, its echo reverberating from the metallic surfaces within—the lamps, the door handles, the window frames and the computers at their desks.

In the aftermath of that explosion, the sound of nearby alarms assailed the air, exacerbating the ringing in the ears of the people who had been caught up so close to the exploding baby stroller.

IN THE STAIRWELL BEYOND, Pretors Corcel and Cáscara were thrown off their feet and now found themselves sprawled on the stairs, with Corcel sporting a bloody cut to his left temple where he had been thrown against the banister on his way down.

Cáscara was the first to rise, pushing herself warily up onto her knees, her head dipped down and swayed heavily.

"¿Qué pasó?" she muttered uncertainly, looking up at the staircase. One of the lights was flickering where a circuit had been jangled, and the flashing made Cáscara feel slightly unreal. Then she saw her partner lying against the banister, his head bleeding from the cut there.

"Juan, are you okay?" Cáscara asked in Spanish, reaching for his arm. "Juan?"

Juan Corcel nodded heavily. "Head stings," he admitted. "Do you know…what happened?"

"Bomb," Cáscara reasoned without a moment's hesitation. Even as she said it, she was pushing herself up to a standing position, and a moment later she began trotting back down the stairs. "Came from the foyer," she said, calling back to Corcel.

"Go," Corcel told her. "I'll follow in a moment." *Just as soon as I'm able to stand,* he mentally added as he felt a wave of nausea run through his gut.

BEFORE SHE STEPPED through into the foyer, Emiliana Cáscara pulled her Devorador de Pecados 9 mm pistol. The weapon had no safety, as that precaution had been deemed unnecessary when the Pretors had taken charge of enforcing the law decades ago. They were the ultimate authority in post-holocaust Spain.

She punched in the electronic code on the keypad beside the stairwell's door, and it unlocked with a soft click. The door featured narrow slats of reinforced glass, and although these had held, two of them now featured a spiderweb of cracking across their surface where they had caught the shock wave from the explosion.

Warily, Cáscara stepped through into the foyer, her blaster held up and ready. The scene that greeted her was carnage. The walls had been charred by the explosion, radiating circles of smudged black, concentrating at the external doors. Those doors were cracked and hung cockeyed, and one of the hinges had melted so that it was now a smoking glob of brass.

People were strewed across the space, Pretors and civilians, caught up in the shock wave, thrown to the floor. Among them, Cáscara spotted Grant and Shizuka—he lying atop a light-haired woman with her skirt hitched halfway up her thighs, Shizuka lying just to the side of the doors that led onto the street.

Cáscara's eyes stopped moving as they spotted the gun lying on the ground beside Grant and the woman, and she trotted over toward it, her own weapon held ready, before kneeling down to snatch it up and pocket it. As she did so, Grant groaned and began to move.

Good, Cáscara thought, *he's alive.*

Grant's eyes flickered open and he saw Cáscara leaning over him, her dark hair fallen down over her shoulders, framing her striking face.

"Is something ringing?" Grant asked in a bewildered tone. "I can hear—"

"There's been an explosion," Cáscara told him in a soothing voice. "Did you see—"

Grant coughed, swallowing a mouthful of dust that had been disturbed by the explosion. "Stroll—" he began, then coughed again. "Lady with a stroller. No kid, just a bomb. I…I dunno…"

The glamorous Pretor's gaze raced around the room, searching for the stroller that Grant spoke of. It wasn't here, which meant it had either been utterly destroyed in the explosion, or it had been moved elsewhere. Cáscara's glance settled on the woman who lay sprawled beneath Grant's hulking frame. "You saved her?" she asked.

Grant seemed momentarily confused, then realization dawned. "No," he gasped. "She came in with a gun. Shouted something—something about death."

Cáscara glanced back over Grant and the woman he was slumped against. He looked okay, just a few smears of dirt where debris had caught him; the woman meanwhile was unconscious—she could wait.

Cáscara stood up, scanning the room. Other people were groaning now, just recovering from the unexpected explosion. Her partner, Juan Corcel, came walking into the room from the stairwell, his face pale with shock but otherwise looking steady. "Anything?" he asked.

Cáscara nodded solemnly. "Bomb," she said, and she pointed at the woman lying beneath Grant. "Says she brought it. There was a gun, too—a Firestar M40."

Corcel nodded, and regretted it immediately as he felt suddenly unbalanced. "You have the blaster?" he asked.

Cáscara confirmed she did before pacing across the room to the outside doors. She waited there a moment, her own blaster raised in readiness, listening for signs of a follow-up attack. Then, tentatively, she pushed the double doors open a crack and peeked through the space.

There was a small porch area there, sheltered from the sun and just two strides across, beyond which was a flight of three stone steps and a ramp leading down to the street. The mangled remains of the baby stroller stood in the center of the space, metal struts jagged and twisted, the whole thing belching thick black smoke. The walls of the porch were blackened with smoke, too.

So that was where the cart had ended up, Cáscara realized, although it didn't explain how it had got here. Grant had suggested that the woman had brought it inside the foyer—but how had it got out through the doors again without ripping through them?

Beyond the porch, a crowd was amassing in the bright morning sunshine of the street, eyeing the Justice Hall and the smoking debris there, keeping a wary distance for fear of further explosions. Cáscara pushed the door wider and stepped outside to address the crowd.

"Everyone move along," Cáscara instructed in a loud voice. "Keep this area clear." She was worried that there might be another bomb or another gunman, worried about everyone's safety—but she didn't want to panic the crowd either, just keep them out of harm's way.

The crowd began to shuffle reluctantly away. Liana Cáscara watched them carefully, trying to detect any hint of someone who was perhaps behaving suspiciously.

INSIDE, GRANT WAS just shaking off the effects of the explosion, his ears still ringing. Pretor Corcel joined him, offering a few words of sympathy that Grant couldn't entirely make out. At the same time, Corcel reached for his cuffs and slipped them over the unconscious woman's wrists where she lay against the floor.

"You did well," Corcel said, smiling warmly at Grant. "Maybe even saved some lives today."

Grant acknowledged the words with a nod before turning his head to look for Shizuka. She lay sprawled just a few feet away, arms over her head, fingers laced tightly together. There was detritus scattered on and around her, a scattering of broken glass flecks along with flakes of paint and chips of wood that had been wrenched from the doors. Grant reached forward and brushed the worst of it from Shizuka.

"Hey, pretty lady?" he urged, stroking her face gently. "Can you hear me?"

Shizuka's closed eyelids fluttered open after a moment, and she smiled when she saw Grant poised over her.

"Did I get it?" she asked. "The bomb?"

Ninety seconds earlier

SHIZUKA SAW GRANT race across the room toward the woman who had just entered. The woman was drawing a compact pistol from beneath her skirt—six and a half inches of gunmetal-gray barrel with silver highlights—and she began shouting something in Spanish.

"¡Los cadáveres de mi amante!"

Grant was already knocking the intruder from her feet as the gun spit its first bullet.

Behind the woman a baby's stroller was just coming to rest on its silver-spoked wheels, a bundle of blankets poking from within. Shizuka's mind focused on it, realized the danger it represented—either a child was in the line of fire or the stroller contained more weapons, or something even more deadly.

Shizuka leaped immediately, propelling herself across the foyer in a blur of motion, her feet skipping on the tile-clad floor as she raced toward the baby stroller. She moved with the uncanny grace of a warrior borne, years of martial arts training ensuring that her body functioned like a well-oiled machine. She was on the stroller in an instant, even as beside her the woman who Grant had tackled to the floor reeled off a second blast from the Firestar, burying a bullet in the ceiling high above them.

Shizuka did not hesitate. She slapped her hands against the bar-like handle of the baby carriage and pushed, forcing it out through the double doors of the Justice Hall even as Grant's shouted warning echoed in her ears.

"The stroller!" Grant yelled as Shizuka pulled the doors inward again, closing them off from the cart. "Somebody—"

And then the bomb in the baby carriage went off, sending its booming shock wave through the porch and the foyer beyond.

GRANT NODDED, A broad smile materializing on his face as he stroked Shizuka's face. "You got it," he assured her. "Looks like it did some damage out there," he said, nodding in the direction of the doors, "but nothing on what it would have caused in here."

Pretor Cáscara came striding back through the porch doors at that moment, her brow furrowed in concern. She

was clearly alert, on edge and ready for anything, her
pistol gripped in her hand. "I think the immediate crisis
is over," she announced in Spanish. "Let's get this place
cleaned up and tend to any wounded."

The man at the desk began giving orders and checking
his comms board as more Pretors arrived to respond to
the explosion and its aftermath. It had been two minutes
since the bomb had gone off; two minutes since the rules
of the game had changed.

A LITTLE LATER Corcel and Cáscara sat in a back room
with Grant and Shizuka, a short distance from the hub-
bub in the foyer where a cleanup op was now under way.
The room was painted white, its overhead light harsh, two
notice boards on adjoining walls pinned with various no-
tices, updates and warnings, a hissing and huffing coffee
machine in one corner and tired-looking plastic chairs arranged untidily about the place. Grant and Shizuka were
encouraged to take a seat each, and the two Pretors brought
their chairs over to sit opposite them.

Shizuka had suffered a few scratches when the doors
had taken the shock wave, including a little bruising across
her chest from where she had been thrown against the
floor, but she and Grant were otherwise fine. The ringing in Grant's ears had stopped after about five minutes;
now he just felt washed out in the aftermath of the adrenaline burst.

"I believe we owe you an apology," Corcel began. He
had a bandage over the scratch on his forehead now, and
it had been cleaned up with antiseptic by one of the medical staff on-site at the Sector Hall. "Because of the circumstances we met, I had misjudged you, Grant. What
you did in there, disarming the woman, and you, Shizuka,
ejecting the bomb—that was very brave."

"Very brave," Cáscara echoed with a nod.

Grant looked indifferent. "I saw the gun and I reacted," he said. "I was in the line of fire as much as anybody."

Corcel was shaking his head in disagreement. "From what the Desk Pretor saw, you were very professional in your action. You, too, Senorita Shizuka.

"You told me that you were once a Magistrate—that is correct, yes?"

Grant nodded. "A long time ago."

"What is it that you do now?" Corcel pressed.

"I'm…freelance," Grant said vaguely.

Corcel nodded thoughtfully. "You obviously keep yourself active," he said. "We have a problem here, one which you have already encountered with the incident in the Gran Retiro. Right now, you are my best witness to what caused it, the people who we think are behind it. I am wondering now if you might consider assisting us in our investigations, strictly in your freelance capacity?"

Grant raised his eyebrows in surprise. "You want my help?" he clarified.

"We need your help," Cáscara spoke up. "I think."

"Perhaps in sharing information," Corcel proposed, "we will be able to reach a mutually beneficial position."

"Perhaps," Grant said encouragingly.

"Then let me start at the beginning," Corcel said. "My name is Juan Corcel, and my partner, Emiliana Cáscara—and as you already know we are Zaragoza Pretors, the equivalent to your American Magistrates.

"Three weeks ago, something happened in the city," Corcel explained. "A group of people were discovered, all dead, in a room of the Basilica of Our Lady of the Pillar in the town center. They were arranged as if they were there to see a sermon, and yet it seemed that they were the performance—"

"Like an art exhibit," Cáscara elaborated. "All of them poised, awaiting death like so." She mimicked the expression of fear and shock on their faces, widening her eyes and sticking out her tongue.

"You think someone did this?" Shizuka asked. "Deliberately?"

"Theories circulated," Pretor Corcel told them. "About a suicide cult, or some kind of prank gone horribly wrong. But they were just theories. No one could be found who had any insight. Emiliana and myself were assigned to investigate along with another Pretor, a man named Herrero."

"A good man," Cáscara lamented.

"We had further incidents," Corcel continued. "One hospital ward of elderly patients became a carnal house. A nasty affair at a local school. Deaths, you understand, mass deaths, but not murders in the traditional sense— almost like suicides, but en masse."

"That's worrying," Grant agreed, "and it sounds a lot like what we saw in the ballroom."

"Yes, it does," Corcel asserted. "We began to put together things, eyewitness reports about people in the area. Two people survived the attacks—we found them both near asphyxiation in a theatrical performance where the rest of the audience died—"

"Ninety-seven people in total," Cáscara elaborated.

Corcel nodded. "Quite. And the survivors spoke of a feeling, a sense of well-being, that had settled in their heads," he explained. "They said they saw things in those lost moments when they had tried to hang themselves."

"What did they see?" Shizuka asked, her voice quiet with awe.

"Colors, shapes, magical things," Corcel said. "When they described them the images defied logic."

Cáscara picked up the story. "We found something at that scene," she said. "Unusual but not substantially so—a feather. We did not realize its significance at that time."

"The woman I chased dropped a feather," Grant recalled. "I picked it up."

"We have it. A red feather, the color of blood," Corcel stated.

"Yeah, but not at first," Grant told them. "She wore it on some fantail arrangement attached to her butt, like something a carnival dancer might wear, and while it was attached to her it was white. Only when it dropped did its color change."

"So the color changes over time," Corcel noted. "That's interesting."

"It's unprecedented, Grant-san," Shizuka observed. "I've never heard of anything like that before."

"Me either," Grant agreed. "And you say you don't know what you're up against here."

"Sightings of several people seen in the vicinity of these incidents began to match up," Corcel said. "Three people were spotted at the scenes—the same three people, two men and a woman, over and over. The men were dark-skinned, while the woman was only fleetingly glimpsed. Pretor Herrero came close to apprehending the group on an occasion six days ago. It was not to be."

"What happened?" Grant asked.

"You saw the discs that they use," Corcel said. "He was on the receiving end of one of these. It cut his stomach wide-open."

"He could not be saved," Cáscara added.

"I'm sorry," Grant said solemnly. "So what does it all mean? Some kind of nutty suicide cult?"

Corcel shook his head. "There's no pattern, no logic. The deaths are random, although they always involve masses of people all at once."

"You've analyzed the feathers and the discs, I take it?" Grant checked.

Cáscara nodded. "The discs are steel, sharpened along

their edges, nothing special," she said. "The feathers are a little more of a mystery. They share some of the properties of hen's feathers, but the DNA is not an exact match. Our experts have been unable to place it."

"Rogue DNA," Grant muttered, shaking his head. He wondered if Cerberus might have more success in analyzing it, for they had vast databanks, including hands-on experience in dealing with extraterrestrial threats. Cerberus primarily operated below the radar, which worked well for the kind of threats they usually tackled. To go public could compromise them. On the other hand, there was a possibility that this case was the very thing that Cerberus tackled—only by looking into it further might Grant find out for sure.

"We can help you," Grant decided. "I work with something—an organization—that has experience in this field."

"Which organization?" Corcel asked.

"It's called Cerberus," Grant said. "You've probably not heard of us, and that's kind of the way we'd prefer it."

"American?" Cáscara asked.

"Yeah." Grant nodded. "But we go all over. Don't like to limit ourselves."

Corcel turned to Shizuka. "And you?"

"I work with Grant sometimes," Shizuka told them.

"You can trust us," Grant said.

"I hope so," Corcel said. "Just now you're our only breathing witnesses."

Chapter 11

Twenty-five miles south of Zaragoza

The morning sun was already high in the sky, peering down on the desolate scrub of an uninhabited region of the Spanish countryside. The ground undulated pleasantly, a mixture of sand and scratchy long grass, occasional bushes with thorny spikes and leaves that were colored a sickly dark green and had not seen water in weeks. Patches of green ran up the slopes, dotted there like marching armies, spiraled bushes whose branches twisted in on themselves like old, arthritic men.

A single lane of blacktop ran through the desolation, the shifting sands sprinkled across it, grains dancing there with each hot breath of the wind.

A Pretor Sandcat was driving along the blacktop, its sleek, armored sides reflecting the white orbed glare of the sun. Painted black with red detailing, the Sandcat was an armored vehicle with a low-slung, blocky chassis supported by a pair of flat, retractable tracks. Its exterior was a ceramic armaglass compound that could repel small-arms fire, and the vehicle housed a swiveling gun turret up top, which was armed with twin USMG-73 heavy machine guns. The vehicles were exclusive to the law-enforcement divisions.

Inside, three Pretors were running a patrol, checking these barely populated areas for incursions by muties or insurgents opposed to the current Pretor-led regime. Muties had been a problem in these parts before now.

Initially appearing after the nuclear conflict that had torn down Western civilization, muties were creatures with cruelly twisted DNA care of the radiation that had blanketed much of the Earth. Some were feral, some more intelligent—almost human, in fact—but it was the subhuman strands that were the biggest threat. For a while, those mutants had run roughshod over the remains of civilization, taking what they wanted and murdering any who were foolish enough to stand in their way. But society had grown up again, and the rise of the Magistrates in North America and the Pretors out here in Spain had curtailed the mutie expansion, creating new and safe communities for the humans and resettling ones that had been abandoned during skydark.

These days, muties were an occasional sight, and many of the younger Pretors had never even seen one.

On board the Sandcat, a young Pretor by the name of Ramos was asking his older companion—Casillas, the driver of the vehicle—about a legendary encounter the Pretor had had with a gang of muties.

"Their eyes glowed in the twilight," Casillas explained in Spanish, his thick, drooping mustache working up and down as he spoke, "and they howled at one another like wolves. It was then that my Devorador jammed and, I swear, boy, I thought I was cashing in my ammo right there."

"And what happened?" Ramos asked, hanging on every word.

"First one comes at me," Casillas said, "still reluctant because he's worried I'm going to shoot him. I'm trying to reload but the blamed Devorador's stock has got jammed up tight and I can't get the dead clip out of the bastard thing. So, the mutie reaches for me, claws on his hand like steak knives, and I did the only thing I could. I threw the pistol at his head, whacked him right in the forehead hard enough I'd swear I heard the monster's skull crack—"

Ramos began laughing at that.

"—and then—*wham!*—I kicked the creature in the gut," Casillas continued, "so hard that it doubled over. As it began to fall back, I hit it with a right cross—used to box for the Pretor league back in those days, and I was ranked when I was young. So I hit this creature and its jaw exploded, teeth spraying out of its mouth. Not normal teeth, you understand…"

"They were curved like fishing hooks," the turret gunner whispered in time as the older man continued regaling their charge. The gunner was called Torres, and he had been partnered with Casillas long enough that he knew all of his stories by heart now. Still, they were good stories, even though Casillas tended to add to his myth with each retelling. Torres smiled. Let the old guy have his fun!

"Six of them came at me at once then," Casillas was saying. "My partner was down and all I had was my fists. So I punched the first—socked him right in the nose, blood everywhere. The next one figures he's going to get the jump on me but I grabbed him in a headlock—" the Sandcat swerved a little as Casillas demonstrated the move "—and flipped him over so that he knocked two more muties down like ninepins."

"Which meant you still had two left," Ramos counted.

"Oh, yeah, but they were scared now," Casillas bragged. "And let me tell you something—a scared mutie is a whole lot more dangerous than a—"

"Casillas!" Torres called from the turret, interrupting the man's reverie.

Casillas glanced at the mirror, eyeing his partner. "What is it?"

"On our nine," Torres said, his voice grim. "Looks like a…building maybe?"

Casillas eased his foot off the accelerator and glanced over to his left, out through the Sandcat's tinted window. For a moment all he could see there was rolling hills, undulating in gentle slopes to a few dozen feet above the strip of blacktop. Then, through a gap between the hills, he spotted a structure colored a deep indigo. "What is that?" he muttered.

"You see it?" Torres checked.

Ramos was leaning over from the passenger seat, trying to get a clearer view. He snatched up the onboard binoculars and pressed them to his eyes.

Another gap appeared between the slopes and Casillas drew the Sandcat to an abrupt halt, pumping the brake. Through the gap the three men could see a tall structure, taller than the lower slopes, curved on its apex and midnight blue in color.

"What is it, can you see?" Casillas asked aloud.

Ramos eyed the strange structure through the binocular lenses. It was hard to see much, most of it was obscured by the scrubland slopes, but he could see vein-like patterning on the surface, lined like the petals of a flower.

"Torres? Ramos?" Casillas asked.

"It's tall," Ramos said, "and it's…been painted, I think."

"Any sign of activity, boy?" Casillas barked.

"No, sir," Ramos confirmed after a moment's observation through the glasses.

Casillas pumped the accelerator and turned the steering wheel, bumping the Sandcat off-road and turning in the direction of the mystery structure. "Then let's take a closer look," he said.

Ramos cheered with excitement. Yeah, this was what hanging with the old Pretors was supposed to be about— fearless investigations, procedure be damned.

The Sandcat bumped over the rough terrain, tracks gripping the shifting dirt as it ascended one of the bush-dotted slopes. As it came to the top, the mysterious structure that lay beyond came into full view.

Standing there amid the wastes, it looked like a gigantic flower. It was organic with black petals, blue veins running up their centers and edges, folded together like a crocus. Each of those petals was as large as a house.

"What the hell is that?" Ramos spit, leaning forward in the passenger seat.

Casillas shot him a look. "Armor up," he said, "and stay on your guard."

On the turret up top, Torres trained his guns on the looming flowerlike structure, gripped by a sense of uneasiness. The thing was otherworldly, its proportions almost too much to comprehend. Where had it come from and how had it come to be here? He switched to well-practiced responses as the Sandcat drew closer to the colossal structure. "No signs of movement," he announced. "No life."

In the passenger seat, Pretor Ramos was shaking his head. "No signs of life," he muttered. "The whole thing looks freaking alive to me."

As the Sandcat drew even closer, kicking up a plume of dislodged dust in its wake, the Pretors spotted an opening at the foot of the plantlike construction, a dark gap where the petals crossed. The gap was easily tall enough for a man to walk through—in fact, it was as tall as three doors piled one on top of the other.

Thirty feet away, Casillas applied the brake, pulling up short of the towering blue-black leaves. "Me and the lad will go check it out," he told Torres. "You keep us in your sights, okay?"

Then Casillas grabbed up his helmet, securing it to his head by the clip arrangement at the high collar of his uniform. Beside him, Ramos had already done the same.

The Pretor helmet design featured sleek curves with red flares streaked across the black surface in two single, widening horizontal lines. The effect gave the impression of a bird of prey's head, tapering backward to a slight ridge at the rear below the crown. The helmet stopped above the eye line where a tinted visor began, covering the wearer down to the base of the nose and leaving their mouth and chin visible. A chin strap on the underside featured a built-up structure that protruded to an inch-long point at the center of the chin, designed as a last-ditch weapon if needed in the heat of battle.

The two men checked their Devorador de Pecados pistols before opening the gull-wing doors to the Sandcat and stepping outside. They emerged on either side of the Pretor vehicle, weapons held low but ready, eyeing the otherworldly structure that loomed ahead of them.

Outside the confines of the air-conditioned Sandcat, it was warm and balmy, the rising sun and lack of shade making the whole scrubby plain hot as an oven.

As one, the two Pretors surveyed the area all around and behind them, scanning it with alert eyes before closing the Sandcat's doors. There appeared to be no one around, and all that they could hear was the susurrus of the breeze over the scrubland.

Moving in unison but keeping a wide distance of roughly ten feet apart, the two Pretors warily approached the mysterious, flowerlike structure. The gap in the front seemed taller now that they were closer to it, but its dark depths remained impenetrable.

Casillas raised his blaster and halted, silently instructing Ramos to proceed ahead while he covered him. Ramos nodded, then stalked ahead on light tread, his weapon held ready. He reached the gap between the petals a few seconds later and, gingerly, peered inside.

It was a tunnel, with high narrow walls leading deeper

into the structure of the flower. It was dark, but this close Ramos could see a subtle lighting to the walls, a kind of soft reddish glow like the embers of a fire. Distant noises echoed from those walls, unidentifiable creaks and scratches, which made him suspect something was alive within.

Ramos glanced back, using his free hand to indicate to his partners that he intended to go deeper inside. Casillas nodded, proceeding forward to cover the entryway while Ramos disappeared within.

The tunnel was cooler than outside, the shade bringing the temperature down at least ten degrees. It smelled faintly of decaying plant matter or mulch. Ramos moved swiftly along the tunnel, eyes flicking left and right as well as watching what was up ahead. The walls were patterned with veins, just like the exterior, and there was a glow deep beneath them that backlit them so that the veins stood out like splayed fingers held before a spotlight. The glow was a warm red, the color of blood seen through the skin. That glow was the only source of illumination here, but up ahead Pretor Ramos could see a flickering light casting swirling patterns across the ceiling, like the reflections of sunlight on a *laguna*.

The tunnel stretched twenty feet before it opened up into a chamber, of which Ramos could only see the ceiling until he was almost at the end of the narrow tunnel. As Ramos got closer to the tunnel's end, he heard the sounds increase, noises of splashing and tapping of uncertain origin. He raised his blaster and paused before the entrance, steadying himself and listening to the strange sounds carrying up from below.

Cautiously, Ramos took another step forward and peeked out into the chamber that lay beyond the end of the tunnel. It dropped down in a series of steps, which was why he had only been able to see the roof of the cav-

ern until now, he realized. The steps wound down ten feet
before opening onto a vast chamber formed in an irregular circle. The chamber was dominated by a pool that was
thirty feet across. Ramos estimated that that pool took up
at least three quarters of the floor space.

The pool was surrounded by a series of dark blue columns that held the roof aloft and was lit by softly flickering flames. The columns were knotted and twisted, like
gnarled old tree trunks, each one unique. But it was the
pool that caught Ramos's eye. Within its vast proportions,
a woman was bathing with her back to him, only her head
and shoulders visible above the flickering surface. The
woman wore a towering headpiece that looked like twisted
branches, or perhaps the horns of a stag. There was something strange about the pool's surface—it swished like
water but it was too dark. And then Ramos noticed how
the contents drained on the woman's bare shoulders with a
trickle of red. Blood, he realized with a start. The woman
was bathing in blood.

Ramos could not hold back the gasp as that realization dawned, and although it had been quiet he saw the
woman's head turn to look at him, her lustrous dark hair
falling over her face to partially conceal it. She was beautiful, Ramos saw—dark eyes full of exotic promise. He
was transfixed.

The woman kept her eyes on Ramos as she swam across
the red pool, making her way toward the edge. As she
swam, she ducked her head down once, dipping beneath
the surface.

Behind her, almost hidden beside several of the twisting columns that held the cavernous roof aloft, three people were kneeling before what appeared to be waterfalls,
their glistening content filling the pool below. The people
had come from the Gran Retiro Hotel and were a honeymooning couple and an older woman who had been on her

first visit to Zaragoza in a decade. Now they were dead, yet still they crouched by the waters, feeding them with their own life's blood.

When the bather emerged there was red on her mouth, a line of blood running from her bottom lip where she had drunk a little of the pool's contents. A moment later, she emerged from the depths, taking haughty strides up a series of steps that were hidden below the surface, her naked body glistening with blood, the weird, towering crown she wore bobbing up and down as she emerged.

Ramos watched, still transfixed by the sight before him. She was tall and elegant, almost six feet in height with another foot and a half granted to her by the towering structure she wore atop her head. The woman's flawless body was entirely hairless, with high breasts and long, shapely limbs. She walked regally, no hurry to her movements, each stride poised and balanced as she paced across the cavern toward Ramos, her eyes never leaving his. But there was something else about her, too, something that swayed behind her, a trail of pale feathers attached to her posterior like a fan.

The woman twirled as she walked toward him, displaying her body with no hint of modesty, limbs moving fluidly like a ballerina on the stage. Ramos could not take his eyes from her, and as he watched it was almost as if she was beginning to glow with a halo of impossible light and color.

The woman passed behind one of the towering pillars that lined the room, and in that moment Ramos felt the spell break. He shook his head, eyes scanning the rest of the chamber where the pool lay, and saw two more figures emerging from the shadows there. They were two men, almost identical, with dark skin and shaven heads, bare-chested and wearing dark pants and boots. They were striding swiftly across the chamber toward

Ramos, looking up at him where he was partially hidden in the tunnel.

As Ramos watched, one of the men reached behind him, pulling something from his waistband at the small of his back. An instant later, the man's arm swept forward, and Ramos saw something glisten in the flickering light as it left his hand. A second later, that same something struck Ramos hard in his chest with a crack of breaking bone, cutting into the Pretor armor and knocking him back until he crashed against the floor on his back.

Winded and with a burning sensation running through his chest, Ramos gasped and tried to get up. As he did, he saw the thing protruding from his chest, lodged high in his breastbone. It was metallic and circular with a jagged edge, three inches across and made from some silvery material. As he watched, blood began to bloom from around the disc-like projectile, and Ramos suddenly felt breathless.

Then the beautiful woman with the feather train stepped up into the tunnel, striding over Ramos's fallen body. He watched her, and her body seemed to glow with impossible light, patterns dancing across his mind's eye, changing what he saw into something magnificent and scary and real.

"Die now," the woman breathed, leaning down to touch Ramos on the midpoint of his protective helmet, where the center of his forehead would be.

Ramos smiled at the prospect, sending the hidden signal—the one programmed into all living things—from his brain into his body, instructing it to give up the fight for survival, to die for his new mistress. As his breathing stopped and his heart ceased its beating, Ramos felt a wave of euphoria running through his slowing brain.

The woman strode onward through the tunnel, toward the exit where the two Pretors waited, accompanied by her two Terror Priests, who gave protection as she went about her dark business. Her name was Ereshkigal and she was alive once more, walking the Earth for the first time in three millennia.

Poised outside in readiness, the two Pretors had no comprehension of what was about to hit them, of how they would beg with tears of joy for their lives to be ended for the woman with the feather train—until they saw the naked woman emerge and begin her dance of death.

Chapter 12

There was something wrong about the woman, Pretor Corcel considered as he watched the would-be bomber through the one-way glass of the interview room. She had been cuffed to the table there like Grant had the night before, beneath the bright fluorescents that cast her skin in the pallid shade of sour milk.

It wasn't obvious, Corcel thought, but it was clear from her eyes. Not obvious, and perhaps more unsettling because of that. Her eyes were too small. The pupils and irises the color of chocolate were overwhelmed by their whites, like two birds' nests floating on a vast river of rapids.

She waited there, not complaining but just twitching now and then and scratching at herself as if there were bugs crawling beneath her skin. Her pale, pale skin. *That's the light,* Corcel tried to reassure himself. *No one looks good under fluorescent light.*

He was right—no one did. But that wasn't it. There was something more to it, like looking at sickness, at death.

Emiliana Cáscara joined him outside the interview room carrying a thin manila file of paper. Her hair was as perfect as ever, her suit spotless—the opposite of the decaying woman waiting behind the glass.

"Find anything on her?" Corcel asked.

"No ID," Cáscara lamented, "but she matches the description from a missing person report filed a little over a week ago."

Corcel raised his eyebrows at that and Cáscara showed him the report she carried. It featured just a single sheet printout with a blurry photograph and a description.

"Bella Arran, café waitress. Lives on Camino Ancho, went missing eight days ago, approximately 11:30 p.m. on her way home from work," Cáscara summarized.

Corcel peered at the picture, narrowing his eyes past the blur. "Could be her," he agreed. "Let's see what the Americans make of it."

A few moments later, Grant and Shizuka were allowed entry to join the two Pretors in the secure area beside the interview rooms.

"What do you have on her?" Grant asked.

"Possible missing persons," Cáscara outlined, running through the information she had dug up.

"And you think this is her?" Shizuka queried.

Cáscara bit her lip. "You tell me. It's our starting point anyway."

The four of them entered the interview room. As they did, Shizuka was struck by the smell on the air. She turned to Grant, halting in the doorway as the two Pretors continued on inside. "You smell that?" she asked quietly.

Grant shook his head briefly, just a fractional movement. He had had his nose broken so many times that his sense of smell was compromised. He could smell strong scents, but anything faint was lost to him.

Shizuka sniffed again, her nostrils twitching. "Like rotting meat," she said quietly, "the way a smilax gets."

Grant nodded an acknowledgment. The smilax was a type of carnivorous vine found in North America that let off a scent like rotting meat to attract its prey. "Strong?" he asked.

Shizuka shook her head. "No, but it's there. Something caught in the air-con, maybe."

"Maybe," Grant said, eyeing the AC grille high on the

wall. He wasn't so sure. His eyes couldn't help but be attracted to the pallid form of the woman who had set off the bomb in the baby carriage just a few hours before. There was something very off about her.

As the Pretors sat down, immediately the woman who may or may not be Bella Arran looked up with those disconcerting eyes of hers. Corcel took the lead, introducing the other people in the room. And then he asked her name.

The woman glared at him and spit on the desk she had been chained to.

"Nice," Grant muttered, from his position standing beside the door with Shizuka. Waiting there, the two of them looked a little like bouncers.

Corcel looked at the spittle on the desk for a few seconds. It had flecks of gray in it, like ash from a cigarette. "*That* won't get us anywhere," he told the woman in Spanish. "You're here until I say you leave, so the sooner you answer our questions, the sooner we can be done with all of this."

The woman's pinprick eyes flickered from Corcel to Cáscara on the chairs, and then over to Grant and Shizuka by the door behind the Pretors. Slowly, her expression changed into a sneer of superiority.

Cáscara picked up the questioning. "You can speak, correct?" she asked.

The woman glared at her, saying nothing.

"She shouted something when she came through the doors," Grant remarked helpfully. "'Corpses for my mistress.'"

"You can speak?" Cáscara asked again, more insistent this time.

"Yes," the woman replied tonelessly as if this was the first time she was being asked.

"Please give us your name," Corcel asked gently.

The woman continued to glare at him, her mouth sealed tightly.

"A woman went missing a little over a week ago," Cáscara began after thirty seconds had passed. "Stop me if this begins to sound familiar. She was a waitress at a café on fiftieth called Oscuro. The woman's name was Bella Arran. Do you want me to stop yet, or should I continue?"

The woman watched Cáscara with pinprick eyes, her expression unreadable.

"Are you Bella?" Corcel asked. "We suspect that you are and that perhaps you are in trouble."

"Trouble which we may be able to help you with if you will speak to us," Cáscara added gently.

The woman's eerie gaze switched back to Corcel, watching him with that piercing stare. "You believe that I am her," she said at last, "the woman, Bella Arran?

"Bella Arran is dead. But what came afterward, that is me. I see now how life was wasted, its purpose rudimentary, banal and pointless. My mistress showed me the true worth of the soul, and I followed her down into the darkness of the womb's embrace. I remembered as I went into that darkness how life had begun and how its promise had been squandered, over and over, year after year. How what I had been was as nothing to what I could have been, to what I still can be. And she showed me how all I needed to do was give myself to her and die and then I could be happy."

"And are you?" Cáscara asked. "Happy?"

"I feel happiness now the like of which I could never describe," the woman who had been Bella Arran said, her voice wistful. She closed her eyes as she spoke these words, pale eyelids dropping down before her unsettling gaze like a store's shutters. The lids were too pale and too thin—they looked as though they had been poorly cut from tracing paper.

"I embrace the light behind the darkness that waits at the grave," Arran said, "for only with light can the darkness ever be seen. I am future, while your past is already racing away."

"She says she's dead," Grant translated into English for Shizuka as he listened to the Commtact's translation.

Shizuka looked at him with concern, saying nothing.

"You've spoken of your 'mistress,'" Corcel said. "Who is she?"

"The great lady under the earth," the dead woman replied, her eyes remaining hidden behind those awful tracing-paper lids. "Your judge in the world that is coming. You are corpses-in-waiting, flowers to be plucked by my mistress, Ereshkigal."

As she spoke the name Ereshkigal, something seemed to change in the woman's physical makeup. Before the startled eyes of the two Pretors, Grant and Shizuka, the woman's previously pallid flesh began to glow in patches, like paper catching light. A moment later and without warning, her whole head was engulfed in a plume of black smoke through which only the licking flames could be seen. The flames and something else—the bright teeth of her widening smile. Her exposed skin billowed smoke, filling the air above her like ink dropped in water.

Closest to the fire extinguisher located at the far side of the door, Grant grabbed it, hefting it up in both hands and clamping down the firing nozzle even as the two Pretors leaped out of the way of the expanding cloud of smoke and flame. A jet of white foam emerged from the fire extinguisher, spraying across the room as Grant targeted the burning woman.

"My mistress shall come for you soon enough," Bella Arran stated quietly from behind the curtain of smoke, her voice unhurried, its tone eerily normal.

As the flame-retarding chemicals struck the woman,

her eerie voice chided them from behind the curtain of black smoke. "You cannot avoid her steps. And when she comes, her love will be all that you shall know."

Shizuka pulled at the door handle but the room had locked automatically when it had closed, sealing in the prisoner and interviewer as a safety feature in case the prisoner somehow overpowered the Pretor. A request was needed to open the door, which was monitored at all times.

Corcel was at Shizuka's side in a moment, hammering against the reinforced glass panel in the door to call the attention of his fellow Pretors outside.

"Let us out," he shouted. "Quickly—there's a fire in here."

With Pretor Cáscara behind him, Grant continued dousing the burning woman with the extinguisher, the sound of its loud jet muffling her chanting voice so that he only heard fragments of her words. "You are corpses-in-waiting, every one of you," she said. "Each of you shall know bliss and shall embrace that bliss with absolute love and absolute joy. You shall embrace the grave willingly and only then will you know the loving touch of Ereshkigal."

The room was filling with the thick, noxious black smoke that was billowing from the burning body. It reeked of burning fat, hissing and cracking as the skin blistered and the flesh beneath it cooked.

A moment later, the door to the interview room opened with a click as the magnetic seal was unlocked from without.

"Go! Go!" Pretor Corcel shouted, ushering Shizuka outside past the shocked faces of three Pretors waiting by the door.

"Liana?" Corcel encouraged as he stood in the doorway, holding the door open with his back. His partner backed away from the burning figure at the desk, trotting out through the open door as one of the uniformed Pretors entered with another fire extinguisher.

"Grant?" Corcel called.

Grant continued to douse the burning body for a few more seconds, but the flames were out now and it was just smoke billowing in thick, inky clouds from the body. The voice had stopped chanting, the white teeth still visible, locked in a rictus grin amid the blurred blackness of the head. "She's out," he said.

"Come on," Corcel encouraged. "Don't breathe any more of this ash."

Grant nodded, striding across the room and placing the spent fire extinguisher on one of the chairs that the two Pretors had been using. "Thanks, man," Grant said, coughing to clear his dry throat as he exited the room past Corcel.

Corcel waited a moment longer in the doorway as more Pretors were hurrying along the corridor outside to assist. The Pretors carried firefighting equipment and wore breath masks and oxygen packs.

Bella Arran's body had slumped back after the fire, her head fallen back as far as it could go, exposing her charcoal-black throat so that it was almost in line with the ceiling. Her clothes had burned away along with her skin so that she was just a mangled mire of bones and burned flesh now. Dark smoke rose from the corpse, leaving the stench of burning meat on the air.

Corcel turned away, letting the cleanup squad do their job.

Chapter 13

"Well, that was downright creepy," Grant stated grimly. He was standing by the window in a communal room in the Hall of Justice, taking the disposable cup of coffee that Pretor Corcel had just poured him.

The room was small with green-painted walls that reminded Grant of pond weed and an arrangement of low, comfortable seating that had seen better days. A coffee table dominated the center of the room, and Pretor Cáscara had taken a seat opposite Shizuka while Corcel worked the percolator in the corner. The room was two stories up with a barred window overlooking the rear of the building. The window looked down on a service road that ended in an underpass leading into the multistory parking garage at the side of the building and featured a locked area where trash cans were stored for pickup.

The smell of smoke hung heavily on everyone's clothes.

"She had nothing on her to trigger that," Corcel confirmed. "We checked her pockets before she was put in the interrogation room. She was clean."

"Have you ever heard of spontaneous human combustion?" Cáscara asked the room.

Shizuka was sitting opposite her, erect on one of the sagging seats, her body poised, alert. "Mr. Krook in *Bleak House* by Charles Dickens dies in such a way, if I recall correctly."

Cáscara nodded. "It is a documented phenomenon, although of questionable veracity. According to the reports, a human body combusts without any external source of ignition—no wick, no fuel."

Grant turned from the window. "And you think that's what our suspect, Bella Arran, just did?"

Cáscara fixed Grant with a stern look. "Do you have a better explanation?"

"Scientific evidence for spontaneous human combustion is a gray area," Corcel chimed in, taking a chair beside his partner. "While there have been multiple reports dating back hundreds of years, the real reasons for the phenomenon have never been satisfactorily confirmed. For a body to just—*pop!*—set alight without an external trigger defies all that we understand about science, surely."

"Does it matter why it occurs?" Shizuka asked. "The fact that we just saw…something happen in front of our eyes cannot be denied. That woman set alight, and there was no external source to trigger that."

"It was as if she willed it to happen," Cáscara observed.

"Yeah, after she'd said the name of her mistress," Grant added. "Ereshkigal. Whoever *she* is. You know her? She a local player?"

Cáscara shook her head and so did Corcel. "I don't recognize the name," Corcel confirmed, and his partner agreed.

At that moment, a Pretor's head popped around the edge of the open doorway, drawing everyone's attention. The Pretor was young and female with round, freckled cheeks and blond hair neatly tied back in a bun. "Juan, Emiliana—your subject is dead," the Pretor said. "Couldn't be revived. It was pronounced by Baroja two minutes ago."

Corcel nodded. "Thanks, Dor."

The uniformed Pretor departed, leaving the group to their discussion.

"You think she was alive?" Grant asked bleakly after a moment's consideration.

The two Pretors looked at him strangely.

"Before the fire?" Corcel queried. "Are you suggesting that Ms. Bella Arran may have already been dead when we interviewed her?"

"That's what she told us, isn't it?" Grant asked. "No reason to question that, is there?"

"There's every reason, Grant," Corcel said. "Dead people are dead. They don't answer questions."

Grant was shaking his head. "Now, that's a very narrow view of what it constitutes to be alive or dead," he said. "I've seen reanimated corpses move under their own power. Never had cause to interview one, but that doesn't mean they couldn't speak."

Corcel laughed uncomfortably. "You have alluded before to a rather colorful history," he said, "but this? Well, it sounds preposterous, if you'll forgive my saying so."

Grant sipped his coffee before speaking. "I won't deny that it does," he agreed, "but you have to admit that something wasn't right about that woman. She spoke about already being dead and, from what we just saw, she commanded her own body to combust, ending any chance we might have had to learn more."

"Not ending any chance," Cáscara piped up. "There are three survivors of the hotel incident who have been placed in recovery in the medical center. Hospitalized, but alive."

"Three," Grant acknowledged. "What about the bodies?"

"They're there, too," Cáscara told him. "In the morgue."

"Maybe we should go examine both sets," Grant proposed.

Corcel nodded. "You sure you're both up for this?" he asked, and his gaze rested on Shizuka.

"Wherever Grant goes, there, too, go I," Shizuka told him.

"Yeah, let's see what we can find out," Grant said.

"Good," Corcel said.

"But since we all smell like fire-damaged stock just now," Cáscara added, "I think we all need to change clothes and freshen up." She looked at Grant and Shizuka, addressing them. "There are showers on-site and I'm sure we can find something for you to wear. What are you, Grant—XXXL?"

Before Grant could answer, Shizuka raised her hand. "We have clothes at our hotel," she said, "and it would be convenient to use this time to pick up something I have left there."

Grant nodded. "Good idea."

"I'll arrange a patrol wag to run you over," Corcel told them both, "and we'll reconvene in ninety minutes outside the hospital. I'll give your driver the details."

"Sounds good, thanks," Grant said. He was already thinking about something he intended to pick up from his hotel room, but he also planned to use the time to check in with Cerberus and see if he could gather any information on the name Ereshkigal. He suspected that the two Pretors would be doing the same.

Chapter 14

"Ereshkigal," Brigid Baptiste read from the computer screen in the Cerberus redoubt, "was the queen of the underworld in Mesopotamian myth." The screen showed a transposed copy of an ancient book, detailing the fragmentary myths of ancient Babylon and its surrounds.

Brigid looked very different from the woman of action who had helped topple the land pirate walker just one day earlier. Now she wore a pair of square-framed spectacles, and her brows were furrowed as she read.

She was working at a computer terminal in the busy Cerberus operations room, located in a hidden redoubt within a hollowed-out mountain of the Bitterroot Mountain Range in what used to be Montana. The room was a vast space with a high roof and pleasing, indirect lighting. Its ceiling looked like the roof of a cave. Within that space, twin aisles of computer terminals—twenty-four in all—ran from left to right, facing a giant screen on which material could be flagged. A giant Mercator map dominated one wall, showing the world before the nukecaust had reshaped the coastlines of North America and other locales. The Mercator map was peppered with glowing locator dots that were joined to one another with dotted lines of diodes, creating an image reminiscent of the kind of flight maps that airlines had given to passengers in the twentieth century. The indicated routes were not flight paths, however, but rather they showed the locations and connections of the sprawling mat-trans network. Developed for the US military, the majority of the units were located within North America, but a few outposts could be seen farther afield.

A separate chamber was located in one corner of the room, far from the wide entry doors. This chamber had reinforced armaglass walls tinted a coffee-brown color. Contained within was the Cerberus installation's mat-trans unit, along with a small anteroom that could be sealed off if necessary.

Right now the mat-trans chamber was empty, but the main ops room was buzzing with life as Cerberus personnel hurried about their business, the dedicated surveillance and protection of humankind.

The redoubt was built into one of the mountains in Montana's Bitterroot Range, where it was entirely hidden from view. It occupied an ancient military base that had been forgotten and ignored in the two centuries since the nukecaust that initiated the twenty-first century. In the years since that conflict, a peculiar mythology had grown up around the mountains with their mysterious, shadowy forests and seemingly bottomless ravines. Now the wilderness surrounding the redoubt was virtually unpopulated, and the nearest settlement could be found in the flatlands some miles away consisting of a small band of Indians, Sioux and Cheyenne, led by a shaman named Sky Dog who had befriended the Cerberus exiles many years ago. Sky Dog and his tribe helped perpetuate the myths about the mountains and so kept his friends undisturbed.

Despite the wilderness that characterized its exterior, the redoubt featured state-of-art technology. The facility was manned by a full complement of staff, over fifty in total, many of whom were experts in their chosen field of scientific study and some of whom had been cryogenically frozen before the nukecaust only to awaken to the harsh new reality.

Cerberus relied on two orbiting satellites at its disposal—the Keyhole Comsat and the Vela-class reconnaissance satellite—which provided much of the data for analysis in their ongoing mission to protect humankind. Gaining access to the satellites had taken long man-hours of intense trial-and-error work by many of the top scientists on hand at the mountain base. Concealed uplinks were hidden beneath camouflage netting in the terrain around the redoubt, tucked away within the rocky clefts of the mountain range where they chattered incessantly with the orbiting satellites. This arrangement gave the personnel a near limitless stream of feed data surveying the surface of the Earth, as well as providing the almost-instantaneous communication with its agents across the globe, wherever they might be. Just now, the agent on the receiving end of the communication was Grant.

Sitting beside Brigid in the ops room were Lakesh and his second in command, Donald Bry.

Lakesh—or, more properly, Mohandas Lakesh Singh— was the leader of the Cerberus operation and a man with an incredible history with the mat-trans project and this redoubt. A theoretical physicist and cyberneticist, Lakesh had been born in the twentieth century, where his expertise had been applied to the original development of the mat-trans process. Lakesh was of average height and had an aquiline nose and refined mouth. His black hair was swept back from his face, a sprinkling of white showing in the black at the temples and sides. In contrast to his dusky skin, Lakesh had penetrating blue eyes that were alert to every detail. Though he looked to be in his fifties, Lakesh was far older than that—two hundred years older, in fact. A combination of cryogenic hibernation and organ replacement had seen Lakesh emerge in the twenty-third century as the leader of what had begun as a covert rebellion against Baron Cobalt but had ultimately developed into something even more noble—the Cerberus organization.

Bry was a young man in his thirties with a curly mop of ginger hair and a permanent expression of worry on his face.

Standing beside these two men, propped against an unmanned desk in the impressive ops room, was Kane. He was dressed in muted colors and had washed and shaved since their encounter with the land pirates in Samariumville. All of them had been connected to Grant via the linked network of Commtacts, and right now, halfway across the world, Grant was listening to Brigid's voice as she summarized everything she could find or recall about the mysteriously named mistress of the dead bomber.

"Her story varies from myth to myth," Brigid explained as she scanned the text, "but they by and large agree upon her role. She was the queen of Irkalla, the land of the dead or the underworld in Mesopotamian legend, a little like Hades in Greek mythology. Considered a goddess, Ereshkigal passed judgment for the underworld and set its laws.

"According to the *Doctrine of Two Kingdoms*, the dominion of Ereshkigal was markedly different from the natural world of her sister Ishtar, and so formed opposites—life and death."

"With Ereshkigal being the principle for death," Lakesh clarified with a grim nod. "It seems, then, that you were right to contact us with your concerns, Grant," he stated into the Commtact pickup mic he wore on a headset. Lakesh did not have a Commtact surgically embedded beneath his skin like the field agents, so relied instead on plug-ins like this one to communicate. "This matter you've happened upon in Spain appears to concern the Annunaki."

"Wouldn't it just," Grant growled over the Commtact, the despair clear from his tone.

The Annunaki had caused no end of trouble for the Cerberus warriors, dating all the way back to before the official formation of the Cerberus organization when an Annunaki overlord called Enlil had masqueraded as the Baron of Cobaltville. An incredibly long-lived race, the Annunaki came from the distant planet of Nibiru thousands of years earlier. Once on Earth, their technology had given the appearance of magic to primitive humankind. They had been elevated to the level of gods in myths that had survived for over six thousand years. The Annunaki's control of humankind had receded over time, but they had made a new stab at absolute control in recent years, leading to the destruction of their starship, *Tiamat*, and the apparent death of the last of their number. The Cerberus warriors had been there to witness both events and were responsible for the campaign that had seen the end to the Annunaki's influence, but they knew better than to believe the Annunaki to be dead. The hateful race had a remarkable talent for surviving against impossible odds and an irritating habit of being reborn when things went sour. Ereshkigal, however, was a new name to most of the Cerberus team, and they had never encountered her before.

"Enlighten us, Baptiste—what can this Ereshkigal bitch do?" Kane asked with a sneer.

"Here," Brigid said as she tapped out a quick pattern on the computer's keyboard. An image came up on screen showing a stone carving that clearly dated back thousands of years. Weatherworn and simplistic, the carving showed a stylized image of a bare-breasted woman with large eyes and a crown or headdress of narrow spikes. Two wings spread out behind her, low to her shoulders.

"Ereshkigal was worshipped in ancient Mesopotamia," Brigid explained, "and there is documented evidence to suggest that she had a temple in the city of Kutha, which was located on the eastern branch of the Upper Euphrates, north of Nippur."

"Enlil's city," Kane recalled.

Brigid nodded. "And close to Babylon also, in modern-day Iraq. A nineteenth-century archaeologist called George Rawlinson found the first references to this—a brick of King Nabu-Kudurri-Usur of the Neo-Babylonian Empire. Nabu-Kudurri-Usur—or Nebuchadrezzar II, if you prefer—was the man responsible for the fabled Hanging Gardens of Babylon as well as the destruction of Solomon's temple in Jerusalem. He features in the Bible in the Book of Daniel."

"So, she was loved and worshipped by people in high places," Kane surmised. "But what did she do?"

"Yeah," Grant chipped in over the Commtact link. "What are we up against here?"

"The myths vary," Brigid admitted, "but one thing is clear—the other gods feared Ereshkigal. She had power that they didn't—power over death."

"So this is the god that gives the other gods nightmares," Kane reasoned. "That can't be good."

"No, it can't," Brigid agreed. "At various times, Ereshkigal was the ruler or joint ruler of the underworld along with her husband, Nergal. Nergal, the god of plague, was forced to marry her after he had insulted her representative at a banquet, who was also her son—although in taking joint control of her kingdom it may be said that he gained more from the marriage than she did."

"You said plague," Grant muttered over the Commtact.

"Never good," Brigid acknowledcdgcd. "Shc had thrcc children—Nungal, Ninazu and Namtar. I don't want to worry anyone, but the latter's father was Enlil."

"Had to be," Kane grumbled, shaking his head in irritation. "Damn inbred family if ever there was one."

"I think she was maybe a little bit unhinged," Brigid said. "She tried to kill her own sister, and the reports vary on whether she succeeded."

"She wouldn't be the first Annunaki to try to assassinate a sibling," Bry pointed out reasonably.

"True," Brigid agreed.

"So we've got a reborn Annunaki goddess," Kane stated, "who rules the land of the dead, scares the other Annunaki shitless and is maybe on a recruitment drive. Like there ain't enough dead people around, she's gotta add extra."

Brigid tilted her head sympathetically. "We don't know why," she reasoned.

"Do these guys ever need a reason?" Kane growled angrily. "Seems like every Johnny-god-come-lately can't wait to start screwing with the human race at the drop of a hat."

"No, there's always a plan," Lakesh said, "a pattern."

"Lakesh is right," Brigid confirmed. "Enlil wanted to subjugate mankind for adoration. Ullikummis came to kill his dad, building an army of human cannon fodder to help him achieve that. Lilitu wanted to regain full possession of her body," she recited, reeling off their three most recent encounters with the Annunaki. There were others, but the point was made.

"So, what do you think Little Miss Underworld is after?" Kane asked.

"The physical makeup of the dead body," Lakesh mused.

"That would be the same chemical structure by and large as a living body," Bry pointed out.

"But easier to control," Lakesh stated.

"Something in the physical body, then?" Brigid proposed. "Fuel, maybe—nutrition or… I don't know."

"In my experience, reborn gods have a habit of being unfulfilled," Lakesh said. "They are born with aspects missing, still forming. A problem with being brought to full term as an adult, I suspect."

"This is all real interesting," Grant's voice growled over the Commtact frequency, "but I need to know how to tackle this woman. Seems she can get inside people's minds like an infection. And her people throw blades at anyone who gets in her way, don't forget. Well?"

"Don't tackle her," Lakesh said. "Not yet."

Kane nodded. "Lakesh is right. We've taken on Annunaki before but it's not easy. You try to do that alone and you'll get crushed."

"I don't crush easy, partner," Grant reminded him.

"Never said you did, partner," Kane assured him. "Just be careful until we can get out there."

Brigid continued to go through the documentation, describing to Grant the image of the stone carving she had found.

GRANT GRIMLY LISTENED to Brigid's recital. He and Shizuka had returned to their rooms at the Hotel El Castillo on the west bank, care of the Pretor escort provided by Corcel and Cáscara. The local Pretors had the discretion to wait outside while Grant and Shizuka went to their suite, ostensibly for a change of clothes and a shower.

While Grant discussed the matter of Ereshkigal with his teammates at the Cerberus redoubt, he was also checking through his travel pack for two items—his shadow suit and his preferred handgun, an old Magistrate Sin Eater, which could be affixed in a wrist holster that he then strapped to his arm so it could be hidden beneath the sleeve of his jacket once he had replaced his clothes with the shadow suit.

Shizuka, too, was switching her attire. She chose a loose cotton jacket from her wardrobe colored a creamy yellow with a brocade pattern that emulated the leaves of the lotus flower. Beneath this she wore a white sleeveless top, loose-fitting pants and shoes that were like ballet flats. She placed a shoulder rig over her arms, specifically designed to hide a weapon under the left arm sufficiently that it would be disguised by the hang of her jacket. The leather holster was decorated with an intricate pattern showing cherry blossoms floating on the breeze past an ancient Japanese pagoda.

The shoulder rig was made to hold a very specific weapon, which Shizuka withdrew from a hidden compartment within her travel case. Contained inside a long scabbard was her katana sword, twenty-five inches of razor-sharp steel with a molded handle that was beautifully decorated with golden filigree. Beside the sheathed sword in the travel case was a small wooden casket, just six inches by three, like a musical box.

She drew a cover from the bed behind her and laid it down on the floor, flattening it carefully. Onto this, Shizuka lay out the sword and the box, sitting cross-legged before them and stilling her mind, zoning out the sound of Grant talking to his allies via the Commtact.

Then Shizuka's delicate hands pushed open the lid and reached inside the box. The contents had been placed carefully within specific compartments that were a masterpiece of simple design and an economic use of space. There were sheets of thin rice paper, a soft square of cotton, a lightly chalked powder ball and a small bottle of oil. In the front of the compartmentalized box, resting across its longest length, lay a tiny brass hammer, held separate from the other items in the sword cleaning kit.

Shizuka reached forward, taking the sheathed katana from where it rested on the blanket. Gripping the hilt of the sword with her right hand, she pulled at the scabbard with her left, drawing the blade out into the open where its polished steel surface reflected the rays of sunlight through the balcony window. The graceful movement was automatic, practiced so many times as to be a part of Shizuka's muscle memory, the weight of the sword moving effortlessly as if it were just another natural appendage of her body. She eyed the blade for a moment, scanning its length, observing the grain of the steel, checking for flaws. Then, careful to hold the sharp edge of the blade away from her, Shizuka took a single sheet of crackling, wafer-thin rice paper and began to slowly stroke the blade with it.

This was a necessary process, a chore that every samurai going back to the days of feudal Japan had performed to ensure that their katana—a weapon that was often referred to as the soul of the samurai—remained strong and clean, free from defects that might hinder a warrior in battle. But it was also a ritual, one that served to fill and calm Shizuka's mind after the disturbing events at the Pretor Hall of Justice.

Shizuka finally discarded the rice paper and began tapping the length of the finely honed blade with the powder ball, running a dusting of chalk along its flawless surface. Thoughts of the woman who had—died, killed herself, combusted?—ran through Shizuka's head with each tap of her sword, but she willed them from her mind, letting her thoughts still in meditation. If she and Grant were to face this Ereshkigal, with her monstrous and unfathomable ways, and survive, then she would need to be at the very top of her game, a modern-day samurai in tune with every sinew, every fiber of her being. For Shizuka knew that a warrior was defeated not by the enemy but by their own shortcomings.

Shizuka ran another sheet of rice paper along the length of her katana to brush away the powder, then reached for the bottle of oil contained in the box and dribbled a few drops along the katana blade. Then she tilted the sword so that the oil ran along its length. With her free hand, Shizuka took the cotton square from the wooden box and began to clean the blade in a long, sweeping stroke down its length, following the lines of the grain of the steel.

Shizuka waved her blade before her, feeling its familiar weight in her hand as it swept through the air. She was ready now, ready for anything. She replaced the contents of the little wooden box and rested it back inside the hidden compartment of her case along with the empty scabbard that had held the katana. Assuming a standing position, she slipped the naked blade through the shoulder rig until it rested within the sheath there. When she turned she saw that Grant was watching her. He had changed, too, and was now wearing the shadow suit under street clothes. Shizuka detected the familiar bulge of the Sin Eater in its wrist holster puffing out the sleeve of his jacket—subtle and easy to miss unless you were made aware of it.

"We have an appointment at the Zaragoza Hospital," Grant was outlining over the Commtact.

"We'll get out there as soon as we can and come find you," Kane assured him over the Commtact. "Think you can stay out of trouble 'til then?"

"I'm not you, Kane," Grant replied, his voice dripping with sarcasm. "I manage to avoid trouble almost every day."

"Yes," Brigid spoke over the Commtact, cutting off the verbal sparring of the two friends, "well, see that you do. Annunaki trouble is too big for any one of us to handle alone. Even with Shizuka's assistance."

Grant looked up at Shizuka as Brigid spoke the woman's name, and for a moment he couldn't help but see how frail her petite frame seemed; especially so when put in context with the towering Annunaki sadists they had clashed with before. "I'll take care," he concluded before cutting the communication.

Then Grant caught Shizuka's eye. "All set?" he asked.

"With reluctance, I am, Grant-san," Shizuka assured him. "I heard you speak of the Annunaki. It seems we may never be rid of their baneful influence."

"Yeah," Grant agreed with a shake of his head. "Not quite the vacation we had in mind, huh?"

"It seems that destiny had another vacation in mind for us," Shizuka told him, "one it would be churlish to reject."

Together they exited the hotel and joined the Pretors waiting in the patrol vehicle.

Chapter 15

Elsewhere

Surrounding the entire city of Zaragoza was a twelve-foot wall that had been built during the dark days of the era known as Deathlands. Following the nukecaust, the population had been culled to just ten percent of what it had been before, and found itself in a newly hostile environment characterized by radioactive hot zones, mutated plants and animals, and, worst of all, mutated things that had started life as men. Stickies, scalies, swampies—the list of mutants was almost endless, and their mutations ran the gamut from useful adaptations, like the dual circulatory system of the swampies, through to picturesque but largely useless twists of the human DNA structure, like semi-sentient hair. To survive, humanity had had to battle with all of those threats and one more besides: itself.

Man could be the cruelest threat of all, his own worst enemy in times of struggle. The greatest survivors, the most adept, had gathered about them men of similar standing, and once they had banded together, many of those men had taken to ransacking the crapped-on, dust-strewn, ash-stained remains of the civilized world and woe betide anyone who got in their way. This behavior had led to the emergence of the villes in the USA, walled settlements that had offered protection and security for such men and their families, tiny fiefdoms where cruelty and submission were often the norm.

A similar pattern had been followed in Europe, and the older cities—or those that had survived—had been cut up and fenced in, baron hiding from baron, playing out tiny wars over food and space and jealousy, the little things that wars are always fought over. Zaragoza had been walled protectively in spits and spots during this period, until the emergence of the grand ville, protecting its ancient architecture from the depredations of would-be attackers.

Around Zaragoza, the wall remained. It had been built tall and it had been built strong and it had been reinforced over and over back when the threat of mutie men taking your wives or your daughters had seemed very, very real.

Now those walls were guarded by Pretors, uniformed and armored, carrying their pistols in smooth underarm holsters from which the weapons could be launched into the user's hand in a fraction of a second. The Pretors worked in teams, four to a gate, placed evenly around the city at the cardinal points of the compass. There were guard posts at these points, with heavily armored walls and mounted railguns for use against possible attack. While the threat of a mutie army breaching the walls had subsided, the old precautions—and the old wariness—remained.

It was to one of these guard posts, the one to the south of the city, that the woman and her two assistants came, striding out of the heat haze of the barren desert, where dust-dry plants vied for space in the shifting sands, clinging obstinately to life long after the battle seemed to have been lost. The tanned woman came barefoot toward the guard post. Her dark-skinned retainers were barefoot, too. She wore a smear of blood and oil across her breasts, a train of feathers attached to her rounded buttocks and the crown of twisted antlers affixed atop her head. The tarmac of the road they walked on was already as warm as the outside of an oven from the sun, but the woman did not flinch when she stepped on it—she walked instead like an actress striding the red carpet, the fan of feathers whipping behind her in the wind.

The two men with her were dark-skinned and muscular and wore only pants, no shirts or shoes. Their expressions were fixed and vacant, their eyes staring straight ahead. One's bare chest showed dark marks like the imprints of insect shadows on his flesh. It may have been tattooing or it could have been some disease; it was hard to be certain. Where the woman seemed animated by the wind itself, dancing and twirling as she paced light-footed toward the guard post, her associates barely moved at all— they were more like rocks being rolled along the road than people walking.

Pretor Cadalso watched them approach through the bulletproof glass of the guard post's window, a smile of disbelief forming on his lips. "Hey, you see this?" he asked, calling across to his fellow Pretors where they were monitoring traffic flow, checking weather reports and otherwise working at their designated duties.

The other Pretors in the post looked up. They were two women and a man. The man, Pretor de Centina, was older than the others, in his midfifties with a face that showed scarring from a cancer scare he had had two years before. He had been a Pretor for thirty years and was pretty well inured to have seen everything he could have seen on the job and not be stunned. The women, Pretors Ruiz and Bazán, were younger and had less experience between them than de Centina alone. Ruiz had short hair, close-cropped to her head like a sheen of black oil, while Bazán had tied her strawberry blond hair back into a braid that could be slipped neatly under her uniform helmet.

"My, oh, my, what do we have here?" de Centina asked rhetorically as he spied the svelte figure moving gradually toward the guard post. She moved like liquid flowing, muscles flexing effortlessly as she crossed the empty highway, spinning in slow delight on the third step or the fourth or the fifth.

"They look like refugees," Bazán opined, plucking her helmet from a hook on the wall of the guard post. "No shoes, no shirts. Maybe they survived something."

"Survived what?" Ruiz asked. "I haven't heard of anything going on out there."

"Out there's a big old world, people," de Centina reminded them all. "Let's not let our guard down just yet."

Pretor Cadalso checked his blaster before stepping toward the guard station's door. "I'll check it," he announced. "Find out what their story is."

Bazán joined him at the door. "I've got your back," she said.

And so they exited, and walked into the path of a reborn goddess who was perfectly capable of tearing through them like a force of nature.

"May I help you?" Cadalso asked the woman and her entourage, striding over to meet them twenty yards away from the guard post.

The woman, Ereshkigal, fixed him with a look. Her eyes were a pale brown, like caramel, though at their edges they seemed to contain the red of blood. "I'm here to give you something," she cooed, luscious full lips oozing over every word with each movement of her mouth. "A memory of beauty."

Pretor Cadalso eyed the woman up and down appreciatively. "And what a memory it is," he said.

Ereshkigal turned her attention on his partner, the woman called Bazán. "Do you like the things you see with your eyes?" she asked.

Bazán's lips curled in a sarcastic smile. "I'm not as easily swayed as my colleague, ma'am. Even," she said, glancing to the woman's shirtless assistants, "when the window dressing is finished so nicely."

Without warning, Ereshkigal twirled on the spot, gracefully spinning before the two Pretors, twice around. When she had finished she told them in a quiet tone, "Memories of beauty are within you already, locked inside you, held close to your hearts. Release them now, and feel the joy flood your veins."

WATCHING THROUGH THE window of the guard post, de Centina shook his head. "What are they? Some kind of dance troupe?"

"They haven't asked for entry yet," Ruiz noted, watching the performance from over the older man's shoulder. The guard post was here to vet potential entrants to the ville, checking them for threats and also for less obvious things, like disease, that could not be allowed through the gate.

"They're not traveling with anything," de Centina pointed out. "Just the clothes on their backs, and those just barely."

"Maybe they got rolled on the way and had their possessions stolen," Ruiz proposed.

"They don't look like people who've been rolled," de Centina told her. "They look more like drug types who're high on something. Take it from an old man who's seen it all before."

The two Pretors watched a moment longer as the woman with the feather train leaned forward, standing on tiptoe and arching her whole body into the move, and beckoned their colleagues closer. Then she spoke to them in a whisper, words that neither de Centina nor Ruiz could hear. The next thing they saw, Cadalso and Bazán staggered back as if they had been shot or stabbed, walking away from the woman in the headdress in a confused pattern. They looked as if they were standing on the deck of a boat during a fierce storm.

"What's happening out there?" de Centina muttered, grabbing for his protective helmet without bothering to look.

OUTSIDE, ERESHKIGAL HAD told the two Pretors the secret words that unlocked the thing inside them, unhinging it from its hiding place and calling it into action. The words were the same as the day she had first discovered them, over six thousand years before.

Pretor Cadalso saw it as a series of great lights, playing before his eyes in a brilliant display like the stars in a clear night sky. They were stars that seemed to swirl and dance, growing ever brighter, ever more intense. He wanted to be closer to those stars, and with each breath he felt them enter his system, budding inside him, clumping together in great chunks of deific brightness. They seemed to be replacing his fleshy organs, turning his insides—all blood and bone and gristle—into something magical, as weightless as helium. He was ascending, the breath of a goddess within him, filling his insides.

Pretor Bazán saw it as a trail of colors, fluttering through the air like a gymnast's ribbon; a streak of paint across her vision. It was just one line but its color was changing along its length as she turned her head to watch, blue replenished by purple replenished by red replenished by orange replenished by yellow—and on and on, a circular spectrum running an infinite, Ouroborus length. She felt that fluttering strip of color encompass and draw her, spinning around her so fast that she could not keep up. She reached for it, not just with her heart but with her breath, expelling everything within her just to try to snag it and draw it close.

To outside eyes—specifically those of Pretors de Centina and Ruiz—it appeared that the two Pretors were hallucinating, for they were reaching out for things that could not be seen, staggering after them and turning this way and that as they grabbed at the air.

Stepping from the guard post, Pretor de Centina commanded his Devorador de Pecados 9 mm pistol into his hand from its forearm sheath and targeted the woman in the headdress. Behind him, Ruiz brought her own pistol to bear, carefully watching the two dark-skinned men who remained standing impassively to either side of the scantily clad woman.

"Don't move," de Centina ordered, stepping slowly forward. "Just get your hands in the air where I can see them."

Ereshkigal simply smiled, a thin-lipped, reptilian smile. In that moment, de Centina thought he saw something of the snake scale about her skin, a slickness and luminescence that was not strictly human.

"Didn't you hear me?" de Centina demanded. "Hands up—right now!"

Beside Ereshkigal, her two shirtless cohorts had their hands behind their backs. In a flash, their hands appeared, flicking up into the air in a heartbeat-fast parody of raising their hands in surrender. De Centina did not even see the flash of metal as the two men moved their hands, launching four throwing discs at him, one from each hand. He felt the discs impact against his chest armor, though, impact and cut through into the flesh beneath.

De Centina's legs gave out from under him, and he collided with the dirt an instant later. He tried to say something as he fell but his vocal cords wouldn't work and his tongue seemed to have swollen in his mouth so that he merely blurted out an animal sound of pain as he flopped backward. There was blood on his chest, seeping into the material where the four throwing discs protruded from their deep cuts into his body.

Ruiz fired without hesitation, pumping the trigger of her blaster and sending two shots in the direction of the two men, targeting their legs in an effort to disable rather than kill, the way she had been trained. The shots rang loud across the desolate plain outside the ville. The first shot was true, drilling into her target's right leg so that he tumbled over himself in a sprawl of limbs. The second should have hit the other man's hip—Ruiz had graduated high in her class for marksmanship—but he stepped into the shot at the last instant, drawing his body low and taking the bullet to the gut instead of the hip. The man's belly burst into a shock of blood, painting the air with red.

Ruiz moved as she blasted again, scrambling over to de Centina's fallen body and dropping to one knee as she sent another shot toward the woman who now stood between her falling colleagues. Time seemed to stand still for Ruiz in that moment, and she watched as the woman in the elaborate headdress seemed to follow the bullet with her eyes as it arrowed toward her. The 9 mm slug was rocketing through the air on a collision course with her right hip. The woman moved her right arm without effort, cutting across the bullet's path as it was about to strike her. Ruiz watched in horror as the bullet seemed to go hurtling away, glinting in the sunlight. The strangely garbed woman was still moving, her arm finishing its sweeping arc where she had—*what?*—cut the bullet from the air? No, that wasn't it, Ruiz could see the bruise budding on the side of her hand where the bullet had hit before being flicked away.

The woman strode across the hot tarmac, the smile disappearing from her ruby lips as she marched toward Ruiz. As she reached her, she stretched out her hands, grasping for the Pretor's head even as Ruiz tried to back away, squeezing her blaster's trigger again. Her shots struck the woman in the side and just below her breast, struck and ricocheted away as if they had hit armor plate. Ruiz wondered, in that shocking instant, just what the woman's flesh was made from. Then the mysterious woman's hands were locked against Ruiz's temples, pressing hard until she had raised her from her knees up to her feet. Then she dragged the female Pretor forward, so that the toes of Ruiz's standard-issue boots slipped along the tarmac. Ruiz was trapped somehow, unable to free herself or to really move.

Seconds.

She wanted to shoot the woman again, but the angle was wrong. She couldn't seem to get the blaster up.

Holding the hapless Pretor, Ereshkigal leaned close and spoke, her words as light and warm as the Spanish sirocco.

"Círculo alrededor del cuerpo,
Guarda silencio a moverse más.
Gire vida lejos,
Gire aliento.
Abrazo fauces del infierno."

Ruiz felt an uncanny pressure in her chest at that, like the flutter of butterflies in the earliest stages of love. It was beautiful and terrifying and curiously addictive all at once. The words, too, were beautiful, though they had already passed out of her mind. She felt the release of the struggle inside her, the struggle she had never really realized she was in, the struggle between living and just giving up.

Ruiz shifted the gun in her hand, turning it fully 180 degrees until it pressed against her own flank, twisting her wrist until she had the muzzle pushed between her second and third ribs. Hearing the whispered words of Ereshkigal, Ruiz gave up, seeing now how wrong she had been to try to live, to cling to something so fleeting and so very full of pain. She pulled the trigger, sending a continuous burst of fire into her own chest from point-blank range, glorying as it ripped through the armor of her uniform and into her flesh.

Ereshkigal let go of the dead Pretor, watching in satisfaction as the woman slumped to the road, her blaster silenced in an instant. She remembered in those moments, the first time she had discovered this secret, the way to kill an apekin human, millennia ago.

Her two assistants—Namtar and the Edimmu called Tsanti—were sprawled on the road before Ereshkigal. As she approached, Namtar, whose body was afflicted with the black marks of the scarabae sickness and who had taken the blast to his leg, lifted himself up, moving to a standing position in an inhuman shift of muscles beneath flesh. The wound to his right leg showed where his pants had torn open. The wound did not bleed—instead it looked like a dent against metal, the skin puckered inward where the bullet had struck. He took a hesitant step forward, testing the leg and confirming he could still walk on it. Then he fell to his knees before Ereshkigal, offering himself to her.

Ereshkigal moved past him, standing over the prone form of the Edimmu Tsanti. Tsanti lay still, the bloody wound of his gut like the aftermath of surgery gone wrong, struts of bone and gobs of flesh mixed in the redness of the wound. The Edimmu were ghosts come to haunt the Earth, but they could still die.

Ereshkigal bent down, running her hands down her bare legs until they reached her ankles, holding them there and bringing her head almost in line with the dead Edimmu's. Then she formed the words of the age-old formula and whispered it into Tsanti's ear before rising and stepping back.

Beside Ereshkigal, the Edimmu called Tsanti opened his eyes, two yellow-white, featureless orbs, and drew in a breath. He had come back to life, the wound in his belly dried and crusting over with scabs, his muscles reknitting sufficiently to let him function. Still on the ground, he bowed his head in appreciation of his mistress's favor, touching his forehead once to the hot tarmac before rising to his feet. She had turned away now to face the guard post and the wall behind it. Tsanti rose, moving awkwardly as he adjusted to the new growth of muscle around the dried wound.

Ereshkigal led the way toward the guard post through which she would enter the city of Zaragoza. Namtar and the Edimmu took up their places beside her, striding purposely along the road.

All around them, the figures of the once-dead Pretors began to rise, joining the mismatched group as they prepared to enter the city.

Chapter 16

Ereshkigal was a mathematician.

She was a member of the Annunaki, the race of reptilian creatures who had arrived on Earth during humankind's prehistory, and who now lived liked gods, equally worshipped and feared by the local population of human apekin. Ereshkigal was tall and reedy, over six feet in height with a crest of spines that towered another eight inches above her head. Slender of form but muscular as was in the nature of all Annunaki, her pale skin looked almost white in the sunlight, ghostly and scaled in the manner of a snake's hide. She had eyes the color of molten caramel, black iris slits running in thick vertical lines down each eye like the eyes of a lizard.

In the days when she was young, before her presence had become known to man, Ereshkigal would sit naked in the courtyard of the Royal Palace of Nippur soaking up the sun, reading and filling in books with long and complicated sums in her precise, spider-thin script. The sums would often run over several pages, and Ereshkigal could often be found switching these pages with one another until she smiled anew, creating a whole new mathematics out of the detached pieces of the old.

Lord Enlil found her sitting on a stone bench by grapevines that climbed against the south wall of his courtyard one afternoon. He considered her a strange child, but pretty. The vines were rich with fruit, great bulbous green grapes the size of eyeballs, drooping from every straining stem.

"You seem pleased with your labors," Enlil said in a duo-tonal voice that seemed to echo as if spoken through a metal pipe.

A member of the Annunaki Royal Family, Enlil was a tall figure, muscular with scales like metal plate, colored like bronze washed in blood. He had a towering crest over his head and his golden eyes were almost hypnotic as they gazed at this female who was a few years younger than he. Enlil had taken to wearing a red cloak over recent months, long enough to brush his ankles and dyed once a week with sheep's blood to retain its lustrous color. He felt it augmented his appearance as a ruler and a god to the simple race whose planet this had been. This was his palace, all golden walls and stone carvings, potted plants growing in long troughs along every wall and rooftop, bringing green to every alcove, every shadow in celebration of his godhood.

Ereshkigal did not peer up from her work as she swapped another page around, replacing it with a new leaf whose calculations ran in a curving line so swiftly had she desired to get them written down.

Enlil waited, watching a gull pass by overhead, listening to the way the wind whispered through the columns that supported the covered section of the courtyard. "Ereshkigal," he said after a moment. "I said that you seemed pleased. Have your labors borne fruit?"

Ereshkigal looked up at Enlil, acknowledging him for the first time with a brief nod of her surf pale head. "My lord," she said, before returning to her calculations.

Enlil sat down, taking up a position beside her on the stone bench. It was hot to the touch, and he wondered how it must feel against her naked form. His eyes roved over the muddled sheets of calculations, then followed the curve of her legs, her buttocks, the swell of her breasts. "It looks complex," he said, his lizard's eyes still fixed on her breasts.

"Logic has no complication," she replied without looking up. "It is merely a case of fitting the parts together."

Enlil wondered about fitting *their* parts together, but chose not to voice that. Although he could not know it, before the decade was over, Ereshkigal would be carrying his child, Namtar, who would be considered by the apekin to be the god of death. Instead he said, "What does your logic reveal?"

Ereshkigal looked up then, fixing Enlil with her luminous eyes. "That there is an equation written into all living things on this planet," she said with some excitement. "It informs them of how and when to grow, and also when to stop. Otherwise, the apekin might keep growing to heights of twenty or thirty feet or more. Can you imagine that?"

Enlil flashed her his smile, perceiving the humor in her example. "All living things must have their limits, and all must be careful not to exceed them," he observed.

"But, you see, the equations can be bent," Ereshkigal whispered confidentially, though there was no one else in the courtyard. "I believe that they may be altered to generate new results."

Enlil was intrigued. "What kind of results?" he asked. He had been at war with his relatives, on and off, since birth, vying for power, fighting over one spit of land or another. He had considered breeding a creature that might tip the balance in his favor, an assassin, his hand-in-darkness. Perhaps this equation, if it could really be used to alter the genetic makeup of a living creature, might hold the answer to his desires.

"I am uncertain as yet, my lord," Ereshkigal admitted with the honesty of a child. "Death, perhaps."

"Death?" Enlil questioned.

"A formula for life is a formula also for death," Ereshkigal explained. "It needs only to be reversed."

"And you believe that this is possible?"

Ereshkigal nodded slowly, flipping to one of her reams of notes. "There should be a way, a formula, with which one could instruct a body to die," she said. "It's mathematics, pure mathematics. You simply need to know what the input is, numerator to denominator, you see?"

Enlil thought that he did. "So you might kill the apekin with—what? An instruction?"

Ereshkigal looked at him thoughtfully. "They are our playthings, are they not?" she said. "I shall take some to my lab and experiment awhile. Perhaps I will be able to introduce new deaths to them."

"New deaths," Enlil repeated, rolling the words around thoughtfully in his head. "Could this be applied to us, the Annunaki, do you think?"

A smile materialized on Ereshkigal's face as if this thought had not occurred to her before. "It depends on how robust the equation is, I suppose," she said.

Enlil eyed the girl more warily. She was still a child really, barely out of her teens, and all she seemed to enjoy were her formulae. She would bear watching this one, in case she should turn on him or make a bid for his throne. "I would contend that such experiments necessitate prime facilities," he proposed. "Not the tiny suite of rooms you have here but something more suited to your purpose.

"Come, dear Ereshkigal. Let us draw up a map for your new laboratories," Enlil said solicitously. "Somewhere out of the sunlight where you might better concentrate." He knew just the spot—below the ground, well away from the terrain of Lords Marduk, Zu or Lilitu, who had been sniffing out his weaknesses over recent months. Let the girl work out of sight for a while and create her death formula for him.

Chapter 17

Traffic on roads. Hustle. Bustle.

The Zaragoza streets were busy with land vehicles. Spain, it seemed, had progressed further than the bombed-out United States of America in its climb back to a livable society after the nukecaust. There were small one-man mopeds, larger two-man wags with plastic coverings that left the sides open and full-on automobiles carrying whole families to and fro on the road network of the walled ville.

Grant was glad he wasn't driving. Sitting in the back of the Pretor patrol Wheelfox—a kind of abbreviated Sandcat with a single, centrally mounted, gyroscopic rear wheel that was four feet high, providing admirable maneuverability and stability—he watched as the driver weaved through the traffic, avoiding snarl-ups and ignoring the constant bleat of honking horns.

The patrol Pretors were amiable on the journey through town. Both had removed their helmets, housing them in the well between the driver's seat and the passenger's. Both men were in their thirties, the one to the right wearing a pencil-thin mustache and perfumed hair oil that gave off a lavender scent, the one to the left sporting a shaved head that had begun to regrow with a five-o'clock shadow to match.

"You're not from around here, then?" the man in the passenger seat asked in passable English, the Spanish accent loaning his words a cheerful quality. "American, right?"

"I'm American," Grant confirmed, "but she's from New Edo."

"An island in the Pacific," Shizuka elaborated when she saw the uniformed Pretor frown.

"You vacation here, get mixed up in some mess," the driver said, glancing behind him even as he steered around a stalled moped on the four-lane roadway.

"Yeah," Grant said. "A whole lot of mess. Your colleagues asked if we could help out."

"Real honor," the Pretor in the passenger seat remarked. "Juan C doesn't partner up easily."

"We'll remember that," Grant said with a nod and a forced smile.

The Wheelfox drew to a halt outside the hospital complex, dropping Grant and Shizuka at the main doors, a triumph of glass and metal. The hospital was a large, white-stoned monstrosity that took up a city block and was surrounded by a desert of tarmac populated by shrubs in bricked-in pots and abutted by a multistory parking garage. Corcel and Cáscara were waiting for them in their own patrol vehicle and came striding across the tarmac toward the jutting porch when they saw the Pretors pull up.

"Feel better?" Corcel asked, eyeing Grant and Shizuka and handing them both a clip-on badge—a Magistrate-style shield finished in metallic blue. He and Cáscara wore similar shields attached to their belts, although theirs were gold.

"Cleaner anyway," Grant said, taking his shield. "What's this?"

"Your jurisdiction. These are temporary," Corcel told them both as they clipped them to their clothes—Grant's to his belt, Shizuka's to a lapel on her jacket. "Don't start throwing weight around that you don't have, and don't go arresting anyone without my say so, you understand?"

"What about shooting a suspect?" Grant asked with mock seriousness.

"I'd advise against that also," Corcel told him in a voice that suggested he hadn't gotten the joke.

"I managed to get a few insights into who this Ereshkigal is," Grant said.

"The name of some old goddess," Cáscara said, "so most probably a gang leader with a sick sense of humor."

"I'd go for the former," Grant told her solemnly. "Goddess. Drawing from experience."

Cáscara's perfectly shaped eyebrows rose in surprise. "Do you meet a lot of old goddesses, Grant?"

"More than I'd like," Grant told her. "Long story. Series of them, in fact. Let's say that most of those old myths have some basis in reality, and over time a lot of them are refusing to stay dead."

"It appears that you live a very interesting life with these Cerberus people you mentioned," Cáscara said archly.

"*Interesting*'s one word for it," Grant said as they passed through the revolving glass door and into the hospital's lobby.

INSIDE, THE HOSPITAL had the universal smell of all hospitals, a mixture of vinegar and citrus fruit and recycled air masking an underlying stink of sweat and sickness.

The hospital lobby was meticulously clean to the point of sterility and was lit by overheads, bright but not overpowering. The gold finish of Corcel's and Cáscara's shields caught the light of the overhead fluorescents in firework flashes. People were waiting on side benches that had been placed in two semicircle patterns around some potted plants, while trolleys were wheeled through containing files and vials.

A young woman dressed in white, with olive skin and hair a midnight black so dark it was almost blue, glanced up at the Pretors' approach from where she had been filing a printed chart behind the long, bar-like desk. "Can I help you, Pretors?" she inquired, speaking Spanish.

Corcel flashed the woman a dazzling smile. "A group of people were brought in from an incident at the Hotel Retiro last night," he explained, adding a case number. "Would you be able to guide us to them?"

"Certainly," the administrator told him before consulting a computer. Swiftly, she gave Corcel a floor and two room numbers that associated with the survivors of the weird attack. "Three survivors, the others are in the morgue."

"We'll find our own way," Corcel told the white-clad woman as she began to look around the lobby for someone to help.

"As you wish, Pretor," she said.

Corcel led the way to an elevator bank located roughly behind the lobby desk.

"I'll handle the interviews," Corcel stated. "Right now you two are the most reliable witnesses we have. Hopefully, this will change that."

Grant nodded. "I'd like to check in on the bodies that were brought in," he said.

"Here, I'll show you," Cáscara said.

"You guys come here a lot?" Grant asked as they waited for the elevators to arrive.

"It can be an unfortunate necessity in our line of work," Cáscara answered, her expression solemn.

"Yeah, I remember," Grant said, recalling his days as a Magistrate in Cobaltville. He thought, too, of his more recent experiences with Cerberus and tried to count the number of times he had ended up waiting in the medical area of the Cerberus redoubt while one or other of his colleagues recovered from injuries sustained in the line of service. He had waited on Shizuka in that situation more than once and knew that she had waited on him at least as often as he had her. Risks of the business, he lamented.

"Oftentimes, it seems that we are shuffling the cards at the fringes of life and death," Corcel said, his thoughts mirroring Grant's. "And yet we never seem to know who'll be dealing our next hand."

While they waited for the elevators, Grant outlined what he had gleaned about Ereshkigal from his discussion with Cerberus. "In essence, the Annunaki are bad business, and Ereshkigal sounds like the baddest business they got," he concluded.

"Sounds delightful," Cáscara deadpanned as the first elevator arrived and its doors inched open. "Morgue's downstairs. Shall we?"

Grant nodded, following the female Pretor into the elevator just as the second one arrived. Shizuka joined Pretor Corcel in the second elevator, riding up to the third floor while Grant and Cáscara descended to the basement.

THE THIRD FLOOR featured pale walls and the same antiseptic smell that permeated the whole building. Shizuka wondered if anyone had ever opened a window here—it felt as though they hadn't, not once since the construction of the building over a decade ago.

A nurse on call waited at the near end of the corridor, just to the right of the elevator bank. She was young, with long blond hair that she had clipped back so that it fell away from her face. Shizuka guessed she was beautiful when she had had enough sleep and her white uniform wasn't showing the creases of a two-day-long shift. Right now, however, she looked something beyond tired.

When the young nurse saw Corcel she stood to attention, a furtive expression on her face. "P-Pretor," she said, her hands twitching nervously at her desk—a small wooden unit housing a flat computer screen with just enough room beneath it for one person to put their legs. "May I—may I help you?"

Used to this reaction—and knowing it was to his badge of office, not him—Corcel offered the nervous carer a winning smile, a row of white teeth materializing in his tanned face. "Three people were brought in yesterday," he said before giving their names.

"Th-through here," the nurse stuttered, leading the way down the clinically clean corridor. The corridor, like much of the hospital, was lit by fluorescents located behind grille-like tiles.

Inside the patients' room, the atmosphere was still. The blinds had been drawn, painting the room in a semidark gloom. Two people shared the room, both of them men, lying in two beds that had been set five feet apart. Both men appeared to be asleep.

"Zorrilla is next door," the nurse explained in Spanish before leaving Corcel and Shizuka alone in the room. Shizuka regretted not being able to speak the language.

Keeping his voice low, Corcel had the good manners to translate for Shizuka. His English was flawless but accented in such a way that the hard edges of syllables seemed to have been planed down. "These two look to be asleep," he said quietly, stepping between the beds.

Shizuka paced across to the head of one of the beds. The man there had a lined face and looked to be in his fifties or perhaps his early sixties. His eyes were closed, his expression serene, but there was bruising around his throat where the noose had been wrapped before he had been cut down. She turned her attention to the occupant of the other bed. This one was younger and appeared well built from the span of his shoulders that was visible under the covers. He had dark hair, sleep-ruffled now, but obviously trimmed neatly. Like his fellow patient, his eyes were closed and there were dark bruises across his neck.

"I wonder what they are thinking of," Shizuka said quietly.

"We'll only know that when they wake up," Corcel said, glancing at the monitors that were wired to the two patients.

One of the men stirred, but when Corcel tried to speak to him he only grunted and turned his head away.

"We'll try the other patient," Corcel told Shizuka, leading the way quietly to the door.

IT WAS NOT clear that they had entered the basement level, Grant thought, as the elevator doors drew back to reveal a starkly lit corridor painted in a pastel shade. The floor, too, was pastel, a barely there green color that had so little confidence it looked like a shirt that had been washed a thousand times until the color was almost gone. It was just like every other corridor of the hospital, and similar to every corridor of every medical facility that Grant had ever attended.

"No bold colors," Grant said, addressing Cáscara. "You ever wonder about that?"

Pretor Cáscara's brow was furrowed when she looked at Grant. "Huh?"

"They never paint hospitals in bright colors," he told her as they trudged along the airless corridor. "It's always soft shades that look like they spent too long in the sun."

Cáscara shrugged. "Maybe they're afraid that anything too bright will scare the patients," she suggested. "No fear of that happening here, though," she added, directing Grant toward a set of double doors that led into the morgue. The doors featured glass roundels at head height, just enough that one could see who was approaching but not look into the room itself.

Within, the room felt cold. Despite his shadow suit, Grant felt the temperature drop against his bare hands and face.

The room was large and featured three walls of drawers running floor to ceiling, each door big as that of a filing cabinet. The fourth wall—the side from which Grant and his companion had entered—was blank with a long mirror running its length, before which stood a small desk with an anglepoise lamp, a computer and a mobile tablet. A man sat at this, his expression haggard, his hair prematurely thinning, staring into the computer screen as the Pretor and the Cerberus man entered his domain. He looked up and smiled when he saw Cáscara, self-consciously brushing at the hair on his head. "Pretor Cáscara, h-how are you?" he said in Spanish. "I—I mean, what are you doing here? Which is to say, can I help you with why you are here?"

"Julio," Cáscara replied, "are you busy?"

The man called Julio shrugged. "So-so," he admitted. "The dead keep on dying."

"Would you have five minutes to show us the bodies that came in last night from the hotel incident?"

"For you," Julio said with a blush as he stood up, "I can make time. Who's your friend?"

"This is Grant," Cáscara explained.

Grant saluted casually.

"He's American. Helping us on a case."

"Lucky stiff," Julio said as he led the way to one of the banks of drawers. He counted them in his head, despite the fact that each was labeled, then pulled at one of the handles that was just below hip level, one up from the bottom. A drawer slid out on runners, long as a bed and containing the figure of a man in his midforties, naked and with a deathly pallor, his eyes closed.

"Looks dead, sure enough," Grant said, peering at the body. He thought he maybe recognized the corpse from the night before as one of the hanging suicides. As he looked closer, he saw the darker skin around the neck and throat along with a little chafing.

"You see the wound around the neck," Julio observed. "Consistent with death by hanging."

"I know," Grant replied.

"Are you a doctor?" Julio asked, surprised.

"No," Cáscara told him. "He was there."

The morgue technician did a double take. "Seriously? That must have been some nasty, nasty business."

Grant didn't answer the man, just gave him a grim smile that said he had seen it all before.

"There are more?" Cáscara checked.

"Twelve in here," Julio confirmed, "with two in the theater waiting for final report.

"Let me close up Frankie here," he continued, reaching for the handle to the drawer, "and then I can—"

The technician stopped as Grant's hand gripped his wrist.

"Wait," Grant said. He had seen something. A movement in the body, just a minute twitch of the fingers. "You see that?" he asked. "He moved."

"Bodies will often shift position as they begin to decompose," Julio explained. "You think you can let go of my arm, man?"

Reluctantly, Grant let go.

And then the dead man moved again.

THE WOMAN IN the second room was awake and, thankfully, far more loquacious than the other patients who had been recovered from the hotel. In her midfifties, she lay in her hospital bed with a frizz of dyed red hair that encircled her head like a bird's nest and spoke to Corcel and Shizuka with a husky voice caused by the previous night's hanging.

"I heard music," she said.

"There was a band there," Corcel told her, "a quintet."

"Yes, I recall," the woman, whose name was Maria Zorrilla, said, "but this was different. It was better than the music that they played, more…sensual. I felt it here, in my—" she tapped her chest "—heart."

"What kind of music?" Shizuka asked once Corcel had translated. He translated her words for Zorrilla.

The woman in the bed spoke rapidly as she reached for a glass of water beside the bed. *"Era exquisita."*

"The music was absolute pleasure, a thing of absolute beauty," Corcel translated. "It was exquisite."

Shizuka studied the woman's face, saw the sincerity there.

"I would return to it in a heartbeat," she said. And then, without warning, she shattered the glass against the bedside cabinet, breaking it with a vicious strike so that the top broke into a jagged line, spilling water everywhere.

Shizuka leaped back as the water struck her. She and Corcel watched in stunned horror as the woman called Maria whipped the jagged remains of the glass up and drew the sharp edge across her throat in a deep gash. *"Era exquisita,"* she said as the sharp edge drew blood.

OUTSIDE, ON THE streets of the ancient city of Zaragoza, the church bells had begun to chime. They sounded in a slow drone, regular as a heartbeat but with each note characterized by almost a minute of silence between each sound— a very slow heartbeat, then. The noise had begun at one church in the south, close to the walls that surrounded the city. However, with each slow chime, the noise seemed to spread, the beat being picked up and mimicked by the next closest church, spreading across the city like a virus as each new church tower picked up the call. By the time it reached the center of the city, where the hospital stood, over a dozen churches were ringing their bells, and the streets seemed to be quietening in their wake.

"He moved," Grant insisted as the dead man's arm shifted on the cold bed of the morgue drawer.

Before Grant could say more, the whole body of the dead man whom the lab tech had called Frankie shifted, rolling in place and reaching his right arm up to grab for Julio. Dead Frankie snagged the lab technician around his left wrist and drew him close with a powerful yank, dragging him off his feet and pulling his whole body down until he was sprawled across the dead man's lap.

Julio screamed.

The dead man's eyes were still closed, pale lids over the eyeballs like a veil.

By then, Frankie was sitting up, and he pulled Julio farther until he was almost lying across his knee. He was strong, then, Grant assessed, darn strong. He was moving Julio like a puppet.

Grant and Cáscara responded in the same way. Two seconds into the attack and both of them had stepped back to put a little distance between them and the moving dead man, and both of them drew their blasters, commanding pistols into their waiting hands.

"Let him go!" Cáscara demanded, training her long-snouted blaster on the moving corpse.

Julio continued to scream, too panicked to even fight the corpse off.

Grant stepped forward again, Sin Eater raised and ready, and reached for the lab technician with his free hand. "Hold on to me," he said, and Cáscara translated it into Spanish a moment later.

As the female Pretor spoke, Grant detected a waver in her voice. She was turning, looking at the other drawers in the room—they were beginning to rattle on their runners. Whatever was inside the morgue drawers was trying to get loose!

Chapter 18

Outside Nippur, Mesopotamia
Circa forty-fifth century BC

She would use the repetitive nature of music, Ereshkigal concluded as she stood in the ventilation room of the underground complex that served as her home and work space, listening to the rhythm of the nearby river. It was a spot in her laboratory complex where, if she listened carefully, Ereshkigal could hear the churning sound of the mighty River Euphrates. She loved the sound of the rushing water, ceaseless as the Annunaki but ever-changing in a way that the Annunaki struggled to replicate.

Ereshkigal had been working on her sum, figuring out the involved mathematics that would shift the living to death without a physical breach. The apekin were easy enough to physically breach, of course, but that was hardly the point. This was an attempt to prove that the living things could be made dead things by altering and reversing the equation that made their lives proceed, that triggered growth from baby to adult. A living human and a recently deceased human weighed the same and had the same basic chemical components—there was no reason that the formula that moved one state into the other could not be tapped, shunted and even reversed. It was just mathematics; that was all.

The complex had been built on land given to her by

Lord Enlil, and constructed by slaves to her specifications. Located twenty steps beneath the surface, the complex ran a quarter mile underground, with tunnels leading to different hubs where Ereshkigal could pursue her experiments in solitude.

One room of the vast complex had been given over to her experiments with the life/death equation she had stumbled upon. Thirty paces from wall to wall, the cavernous room was perfectly round with a sloped ceiling that rose to a peak in the center. Being inside it was a little like being inside a volcano. It was lit by a complex system of mirrored surfaces that were used to reflect natural sunlight during the daytime and turned over to torchlight after dark.

Like the rest of the complex, this room was warm, kept at a consistently balmy temperature. Ereshkigal liked heat; like all of her race, she was cold-blooded, so heat was a luxury she reveled in whenever she was able.

Ereshkigal came striding into the laboratory now, her expression serene. Her wings had flourished in the six years since she had descended into this underground complex, budding from her back in twin lines so that their feathers now trailed behind her like a cape as she walked. They were artificial, created by the bioengineers of the Annunaki, built by Ningishzidda from her designs. Ereshkigal liked the way that they moved, following perfect wave forms whose complex logarithms belied the grace they sought to produce. When she watched them flutter, she saw the math behind the movement, each formula a thing of wonder and beauty.

As she descended the steps, Ereshkigal was thinking about the rhythm, working out the way in which her formula could be adapted to create its shapes, its beats. The apekin were simple, she knew—they responded well to rhythm. If she could shape her equation into a rhyme that could be sung, then she could deliver it with all the surety of a sword blow, sending the instruction straight to her victim's brain.

She would still use her papers—she was a mathematician after all—but every calculation began in her head, committed to writing only when she had need to shift its planes and dimensions, to make the figures bisect and form new geometric shapes in her mind's eye.

An Igigu harpist began to play from one corner of the lab as Ereshkigal entered, for she preferred to work to music—she found it drowned out the pleas and moans and screams of the apekin upon whom she experimented. The Igigu was a reptilian humanoid and moved with abundant grace, plucking at the taut strings of the harp with the subtle care of a mother cleaning its young. The Igigi were servants to the Annunaki, described by the humans as "those who watch and see." Physically, they lacked the musculature of their masters, and mentally they lacked the Annunaki's cunning. They served the Annunaki not from fear, however, but out of love, believing the Annunaki to be enlightened, and hoping that close proximity might confer enlightenment upon them.

Ereshkigal watched the Igigu harpist for a moment as she stood at the bottom of the steps. Then her attention shifted, caramel-brown eyes switching to the three figures affixed to the tables that stood in a line across from the single doorway. They were apekin—"humans" in their own parlance—two males and a female, all held naked with their arms stretched tautly above their heads, their ankles strapped down with intelligent nano-fiber cord that responded to their movements to ensure they would not pull themselves free. One of the males grunted something as Ereshkigal entered, and the other two looked up and began mewing in the irritating way of their race.

Ereshkigal strode across the laboratory to the strains of the harp, the tune reminding her of the cascading artificial waterfalls that flowed from Enlil's Royal Palace in Nippur.

"Please let us free, goddess," the human male to the left cried, his voice coarse to Ereshkigal's ears.

"Our devotion is absolute, goddess," the other male added.

"No, don't listen to them," the woman shouted, her voice already raw from crying out for so long. "I am the most devoted. The adoration of these two is nothing compared to my adoration of you. Please let me free that I may spread your love—"

"No, me! Let me free!" the man who had spoken first cried.

"It should be me," the other male cried out. "I have a family. They need me."

Ereshkigal affixed her three prisoners with a look that could turn milk. The apekin continued to whine, their voices sounding like cats being slaughtered to Ereshkigal's ears; which was ironic in so much that cats she had time for, for they were their own masters and required no one to look up to to give them a sense of worth.

Ereshkigal looked down at the female. The female's body was red and clammy with sweat, long, dark hair clinging to her forehead and the sides of her face. "You say that your adoration is richest, Kalumtum?" Ereshkigal asked, her voice soft and rich as warmed honey.

"Yes, my goddess," the woman replied. "Oh yes."

"And you beg of my favor?" Ereshkigal asked.

"Yes," the woman replied, her body arching as she strained frantically against the bonds that held her on the examination table. "I would do anything if you would only let me free. Please, I beseech you. Show mercy on me."

"I propose an experiment," Ereshkigal said, her eyes locked with the female's. "I shall speak, then I shall ask you to remember my words and hold them tightly in your head until I ask that you repeat them. Do you understand?"

Still straining at her bonds, the woman nodded, though she was obviously confused by what Ereshkigal had said. Beside her, the other humans were straining to see, pulling against their bonds as they tried to look past the standing figure of the underworld goddess.

With a gesture, Ereshkigal silenced the harpist, who sat waiting patiently, staring into the middle distance until his services were needed again. Then she leaned close to the woman and spoke the words of the formula into her left ear, so close and so quiet that only the woman could hear. Ereshkigal had spent long hours stripping the sum down into grunts that the ape-descendant could easily remember. She had used rhythm and rhyme to make them more memorable.

"Now, you are to hold these in your head, repeating them over and over without saying a word aloud," the Annunaki instructed.

The woman lay there, eyes wide, running through the words in her head. Her brow was furrowed in concentration as she tried to ensure each word was correct.

Ereshkigal took a step back and waited, watching the expression on the woman's round face. The woman was staring intently, her lips tight, running through the rhyme—the secret equation—in her head. Her eyes seemed to grow wider as she continued to run the words of the equation over and over in her mind, and Ereshkigal's lips rose slightly into a smile as she noticed that the woman had stopped breathing because she was concentrating so hard.

"Recite the words I told you," Ereshkigal urged. "Loudly, so that I may hear you."

The apekin woman opened her mouth and spoke, the first words coming slowly.

"Circle…around…my body…"

Ereshkigal's thin-lipped smile grew wider as she saw the woman's expression break into something that encompassed both pleasure and fear. Her eyes had become so wide that it seemed as if they might burst free of their sockets. Her mouth pulled open at each successive word she spoke and it seemed to be a struggle to bring her lips back together to form the next word in the recital.

"Be still—" the woman continued "—to…to move…"

"Go on," Ereshkigal encouraged.

"To move…" the woman said, her face strained in rapture, "no…more."

Ereshkigal watched in fascination as the woman's face seemed to draw in on itself, her cheeks sunk, her lips cracking as if suddenly dry. Her eyes had become bloodshot in a matter of seconds, and dark circles materialized below them. Her ruddy skin, rosy from the warmth of the room, became pale and drawn, the flesh on her body suddenly losing its luster so that it seemed to be taut like the skin on a drum, showing every muscle and bone. The woman's belly, where it had been rounded just moments before, sunk down as though it had collapsed, its curve switching from convex to concave before Ereshkigal's eyes.

The other test subjects in the room were howling fearfully, unable to comprehend what it was that they were seeing.

And all the while, the woman's smile grew more desperate, more forced. Was it because she wanted to please Ereshkigal, or was it something else, something in the equation that had made the act of self-immolation pleasurable?

Ereshkigal watched as the woman struggled for another breath, the smile still on her face, tears welling in her eyes. The woman strained and a strangled squeak emerged from somewhere deep inside her throat. Then she stopped, the look of bliss fixed on her face, her body losing all tension, sinking down against the surface of the table on which she was resting. She was dead.

Ereshkigal gestured to the Igigu harpist, and immediately the music began to play once more, a cascade of plucked notes running up and down the musical scale like raindrops on armor plate. The music helped mask the startled cries of the other apekin in the room, who were asking what had happened, whether the woman had died, whether either knew what was going on. Listening to the music, Ereshkigal tuned the shrill voices of the apekin out of her mind.

The recital was incomplete, Ereshkigal knew. The apekin woman had spoken as much of it as she could force through her throat before the throat had closed up, cartilage rings tautening to the point where no further sound could be expelled.

Death was possible then, Ereshkigal ruminated. By committing a mathematical equation to the subject, it was possible to reverse the life in them. Could that process be reversed a second time? she wondered. Could the newly dead be made to live again by imparting the same equation—albeit reversed—to the body? That was worth exploring, certainly.

But that was for later, she realized, bringing her thoughts back to the here and now. Anu had taken an interest in her over recent months, and his patronage was as valuable as that of Enlil himself. She would give him her body for a while, that she might access his resources on the mother ship, *Tiamat*, the better to continue her research into the mathematics of life and death.

Chapter 19

The drawers in the hospital morgue were rattling. They sounded like cowbells or drumbeats as the metal doors shook against the hinges, the drawers within shuddering on their runners.

The corpse called Frankie held Julio, the lab technician, across his lap. He was hefting Julio bodily up to get him into place for—*something*, Grant couldn't guess what. Julio was screaming himself hoarse, unable to mentally process what was happening.

"Sir, you have to let him go, please," Pretor Emiliana Cáscara was shouting in Spanish. "There's been some mistake. I'm a Pretor. I can help you."

Grant had his Sin Eater primed and ready, and he was reaching for Julio's struggling form.

"Take my hand!" Grant urged, reaching forward with his free hand and grasping Julio beneath one arm.

"What's happening?" Julio screamed and shook Grant away in his panic. The strained note of his anxious voice was as penetrating as a knife, and it seemed to cut straight into Grant's gut. The other man—the corpse—wasn't answering Cáscara's pleas, he didn't even seem to hear them. He just shifted Julio's body where he balanced it across his lap, sitting up and looming over it, legs still stretched out on the metal slab.

Corpses that moved. Grant had seen this before. Maybe this time it was an error—maybe the guy had been put in the morgue by mistake, one of those believe-it-or-not medical stories that you heard from time to time. Or maybe it was something much nastier. Maybe some dead chump had just come back to life and was now thinking whatever the dead thought when they'd spent twenty-four hours waiting to get in the grave, just like Bella Arran.

Grant reached for Julio's quivering hand again, even as the corpse known as Frankie drew the morgue technician closer. But suddenly the corpse had pulled Julio up and he sunk his teeth into the living man's throat.

There was a spurt of blood. Grant watched it from just two feet away, saw it in all its hideous glory. Blood pumped from the severed carotid artery in Julio's throat and sprayed against Frankie's corpse-pale face, washing him with its deep, dark redness even as he placed his mouth against the hole he had made as if to seal it. His mouth over the wound, Frankie started to drink or eat, Grant could not tell which. He saw the corpse's throat move as it swallowed.

The whole thing had taken seven seconds, from Julio being snatched to his throat being bitten. Even if Frankie was alive, one of those medical quirks Grant had heard about, there was no reasoning with a man who bit into a helpless victim's throat.

There was a time to reason and a time to act—and Grant knew just which this was. In an instant, Grant shot the corpse, delivering a 9 mm bullet from his Sin Eater's barrel into the side of the dead thing's head. The corpse's head took the bullet below the left temple, just above the eye, and his skull caved in a sudden entry wound a split second before the bullet emerged from the back of his head. The dead man shuddered, then dropped back onto the cold metal surface of the morgue drawer, accompanied by a sound like a trash can lid being dropped.

"Dead boy's…dead," Grant stated, glancing back to where Cáscara was scanning the drawers.

"Was he dead before?" she asked uncertainly.

Grant looked at the beautiful Pretor, reading her body language. The tension in her pose was pronounced—she was spooked. "What's that noise?" Grant asked, noticing the rattling for the first time.

"The drawers," Cáscara said, indicating with a twitch of her blaster's barrel.

There were drawers on three sides of the room, floor to ceiling, each one designed to hold a body like Frankie's. Grant scanned them in an instant, estimating that there were somewhere between forty and fifty drawers in this room alone—potentially holding forty to fifty corpses. He could see some of the metal doors shaking, the overhead light bouncing from their surfaces as it caught them. It wasn't happening to all of them, maybe two or three on one wall, another four here, more on the far wall.

"Julio, you still with us?" Grant asked.

No answer.

Grant glanced back at the open drawer where the morgue tech lay across the dead body of his attacker. There was blood down one side of his neck and he was not moving. "Julio? Damn. How many victims of the hotel incident did he say he had here?" Grant asked. "Twelve, wasn't it?"

"*Sí*, twelve," Cáscara agreed.

Grant began to say something else when one of the drawers came crashing open, bursting from the wall to their left like a champagne cork. Already at floor level, it slid across the floor tiles, crossing the room with such speed that it almost knocked Grant off his feet—he only just leaped aside in time to avoid being struck. Inside the drawer lay a man—or more accurately, a corpse—naked with a blue tint to his sickly pale skin, eyes closed, a head of thick white hair that reached down past his shoulders.

The back end of the drawer looked as if it had been sheared from the wall, and part of the runners on which the drawer slid had come with it as it had burst from its housing.

Cáscara had her blaster trained on the dead man in an instant. "Don't—" she began.

But already the figure was up out of the drawer, moving with a swiftness that seemed superhuman. He stalked across the floor in a low crouch, charging towards Cáscara.

"Shoot it!" Grant urged.

But Cáscara did something else. With perfect timing, she stepped just out of the corpse's path, turning backward on her right heel so that she continued to face the dead thing even as he charged past the spot where she had been. He missed her by inches, and as he passed, Cáscara whipped her left foot in to trip his trailing foot, hooking it up and back so that White-Hair lost his balance. Still charging forward, the man suddenly fell over himself, his head and torso tumbling forward as his legs were whipped out from under him, until he smashed jaw-first against the solid floor beneath him with a loud smack. The rest of his body followed, toppling to the floor like an avalanche.

Cáscara had her gun trained on the man's head in an instant. "Don't move!" she shouted.

Grant looked around, checking the walls and their shaking drawers. There was no time to be impressed by Cáscara's move; he had to remain alert.

"Are you okay, sir?" Cáscara was asking. "Were you trapped in there?"

Arching his back, the white-maned figure turned his head slowly, staring at Cáscara with deep-set eyes that were surrounded by dark circles. Except the eyes were still closed, sealed tight. Then, a sinister smile appeared on his face, and he opened his dark-lipped mouth to speak. *"¡Los cadáveres de mi amante!"* he cried from a crackling throat that had no saliva in it.

Grant knew those words all too well. They had lodged in his mind the last time he had heard them, when the bomber had tried to blow up the Pretor Hall of Justice that very morning. Even without the Commtact's instant translation he would have been able to recite the words in English: "Corpses for my mistress!"

LYING IN THE hospital bed, Maria Zorrilla drew the shard of broken glass from her throat. A thin line of blood materialized in its wake, becoming thicker even as it clotted.

Shizuka gasped as she saw that self-inflicted wound materialize, her eyes drawn to it like a moth to a flame. "What is she…?" she began, unable to process what she was seeing. Shizuka came from a tradition of seppuku, the ritual suicide committed by samurai for failure. Even so, this sudden move by Zorrilla was so unexpected, so awful, that it made Shizuka feel queasy.

"Medic!" Pretor Corcel shouted behind him, scrambling across the room to the bed and reaching for Zorrilla's hand. "Give me that, Maria—it's okay," he insisted. "Medic!"

Still clutching the jagged shard, Maria Zorrilla jabbed out with it, using it like a knife to stab Corcel squarely in the chest. Corcel's eyes widened with the blow, and he lurched to one side, reaching up for his chest. Shizuka saw the shard of glass protruding from the center of his chest like a dagger, low to the pectorals, a bloom of red blood expanding rapidly on his white shirt.

"Pretor?" Shizuka said, her attention flicking between Corcel and the demented woman in the bed. She turned to the open door and shouted for help, hoping that someone on staff understood English or would at least respond to the urgency in her tone. "Help! Please help! We need a doctor or a nurse here right—"

Her words were cut off as a heavy blow struck Shizuka

across the back of the shoulders at the base of her neck. She tumbled forward, sinking to her knees and slamming her forehead against the metal frame of Maria Zorrilla's bed with a hearty clang.

Chapter 20

Shizuka was an old hand at combat, and her survival instincts kicked in in the instant between her being struck and her striking the bed. Though her head was reeling, she rolled forward, scampering in an ungainly fashion away from her mystery attacker. As she scrambled, she looked behind her and saw the man standing there—dark-haired with broad shoulders and a healthy Mediterranean tan, dressed in pajamas whose open neck showed the dark bruising that ran across his throat. It was one of the victims from the other room, the one who had been asleep when Corcel and Shizuka had tried to question him.

Across the room, Pretor Corcel was lying in a heap on the smooth floor tiles, head pressed against the floor and eyes open widely in shock. His mouth was open, too, and Shizuka could hear his breathing as he lay there. The breathing was heavy and strained, but at least he was alive.

Shizuka's attacker was striding across the room toward her, hands bunched into fists, a look of insane drive in his wide eyes. "Going to show you the wonders of the grave," he muttered in Spanish. "Going to bring you to the brink of death where absolute joy awaits."

Thinking fast, Shizuka scrambled under the bed as the man reached for her, slipping across the floor and popping out again on the other side.

Shizuka got her bearings as she stood, eyeing the dark-haired man who had been caught up in the hotel atrocity.

"You don't want to do this," she said, holding her hands out before her in a placatory gesture. "Just try to calm down." She hoped he could speak English.

The man's lips curled back to reveal a grim snarl, while his brows knitted darkly over closed eyes. "Corpse in waiting," he said in accented English. "You only postpone the inevitable." Then he came striding swiftly around the metal-framed bed toward Shizuka.

Shizuka glanced around. There were two beds in the room, one with Maria and the second one unoccupied.

Then the man was reaching for her—and he had a long reach, the kind a championship boxer had. Shizuka leaped aside, ducking beneath a second grab and then butting up with her outstretched palm to strike the man in his jaw with the heel of her hand. The blow connected with a slap, and for a moment the man just stood there, shaking off the momentary rush of pain.

Shizuka readied a follow-up move, offering the man a warning first. "I hope you can understand me, Pajama Party, because I'm going to have to disable you unless you back off."

Then, unexpectedly, Maria—the woman in the bed— threw herself forward, wrapping her arms around Shizuka from behind. The man with the bruised neck came at Shizuka, grinning like a maniac, his eyes closed tight.

DOWN IN THE ice-cold morgue, the white-haired figure caromed toward Cáscara, reaching for her with grasping hands. *"Corpses for my mistress!"* he repeated in that dry-throated rasp of a voice.

Cáscara was fast. She managed to sidestep the naked man's attack and grab his right arm, drawing it sharply up and around so that she was standing behind him with his arm in an armlock.

"Don't make me hurt you, sir," she insisted in Spanish. "You've obviously suffered a trauma and—"

Another drawer broke open from the wall, its front splitting down the middle as something forced its way out with one devastating blow.

Grant turned his Sin Eater toward it in a two-handed grip, ready to blast whoever or whatever emerged. A hand appeared from the crack, then an arm, both of them deathly pale. But before anything else appeared, another of the drawers—this one located on the wall opposite—came propelling from the wall. It landed on the floor with a clatter of cold steel on slate, disgorging the naked figure of a svelte woman in her thirties, with skin so pale it held a blue hue, and a tangle of dark hair that looked like a rose bush in bloom. She leaped from the drawer even before it had finished bouncing on the tiles, landing in a dead run and powering toward Grant.

Grant took two steps forward, angling his shoulder low and meeting the woman just before she planned to meet him. As they met, Grant flipped the woman with an almighty shove. The woman skimmed against the ceiling as she went up into the air, knocking one of the depending fluorescent tubes so that it pitched and yawed, its illumination rolling across ceiling, walls and floor.

The dead woman crashed down against a bank of drawers, even as another one burst open to discharge a dark-skinned man with a potbelly and a balding pate.

Meanwhile Cáscara was trying to hold on to her own attacker as he writhed in her grip. There came a cracking sound from his shoulder and suddenly the limb hung loose in Cáscara's hand—he had dislocated it. In a flash, the reawoken corpse had thrown Cáscara over his shoulder, tossing her down onto the deck with a loud slam.

Cáscara rolled, trying to catch her breath as she avoided

the man's attempts to stomp on her head with his bare, pale foot.

"How can dead people be attacking us?" Cáscara demanded, desperation in her voice. "How?"

"Don't ask," Grant replied, targeting the potbellied figure who had emerged beside him. "Just shoot." With that, he squeezed the trigger of his Sin Eater, planting a 9 mm slug in the man's forehead. The man's head was knocked painfully back on the stem of his neck and he stumbled back under the violent impact.

"Is it really possible to shoot the dead?" Cáscara asked as she pulled herself up into a crouch and blasted at her attacker.

Grant turned so they were back-to-back. "To shoot? Yes. To kill? Jury's out," he told her grimly.

Cáscara's shots hammered into the white-haired figure who had dislocated his shoulder to be free of her, drilling—one, two, three—down the pale expanse of his torso as he strode across the slate floor. With the second shot, the walking corpse stumbled a little and with the third he turned in place, falling to the floor in a tangle of limbs.

"Cáscara, what's our quickest route out of here?" Grant asked, watching as his potbellied target writhed on the floor, his head a bloody ruin.

Cáscara glanced over to him. "The way we came, back to the elevator," she said.

"Okay, let's—"

Then something very odd happened. Grant had been backing away, skipping across the room past the gurney-like drawer where the corpse called Frankie still lay, ready to pluck Julio from the floor and keep moving. But as he reached for Julio, Frankie reached out for him, one arm extending—literally extending—to grab Grant by his arm.

Grant yelped as he was wrenched off his feet, flipping almost double over himself.

Cáscara turned at the sound and saw something she could barely comprehend: corpse Frankie was stepping from the outstretched drawer that had been pulled from the wall, still clutching Grant by one hand. His face was marred by a bullet wound to the forehead, but it was his arm that drew Cáscara's horrified attention. The right arm—the one which held Grant—was much longer than any arm she had ever seen on a man. It reached all the way down to the floor, muscles elongated like warm taffy, the pale skin stretched taut over them. Cáscara watched in horror as Frankie loomed forward, his other arm extending toward her like the tentacle of an octopus.

SHIZUKA FOUGHT AGAINST Maria Zorrilla's grip as the man with dark hair came at her, the gleam of insanity in his crazed expression.

"Era exquisita," the man hissed, reaching his hands around Shizuka's throat.

Shizuka kicked out, swinging her right leg up and into the man's groin as his fingers reached for her neck. The man grunted, expelling the breath through his clenched teeth as he staggered one step backward.

Shizuka kicked out a second time, struggling to break free of the gripping arms that held her against the bed, right leg scissoring back and forth to snap toe and heel into her male attacker's face in a quick one-two. The man hissed something in annoyance as his nose broke and his blood began leaking down his face.

Shizuka rolled her shoulders, shifting her weight enough to break free of Zorrilla's grasp. An instant later she had spun, stepping away from the bed and her two attackers.

Lying in the bed, her throat bleeding, Maria Zorrilla threw back the bedcovers and stretched out one leg until it hung over the side. Then she swiveled, preparing to sit up and get out of the bed.

"Stay where you are," Shizuka ordered. "Both of you."

Zorrilla ignored her, shifting her weight so that both legs hung over the side of the bed, feet touching the floor on tiptoe.

Beside her, Dark-Hair wiped the leaking blood from his nose, smearing it across the side of his face like war paint as his eyes gradually opened to reveal pale slits. "Don't fight it," he said in his accented English. "You cannot comprehend the joy you will feel when you let go."

At that moment, a figure appeared in the doorway— a nurse, dressed in white with her long dark hair pinned up beneath a neatly pressed hat. "Is there a problem?" she asked in Spanish.

Shizuka had almost forgotten that she and Corcel had called for help; the past thirty seconds had been a blur.

As she spoke, the young nurse saw Corcel's body lying on the floor, and she took in the whole scene with a wide-eyed stare. "What's happening—"

Her query was cut abruptly short as something came bursting through the pressed white linen of her smart uniform, sharp and bloody and wide as a meat cleaver. Shizuka watched in shock as the nurse collapsed to the floor, emitting a stifled gasp of pain from her taut lips. Standing revealed behind her was the other occupant of the room next door, the white-haired man who had been caught up in the hotel attack the day before. He wore gray pajamas and held a length of metal in one hand at the near end of which was an anglepoise lamp. The metal was slick with blood where he had forced the screw-in end through the nurse's body from behind.

"What are you?" Shizuka asked, her words urgent, breathless.

"The future," the white-haired figure told her without

a trace of an accent. "The future of the world." His eyes were open but uncannily pale, as if the irises were merging with the whites.

The three patients began to advance on Shizuka from all sides, leaving her with nowhere to run.

DOWN IN THE MORGUE, Frankie slid from the drawer, still holding Grant as his bare feet met with the floor. One arm extended inhumanly toward Pretor Cáscara, its length growing impossibly as she watched, bones and joints shifting in nauseating configurations.

In her role as a Zaragoza Pretor, Emiliana Cáscara had seen a litany of disturbing things. Crimes committed on people, on animals, on children. She had seen the devastating results of random gunfire, seen car accidents that would turn a surgeon's stomach, and even walked in on a killer as he was butchering his wife to death. And seeing all those things, she had, she liked to think, become just desensitized enough to make her better at her job. But seeing a man's limbs extend beyond all human proportion was so unsettling, so weird, that she was just left standing stone-still in shock.

The lengthening arm reached for Cáscara's head, index and middle finger extending to jab her in the eyes. Cáscara watched, brain knowing she had to move but somehow failing to pass that instruction on to her body, her limbs.

A sudden burst of gunfire shook Cáscara from her trance. Clutched in the dead man's other arm, Grant was holding the trigger of his Sin Eater down, drilling bullet after bullet into his attacker's leg—the only target he could reach.

In an instant, the dead man stumbled, lurching forward on the ruined leg, his grip loosening from around Grant's torso.

Grant slipped from the man's grasp, spun and aimed his Sin Eater at the corpse's head as the man dropped to the floor. "Playtime's over!" he snarled, holding down the trigger.

A moment later, dead Frankie's face had become a mess of ruined flesh and bone, and he lay writhing on the floor like a hooked fish.

Grant stepped away from the shuddering corpse, reaching for Julio where he now lay on the floor beside the open drawer. "Come on," he told Cáscara. "Let's get moving."

THE THREE FIGURES were advancing on Shizuka as she stood on the far side of Maria Zorrilla's vacant bed. There was nowhere for Shizuka to escape—the room's sole window was ahead of her, blocked by the dark-haired man whose nose she had just broken, while the exit door and en suite were next to one another, blocked by the white-haired man who was striding across the room wielding the blood-drenched anglepoise lamp.

Not that Shizuka needed to run. She bent slightly at the waist, bringing her center of gravity down as the menacing figures approached. Then she pounced, moving with the fluidity of a cat stalking its prey.

Zorrilla was the closest to Shizuka, having just emerged from the bed. Shizuka stepped forward, driving her right hand out in a ram's-head punch that clipped the woman across the jaw. She may be an innocent—in theory they all were—but they were caught up in something that went beyond Shizuka's understanding just now, and every moment they delayed her was another moment that Pretor Corcel was bleeding out on the floor.

Shizuka's blow struck the woman like a thunderclap, and she was thrown backward, stumbling against the bed with a shriek of surprise.

The dark-haired man was on Shizuka then, driving one of his meaty fists at her face. Shizuka spun, twisting out of his reach as the blow sailed past, feeling its breeze rush against her cheek.

Now Shizuka was facing the blank wall by the bed, and she kicked out, pressing one foot against it to launch herself in the opposite direction to where Dark Hair was still recovering from where his attack had missed. Tucking her head, Shizuka struck him with the crown of her head high in his ribs, knocking the wind out of him and driving him back in a graceless stumble of his unsteady legs. The man fell a moment later, three steps into his awkward dance. Shizuka rolled on the floor, flipping up as she untangled herself from him.

Three feet away, the third man swung the anglepoise lamp at her head. Sensing the movement, Shizuka ducked, and the bloody struts of metal raced over her head, momentarily entangling in her hair before tearing free and striking the wall to her left.

Remaining low, Shizuka swung her fist out and up, striking White-Hair in the gut. The blow was poorly executed, however, the angle wrong, and White-Hair just spit out a breath before reaching down for Shizuka with his free hand.

Throat caught in the man's grip, Shizuka found herself being pulled forward, and she lost her balance as she went skittering across the floor tiles. He let go an instant later and Shizuka went flying across the room before connecting with the far wall.

The man with the anglepoise lamp was on her in a second, swinging his makeshift weapon at her head, using the weighty metal shade and bulb like a club.

"Shit!" Shizuka gasped, rolling out of the way of the assault. The heavy lamp struck the wall behind her with a crash, the bulb shattering on impact.

Shizuka moved swiftly then, her body responding to the hours of training she had put in to become a samurai. She kicked out, leg swinging to catch her attacker behind his knees, forcing him to step forward or lose his balance entirely. He stepped forward, arms outstretched to remain standing. The move had forced the man to step closer to Shizuka, meaning he was much less able to use the hefty weight of the anglepoise lamp as a weapon.

Shizuka stepped in closer still, reaching one arm behind the man's head even as her other hand grabbed ahold of the lapel on his pajama top.

Before White-Hair knew what was happening, Shizuka flipped him over, tossing him over her left shoulder so that he slammed against the wall directly behind her, headfirst.

Shizuka scrambled toward the door, halting momentarily to grab Corcel's arm. "Can you walk?" she asked.

Corcel mumbled something incomprehensible and began to push himself up from the floor. There was a lot of blood on his shirt where the glass shard still protruded.

"I'll help you," Shizuka insisted, tightening her grip on his arm and adding her own strength to his as he raised himself.

A moment later, the two of them were lurching out the door and into the corridor beyond.

Outside, the corridor had descended into chaos. There was blood on the walls and two nurses lay dead or dying, slumped against doors to the patients' rooms.

"What's happening?" Shizuka asked with incredulity. "How—how can this be?"

From the room behind her, Shizuka's three opponents had shaken off her attacks and were striding across the room toward the samurai woman. *"Corpses for our mistress!"* they chanted in unison, the words delivered in Spanish.

With that, all three began to charge toward Shizuka and Corcel, leaving them with no more time to plan.

Down in the basement, Cáscara and Grant hurried to the door of the morgue. Grant had Julio over his shoulders in a fireman's lift, his Sin Eater still held in his right hand.

Before they could get there, another figure shoved its way out from one of the wall-mounted drawers, a tall man with long limbs and a muscular torso. He leaped from the broken drawer and barred the way to the doors.

"I think he works out," Cáscara muttered.

"Or he used to," Grant said.

Another drawer to their left crashed open, then another, and more animated corpses began to pull themselves out of their would-be prisons.

"We're trapped," Cáscara stated. She was right—there were too many walking dead in the path to the door for them to exit easily—they would have to plan a route through them. Brute strength alone would not be enough.

"Go back," Grant suggested, scrambling toward a door on the far side of the room.

Cáscara skipped ahead of him, reaching for the door. It had a large glass pane in it that ran roughly from waist to crown, granting a clear view into the room beyond. It was in total darkness.

Cáscara opened the door and held it for Grant, ushering him through as the animated corpses began to swarm toward them. Another of the morgue's drawers burst open behind them and a pale-fleshed woman came rolling out from within.

Once they were through, Cáscara slammed the door closed, holding it tightly by the handle. "We need to lock this place up somehow," she said, her eyes on the moving figures in the next room. "Does he have keys on him?"

Grant reached up with his free hand and checked Julio's

pockets. The blood was drying on the morgue tech's neck and he was delirious. "Can't find... No, nothing," Grant confirmed. "Just pens and cash."

Cáscara cursed in Spanish, still watching the figures emerging from the drawers in the next room. "If they get free, Grant—"

"Yeah," Grant acknowledged. "Let me try something," he said before switching to his Commtact frequency.

"Cerberus, this is Grant. Kane, do you read me? What's your ETA?"

The response from the Commtact was nothing but silence.

"Cerberus?"

Cáscara looked at Grant quizzically.

"I have a radio comm rig-wired in my skull," Grant told her before trying the frequency again with no result.

"These walls are lead-lined," Cáscara pointed out. "Will your radio penetrate that?"

Grant grimaced. "Evidently not," he admitted. "It sometimes has trouble when I go underground, too."

Automatically, Cáscara reached for the light switch on the wall. The lights flickered on, filling the room with the momentary *tink-tink-hum* of fluorescents. They were in the theater, where the recently departed were examined when there was medical uncertainty about the cause of death. Two metal examination tables dominated the room, and beside each was a podium containing examination implements. A figure was sitting up on one of those tables, a woman, naked with the top of her chest split open and pinned back to reveal the chest cavity. Behind her, a medical examiner in a white coat was hanging from a noose that had been hooked over one of the depending fluorescent lights made from rubber tubing while another man, naked with the skin of his neck pulled back to expose his throat, was standing holding the other end of the noose.

Behind them, through the window set within the door, more drawers were opening, disgorging their once-dead contents, twelve dead men swarming toward the unlocked door.

There were no other exits.

Chapter 21

Twenty-seven minutes earlier

Bells were tolling throughout Zaragoza city.

A graveyard stood beside an eighteenth-century church that was more ruin than building now. The graves were overgrown, their stone engravings mostly lost to the ravages of time. The clear blue sky above remained defiant to the rot below.

Amid this scene, a swirling blossom of color materialized without warning. Like the leaves of a lotus blossom, the upended cone of color seemed to bud from the ground itself. And more—a second cone appeared directly below this one, delving impossibly into the earth in a fracture of reality itself.

The cone was accompanied by no noise, except perhaps the excitement of ionized air particles that arrived in its wake. Its depths held every color of the rainbow, swirling amid a black screen like the night sky, where flashes of lightning like witch fire vied for space.

From this double cone, which defied the laws of physics, there stepped two people—Kane and Brigid Baptiste. Both were dressed for combat, sleek shadow suits hugging their taut bodies, jackets with ammo pouches, grenades and knives finishing the ensemble.

Brigid had a weapon at her hip, her trusty TP-9 semiautomatic, held in an open holster where it could be accessed immediately.

Kane, too, had a blaster, though his was hidden in the familiar forearm holster that tucked beneath his jacket's sleeve, awaiting the command that would launch the weapon into his waiting hand.

As they stepped from the swirling coruscation of light, the cones seemed to shrink, pulling back to their meeting point where they intersected on the line of the ground. A moment later they were gone, and all that stood in their place was a silver pyramidal structure, roughly one foot high with a mirrored surface. This pyramid device was the interphaser, and with it Kane, Brigid and the other members of the Cerberus organization could travel instantaneously across great distances by accessing the quantum interphase window it was designed to open.

Kane looked around warily, alert to danger. "Nice place for a vacation," he deadpanned. "I can see what drew Grant and Shizuka here. Plenty of romance."

Brigid was crouched over the interphaser, shutting down as it finished its sequence. She had brought a carry case with her, a little like a rucksack but with a molded, padded interior where the unit could rest safely when not in use. She sealed up the interphaser in its case and glanced around the graveyard. "Do you think we should take this with us, or hide it here for now?" she asked Kane.

"Leave it," Kane said. "Let's explore first, track down Grant and Shizuka."

A moment later, Brigid had hidden the carry case deep in the overgrown bushes. Then she and Kane made their way through the tangled undergrowth of the forgotten graveyard, emerging through a set of chained and padlocked gates whose hinges were held together by a combination of rust and sheer bloody-mindedness. As Kane led the way through the rotten gates he used his Commtact to hail Grant.

"We've just arrived," he said. "Where are you?"

There was no response.

Kane had emerged on a narrow street on the east bank of Zaragoza, at the end of which he could see the River Ebro. The street was abandoned. The river's waters cast dancing lights on the street as they reflected the sunlight from overhead.

Kane tried his Commtact again. "Do you copy, over?"

Then he stopped moving, glancing back at the graveyard as Brigid pushed her way through a gap in the broken-down gates beside a crumbling wall. "You notice that?" he asked her.

"What?"

"The bells," Kane said, looking up at the ruin of the church. "Someone's working the bells in there."

Brigid shrugged. "Well, it *is* a church," she said.

"Yeah, but look at it," Kane stated with uncertainty. "The place looks like it's about to fall down. Who are they calling to prayer?"

Brigid inclined her head in thought. "This isn't the only church ringing," she said after a moment. "I can hear—"

"Me, too," Kane confirmed, first pointing up the road and into the city center, then gesturing toward the river itself. "And there, too."

"Any word from Grant?" Brigid asked.

"No," Kane stated with a shake of his head. Then he activated the Commtact once again. "Cerberus, this is Kane. Can you triangulate Grant's current position and guide me there?"

Farrell's voice replied over the Commtact a moment later from his position at the comms rig of the Cerberus redoubt. "Gotcha, Kane," he said. "I'm bringing up the data now."

APPROXIMATELY FIVE THOUSAND miles away, in the Bitterroot Mountains of Montana, Farrell tapped out a command on his DDC computer. The screen flashed up the data from Grant's biolink transponder tracking device. Embedded within all Cerberus personnel, the transponder utilized nanotechnology to provide a position locator, as well as reporting back the user's health, including heart rate and brain-wave activity. Cerberus used these devices to monitor team members in the field, and they had been crucial in saving the lives of several agents.

"Got him," Farrell confirmed over the Commtact link as the locator began to broadcast its position on a real-time satellite image of the city. Farrell tapped out an instruction, drawing down a street map overlay on the image and factoring in Kane's and Brigid's positions. He could not locate Shizuka, however—since she was a Tiger of Heaven and not a member of the Cerberus operation, she had never had a transponder surgically embedded.

"He's four blocks to your north and one west," Farrell explained. "Looks like…a hospital."

"Hospital? Shit! How are his life signs?" Kane asked, concerned.

"Look normal," Farrell confirmed after bringing up the relevant information from the transponder. "Heart rate's fast—"

"Can you try raising him?" Kane butted in. "I'm having no success this end."

"I'll try," Farrell said into his headset.

THE STREETS WERE EMPTY. Automobiles stood abandoned, stores open, but there was no one outside, not even sitting at the little café tables that lined the sidewalks outside the eateries. There was barely any traffic noise either, and none of the usual noise of people talking, moving, *living*.

All there was was the sound of the tolling bells, slow but regular, echoing across the city.

"What happened here?" Kane asked as he and Brigid jogged up a street, heading for Grant's position.

"It's still happening, I think," Brigid observed, looking from storefront to storefront. There were people in the stores, she could see, but they were moving slowly—all of them—which was disconcerting.

"Let's find Grant and Shizuka first, before we start figuring this thing out," Kane decided. "If they're caught up in this then—" He didn't finish the statement, just let it hang there, like a threat.

They crossed a junction on foot, and Kane spotted people moving along the cross street. They were hurrying into buildings, apartments located above quaint cafés and clothing boutiques, cars pulling over. They looked scared, as if they were frightened to be seen in the light. Kane watched them, trying to figure out what they were hiding from.

The tolling bells seemed to be getting louder, and with each intersection the echo became more pronounced, a slow beat droning through every street, every alleyway.

Zaragoza was an old city, and inevitably its streets were haphazard and irregular. Kane and Brigid hurried past a side street that was little more than an alley with a decaying stone arch above that linked building to building. As they did so, a figure on a moped came hurtling out of the alley's mouth, engine loud in the silence. He wore no helmet and had his hands off the handlebars and pressed instead to his face. He was shrieking, a strained and painful howl like a trapped animal.

The Cerberus warriors leaped aside as the scooter came rushing past, watched in shock as it slammed into the building opposite, on the far side of the street, striking a brick pillar with such force that it caused the adjacent store windows to shatter. The sound of the collision seemed absolute in the quiet street, and it was followed by a return to silence so abrupt that it felt like a physical thing.

In the aftermath, the biker was left lying on the sidewalk with the scooter wrapped around his legs like a snake.

Kane scrambled across the street toward the rider, calling out to him in English. Brigid followed, repeating the words in Spanish—thanks in part to her eidetic memory, Brigid could speak several languages.

"What happened?" Kane asked as he reached the rider. "You okay?"

The man's hands were still pressed against his face, and now there was blood seeping between the bruised fingers. He wore a shirt and blue jeans, both torn in the sudden fury of the crash, the shirt splashed with a few spots of blood.

"How did you lose control?" Brigid asked, leaning down to look at the bloody rider. He didn't respond. "You're hurt," she said. "Let me look."

Gently, Brigid reached for the man's hands, pulling his right hand away from his face. As she pulled his hand away, she saw his mouth was stretched taut in a grim smile, blood washing across his teeth. His visible eye was bright, staring into the middle distance, not focusing on her at all. His lips moved, the smile never wavering, and Brigid realized that the rider was saying something, barely audible even in the near-silence of the street.

"Is he speaking?" Kane asked as he crouched beside the wounded man.

Brigid nodded. "I think so." After pulling his other hand away, she leaned closer, straining to hear the man's whispering voice.

"'Such joys I see, such joys…'" Brigid translated.

Their Commtacts flared as they puzzled over the man's actions and words. It was Farrell. "Kane, you've stopped moving. Everything okay?"

"Got a little sidetracked," Kane admitted, glancing up the road and all about him. The streets remained almost empty, just a few distant figures hurrying out of the sunlight, the bells chiming very slowly to punctuate the silence. "Anything from Grant or Shizuka?"

"No, he's not answering my hails," Farrell confirmed. "And he's also not moved—he's still at the hospital."

Kane looked at Brigid. "This guy needs to get there, too," he said, and Brigid nodded. "Farrell, how many blocks is it? Two more?"

"One and half," Farrell corrected. "Take the next junction and hang a left. I figure you won't miss it."

"Gotcha," Kane replied as he gently extricated the wounded moped rider from his vehicle. Carefully, paying attention to supporting the man's neck, Kane lifted him in both arms, adjusting his weight gently. The man continued to mutter in Spanish, the words barely more than the whispers of his moving lips.

Brigid was about to question Kane's plan when she saw the look on his face and remembered who he was. Kane had been a Magistrate once, feared law enforcer of the barons. But Mags were also tasked to help the citizens, to assist in keeping order and steering society away from chaos. Saving lives, one at a time, was all a part of their remit. After the baronies, after Kane had been exiled along with Brigid and his brother-in-arms, Grant, he had regained his humanity, the humanity that had been stripped from him by the Magistrates' harsh training program. Kane had retained the old instincts, all those factors that had made him such a great Magistrate, but he had added something else—the burning need to help people, to save innocents. Kane was a pragmatist and a soldier, but he was not a machine—he cared about who lived and who died. That was what he had achieved since leaving the barony's clutches; that was the reward that his work with Cerberus had given him.

Kane carried the bloodstained rider and, with Brigid at his side, made his way to the end of the block toward the hospital. Like the others, this street was deserted, just abandoned cars—not parked, but simply left, doors open, sometimes with wipers and lights still on—a dog tied to a lamppost by its lead, barking forlornly.

"Something's very wrong here, Baptiste," Kane said.

Brigid shot him a look. "You think? Kane, I don't know what we've walked into but it's… I'm finding it very unsettling."

"Ereshkigal," Kane said, reminding Brigid of her research.

"But how does someone clear the streets like this? It's—" Brigid stopped, spying something across the street from where she strode beside Kane.

A young woman in the window of a florist's was hanging herself, using the baling wire to hook herself up on the curtain rail that stretched across the windows. She wore a plain dress that ended above her knees, pale pink in color, girly.

Brigid spotted it first and ran across the street toward the store. Its door was open and she rushed inside.

"Stop," Brigid said in Spanish.

The woman continued in her task, moving in an almost trancelike state.

"Baptiste," Kane called from outside the store.

Brigid ignored him, pacing across the room, hands held up to show that they were empty. "I won't hurt you," Brigid assured the woman. "I'm sure you have your reasons. But please, just—"

"Baptiste!" Kane again, more urgent this time.

Dammit, Kane, not now, Brigid thought as she stepped up to the woman who was preparing to hang herself.

Outside, the bells chimed again.

Brigid reached for the woman's arm; up close she looked as if she was barely out of her teens, maybe not even that. Too young to be contemplating suicide, surely. The young woman didn't even seem to notice her, she was too busy trying to hook the baling wire tightly over the rail. Brigid snatched it back and unhooked it from the rail with her other hand.

"Don't do this," Brigid pleaded. "Whatever it is that's driven you to—"

Brigid stopped as she caught a glimpse of movement in the back of the store, in a darker room behind the counter. Another figure was moving there, sifting through a cupboard. Brigid caught the glint of metal in their hand as they pulled something free. It was a pair of shears, seen partially in darkness, the kind used to clip the stems from flowers. Brigid watched, horrified, as the person in back jabbed the blades of the shears into their gut.

"No! Stop!" Brigid screamed, leaping over the counter and scrambling into the back room. Behind her, the young woman in the pale dress took the dropped baling wire and began to loop it up around her neck and over the rail once more.

In the back room, an older woman, in her thirties with short, dark hair, was bent over double, drawing the blades of the shears slowly across her belly. Blood was beginning to bud there in spots, seeping into the cream-colored blouse she wore. The shears were a poor weapon, their short, curved blades acting like hooks in the woman's flesh. Imprecise—but devastating.

Brigid grabbed the woman's hand and wrenched the shears from it, throwing them across the room. "What's got into you?" Brigid demanded. "Why are you doing this?"

"Baptiste!" It was Kane's voice again, calling from the open doorway of the florist's. "You really need to see this."

Brigid stepped out of the unlit storeroom, her heart sinking as she saw the woman whom she had—helped? saved? stopped?—just a few moments before was already trying to loop the noose back around the rail over the windows. Kane was standing in the doorway, the wounded body of the scooter rider still held in his arms. His face was ashen, his expression grim.

"What is it?" Brigid asked, barely able to take her eyes from the woman in the window.

"I don't know," Kane admitted, leading the way outside, "but it's big."

Brigid followed Kane outside into the street once more and looked up to where he indicated. Up ahead, the colossus that was the hospital building waited. It was eerily still, the streets around it abandoned. On its rooftop, Brigid could see a line of people, all of them waiting at the roof's very edge.

"Oh, sweet baron…" Brigid muttered.

And as they watched, the first of the figures stepped from the roof.

Chapter 22

There were two workmen on the steps of the Hall of Justice, working to repair the ruined door where the bomb had been detonated earlier that morning. The steps and surrounding walls had been blackened from the bomb blast, but the shattered glass from the door had already been swept away. One of the men was nailing a wooden panel in place over where the glass had been damaged, while the other carefully tapped out the glass that remained, dropping it into a dustpan.

Somewhere nearby, the church bells had started chiming, droning on and on in a slow, laborious pattern that seemed to penetrate the skulls of anyone within earshot.

Walking abreast, four Pretors strode up the steps into the Hall of Justice, heading for the door—nothing out of the ordinary. The workman tapping out glass looked up as the shadow of one of the Pretors crossed over his work.

"I'll be just a minute," he promised, recognizing the uniform and the boots.

The lead Pretor reached down without warning and grabbed the man by his collar, dragging him up to his feet with a jerk before tossing him violently aside.

"Hey, what th—" the workman cried.

The intimidating helmet of the Pretor stared back at him, eyes hidden behind a darkened visor that seemed to be boring into his very soul.

The other worker was knocking a nail in place when

the female Pretor kicked him in the chest. He sagged over
with a pained splutter, looking up to see the woman standing over him. Her uniform was torn across the chest as
if she had been shot—in truth, she had—and there was
dried blood there and something else, a kind of weave of
shimmering lights at the edges of a ragged wound that
marred her torso.

The Pretor shoved the workman out of her path with a
vicious kick before leading the way into the Hall of Justice lobby.

The desk Pretor glanced up as the woman entered, accompanied by her three colleagues. He recognized all four
of them.

"Hey, Ruiz," he said turning back to his computer
screen. "You're off shift early, aren't you?"

Pretor Ruiz of the ruined chest raised her Devorador de
Pecados pistol and blasted the desk Pretor in the face. His
head erupted in a burst of blood and bone as the 9 mm slug
penetrated his forehead and shattered his nose.

There were two Pretors at the security door in the building when the shot was fired. The first, a woman in her
early forties who spent a lot of time in the facility's gym
and liked to brag that she had seen everything in her service to the badge, started screaming. Beside her, her partner—a younger woman with auburn locks that emerged
from under her helmet in braids like the snakes of Medu-
sa's hair, looked horrified, her jaw dropping in surprise.

"De Centina, is that—" the younger woman asked, recognizing the old Pretor who had followed Ruiz through
the door. De Centina had left his helmet at the south gate,
where Ereshkigal had killed him. Now his reanimated
corpse was riddled with the cancer that had tried to eat
at his face years before, leaving sparkling lines of newly
possessed disease trailing across his mug like winking
stars in the evening sky.

In answer to the woman's unfinished question, de Centina raised his blaster and shot, sending a 9 mm bullet through her throat, shattering her voice box before she could finish her query. De Centina had been a Pretor longer than almost anyone in the Hall—he had had many years to think about the weak spots of the Pretor armor, and knew just what he was doing when he targeted the woman's throat.

Behind de Centina and Ruiz, Bazán and Cadalso were marching in the door in step, their own weapons armed and ready.

The older woman was still screaming as her partner went crashing to the floor in a heap, her vocal cords a bloody splash where her throat had been. Ruiz swept her gun around and blasted again, delivering a 9 mm bullet to the woman's outstretched hand where it rested against the door frame. The woman yelped in agony as her hand was ripped apart and then stumbled back into the stairwell that waited behind her.

De Centina led the way to the stairs, Ruiz marching just a step behind him.

In the lobby, Cadalso and Bazán made short work of two perps who had been brought in for cautioning and were just waiting for the final records to be completed so that their possessions could be returned. Both died whimpering as the sound of church bells tolled through the open door, masking the reports of gunfire.

There was no one to challenge them on the stairs. Each Pretor was equipped with an identity tag that triggered a sensor at the door upstairs, granting them access to the squad room. De Centina led the way, while the others filed in behind him.

Inside, the squad room was alive with activity. Pretors were working at their desks, interviewing suspects, interviewing crime victims, filing reports, making caffeinated drinks. There were Pretors in full street uniform, others dressed in the light, armor-weave suits of the higher-ranking investigative officers. Several glanced up from what they were doing as de Centina and his team walked in, but they all knew de Centina, no one thought anything strange of his coming through the squad door at this time of day.

Some people could be turned, but many resisted the charms of Ereshkigal's spell, needing her personal attention to receive the formula that would send them to despair and, from there, into the triumph that was the afterdeath. For them, the easiest solution was a quick death after which Ereshkigal could apply the formula at her leisure, reviving the corpses and showing them new ways to live. Her Terror Priests—these newly revived dead—were tasked to create those corpses. *Corpses for their mistress!*

A Pretor called Millas, six years out of training and with an arrest record second to none of his graduating year, looked up again after acknowledging de Centina and his group entering the room. There was something about de Centina's face, he realized.

When Pretor Millas looked again, he saw the sparkling lines like fluorescent tubing had been sewn inside de Centina's face, the way it glistened like moonlight on water. "Hey, de Centina—what happened to you? Is everythi—"

Dead Cadalso shot from behind de Centina, blasting over the older Pretor's shoulder and delivering brutal death to the unsuspecting Millas. Millas's right ear exploded into a bloody spray, and Cadalso's second shot bored through his face in an instant.

The squad room was alerted then and, immediately, trained Pretors went diving for cover and reaching for weapons.

Ruiz, Bázan, Cadalso and de Centina tracked across the room, blasting over and over, felling six Pretors and four

ordinary citizens who moved too slow. It left seven Pretors
alive along with three civilians, six hiding behind desks
while a Pretor and a norm had slipped through the door
on the far side of the room and into the corridor beyond.

The four reanimated Pretors strode through the squad
room fearlessly as Pretors appeared from hiding to blast
shots at them. De Centina blasted another Pretor the moment he appeared from behind a filing cabinet, while
Bazán leaped atop a desk and aimed her pistol straight
down, spraying the space beyond with 9 mm bullets and
executing a Pretor and two civilians in an instant.

Cadalso took a shot to the arm, ignored it and moved on
through the room, blasting in the direction of the shooter.
He was rewarded with a cry from that area as his bullet
met flesh, then disappeared through the doorway and into
the corridor.

In the corridor, a female Pretor called Grosella was
busy loading a Copperhead assault rifle while a female
civilian wearing too much makeup and a short skirt cow-
ered beside her. The Copperhead featured a two-foot-
long barrel, with grip and trigger in front of the breech in
the bullpup design, allowing the gun to be used single-
handedly. It also featured an optical, image-intensified
scope coupled with a laser autotargeter mounted on top
of the frame. The Copperhead possessed a 700-round-per-
minute rate of fire and was equipped with an extended
magazine holding thirty-five 4.85 mm steel-jacketed
rounds. In short, it could create a brisk level of destruction like few other guns in its class.

Cadalso shot the blond-haired Pretor even as she raised
the subgun and fired, watched her head explode as a line of
4.85 mm bullets peppered the wall a foot to his right. Pretor Grosella crashed down to the floor in a blurt of spraying blood, while the civilian screamed in horror.

Cadalso looked at the civilian with disdain, eyeing her

garish clothes and painted face. "Corpses for my mistress," he said as he brought his Devorador de Pecados pistol up and shot her through the forehead.

BACK IN THE squad room, de Centina, Ruiz and Bazán were making short work of the remaining Pretors. Bullets struck them, buried in their bodies, chipped away chunks of their flesh, but they just kept coming. They were beyond death now, in the blissful place that Ereshkigal had introduced them to, her new Terror Priests for the new order. She believed only in death and they believed only in her. The world of man had been judged, and sentence was being passed. Perfect, mathematical sentence.

A Pretor eight weeks from retirement took four shots in the belly before finally slumping over the desk he had used for thirty-seven years. Bazán cruelly made sure, striding over to him and blasting him in the back of the skull from point-blank range even as another 9 mm slug buried itself between her shoulder blades.

Ruiz found herself tackling a Pretor who had unhooked a fire ax from its holding place on the wall, presumably realizing that bullets were doing no good against this enemy. The Pretor—a muscular man with a good foot and half in height on Ruiz—swung the ax with the vigor of a woodcutter, driving it downward, where it cut through Ruiz's left arm. The arm seemed to hang for a moment, drooping from the shoulder and swinging lifelessly. Then, before the Pretor's startled eyes, the arm seemed to extend, the space between shoulder and amputation filling in with new nerves and sinews, twining up and in on themselves as they rebuilt the arm until it was six inches longer than it had been before.

Ruiz kicked the man in the groin as he goggled in surprise, then brought her automatic around and blasted him in the chest, pumping the trigger until her third shot pierced his armor and he finally stopped squirming.

Across the room, de Centina and Bazán made short work of the remaining Pretors, taking several hits without so much as slowing down until they finally overwhelmed the living.

Bazán shoved one struggling Pretor through a water cooler in an eruption of spilled water, before kicking him with enough force to dislocate his jaw. After that, a well-placed shot finished the man.

In the aftermath, the squad room looked like a charnel house, dead bodies strewed across the floor and on chairs and behind desks. The four reanimated Pretors surveyed their handiwork with pale, devolving eyes. Death rewards those who accept it, they knew. Ereshkigal may yet come here to share her gift.

Outside the Hall of Justice, the bells of Zaragoza continued to chime, repeating their eerie, one-note refrain.

Chapter 23

Brigid and Kane watched as one figure stepped off the roof of the hospital and dropped, plummeting like a stone to the pavement below. They struck with the inevitability of nightfall, the sound of their impact carrying across the silence like a peal of thunder. In its wake, the church bells chimed once more, droning once in unison, creating a period to the jumper's death sentence.

Even as the jumper landed, the next one was stepping over the edge of the roof, and in a moment that one was falling, too, careening down the outside of the building toward their inevitable death.

"We have to do something," Brigid gasped, turning away.

Kane glanced down at the bike rider in his arms whom he had rescued, glanced back at the roof of the hospital where people were lined up like lemmings on a cliff. "No time," he said. "We need to find Grant first—"

"No, Kane!" Brigid was insistent. "People are dying."

"Killing themselves," Kane agreed. "But so many— I figure they've been, I dunno, instructed to do this. To commit suicide."

"Why would— How would—" Brigid could not form the question, she was so distraught.

"I don't know," Kane admitted. "Mass death cult maybe?"

Brigid looked sullen. "It's possible," she admitted. "But this is so huge. It's hard to imagine—"

"And that's why we need to find Grant and Shizuka," Kane insisted. "Think! If they're caught up in this, then we could be about to witness one of them jumping off that roof."

Reluctantly, Brigid nodded. She needed no further convincing. "We can't ignore everyone else, though," she said.

"We won't," Kane assured her, trotting toward the hospital with his burden. "But since Grant is here, if he's not caught up in this madness, then he may have some insight into just what the hell's going on."

THE HOSPITAL WAS CHAOS.

Just making their way to the lobby doors, the Cerberus warriors saw numerous distraught faces peering out of stalled automobiles, figures slumped on benches covered in blood from unknown wounds. More figures leaped from the roof, falling on the hard, unforgiving asphalt. Brigid reported what they were seeing over her Commtact, relaying it back to Cerberus HQ in an emotionless monotone. It was the only way she could distance herself from the event.

Inside was worse. Whatever had taken hold of the city had clearly done so in stages, which meant that some people had had time to get here and seek help before they had been entirely caught up in the madness. But by the time they had got here, they had begun to lose all rationality, seeking instead only their own deaths and those of the people around them. Now the lobby looked like a charnel house, with blood lashed against two walls and the windows looking out onto the asphalt strip, and dead bodies strewed across the furniture. At the desk, the on-duty nurse was using a scalpel to cut open her own wrists, drawing a long, vertical line from wrist to elbow, the smile widening on her face as she pushed the blade deeper. There were others in the large lobby space wandering aimless as sleepwalkers, two hanging from nooses that they had attached to a metal sign overhanging the desk.

"I…I don't know what we can do," Brigid admitted, looking around her at the picture of insanity.

Kane spotted an empty—and blood slick—bench and strode across to it, placing the wounded moped rider there. He figured that patching the man's wounds was the least of their priorities just now.

"Keep moving," Kane told Brigid solemnly, "and hope it doesn't catch up to us."

Outside, distant, the bells of Zaragoza chimed once again, sounding the final heartbeats of a dying city. Through the lobby windows, another body could be seen crashing to the ground from the roof, feetfirst, his ankles shattering on impact and turning his legs into jagged geometric shapes.

At the Cerberus redoubt, Farrell had been joined by Lakesh and Donald Bry as Brigid's report came in.

"It's not unprecedented," Lakesh told Brigid reasonably once she had described the scene. He worked the advanced Cerberus database as he spoke, bringing up further information, following his instincts. "There have certainly been documented instances of mass hysteria, wherein whole communities have behaved irrationally," he reported. "Mass hysteria generally begins with one individual who exhibits symptoms during a period of extreme stress. The symptoms then manifest in others, unconsciously copying the first until a full-blown epidemic ensues."

"People are killing themselves, Lakesh," Brigid responded. She sounded withdrawn.

"Mass hysteria has been known to go to the point of self-harm," Lakesh stated. "In Strasbourg 1518 they witnessed the Dancing Plague or Dance Epidemic. Dancing in the streets, often for very long stretches of three or four days. Within a week, thirty-four people had joined the initial dancer, and within a month there were around 400 dancers. Some died from heart attacks, strokes or simple exhaustion. There is no logic as to why people did this—they drove themselves to it, caught up in the mania.

"And then there was the Tanganyika laughter epidemic…1962. A school had to be closed down after most of the student body—almost one hundred in total—couldn't stop laughing. It spread to Nshamba, a nearby village that was home to several of the students. Over two hundred people had what appeared to be laughing attacks, and the epidemic continued to spread. Thousands of people were hit. Lasted over a year. Reports at the time stated that the laughter was frequently accompanied by pain, fainting, flatulence, respiratory problems, rashes, attacks of crying and random screaming."

Bry stared at Lakesh with his usual look of shock. "They laughed themselves to death?" he asked.

"They tried to," Lakesh stated grimly, covering the pickup mic on the Commtact headset.

Brigid's voice came over the Commtact, sounding firmer than it had before. "So there may be a precedence," she said. "Lakesh, are you aware of any specific examples which involve self-immolation or suicide on a massive scale?"

"As a protest, yes," Lakesh said, "or in the case of religious fervor. The Jonestown incident in 1978, for example, which saw extreme paranoia sweep through an increasingly isolated community, preceding a mass suicide.

"All of this has happened before," Lakesh concluded. "We just need to figure out why it's happening now. And figure it out quickly. I know it's hard, Brigid, but let that see you through."

"I will," Brigid replied after a moment.

As the conversation was proceeding, Farrell was running through the tracking data for Kane at his own terminal.

"I have Grant almost directly beside you," Farrell told Kane, mapping their transponders on his computer screen.

KANE LOOKED AROUND the lobby, his gaze halting a moment to take in the faces of the dead and dying who were situated all around him. Grant was not there.

"That's a negative, Farrell," he reported. "Are you sure of his location?"

"Sure as can be, Kane," Farrell confirmed. "I've double checked the readings—you should be able to see him if he's there."

Kane's eyes tracked around the lobby, then beyond to the open doorway that led to the corridor. He glanced back at Brigid. "He's either above us or below," Kane reasoned. "Baptiste? You have a preference?"

"I'll go up," Brigid said, striding with Kane toward the elevator bank that was located approximately behind the wall backing the lobby desk. "Check the roof."

Kane inclined his head uncertainly. "Leaves me with the morgue level. Not sure if that's going to be a better place to be or the worst," he grumbled as he pushed through the doorway that led into the stairwell. He took the carpeted steps two at a time, jogging down a level until he reached the basement.

BRIGID TOOK THE elevator to the second floor, aware of how large the hospital complex was. She wanted to check all the floors, not just the madness on the roof, not in the least because she was afraid of getting dragged into it somehow, sucked in by the mass hysteria that seemed to have possessed the city. Was it a death cult, as Kane had suggested, or something even more insidious? And how did Ereshkigal figure into all this, if she did?

The elevator—a large car big enough to fit two gurneys side by side—rose gently, playing a faint music track from a small speaker located beside the call buttons before stopping at the second floor. Its doors drew back gradually, revealing a darkened corridor.

Brigid stepped out warily, listening intently for any trace of sound. As she stepped out, the overhead lights snapped on—motion sensors, Brigid realized. Which told her something—no one had been in this area for a few minutes, at least. *Maybe they've all gone to the roof,* Brigid thought bleakly.

"Hello?" she called out tentatively. "Anyone home?"

There was no answer, only the low hum of air-conditioning units from the walls.

She paced to the end of the wide space dedicated to the elevators, peered up the corridor there. Like the elevator area, the walls were painted a pale, washed-out blue with a cream-colored stripe running along their lowest portion. The floor looked clean—tiles glinting in the reflection of the overheads—and there were doors peeling off to the left and right while the corridor continued to stretch onward. Twenty feet away, the illumination was still shut off, and Brigid suspected that this floor of the hospital, or at least this wing, was currently not in use. That, or maybe they had been abandoned when the whole mess had started—the people here might even now be the same ones that Brigid had seen throwing themselves from the roof.

Brigid turned around and walked back past the bank of elevators until she reached a second corridor that was located in mirror image to the first. This, too, appeared empty, with lights down the far end still extinguished.

She returned to bank of the elevators and pressed the call button, then waited for an elevator to arrive. One level down, two more to go.

KANE HURRIED DOWN the internal staircase, the soles of his boots hammering against each step like a blacksmith's hammer against an anvil. Kane slowed as he reached the bottom, tuning in his senses to the environment. He was renowned for his pointman sense, his ability to detect danger seemingly before it happened. He needed that ability now.

He stood before a closed door to the basement level of the hospital. "Farrell, you still receiving me?" Kane whispered as he activated the Commtact in his skull.

Farrell's response came through haphazardly, breaking up and nonsensical. Evidently, whatever was located in the basement was screwing with the Commtact's receiving abilities. That could explain why Grant had dropped out of contact.

Kane had hoped to get a confirmation from Farrell concerning Grant's current location but he would have to proceed without further intel. "Farrell, if you can hear me," Kane whispered, "no loud noises, okay?"

With that, Kane reached for the door handle with his left hand, leaving his right free to draw the Sin Eater hidden against his wrist should he need it, and pulled the door toward him.

He halted with a gasp.

What greeted him was a scene of eerie carnage. Behind the stairwell door lay a corridor that had once been finished in a soft, pastel green with green floor and white tiled ceiling. Now it was red; the rich, wine-dark red of freshly spilled blood.

There was blood splashed across every wall and drizzled along the floor, layered in great swathes across the once clean surfaces.

"What happened here?" Kane muttered, astonished.

As he spoke, a white-coated figure shambled into view—a doctor? His coat was splashed with red and he had a pair of scissors protruding from his left eye socket, shattering one side of his spectacles, while his other eye was narrow, almost closed. His hair was dark and patchy, matted against his head by sweat…or something else, maybe. He appeared to be bare-chested beneath the jacket. The way he staggered, he seemed to be drunk, lurching across the wide section of corridor where the elevator bank was located.

Kane hurried over to the man and stopped before him, grabbing him by the top of his arms. "What happened here, man? Speak up," he demanded.

"The patients…" the white-coat said, his words strained and hollow-sounding.

"What about them?" Kane urged.

"They're…"

Kane felt the doctor's body tense at that very moment, and something else, too—he felt something wrapping around his leg. He looked down, pushing the white-coat away so that he was at arm's length. Wrapping itself around the lower part of Kane's leg was something that looked like an octopus's tentacle. Only it wasn't an octopus—it was the doctor's arm, elongating impossibly and contorting as if it had no bones inside it, like uncooked dough.

BRIGID BAPTISTE CHECKED her wristchron as the elevator ascended to the third floor. It had been twenty-six minutes since she and Kane had materialized via interphaser in the overgrown churchyard on the east bank.

The elevator came to a gentle halt and its doors drew back on hidden runners. The second floor had been empty, abandoned.

The third floor was different.

There were people all over, a lot like the lobby, and they were hurting themselves and each other, ripping into one another with blades and pens and syringes and anything else that might be used as a weapon, even bedpans and crutches. It was a sickness on a grand scale. But no one moved when the elevator doors slid open. They had been moving, Brigid felt sure, but they stopped moving when the doors pulled back, standing like statues, midcarnage.

Brigid realized that these were the first people that she had seen since she and Kane had exited the blood-daubed lobby of the hospital complex. And it appeared that every single one of them was intent on killing themselves or the person next to them.

As she looked across the wide communal area that led to patients rooms, Brigid saw a familiar figure step from one of those doors. It was Shizuka, and she was assisting the stumbling body of a handsome dark-haired man with blood on his neatly tailored suit, a chunk of glass protruding from his chest.

"Shizuka?" Brigid called.

At the noise, everyone in the lobby turned, almost as one, their faces marred with blood and cuts and bits of glass hacked into them, turning together to look at Brigid Baptiste where she stood framed in the widening doorway of the elevator car. No one looked happy.

KANE SHOVED THE doctor away—hard—with his left hand, lifting his leg out of the eerie, tentacle-like grip. The tentacle slithered back around Kane's leg, tightening its grip even as it rose past his knee.

"Get off me," Kane snarled, commanding the Sin Eater into his right hand with a practiced flinch of his wrist tendons.

The doctor—if he even was a doctor—found himself

staring down the thirteen-inch barrel of the weapon with Kane's glaring eyes focused on him.

The tentacle-like arm wrapped tighter around Kane's leg, while his other arm seemed to extend even as Kane watched.

"That's it," Kane hissed and squeezed the trigger of his blaster, sending a round of 9 mm fire into the doc's upper left arm. The man fell with a groan, dropping back until he struck the floor. His left arm remained wrapped around Kane but its grip was faltering, and it was a matter of a few seconds for Kane to extricate himself from it.

With the discharge, Kane figured all pretense at stealth was gone, so he called out as loudly as he could. "Grant? You down here?"

It had been twenty-seven minutes since he and Brigid had arrived.

GRANT HEARD THE call from the back-room theater that led into the morgue. He was wrestling with the naked woman with the open neck while Cáscara reloaded her blaster, having already drilled a full clip into the broad-shouldered bruiser holding the noose. Bruiser had stumbled but not fallen, and like Frankie in the morgue drawer, he had reached for her in response with fingertips that grew far beyond their natural extension, spiraling through the air toward her like seaweed.

Cáscara had thrown herself aside, ducking behind one of the examination tables, pressing her back against it as the elongated fingers wavered in the air just inches above her. *Reload*, she told herself. *Don't think about it—just reload*.

Grant had dropped Julio's body gently on the floor even as the woman with the open chest turned and hissed at him. "Be cool, kid," Grant told Julio as he rose again to meet with the animated corpse.

Open-chest kicked out at Grant, swinging her leg high. Grant ducked, drawing a bead on the woman with his Sin Eater and snapping off a shot in the same instant. She may be dead or not dead, but Grant would bet that he was the only one of them trained for combat as a hard-contact Magistrate.

The bullet streaked through the chill air of the surgical theater before embedding in the woman's torso, just to the left of her breastbone—a perfect heart-shot. The woman flinched at the impact, her outstretched foot coming down again in a stuttered drop.

Grant leaped at her then, driving at her with all his weight, shoulders down, and knocking her back before she could catch her balance. She went caroming into one of the surgical tables, flipping onto it then dropping down over the other side. Grant went with her, rolling free as they struck the table and hauling himself up in a lurching kind of landing. Didn't matter—he was on his feet and she was still on the floor; the advantage was his.

It was somewhere during that brief altercation that Grant had heard the gunshot and then what sounded like his partner, Kane, calling his name from beyond the room. He turned, head jabbing around momentarily to take in the scene through the glass pane of the door, before whipping back to face his opponent again.

What he had seen through the window was the morgue door opening and a figure moving through. He had only stolen a glance but he was pretty certain that it had been Kane, dressed for combat with a Sin Eater in his hand, blasting merry hell out of the swarming corpses as they charged him in the doorway.

Corpse woman was still on the floor, but her body seemed to writhe, muscles showing clearly beneath her naked flesh. Grant's eyes widened as the woman physically expanded, arms and legs lengthening, fingers and toes becoming longer, like time-lapse photography of a plant's growth.

"What the hell?" Grant muttered, bringing his Sin Eater up again. He fired, blasting another 9 mm bullet from the chamber into the woman's forehead. As if that would matter—but he figured that shooting a dead person in the head made about as much sense as anything else he had seen here this past quarter hour.

Beside him, Cáscara reached up from her hiding place and snagged the extended fingers of her own "playmate," grabbing them as they withdrew across the surgical table. Then she was up on her feet, bringing her Devorador de Pecados pistol up and ramming it against the weirdly extending forearm of her opponent. A second later she fired, drilling a bullet into the man's wrist from point-blank range. The arm seemed to go limp in her grip.

KANE COULD HEAR the noises from outside the morgue. He entered warily, turning the door handle to unlatch the door, then stepped back and held his pistol up and ready. He could hear the sound of movement from within, shuffling feet, scraping metal. He kicked the door wide-open in a single swift movement so that it struck the back wall with a crash.

A set of naked figures turned at the noise. There were fifteen in all and they were pallid and drawn, four of them clearly in the early stages of decomposition. They looked at Kane with cruel expressions, though not one of them had his or her eyes open—instead, the eyelids were sealed over the eyes.

"Nobody move," Kane instructed from the open doorway.

The corpses moved, trudging toward him—at first slow, then picking up speed with every subsequent step until they were rushing at him like a swarm of insects.

Kane fired, flicking the Sin Eater to triple burst as he squeezed the trigger.

Shots rang out. Struck across the chest, the first of the corpses—a man of indeterminate age with marker pen lines down his flank surrounding a line of black stitches—shuddered in place and dropped to his knees. Behind him, the next two corpses felt the fury of Kane's blaster, a woman taking two bullets to her left shoulder, striking with such force that she was spun almost entirely around; her companion, a heavyset male showing the potbelly of some impressive middle-age spread, took a bullet to the chest and just halted, as if he had struck a wall.

But still they kept on coming.

Kane spotted targets, sending out a single burst of fire at each before moving on to the next. Two more figures dropped under his hail of fire, while another went caroming into his neighbor as a 9 mm slug ripped away the right-hand side of his face.

Then they were upon Kane, and he went down beneath a cavalcade of bone-dry arms and legs. As he struck the floor under the weight, all that Kane could see was dead skin and eyes that had sealed shut.

Chapter 24

Darkness.

A pain in the back of his head.

The smell of formaldehyde so strong he could taste it.

Something pressing against him. Many somethings, all pressing from different sides, pushing against his ribs, his arms, his legs, his face.

It came back to Kane in a disordered jumble: what had happened, where he was, how he had come to be here. He was in the hospital morgue, he remembered, shooting things that didn't seem to realize that they were dead, and something had struck his head. He was lying on his back, and there was something writhing on top of him, moving around him. One thing or many things, he could not quite be certain.

The dead walkers had smothered him, overwhelmed him by sheer weight of numbers.

The Sin Eater was still in his hand, clutched there the way a drowning man clings to a life buoy. He squeezed its trigger, cursing even as he felt it press against something solid and doughy, a dead body that somehow still knew how to move. The blaster kicked in Kane's hand, but he knew that it was like shooting hunks of meat—the very best he could hope for was to whittle his attackers down, chunk by chunk.

Meanwhile, they had him overwhelmed—numbers, relentlessness, everything was on their side. Things that couldn't die, couldn't stop. Now he could feel them clawing at him, their hands on his mouth, pressing at his face, his eyes.

Eyes.

It came to Kane unexpectedly, the eureka moment, barely formed. The realization that they all had their eyes almost closed. What it meant, he did not know. But it gave him the idea.

Kane shifted, constricted by his attackers, reaching desperately into his jacket pocket with his left hand. He could not reach, his fingertips just brushing against the edge of the items there. He shoved with his elbow, pushing at the weight of bodies on top of him, jabbing at them with the barrel of the Sin Eater in his other hand. But still he could not quite snare what he was after.

The second thought was perhaps even more inspired than the first. He needed space to work, just a few inches of room so that he could get his hand into that pocket and snag the device he needed. So he pushed up with his right hand, the one holding the Sin Eater blaster, and flinched his wrist tendons to send the weapon back to its hidden, spring-loaded holster. The gun disappeared in an instant, and that instantaneous shift left a momentary gap within which Kane could wriggle. His left arm pulled a little farther, fingers reaching for and priming one of the two-inch spheres that resided in his pocket before pulling it free.

Three...

Kane closed his eyes, even though his view was entirely obscured by his attackers.

Two...

He shoved out with both arms, using all his strength to generate more space under the scrimmage of writhing corpses.

One...

Kane released the device, letting it roll from his hand.

He felt it butt against his side, between the third and fourth ribs on his left flank, and he screwed his eyes shut tighter.

Boom!

Powder keg!

The flash-bang went off. Its usual bellow of furious sound was muffled by all the bodies, sounding more like an explosive charge detonated underwater. But the light was revelatory—a great burst of pure whiteness amid the scrum of pale, dead flesh. Kane saw it even through his closed eyelids, and he hoped that the same would be true for his opponents.

There was a loosening of the pressure on Kane as a ripple of shock seemed to run through the bodies pressing against him. So they had seen it then, somehow.

The eyes of the corpses were like those of a baby bird. Behind the lids, retooled, their eyes were not properly formed. Their newly rewired ocular nerves could not handle the sudden burst of light that the flash-bang emitted.

What happened next happened fast. Kane blinked back the afterimage of the explosive, rolling his body to scramble free from the cluster of corpses who threatened to overwhelm him. His feet pressed against the floor, and his arms wavered and shifted beneath that press of bodies. If one could have applied an X-ray at that moment, it would have looked for all the world as if Kane was swimming, doing the back stroke amid a tide of bodies.

It was momentary. Those corpses closest to the flash-bang had reared back, but they had still been pressed down by the others around and above them. Kane took the brief ease in pressure to make enough space for himself that he could reach for more of the devices. His hand rummaged in his jacket pocket and gripped two more of the spherical pods. He primed one with his thumb, the second with the heel of his hand, gripping and turning with desperate urgency.

Kane dropped both flash-bangs, turning his head as they went off. This time the explosion was louder, the press of bodies against him was easing, and Kane's hearing popped the way it did when traveling in a high-speed jet.

Around him, the pressure of bodies had eased almost entirely, and words were being growled in Spanish, words that Kane's Commtact was picking up and translating even though he could not hear them directly.

"Pain!"

"Pain!"

"Why would she let us suffer so?"

Kane pushed free of the scrimmage, scrambling backward on his butt, legs working double-time to get him away from his attackers. The Sin Eater materialized in his hand even as he broke away from the mob, and as it struck his hand his finger was pressing against the trigger, sending out a rapid burst of fire at a woman's corpse who still clutched on to Kane's booted foot. The woman's face was peppered with bullets in an instant, pallid flesh tearing away like cobwebs. She let go and Kane was finally free.

JUST ONE ROOM AWAY, Grant had been dodging attacks from the woman with the open chest wound while Pretor Cáscara kept out of reach of the dead man with the extending fingers.

The dead woman now had a perfect circle drawn on her forehead where Grant's bullet had broken skin and entered her brain, but somehow she just kept coming.

"Need to change tactics," Grant muttered as the woman hissed something at him in whispery Spanish. His gaze raced around the room, searching for something to use as a defense.

The woman paced toward Grant, her arms raised as if to strangle him. He kicked out as she came close, delivering a solid blow to her abdomen. Beside him, Cáscara was doing something similar to her own foe, just trying to hold him off.

Grant sidestepped as the female corpse struggled to regain her balance, scrambling across to where one of the surgical tables stood. The table was fixed—which was a drag because Grant had hoped he might be able to use it as a battering ram to drive the woman back. No matter, the table still had instruments laid out on it that he might utilize.

Grant snatched up a one-pint bottle of ether as the dead woman came marching toward him, those ghost-pale eyelids sealed over her eyes. He threw it from just a few feet away, watched as the bottle shattered when it struck her forehead, spilling its contents across her face, broken glass in her hair. The woman did not even slow, but that did not matter—Grant was already bringing his Sin Eater up to her face and he squeezed off a shot as she reached for him, delivering a 9 mm slug into her left cheek as the gun rose in an arc.

The bullet struck the spilled ether, igniting it in an instant. It was like watching a fireworks display.

Suddenly, the woman was a ball of flame hurrying at him, while Grant skipped backward, his left arm up to shield him from the heat's intensity.

The woman was still coming, striding forcefully across the tight space of the examination room, even as her body began to burn from the head downward, the flames spreading with her every step. Beneath his clothes, Grant's shadow suit compensated for the sudden rise in temperature, but it couldn't prevent him from feeling the radiance of the human inferno against his face. Grant shot again, sending another bullet into the flaming maelstrom, aiming for the woman's heart. The bullet seemed to catch fire as it streaked at her, spreading the flames with an almighty "woof" of sound.

The corpse woman slowed then, as the flames caught one of her legs and began to burn more fiercely. Grant took the opportunity, turning on the spot before delivering a perfect roundhouse kick to her burning torso. The kick hit her with a crack of bones, and the animated corpse fell back from the force of the blow, crashing against the floor like so much discarded junk. Dark, acrid-smelling smoke billowed from the burning body, casting the ceiling in a smear of charcoal black. The fire had stopped her at least.

Grant had stepped back, watching his opponent burn, even as, across the room, Cáscara was using her handcuffs to affix her own attacker to the other table by his ankle.

Grant smiled—maybe they had managed to stop these impossible dead things after all? Then he felt a sudden strike across the back of the neck and he sank to his knees. As he did so, he felt something grip around his neck, tightening in a fraction of a second.

Cáscara was reaching for the room's fire extinguisher to douse the burning corpse before its flames could spread. She heard Grant's knees slam hard against the floor tiles, turned and saw that he was being attacked by the medical examiner who was still hanging from the ceiling by a rubber-tube noose.

"Grant, look—" Cáscara's cry came too late. But she was drawing her pistol around to target the dead man hanging from the ceiling. Dead? Or maybe dying? Maybe he needed help. Oh, shit.

"Please let go of him," Cáscara reasoned, the blaster never wavering in her grip, "so that I can help you down."

"Corpse in waiting," the hanged man sneered in response, his voice strained. "Corpses for my mistress."

Cáscara pulled the trigger, sending a 9 mm slug into the depending man's body, then another and another. The bullets embedded in the white-coated figure but he continued to cling to Grant, legs wrapped around the ex-Magistrate with incredible inhuman strength.

Grant pulled at the man's legs, trying to speak, trying to call out, but he could not get them loose. It seemed that with each pull, the legs bent further, twisting into impossible knots around Grant's neck.

And then the door to the theater crashed open and Kane came striding in, Sin Eater held out before him and reeling off a shot even as he assessed the situation. Kane's bullet was aimed high, targeting not the hanged man but the strip of rubber tubing that had been used to hang him.

The tubing broke apart as the bullet cut through it, and the hanging man tumbled to the floor, abruptly loosening his hold on Grant. Grant ripped the entangling leg away—now more like a squid's appendage than a human's—rolling free from the freak's grip. As he rolled, he saw Kane striding into the room, blaster trained on the fallen figure, left hand holding a familiar silver sphere.

"Close your eyes," Kane said before triggering the flash-bang.

Grant turned his head away, screwing his eyes shut tight as the flash-bang exploded in a hail of sound and fury.

ON THE THIRD-FLOOR ward, Brigid Baptiste found herself the center of attention as a dozen patients in various states of distress turned to face her. Their eyes were pale—uncannily so—and they displayed the coordinated movement patterns of flocking birds, with each member of the group turning to face Brigid in unison.

Farther along the broad corridor, Brigid could see Shizuka helping a man whose white shirt was marked with blood.

The blood-streaked patients began to congregate toward Brigid, their expressions gripped with unutterable joy. In moments, Brigid found her way blocked, the gaunt faces of the sick pressing all around her. Then one reached for her, a woman with long blond hair and dressed in a hospital gown. She grasped for Brigid's clothes, pawing at the lapels of her jacket.

"Get away from me," Brigid instructed, speaking in Spanish and batting the woman's hand away.

Another patient, this one a man with a balding pate, reached for Brigid's hand as she brushed the woman away, while a third grabbed her hair from behind, yanking her back.

"Corpses for the mistress," one of the women chanted as Brigid struggled against the onslaught. A moment later the chant was taken up by all twelve patients.

Shizuka saw what was happening from the far end of the corridor where she was helping Corcel from Zorrilla's room. She glanced down at Corcel where he was slumped against her, saw how pale his face had become, how his eyes seemed to be drifting in and out of focus.

"Stay here," Shizuka instructed, helping Corcel to a chair beside the nurse's station.

Then she drew her katana sword from its hidden sheath beneath her jacket. The blade emerged from its scabbard with a whistled note, the sound of perfectly smoothed metal.

The sword swished through the air, flashing like a streak of lightning as it caught the overhead lights. "Back off!" Shizuka warned in English, striding toward Brigid, the sword held ready. "Everyone!"

The group of possessed patients seemed bemused by the samurai woman's order—though there was no mistaking her intention. As one they turned to look at her, still voicing their wicked chant.

Amid the crowd, Brigid was being pulled left and right, hands pawing at her clothes and hair, dragging her in two directions at once. In a moment, the mob seemed to part and Brigid was suspended in their center, one group pulling at her left arm, the other pulling her right, both limbs stretched to full extension. Brigid strained as the pressure increased on her shoulders.

"Cadáveres para mi amante," the crowd droned, pulling Brigid's body painfully in two directions. "Corpses for my mistress."

Chapter 25

The patients were trying to pull Brigid apart in a perverse tug-of-war. She strained against them, fighting with every muscle to hold herself together as her arms threatened to be pulled from their sockets.

"Cadáveres para mi amante," the crowd droned. "Corpses for my mistress."

Shizuka strode toward the group, swinging her sword in a brutal arc that ended in the head of the closest mob member. She didn't intend to kill, but the time for diplomacy was most definitely over.

The mob member went down, crashing to the side as his head was struck with the flat of the sword.

The next met Shizuka's blade head-on, his chest echoing as the flat of the sword struck against it once, twice, thrice, until he fell to the floor.

The pressure on Brigid had eased subtly, but she could not relax. These lunatics wanted to pull her apart, for reasons she could not begin to fathom. It was all tied up with Ereshkigal; it had to be. But how? Why? Why did the reborn Annunaki goddess need corpses so badly?

Shizuka's blade swished again, batting at the grasping arms of one of the patients and leaving an angry red mark across the skin. The next patient came at Shizuka, responding to her threat now, his jaw still chanting the words of their sick litany. "Corpses for my mistress."

Shizuka met him with a twist of her body, bringing the

katana blade up so that its pommel struck between the patient's ribs. The man let out a pained blurt of breath and went dancing away, clutching at his bruised chest. Shizuka followed up immediately, reaching up for the man's head with her left hand and twisting so that he turned away from her in a violent lurch. Then her blade came up again, reversed once more to use the pommel as a baton with which to strike his cranium with a loud crack. Broken bones did not matter in this battle, keeping everyone alive was all that Shizuka really cared about now.

Brigid Baptiste was not helpless. Despite her predicament, she remained well versed in combat and was a very capable fighter. Right now she was being held a few inches from the floor, but she could just touch it if she stretched her toes. She did so, right boot skimming against the floor tiles. She leaned, drawing her body that way, forcing the group of four who were tugging at her right arm to lurch just a little, enough to drop her another inch lower. The toe of her boot connected, giving her purchase enough to kick backward. The move threw the balance of both groups who were pulling at her, and they staggered momentarily to one side as they clung on. That tiny change was enough to relax the pressure on Brigid's arms momentarily, and she lifted her feet up and out, kicking with both of them at the legs of the people to either side of her. The kicks were weak but they surprised the possessed patients, finding another chink in their armor and easing the pressure on Brigid's arms a little bit more.

Shizuka, meanwhile, was working her way through the angry patients with swift professionalism. A cut leg here, a slap of steel there, and the crowd started to thin.

As she reached Brigid—the redhead still held by seven patients who were trying hard to rip her to shreds—Brigid got her feet on the ground at last and kicked, springing with as much power as she could muster so that she went high in the air. Five of the people clinging to her let go, two of them crashing into the others at the sudden, unexpected movement, knocking them away. They tumbled like dominoes, and Shizuka was on them in an instant, bringing the razor-keen blade of her katana around in a sweeping arc that dared them to cross it.

There were still two of the chanting patients holding Brigid, clinging to her arms as she ascended. Brigid's body was still in motion, twisting in her opponents' grip to bring her legs upward so that she was upside down. In an instant, her feet slapped against the high ceiling and she pushed, extending both legs to drive herself—and her attackers—back down to the floor. All three crashed to the floor in a jumbled heap.

Brigid leaped away, bounding out of the muddled group and creating a few steps' distance between them before spinning around. Shizuka was at her side in an instant, fending off the remaining crowd members with the flat of her blade.

"What brings you here?" Shizuka asked.

"I was hoping to catch up with an old friend," Brigid replied with a grim smile. "Do you know what time visiting hours are?"

Shizuka slapped her blade against one of the approaching patients, ducked and brought her kicking leg up and out to strike another in the gut, knocking him to the floor. "Any idea what's going on?" she asked, her breath coming fast.

"Not yet, but it's everywhere," Brigid replied, "all over the city. A kind of mass hysteria."

"Then why aren't we affected?"

"Good question," Brigid said. "No answer just yet, I'm afraid. So what's happening with you?"

"Caught up in insanity," Shizuka summarized. "Guy there is Corcel, local law, got stabbed. I was trying to help him."

"Then let's help him," Brigid agreed, kicking a looming patient in the face. The patient struck the floor with a slap.

"THEY DON'T LIKE LIGHT," Kane explained as he helped Grant off the floor of the morgue's examination room.

The hanged man was just lying there, twitching as if hit with an electric current, his legs curling and flopping like an angry cat's tail.

Cáscara, meanwhile, was using the fire extinguisher to put out the woman's burning corpse before it took the whole hospital with it, her own opponent struggling against the cuffs she had managed to snag on his ankle.

"I figure it's something to do with their eyes," Kane continued with his usual sense of understatement. He was shouting a little, having been almost deafened by the first flash-bangs, but his hearing was returning now. As Grant stood up, Kane nodded toward Cáscara. "Care to introduce us?"

"Kane, this is Cáscara, a local Magistrate," Grant said.

"Pretor," Cáscara corrected, acknowledging Kane with a nod, "and call me Emiliana."

"Sure."

"And Pretor—this is Kane," Grant explained. "We've worked together for a long time."

"I save his butt, usually," Kane said, flashing the dark-haired Pretor a smile.

"So I see," she responded, switching off the fire extinguisher.

"We ran into big problems here," Grant summarized. "Corpses coming back to life, their physical properties not as rigid as you'd expect. I tried hailing Cerberus—"

Kane held up a hand to halt his partner's continued explanation. "There's bigger problems than that, buddy," he said. "Outside, the streets are like a graveyard. There's people trying to kill themselves, a lot of people. There's a whole herd of people throwing themselves from the roof here while, out in the street, Baptiste and I were almost run down by a biker who was determined to connect with a brick wall."

"Madness," Cáscara muttered.

"Yeah," Kane agreed, "the worst kind. No explanation, no discernible trigger. Just people going nuts all over. Lakesh suggests it's some form of mass hysteria, says there's historical precedent."

Grant nodded, briefly explaining to Cáscara that Lakesh was their ally back home.

"Any idea what started it?" Grant asked.

Kane shook his head. "Not yet. You're the man on the ground—we were hoping you'd have some intel we could use."

Grant shook his head slowly. "You already know about Ereshkigal," he said. "I'd guess she's involved—if she exists."

"You said you saw a woman—" Kane prompted.

"Yesterday," Grant confirmed. "But there's no way of knowing if that's who's causing all this.

"You said Brigid is with you?"

"Yeah, checking the other floors," Kane told him. "We had you triangulated but Farrell couldn't say what floor you were on."

"Shit," Grant cursed with an angry sigh. "Shizuka's out there, too. I thought it was just the morgue, but if she's got caught up in this—"

Kane held his hand up to calm his friend. "We'll locate her," he said, reassuringly. "Let's get moving, and maybe we can get to the bottom of this."

Emiliana Cáscara shot Grant a sideways look as Kane

stalked back to the door leading into the morgue. "Your friend? He's a take-charge kind of guy, isn't he?" she said.

Grant smirked despite himself. "He gets restless," he said. Then he moved over to where he had placed Julio the lab tech, swiftly checking the man's vitals. His pulse was weak but he was still breathing at least. "You have any idea where we can take this guy?" Grant said after patching up his wound with a strip of gauze.

"Leave him here and lock the room," Kane suggested, standing in the doorway, surveying the carnage in the morgue. "There's no help for anyone outside—trust me."

Grant swallowed hard and nodded. "Kane," he said.

Kane met his partner's eyes. "Yeah, I know. Annunaki. It never ends."

"Never does," Grant agreed.

Together, the trio left the theater, hurried through the morgue and, from there, made their way to the bank of elevators. Around them, the dead bodies of the reawakened corpses were holding their hands to their eyes, hissing in confusion and—perhaps—pain.

ON THE THIRD FLOOR, Brigid and Shizuka had fought their way to Pretor Corcel and managed to drag him to an examination room in the abandoned floor below. Temporarily safe, they closed the door and Brigid got to work tending to the Pretor's cut. The wound was deep and he had lost some blood, but he was hanging on to consciousness.

"You took quite a beating here," Brigid told him gently in Spanish as she cleaned the wound, having removed the glass.

"Just one beating," Corcel replied with a weak smile. "Lucky shot."

Shizuka stood at the door, watching through a gap in the blinds that were intended to grant the occupants privacy.

"Anyone coming?" Brigid asked.

"No," Shizuka confirmed. "I think we lost them when we jumped in the elevator. Lucky you knew this floor was empty."

"We're all barely surviving on 'lucky,'" Brigid groused, using a cotton swab to clean the edge of Corcel's wound. "We need to get on top of this, ASAP."

Corcel nodded, his head moving slowly and heavily. "A whole plague of madness, you said," he muttered to Brigid. "It's baffling. We've seen some group suicides over the past few weeks, but nothing on the scale you've described."

"How many?" Brigid asked.

"A dozen," Corcel recalled, "in two unrelated incidents. *Seemingly* unrelated," he corrected.

"We suspect it's the work of an alien agent," Brigid told him.

"Ereshkigal," Corcel said. "Yes, your friend Grant told us about how he and his people had met with alien gods. I thought he was exaggerating."

Brigid pressed an absorbent pad against the Pretor's skin, tearing off a strip of gauze tape she had taken from one of the cupboards and adhering it in place. "How do you feel now?" she asked as she strapped up the wound.

Corcel winced. "Stupid," he admitted. "I should never have let that woman ambush me like that."

"We were both surprised," Shizuka placated. "She slit her own throat and then attacked Corcel."

Brigid frowned. "Did you say that right?" she checked. "She attacked *after* wounding herself?"

"It doesn't make a lot of sense, does it?" Shizuka agreed.

Brigid sighed heavily. "It makes sense to somebody," she reasoned. "We just have to figure out how."

"We'll return to the Hall of Justice," Corcel proposed, his eyes closed against the pain. "They should be coordinating efforts to stem this. Hopefully they'll be able to give us some insights."

At that moment, Brigid's hidden Commtact trilled to life, and Kane's voice began speaking directly into her ear canal. "Baptiste, I've found Grant. Where are you?"

Turning her head, Brigid answered. "Second floor. I'm with Shizuka and a local law enforcer called Corcel," she explained. "I understand Grant knows him."

"We've run into some serious trouble in the morgue," Kane summarized. "Dead people coming back to life, their physical properties no longer absolute. We got out. We're in the lobby now."

"It's chaos on the third floor, too," Brigid told him. "A group of patients tried to rip me apart like they were in a trance."

At the other end of the Commtact link, Kane cursed. "We need to regroup," he decided. "You able to get here?"

"Oh, Kane," Brigid cried. "What about the people on the roof?"

"Too many darn victims," Kane growled in reply. "We need to find the source."

"Agreed," Brigid said reluctantly. "The Pretor here suggests going to the Hall of Justice."

"Local Mags?"

"Exactly. Pretor thinks they will be surveying the situation and trying to regain order."

"Stands to reason. That's standard protocol for Magistrates," Kane agreed.

"We'll be with you in a few minutes," Brigid assured him, cutting the connection.

Shizuka and Corcel looked at Brigid quizzically. They had, of course, only heard her side of the discussion.

"You have a plan?" Corcel asked.

"Yes," Brigid told him, helping the man to his feet. "Yours. Think you're okay to walk?"

Corcel winced, screwing up his eyes. "I'll be fine," he assured her, taking a tremulous breath. When he opened his eyes once more, the irises were a little bigger and a little paler. Neither Brigid nor Shizuka noticed.

Chapter 26

Outside the hospital was madness.

The sounds of vehicle engines roared in the distance now, echoing through the city like a race track in backing to the slow, gradual chimes of the church bells. There were bodies hanging from the streetlamps of the parking garage, with more people queuing up to do the same. Others were finding even more inventive ways to kill themselves, bashing their brains out on blood-smeared concrete pillars, leaping out of the moving vehicles they drove to high speeds or throwing themselves in front of them, holding themselves under the water of the decorative fountain outside the hospital until they drowned.

All around the hospital, the dead or dying were sprawled on the hard pavement like sandbags from where they had jumped from the roof. Groans emanated from the clumped bodies, and the scene was mirrored up and down the street beyond where the roofs of other tall buildings had been used to similar effect.

Smoke billowed from distant buildings where fires had been set, clouding the sky in towering plumes like dark fingers clawing for heaven.

"This is impossible," Brigid stated as she observed the scene of carnage. "Humans—we have survival instincts. They—we—shouldn't be doing this. It's impossible." She was standing with Kane, Grant, Shizuka and the two Pretors just beyond the grand glass doors that led from the hospital reception area. The doors showed cracks in the glass and there were several bloody smears where people had tried to use those cracks to cut the arteries in their wrists, their necks. One man lay dying on the ground below a bloody smudge, eyes wide and a look of ecstasy on his face.

"It's happening, Baptiste," Kane said pragmatically.

"People have the capacity to kill themselves for many reasons," Shizuka reminded them. "Not just through depression. It can be a gesture of devotion or a mark of honor, for example." She was thinking of her own legacy as a samurai.

Brigid looked at Shizuka as realization dawned. "Devotion," she repeated. "Honor. Dammit, why didn't I think of that?"

"Think of what?" Kane asked.

"These people are killing themselves as a self-sacrifice," Brigid guessed. "To do so in such numbers, that would have to be the most likely explanation. They want to die to achieve something. Something more than death."

"What does Ereshkigal promise?" Grant asked.

Brigid thought for a moment. "I'm not sure," she admitted. "Only fragments of her story survived. She ruled the underworld and was not above killing other Annunaki for revenge. But beyond that, how she interacted with humans…we don't know."

Corcel scanned the parking garage, searching for his Wheelfox. It remained where he had left it but was now abutted by two crashed motorbikes, one of the riders lying dead on the hood. "Come on, let's get to the Hall," Corcel said, leading the way across the body-strewn tarmac. He was bent over a little as he walked, wincing where the pain of the chest wound pulled against him.

"I'll drive," Cáscara told him as the group approached the Wheelfox.

Corcel shook his head. "No, Liana. I may not be good for much just now, but I can still drive."

Cáscara shot Corcel a quizzical look but Corcel ignored her and tapped in the key code to unlock the patrol vehicle. Corcel swung himself painfully into the driver's seat once the gull-wing door opened. As he did so, Cáscara reached for the man lying across the vehicle's hood. The man wore a leather jacket and a bandanna across his head, once blue but now stained with blood in what looked like a slick, black patch. As Cáscara touched his arm, the man flinched and turned his face toward her. His expression was jocular, wide smile amid blood-streaked stubble.

"The joy, the joy!" he trilled in Spanish, twisting to reach for the female Pretor. "Feel the joy!"

Then he had Cáscara by the wrists, pulling her down onto the hood of the Wheelfox with such vigor that she struck the windshield with a loud bang.

Kane interceded in a flash, placing one strong hand on the biker's chest and forcing him back with a shove so that he rolled over the slanted front of the Wheelfox while Cáscara stumbled free.

Shizuka was with Cáscara straightaway, helping her back while Grant and Brigid stormed forward.

The biker was up again in a second, a mad stare in his too-pale eyes, his lips curled in a sneering smile. *Cadáveres para mi amante,"* he cheered. "Corpses for my mistress."

Then the man leaped, springing from where he had fallen, bounding through the air toward Kane with his hands poised in tight claws.

Kane met him with an outstretched arm, delivering the heel of his hand to the man's face in a brutal blow. The man seemed to sag in the air, his body concertinaing as it crumpled against the force of Kane's blow. He dropped to the ground, and Kane spun away.

The moment that Kane was out of the line of fire, Grant unleashed a burst of fire from his Sin Eater—commanded into his hand in the seconds between the man's ambush attack on Cáscara and Kane's devastating rebuttal. Several 9 mm bullets drilled into the man's left kneecap, hobbling him in an instant.

The biker hissed like a cat as the bullets struck him, writhing against their impacts.

Beside Grant, Brigid was ready with her own blaster, the sleek TP-9 unleathered from the holster at her hip, but it was unnecessary.

"Stay down," Grant ordered, his dark eyes fixed on the deranged attacker. Whether the man understood English or not did not matter—Grant figured that his expression and the blaster in his hand should be enough to convey his message.

"I would have cuffed him," Cáscara bemoaned in irritated Spanish.

"I think we're beyond the stage of cuffing people," Kane told her.

While Cáscara took the shotgun seat, the Cerberus warriors and Shizuka bundled into the back via a wide gull-wing door set before the single back wheel. It was cramped, but there was space enough.

Corcel triggered the Wheelfox's ignition and the engine roared to life like an animal unleashed. "Everyone comfortable?" he asked jocularly. He looked drained of color and his eyes were beginning to fracture as the irises merged with the whites. His heart had stopped earlier, when the glass had hit it, but he had bounced back... somehow.

Corcel pressed his foot down on the accelerator and

steered the Wheelfox out of the parking lot, leaving behind the body of the biker who had attacked them.

THE STREETS WERE HELL. Sheer bloody hell.

There were dead bodies and dying bodies and people trying to kill themselves and each other. But what made it worse, as if worse could even be contemplated, was that there was barely any noise—no screams, no shouts, no weeping or groans or shrieks. Instead, the streets were silent but for the ever-present thrum of distant engines accompanied by the slow, metronomic beat of the church bells.

"We've walked into a nightmare," Grant muttered, looking through the window port of the Wheelfox land wag.

Corcel guided the Wheelfox through broken vehicles, burned-out heaps, bodies—so many bodies—that were just scattered across the road. He kept at a steady twenty miles per hour, not racing, just trying to keep moving while people fell from buildings above them, autos crossed intersections in mad games of chicken where the aim was not to survive but to crash and to die.

"How far to the Hall of Justice?" Kane asked.

"Little over a mile," Cáscara told him from the front seat.

"Street's blocked," Corcel chimed in, applying the brake.

Up ahead, a vast group of moving figures could be seen through the windshield, marching in a kind of ragged unison, bobbing like waves on the ocean. They were tired-looking, their clothes torn and stained with blood. Some displayed sickening wounds on their exposed bodies, self-inflicted or encouraged by others. There were men, women, children; young and old; infirm and healthy. Every member of that eerie, unreal mob was smiling with an unnerving, fixed grin of teeth like a shark scenting prey.

The people were chanting something, the sound of all those voices beating against the sealed windows of the Wheelfox. *"Saca a tu vida!"*

"Bring out your living!" Brigid translated automatically.

"What the hell?" Grant muttered.

"Trouble," Kane replied, squeezing himself close to the grille that separated the front seats from the rear compartment, trying to get a closer look.

The wave of people was moving toward them, spreading out and blocking the full width of the street from store to store, striding determinedly. There must have been two hundred or more, each one displaying that unnerving, ecstatic smile, each one joining the chanted words in Spanish. "Bring out your living! Bring out your living!"

As Kane watched, he saw the way the bodies of some of the crowd members seemed stretched or of uncertain proportions, like something made from plasticine. Here a man strode on long, bandy legs that he seemed to fling forward like yo-yo strings, reminding Kane of the legs of a spider. There a woman walked with a torso elongated like an elephant's trunk, her head peering up above the crowd members who surrounded her. Another figure had arms so long they touched the ground before his feet did, and he propelled himself forward on his hands like a child's circus toy.

"Bring out your living!"

Somewhere in back, amid the great torrent of grinning people, the figure of a beautiful woman seemed to be directing them, semi-naked like a carnival showgirl, running bloody hands through her long dark hair, within which was clipped a crown of twisted bones.

"That's her," Grant said, spying the woman momentarily through a brief parting of the crowd. He scrambled forward and pointed. "See there? Flanked by two men?"

Kane nodded, spotting the striking woman amid the swelling crowd.

"That's the woman I saw back at the hotel," Grant confirmed.

"Ereshkigal," Kane said, barely breathing the name.

The crowd was getting closer. "Bring out your living."

"What do we do? We can't run these people down," Corcel stated.

"He has a point," Grant agreed. "An' I don't think we can just waltz into that crowd to get to her—do you?"

"No," Cáscara agreed. She did not sound happy.

"Is there another route?" Brigid asked. "Some other way to get to the Hall of Justice? Coordinate from there?"

"Of course, yes," Corcel said, shaking his head as if to gather his senses. "I was…distracted. I'm sorry."

Flanked on all sides by her faithful, the carnival woman gestured for the mob to proceed toward the stalled Wheelfox patrol vehicle. For a moment, her eyes seemed to fix on the vehicle, jet-black orbs piercing the tinted windshield to peer directly into the driver's eyes, into his soul.

Chapter 27

Corcel shifted into Reverse, and the engine whined as the Wheelfox shot back. Up ahead, the crowd had begun moving faster, jogging toward the vehicle as it hurried away from them.

Still reversing, Corcel spun the wheel, slipping the nimble Wheelfox into a tight 180-degree turn. Now facing in the opposite direction, Corcel shifted into Drive and nudged the accelerator, charging up the body-clogged street before taking a hard right and slipping into an alleyway between buildings. Behind them, they left the sound of the trudging crowd, their slowly marching feet hitting the pavement in step, their voices chanting the same refrain: "Bring out your living!"

The alley was a tight fit, curving around back of one of the ancient buildings and past a church where the bells were gonging their eerie, incessant call.

THE ENTHRALLED COULD sense the burden of the living, sense the sadness life generated like a beacon in the night. It seemed to burn before them with the brilliance of a thousand supernovas, calling them to points in the city where Ereshkigal's release had somehow failed to touch. The dead—her army, her faithful   joined together to hunt these poor souls down, to bring to them the gift in all its glory and wonder and joy.

Beatriz Valle was one such victim. She was twenty-seven, a mother and nursery group helper, whose husband had left her three years before following the birth of their second child. He had left her for an older woman, older and plain-looking, in fact, which had somehow hurt more than if he had left her for someone pretty.

Beatriz lived in a small apartment to the west of the Ebro, the two bedrooms divvied up between herself and her two children. She could not see the river from her window but she could hear it, that reassuring shushing as it burbled its way toward the distant ocean, passing the sights of Zaragoza with all the indifference of water. She would listen to it sometimes when she had finished washing up, craning her head to the open kitchen window and imagining that maybe the river water was the same water that she had used to clean her dishes.

Her children were no trouble. Juanita was a fussy eater but Carlos was self-sufficient at five, happy to play his own games and make his own entertainment that incorporated his little sister in a way that only sibling love could, finding new players for his stories, new princesses and heroes and noble steeds for his sister to portray, emulate or ride.

That afternoon, the children were at their grandmother's—a regular date they shared after nursery one day a week, giving Beatriz a little alone time to pamper herself. She was in the bath, mirror fogged over and windows steamed up, when she heard the bells of the nearby Catholic church. She smiled at the sound—one she associated with weddings and christenings and the joy they brought.

Oddly the bell had chimed just once. She didn't think about that until she noticed its subsequent absence, like waiting for a clap of thunder that never came to follow the flash of lightning. Maybe someone had hit something by accident, she thought, smiling at the slapstick image that the thought conjured in her mind's eye.

And then the bell had chimed again, accompanied this

time by another close by. The bells chimed in unison but their pitches were different, creating a kind of doubling effect like voices in a poorly tuned radio signal.

Lying in the bath hearing those bells repeat, Beatriz suddenly felt cold. Where before the bath water had been warm against her body, now it felt chilly. She glanced around the compact bathroom with its pale yellow walls in need of new paint, its mirror and window misted over. There was so much steam in here, looking into it suddenly seemed like peering into the fog. She lay there in the tub, listening for the chimes again. Waiting.

Waiting.

Waiting.

Chime.

It was eerie. Uncanny. The chimes were too spread apart, too regular, playing an oh-so-slow rhythm she had never heard before yet knew in her heart, knew from before thought, before body, before time.

The cooling water rotated slowly around her, a gradual current formed by the eddies of the wind through a tiny gap in the window's frame. And then Beatriz heard the noise, an urgent, insistent, angry banging at her front door.

She gasped, pulling her hands up to her chest to cover her nakedness, turning to the bathroom door. Her landlord? Surely not, the rent wasn't due for another two weeks.

She strained for a moment, listening for what was going on outside. The hammering stopped, and then there was nothing, just the vacant silence left in its wake, heartless as the grave. She strained, listening harder. Was that movement at the door? Was something scrabbling around out there, just outside her bathroom door? Was it...?

Chime.

The church bells bonged again, loud now, making Beatriz jump.

"That's it," she muttered. "Gotta get out of this bath."

She was up even as she spoke, water draining off her as she vaulted the side of the tub and stood on the bath mat.

There was a chill deep inside her now, a chill that was no chill at all, the cold between planets, the cold of the abyss.

She reached for the towel, drying herself quickly and perfunctorily, with none of the tenderness she would have shown her children at bath time. She just wanted to be dry now, get outside and see what was going on, whether it was just her imagination or—

Chime.

The church bells again, all over the city, chiming the death knell of everyone who dwelled within its once-protective walls.

Beatriz's body was dry. She slung the towel aside, not looking as it wrapped itself around the broken wicker chair that she perched on when she was watching the children clean their teeth.

She was reaching for her underwear when the door to the bathroom crashed open and a figure stepped inside.

Beatriz screamed.

The door was hanging from its hinges, a great hunk of wooden panel poking into the wall like a salacious tongue. A man was standing there, so tall he had to duck to enter the room, shirttails hanging loose, tie wrenched to one side. He was not only tall, but freakish, Beatriz saw—his neck was long like one of those African tribesmen who used rings around their necks to elongate them, only there were no rings. And his torso, too, or at least the upper part, where his ribs started, was also long, reminding her more of an alligator's body than a human's. His face was human enough, dusky skin and dark hair, eyes wide and a toothy smile so joyous it disturbed her to look at it. The eyes were big, blotches of irises that seemed to fracture around their edges, clouding into the whites.

"Exquisita edad," the man said. "Age exquisite."

Then he reached for her with arms that seemed to extend well beyond their natural length, growing even as Beatriz stood there, naked and transfixed. The thought went through her mind then, as those hands reached for her throat and began to squeeze the life out of her—why had this man broken the door when she hadn't even locked it.

The bathroom lock had not worked in the six years she had rented the apartment.

THE ROAR OF the Wheelfox's engine was loud in the interior compartment. The alleyway down which Corcel had taken them seemed to be getting narrower, its turns tighter and leaving less margin for error. Suddenly, the front fender clipped a café table and chairs, knocking them up and over the hood until they careened off to one side. Corcel eased down on the accelerator, powering through the obstruction.

There were a few people here, though it seemed that most had congregated with Ereshkigal on the streets. Washing lines hung high overhead, cinched between the upstairs apartments located above the crowded eateries and cafés. Two bodies hung from one of the lines, dangling in the wind, dead.

Corcel looked pale as he gripped the wheel, eyes staring straight ahead, turning out of the alleyway and stabbing out onto a wide street with a complaining screech of tires.

Then the sturdy patrol vehicle was racing up the main thoroughfare, with the identifying red eye light of the Hall of Justice visible at the end of the street.

The road here was filled with debris, dead bodies, here a dog that had been run over by some heavy vehicle. A circle of people were standing outside a storefront that was billowing smoke, four of them in total, hands locked and staring into one another's faces. They looked delighted as the smoke wafted around them before spiraling up into the sky.

"It's citywide," Cáscara said, blinking in surprise.

"Yeah," Kane agreed. "Looks like it's been spreading ever since we got here."

"The streets were almost abandoned when we arrived," Brigid added by way of explanation. "It was like the bells were warning them to hide."

"Do you think it's affecting everyone?" Shizuka asked. "It can't be, can it?"

Brigid turned to her, seeing the fear on her pretty face. "It's not affected us," she said.

"But there's a reason for that," Shizuka said. "We're not local, we're visitors. That's what we all have in common."

"Except me and my partner here," Cáscara pointed out, "and we haven't been affected. Right?"

Corcel didn't answer. His attention was fixed on the street as he aimed the hurtling Wheelfox toward the entry to the Hall of Justice compound.

"Where were you when the bells started?" Brigid asked, a theory percolating in her prodigious mind.

Cáscara swiveled in her seat so that she could address Brigid. "In the morgue with Grant."

"No Commtact reception down there," Grant told Brigid helpfully.

"Did you hear the bells?" Brigid queried.

Cáscara looked thoughtful, her lips tightening into a pretty moue. "Not until we came out into the lobby," she recalled. "And even then, they were faint."

"Ultrasonics don't need to be consciously heard for them to affect the subject," Brigid mused. "If it was something like that, then the volume wouldn't matter, only the proximity."

"What do ultrasonics do?" Cáscara asked.

"High-power sound waves," Brigid said. "They can be

used as weapons. For example, brown notes, sounds below twenty hertz, can theoretically affect an individual's body, making them involuntarily lose control of their bowels."

Cáscara pulled a face. "Ick, nasty. And you think that this—"

"I think we need a theory," Brigid replied, "and ultrasonic weaponry fits as well as any. It's a starting point at least."

"One we sorely need," Kane averred.

The engine roared louder as Corcel pressed his foot against the accelerator. The Wheelfox zipped off the street and through the barrier that restricted entry to the multilevel garage abutting the Justice building. Designed to respond to a hidden trigger located in all Pretor vehicles, the barrier rose as the Wheelfox approached, just barely fast enough to let the vehicle through.

With its low ceilings and hard surfaces, the garage seemed to be filled with the strange echoes of screeching tires and roaring engine as Corcel's Wheelfox tore along the marked roadway between parked vehicles. Inside, it was lit by dull fluorescents, casting it in a dusky light. Then they took a ramp at speed, bringing the wheel around as Corcel ascended to the second level.

Still talking with the Cerberus team, Cáscara found herself suddenly thrown in her seat, the safety belt digging into her shoulder as she lurched. She turned to look through the windshield and then at her partner. "Juan? You want to slow down…?"

Corcel ignored her, his expression fixed as he stared through the windshield. The chimes of the bells were running through his head now, over and over, bringing with them the rhythm that Ereshkigal had discovered all those millennia ago—the rhythm of life and death. He yanked the wheel around, driving the Wheelfox through the closed-in space at an increasing rate. Parked Wheelfoxes and Sandcats whipped past them to either side in a blur of ceramic shell and armaglass.

In the back compartment, Kane, Brigid, Grant and Shizuka found themselves thrown side to side.

"What are you doing up there, man?" Grant yelped as he was tossed against the door.

Corcel turned the wheel again, and the tires screeched as the Wheelfox took the ramp up to the next level. A moment later the compact patrol vehicle emerged on the top level, above which were the landing pads for the Pretors' Deathbirds and other air support vehicles.

Cáscara was staring at Corcel strangely, trying to make sense of what was happening. In back, the Cerberus allies were unable to do anything but complain. They were not able to reach through the grille, which was designed to stop felons from interfering with Pretors after they had been arrested.

"Slow down!" Cáscara called.

But Corcel ignored any voiced instruction. All he could hear now was the piercing instruction in his mind—the one that demanded corpses for his mistress.

Cáscara glanced through the windshield and saw that they were heading directly to the edge of the garage. There was a low wall there, just a little higher than the front fender, with an open horizontal space above it to bring daylight into the building. Corcel was heading at the wall and he was not slowing down.

Cáscara reached across to grab the wheel, pulling at Corcel's left hand. But it was already too late. The man's foot was rammed against the accelerator and the only course correction that Cáscara could hope to enable was too little, too late.

"Corpses for my mistress," Corcel said in a low voice as they struck the wall.

Chapter 28

Hurtling at high speed, the Pretor Wheelfox slammed into the wall of the split-level parking garage. The crash of impact could be heard four streets away; it sounded like an aircraft had dropped from the sky.

The shock wave reverberated through the body of the vehicle like an earthquake, throwing the driver and passengers in all directions with shouts of surprise and pain.

The wall had crumpled beneath the onslaught but the Wheelfox kept on going as great hunks of concrete and metal broke away and began their brief descent through the thirty-foot distance to the street below. Engines roaring, the Wheelfox followed, smashing through the gap in the wall and careening out into empty air.

The engine's whine assumed a higher pitch as the wheels left the surface, and then the Wheelfox began to fall, tracing a shallow arc that threw it out beyond the edge of the parking garage and halfway across the street beyond, following those huge chunks of falling debris.

For a moment, Cáscara could see the familiar roofs of the Basilica of Our Lady of the Pillar and the Aljafería Palace hurtling past in the distance, viewed from new angles.

Then the Wheelfox slammed into the ground with a second thunderous crash, which could be heard two blocks away, nose-first and accompanied by hunks of wall and metal and a great billow of dust. The engines whined for a moment and the vehicle lurched a few feet forward, threatening to overbalance and flip, before coming down again at an angle where it rested, its rear wheel bent and its back port side touching the road.

THE GODS DEMANDED SACRIFICE. It showed devotion, it showed belief, it showed the insect's awe in the face of a being so much grander than anything that insect could ever fully comprehend.

Ereshkigal stalked the city in beauty like the night. Her body was becoming more lizard-like now, more absolute and rigid, the skin assuming its hard, armor-like coating that she remembered from her first life, lo those millennia ago.

Each step was a step of an age-old dance, her tail of feathers shimmying in time to the secret equation she had happened upon when she was still a youth in Enlil's courtyard. To an observer's eyes, if such there had been, the dance appeared to be a flamenco, a Spanish dance of death.

Around her, the city of Zaragoza was dying. Few who heard the chimes in the secret rhythm could resist, their promise of joy eternal too strong a draw to ignore. People came from their apartments to die, pushing a dagger deep into their heart, diving from their open windows or merely throwing themselves prostrate in the streets before the marching mob to be crushed in its wake. The deaths were glorious. Every one fed her within, strengthening Ereshkigal and supplying the rudimentary genetic material for her to finish her birth that had begun with the dragon's tooth in the hand of that vodun madman, Papa Hurbon.

Around her, a city was committing suicide in the ultimate proof of her perfect mathematical reasoning.

Close by, the cattle pens were being opened in preparation for turning man's city over to the animals, to the wild.

THERE WAS RUMBLING at the very edge of Kane's consciousness, like thunder over the desert. It woke Kane up. He was the first to awaken. He felt like hell. His head ached, his back and shoulders felt cramped and it hurt when he breathed. But he was alive.

The rumbling thunder was still distant, a low drumming punctuated by the sudden chime of a hundred church bells all around the city.

He was lying on something soft. A body. No, a leg. Brigid's leg, black-clad, the holstered TP-9 digging into his flank. Kane moved, hissing breath through clenched teeth, until he was free of the obstruction.

"Sorry," he muttered.

Was the rumbling getting louder? It was hard to be certain, his head was throbbing so much.

He was in the rear of the crashed Wheelfox, which was lurching now to one side, cobwebs of ruin marring the windows. The light from those windows seemed bright, and Kane took a moment to squint at it and catch his breath.

He began turning his head, regretted it, and turned it more slowly, taking a slow breath through his mouth. He wanted to vomit.

Grant, Brigid and Shizuka were strewn about the cabin, Shizuka slumped against Grant's hulking body, Baptiste jammed up against a window with her legs at an awkward angle across two seats, left foot twisted. None of them were moving.

"Hey," Kane called, in a voice that sounded gratingly loud to his own ears. "Hey? Anyone awake? Anyone?"

No one answered, and Kane took a moment to study his allies. They seemed to be breathing; whatever had saved him had maybe saved them, too. Thirty feet is a long way to drop. Thirty feet in a metal box with wheels…? That could either be better or worse depending on what happens to the metal box.

Distant rumble, desert thunder, getting closer. Closer. Closer.

Kane moved slowly, scenting the air. No smoke anyway. Nothing was on fire.

He leaned forward and peered through the grille partition between the passenger area and the cab. The windshield looked like a mosaic made of broken ice; everything seen through it was like looking at a reflection in a shattered mirror.

He saw that both driver and passenger had been flung forward so that they pulled at their safety belts. There was a smear of blood on the windshield on the driver's side. Neither of them was moving.

"Wake up," Kane said. "Hey, wake up."

There was a murmur from behind him. "You okay?" he asked, not knowing to whom he was addressing the question.

"Kane-san?" Shizuka's voice cracked as she spoke, and when Kane saw her in the darkness of the rear, her hair was in disarray across her face, like an old-time shampoo ad.

"Shizuka," Kane began, struggling for a moment to bring her name to the front of his brain. "We crashed, I think. You okay?"

The distant rumbling was louder now, closer.

Shizuka said something in Japanese, pushing her hair from her face. "Back hurts," she said.

"Bad?"

"Won't know until I try to walk," she admitted. "What happened?"

"Kane, that you chatting up my girl?" Grant spoke, his voice a deep rumble.

Kane laughed in a kind of snort of breath. "Yeah, you all right, pal?"

"I think so, yeah," Grant said, shifting in his seat. "Feels like we hit a wall."

"We did," Kane told him, "straight through and out the other side."

"Yeah, now I remember," Grant said with reluctance.

The rumble was loud now, like buildings falling down, bricks thumping against the ground like a waterfall torrent.

Kane pushed at the door to his right. It was locked, standard precaution when traveling in the back of a Magistrate transport. "We need to get out of here," Kane said, "but the doors are locked."

Grant worked the handle on the one to his left, flipping it up and down to no avail. "We need someone in front to work the release," he said.

"Pretors?" Kane began. "Corcel? Emiliana? You guys a—wake?" He almost said *alive*, but thought better of it. Nothing.

Beside Kane, Brigid stirred and mumbled something unintelligible.

"Hey, Baptiste, welcome to the party," Kane greeted her.

She looked at him through lidded eyes. "What happened?"

"Went through a wall and fell two or three stories to the ground," Kane summarized. "Vehicle's immobilized, doors are locked. We're trapped."

Brigid said something in Spanish, tapping on the partition between the driver's area and the rear of the Wheelfox. No one responded.

She turned back to Kane. "No backup system that only Magistrates know?"

"I know Sandcats," Kane admitted, "but I don't know

these local knockoffs." He glanced around the passenger area, running his finger along the seams, but nothing revealed itself. "Looks like we're trapped here for now."

Outside, through the fractured spiderweb of glass, they could see figures moving, walking with eerie purpose toward a destination unknown. The rumbling was loud now, hard to ignore. The bells of Zaragoza continued their lethargic chime, one beat every fifty-two seconds. Brigid tried working the catch on the door while Grant put his back to the seat and tried kicking open the door on the other side. The vehicle was durable, and nothing broke free.

Then there came a groan from the cab, and the Cerberus rebels and Shizuka looked up hopefully. It was Cáscara. She was rubbing her hand gently at her face. "Wha…?"

"Pretor, you hear me?" Kane asked, then Brigid repeated the words in Spanish.

"What happened?" Cáscara asked, her voice sounding woozy. "Juan? Are you—" She stopped, staring at the body of her partner where he was pulled taut against his safety belt. His head was cut open and there was dark, drying blood on his forehead. Cáscara reached across and touched Corcel, stroking his arm. He did not react, did not move. His fracturing eyes were open and staring into nothingness.

"We need to get out of here, right now," Kane insisted. "Don't you hear that?"

The rumbling, like thunder overhead.

Cáscara muttered something—perhaps it was a prayer—biting on her knuckles and stroking Corcel's arm once again.

"I think your partner was possessed by whatever has taken control of the city," Brigid concluded.

"Sí."

Cáscara fumbled around the dash for a few seconds,

reaching past her partner's dead form and toggling a switch on the steering column. There was a click, and the rear doors were unlocked.

Kane pushed at his door, while the others waited. Outside the thunder was deafening, only it wasn't thunder—it was the sound of almost fifty hooves stamping against the ground in a stampede. Kane saw the movement at the far end of the street, a line of black-brown, wavering and getting closer.

Up front in the Wheelfox, Cáscara had worked her own gull-wing door and eased herself out of her seat. She planted her feet on the sidewalk, standing a little woozily.

"You see that?" Kane asked, pointing to the movement in the distance.

"Bulls," Cáscara said, her voice two octaves higher than Kane had heard before. "We have to— Help me… You must… Juan…" She was reaching into the Wheelfox, grabbing for her partner's safety belt and trying to loosen its catch.

"Leave him," Kane said, "there's no time."

The others had exited the Wheelfox via the same door as Kane. With the way that the vehicle was lurching, it was easier that way.

Kane and Cáscara were watching the charging bulls, a dozen in all, their angry heads down, horns pointed toward them, bobbing up and down as they came ever closer. "Move, people, move!" Kane commanded.

"The Hall of Justice," Cáscara said, leading the way toward the steps of the building.

Grant and Shizuka followed along with Kane, trotting along swiftly, glancing over their shoulders.

Brigid tried to hurry, too, but her ankle bent and she staggered with a cry of pain.

Kane stopped, glancing back. "Baptiste? What is it?"

"My leg," Brigid replied, leaning down to press against her ankle.

And then the wave of stampeding bulls was upon them, charging down the street like a hurricane.

Chapter 29

The rumble of stampeding feet was deafening. Brigid did not know where to look because there were the angry, flat faces of bulls everywhere, moving like a wall in one of those old-time adventure serials.

Kane grabbed her by the waist, plucking her up as if she weighed nothing. Brigid was thrown back with the grab, and she found herself hanging from Kane's arms as he ran away from the charging stampede, watching everything upside down as that wall of dark faces glared at her, seeing red.

Then Kane leaped, vaulting onto the hood of the crashed Wheelfox transport, running up its sloping windshield as the bulls reached their position. He stopped when he reached the roof, standing there, panting for breath with Brigid in his arms. Less than a foot below them, the tops of the bulls came charging past, splitting like a river meeting an obstruction as they reached the fallen Wheelfox.

Brigid closed her eyes a moment and let the wave of panic subside while all around her the rumble of thundering feet echoed from the hard surface of every building.

The wave lasted ten seconds, maybe less. Surreally, the church bells of Zaragoza chimed once more in the middle of it all as a wave of angry bulls who had once been used for entertainment hurried past with all the grace of a raging river.

As the bulls passed, Kane looked down at Brigid's face,

her skin pale, the vibrant red hair catching in the wind. "Turning into a damsel in distress, Baptiste?" he asked.

Brigid opened her eyes, two fierce emerald orbs glaring into Kane's. "How many times have I saved your ass? How many times *this month*? *This week?*"

"I don't keep count," Kane told her.

"Think you can give me this one then?" Brigid asked. Was it anger or wounded pride in her tone? Kane wondered.

"What happened back there?" he asked.

"My ankle gave way," Brigid told him as he gently set her down on the roof of the Wheelfox. "The shadow suits likely protected us from that drop, but I must have twisted something in the impact."

"I guess," Kane agreed. "I'm benching you until—"

"No!" Brigid insisted. She tried putting weight on her foot, huffed painfully and shook her head. "If I go slow I'll be fine," she said. "Just don't ask me to vault any high walls."

"I'll keep that in mind," Kane said, helping Brigid down from the roof of the car.

Cáscara, Grant and Shizuka were standing on the steps of the Hall of Justice, its walls blackened where the bomb blast had gone off just a few hours before. Seeing that damage made Grant realize just how quickly things had been moving. It was kind of insane.

"Are you all right?" Cáscara asked in her beautifully accented English. "Was it the fall?"

Brigid nodded. "Armor-weave uniforms," she explained, referring obliquely to the shadow suits that all but Shizuka wore. Shizuka had been lucky that she had been in the rearmost seat when the Wheelfox had made its swan dive; the others had cushioned her from the fall. "But I must have landed badly."

Cáscara led the way up the steps that led into the Hall of

Justice. Kane helped Brigid up the steps, and she favored her right leg as she struggled to join the others.

"Juan's dead," Cáscara told Shizuka as she led the way inside. "He's free of it now."

Shizuka nodded. "He was a good man. I'm sorry."

INSIDE, THE ENTRY lobby to the Hall of Justice looked like a butcher's store at the end of the day. There were three dead bodies, including the desk sergeant, and blood was smeared across the broken glass in the door leading to the main building, where two more bodies lay. The door was open.

"That should be locked," Cáscara said, trotting forward urgently.

Grant was through the lobby and behind the female Pretor by then, a grim expression on his face. He held his Sin Eater ready. "We're behind you," he assured her. He knew what it was to be a Magistrate and to lose brothers-in-arms. The woman had just lost her partner and then to come face-to-face with this had to be hard to take in.

With Cáscara leading the way, the five-strong group hurried up the stairs toward the squad room. A Pretor lay across the banisters from the upper level, slumped over with blood painted across his helmet. The helmet's visor was shattered.

"Damn bloodbath," Kane muttered as he followed Grant and Cáscara to the second story.

Cáscara pulled up short as she pushed through the door into the squad room. There were four Pretors there, each one working on the carcasses of anyone else who remained.

"Welcome to death ville," Grant muttered as he peered over Cáscara's shoulder.

The Pretors turned, sighting the new people with their burning sparks of life.

"Corpses for my mistress," they repeated, the chant now familiar to Grant even when spoken in a foreign tongue.

"Corpse this!" Grant replied, bringing his Sin Eater up in a swift arc until it pointed over Cáscara's shoulder. His finger pressed against the trigger even as the barrel cleared Cáscara's arm, and a rapid burst of fire cut through the room.

A flurry of 9 mm bullets whipped through the air, cutting into the closest of the dead Pretors—the man once known as Cadalso but who no longer had a concept of the individual—and tearing into the flexible, bloodstained armor he wore across his chest.

"Grant, no!" Cáscara shouted even as the dead Pretor went crashing backward into a nearby desk. "They're Pretors."

"Don't you get it?" Grant snapped as Cáscara grabbed his wrist to throw his aim. "They're dead already, Cáscara. All we can do now is try to make them realize it."

Cáscara's face was screwed up in anger as she glared at Grant, but she was distracted from her response by the sounds of weapons being drawn in the room before her. The three Pretors who remained standing—their names once de Centina, Ruiz and Bazán but now just "the devoted"—were drawing their Devorador de Pecados blasters from the hidden sheaths that ran up their forearms. The thirteen-inch barrels extended even as the weapons materialized from their holsters, and in a fraction of a second all three blasters were firing, sending a triple burst of bullets toward the doorway where Cáscara and Grant were standing.

"Get back!" Cáscara shouted, pushing Grant out through the door, back into the stairwell. She threw herself in the other direction, tumbling into the squad room in a swift tuck and roll. The bullets peppered the walls and door where she and Grant had been just a moment before, cutting perfectly circular trails of destruction.

The heavy door on the stairs slammed closed as Grant came tumbling through and he heard the bullets riddle against its other side.

Shizuka was the first to reach his side. "Grant-san, what is it?" she asked, even as their other companions hurried up the stairs to join them.

"Magistrates," Grant summarized. "Dead ones. With guns."

Kane cursed.

"Emiliana's still in there," Grant said, picking himself up from the floor and reaching for the door. "Need to get in there and—" He stopped.

"What is it?" Shizuka asked.

"Door's jammed," Grant said, pushing against it. "No, not jammed—locked."

"Must be a security feature," Brigid proposed. A moment later she spotted the unobtrusive metal box that was attached to the wall across from the door, perfectly in line with it. "There, see?"

"What is that?" Shizuka asked.

"Chip reader," Brigid explained. "Scans subjects as they pass it, unlocks the door for people with the right authority."

"Meanwhile the rest of us are stuck outside twiddling our thumbs," Kane lamented.

"Maybe not," Grant said, plucking the blue shield badge from his belt. He waved it across the reader several times but it did not respond. Clearly, his clearance was not high enough.

Beside him, Shizuka was glancing up and down the stairwell, trying to envisage another way inside.

CÁSCARA SCOOTED ACROSS the floor of the squad room on her backside as shots whipped past overhead. There were four opponents here, she knew, four that she had seen anyway. She needed something quick to disarm them and put them out of commission.

Kane used light, she realized. If they couldn't be reasoned with, then she would have to find some way to replicate his defense.

She needed to get the Pretor reports to try to figure out the pattern of what was going on—if there even was a pattern.

She was behind one of twelve desks located in the squad room, crouching with the chair by her side. There was a dead body on the chair, a Pretor called Drid with whom she had shared a break or two over the past six months. He was a good guy, one sugar in his coffee, and now he was dead.

The shots had stopped. Cáscara could hear booted feet pacing across the room, spreading out in a practiced sweep pattern, the kind she had been taught back in training. It was now or never.

"Pretors, I'm one of you," Cáscara announced from her temporary hiding place. "Here—" and she showed them her shield, holding it above the surface of the desk, having unclipped it from her belt.

The response—a familiar boom of gunfire as two of the Pretors took a shot at her hand.

Cáscara screamed as the shield was hit with a bullet, and she managed to get her hand out of the path of the gunfire just in time. Her fingers felt singed where the shield had been kicked out of her hand by the bullet.

"Okay," Cáscara muttered to herself. "Don't say I didn't try." Then she commanded her Devorador de Pecados pistol back into her hand, crouch-walking across the squad room as the dead Pretors approached.

Cáscara scrambled under the knee space of a desk, crouching there where she could see the other desk she had been hiding behind. Three of the Pretors stopped at the desk, guns trained and ready, sweeping the area for her even as they discovered that she had gone. She recognized them all. The women were Ruiz and Bazán, street patrol Pretors who were both quite new to the service, while the man was an older Pretor called de Centina. The uniform across Ruiz's chest was stretched taut around a mess of dried blood, her flesh visible through the rent. The flesh at the edge of the wound seemed to sparkle, as if glitter had been poured there, and her left arm seemed to bend at a strange angle, as if it had been oddly extended by botched surgery.

De Centina had his helmet removed, leaving his face exposed. His eyes were wide, their irises indistinct, as if they were losing integrity. His face showed the scarring where he had fought with cancer a few years before. Now that scar was wide and dark, oozing with glistening beads of whiteness, like stars inside his face. Whatever had taken possession of these people had reignited the cancer and added to it, Cáscara saw, eating up de Centina from within.

Cáscara poked out from the knee space, bringing her pistol to bear on de Centina. She had liked the old hand—everyone in the division knew and liked him, in fact—and she couldn't bear to see him like this, with his face ravaged with living cancer. She took careful aim and squeezed the trigger, closing her eyes as the bullet exited the blaster's barrel.

De Centina went down in an explosion of flesh and bone, his already ruined face rent apart by the 9 mm slug.

The other Pretors turned, and Cáscara leaped from her hiding place and blasted, sending a triple burst of fire at the dead woman called Bazán. The bullets struck in a rising arc—gut, chest, head—and Bazán stumbled backward amid a cascade of her strawberry blond hair.

Dead Ruiz blasted at Cáscara, who was leaping over the nearest desk to gain some distance. The bullet struck

Cáscara in the right thigh and she felt her balance go even as she slid across the desk and over the side.

"Dammit," Cáscara muttered, feeling the burn at her thigh like a poker.

Didn't matter. She had to keep moving, get the reports and get out.

Cáscara looked around, searching desperately for some weapon to use against the dead Pretors, some way to get the jump on them. Across the room, Cadalso, the man whom Grant had shot less than a minute before, was pulling himself up off the floor. His face was smeared with blood and his eyes had that pale, bled-out look that she had observed in the other victims of Ereshkigal; the one Corcel had begun to exhibit in the end. Behind Cáscara, Ruiz was striding purposefully across the room, her pistol held ready before her as she stalked her prey, over-length left arm hanging limply at her side like a child's lopsided drawing. Living prey in a city of the dead. The beautiful, dark-haired Pretor was trapped on all sides.

Trapped, but not helpless.

Cáscara raised her pistol and fired, targeting the bright red fire extinguisher that resided by the door to the squad room. The moment that the bullet pierced its metal shell, the pressurized gas within blasted outward with supreme force, sending the extinguisher rocketing across the room and knocking Ruiz off her feet with a *clang*.

Cáscara selected her second target, blasting a light fixture above Cadalso's head. It was a fluorescent tube strip light, and the bullet shattered its facade in a burst of lightning-bright sparks. Cadalso was momentarily blinded, shrieking like an animal as the tube light fell from its fittings and struck him across the face.

Cáscara leaped up, shrieking in pain at the bullet wound in her thigh. She ran, a kind of hobble-run, but a run just the same, through the squad door and into the incident

room that was located beside it. There were two more
dead bodies out here, a Pretor and a civilian. There was
a map on the wall of the room, showing the city of Zaragoza with the streets marked in different colors, and beside
that a second map, roughly the same size but showing the
local area surrounding the city. A DDC computer terminal waited on a desk in front of the wall of maps. There
were also rows of chairs arranged in a semicircle, and a
desk to one side with a coffee percolator whose contents
were a dark sludge, a window on the far side of the room
overlooking the service road behind the Hall of Justice.
The room was unoccupied.

Cáscara turned and slammed the door, locking it before striding over to the computer terminal. She tapped a
key and the screen came to life.

She typed in her pass code and then made a request to
see recent reports. A whole list of incidents appeared on
screen, running in reverse time order—the most recent
appearing as the highest on the list.

Which to look at? she wondered.

She stood there a moment, biting her lip as something
tried the door handle.

De Centina!

The thought came to Pretor Cáscara then, inspired by
the action in the squad room. She tapped in another query,
brought up the rota for de Centina. He had been posted on
the south gate of the city, she saw.

Behind her, the door handle rattled again, firmer this
time, followed a crash as someone tried to force the door.

Cáscara's fingers rushed across the computer keys, adding search terms as she hunted for the possible source of an
incursion at the south end of the city. Nothing obvious appeared, but something else caught her eye. A Pretor patrol
squad—a three-man crew with over twenty years' experience between them—had failed to report in after a stan-

dard recce to the southwest of the city. It could be nothing, she knew, but coulds and woulds and shoulds were the things that detective work was made of. She tapped in the command to bring up their patrol route.

OUTSIDE THE SQUAD ROOM, Shizuka and the Cerberus warriors were feeling helpless to assist their ally. Kane had tried a half-dozen times to batter the door down but it stayed rigid, designed to survive a terrorist attack.

Grant and Shizuka climbed up the stairs to look for another way in, leaving Kane and Brigid alone, listening to the sounds of chaos outside the building.

Kane took those moments to check Brigid's ankle. He had been a Magistrate once, and while it was certainly not his area of expertise, he knew a little basic field medicine, enough to strap up Brigid's ankle to help her walk on it, using the sleeve torn from his own jacket as a makeshift support.

"I think it'll hold for a while," Kane promised Brigid. They shared a bond, these two, the *anam-chara* link of soul friends. It was in moments like this, when Kane would suddenly drop everything just to ensure Brigid's safety, that that link seemed to express itself.

"I'm going to slow you down," Brigid pointed out.

Kane met Brigid's eyes, fixing her with a look. "There's more to life than running," he told her. "Now, what do you think Ereshkigal's grand plan is? What's her objective?"

Brigid shook her head. "How would I know?" she said.

"You're the smartest person around," Kane told her. "Think."

Brigid stared into the middle distance for a few seconds, recalling the strange vision of the woman they had spied amid the mob, trusting the perfect recollection of her eidetic memory. "She's unfinished," she said. "Not yet Annunaki."

"You're right, she looked human," Kane said. "Kinda."

"Grant said she was human when he first met her," Brigid reminded him, "but now she's begun to change. Change doesn't happen, it's triggered. It needs some kind of external input to make it occur. You remember the way the Annunaki first reappeared, with the genetic download from *Tiamat*?"

"Yeah."

"Like that," Brigid said.

"*Tiamat*'s dead," Kane pointed out. He had been there at the destruction of the dragon ship, not once but twice, the second time on the banks of the River Euphrates where the great starship had been reforming only to rot from within.

"Even the dead give life to something," Brigid said reasonably. "The worms, the maggots—things thrive on death, even humans."

"New life from old," Kane mused.

"Exactly," Brigid said, "and what could be more Annunaki than *that*? So what if Ereshkigal needs protein, those genetic building blocks from the dead to re-create her own body? What if that's why she's killing everyone?"

"But so many people?" Kane asked and stopped himself as he answered, "Sure, why not? When have the Annunaki ever done anything small-scale?"

Brigid nodded in realization. "It's just like the ancient myths said. She's harvesting the dead, Kane, using them to make herself more powerful."

Chapter 30

Grant found an open window higher up the stairwell. It was not wide enough for him to fit through, but Shizuka, whose petite frame was far smaller than his, found that she could slither her way through it with a little judicious contortion.

Outside was a ledge, two inches wide and overlooking the service road behind the building. Shizuka stood there, two stories off the ground, waiting as Grant passed through the stash of flash-bangs that Brigid and Kane had shared.

"Kane found that these can blind those pre-grave dead folks," Grant explained. "I'll look for another entry. Find a window, a way in, and do whatever it takes to get Cáscara out alive."

"Will do," Shizuka assured him.

"And, Shizuka? Be careful."

"Always," Shizuka said, reaching across from the ledge for a pitted section of wall cladding. A moment later she was gone, traversing the wall in spider fashion until she reached a window lower than Grant could see. She tried it, found it locked and moved on, spanning the surface of the building in rapid fashion.

Cáscara brought up the last report from Casillas and his team, the group of Pretors who had been running a patrol outside the city walls to the southwest of Zaragoza.

A map appeared on the computer screen, indicating their route, including their location when they had filed their last report.

Beside her, the door was rattling in its frame, and Cáscara could hear the report of a gun as someone tried to blast the lock to smithereens.

She watched the door for a moment, praying that it would hold just a little longer. These dead men were drawn to the living the way sharks scented blood. She could not hope to escape them for long.

The beautiful Pretor scanned the report, searching for clues as to where Ereshkigal had come from. Maybe she could help Corcel. She felt certain that the source was outside the city. The appearance of the reanimated gate guards here in the Hall of Justice, their use in destroying the Pretors, hinted as much. Putting that evidence together with the loss of contact with Casillas and his squad suggested that something had entered the city from the south.

At that moment the door gave, and a Pretor came marching into the room with his blaster raised. It was Cadalso. The visor of his helmet was red with blood and there were pockmarks across his breast where he had been shot more than once.

Cáscara dropped to the floor as Cadalso's blaster fired, using the desk as scant cover from the assault. Behind Cadalso, a second dead Pretor was entering the room, the strawberry blond Bazán, her helmet now askew and blood marring her hair.

"Corpses! Corpses for the mistress!" the two Pretors chanted as they fired their blasters.

And then the window exploded in a shower of glass and a burst of sunlight radiance, the illumination casting the room into stark whites and defined shadows accompanied by a near-deafening boom.

Cáscara blinked back the pain in her eyes, spots running across her vision so that she could barely see around them.

Shizuka followed the flash-bang, drawing her katana in an effortless, graceful move, and launching herself across the room like a missile.

The reanimated corpses were writhing in agony where the flash-bang had assaulted their deteriorating eyes even behind tinted visors; eyes whose ocular nerves had had to be reknitted to join the brain after death.

Shizuka struck them in a blur of motion, cutting the man down with a brutal slash across his belly before following the move through so that her sword tip ended embedded in the gut of the woman. She withdrew the blade in an instant as both the dead figures fell back, blood blurting from between their teeth as they collapsed to the floor, eyes screwed shut tight behind their visors.

There were more outside, Shizuka saw. Two figures, both dressed in the uniforms of Pretors, one displaying a terrible facial disfigurement, came hurrying toward the doorway, their Devorador de Pecados pistols raised and ready to fire.

Shizuka stepped forward, bringing her sword up as the first of the bullets launched. She cut the bullet from the air, leaping across the confines of the corridor and slapping at the far wall with her free hand as a second bullet glanced past her. The graceful samurai warrior used that slap to propel her whole body up into the air, legs windmilling as she left the floor.

Another bullet fired from Ruiz's blaster, rocketing down the corridor with the clap of explosive propellant. Shizuka was higher than the bullet, flipping her whole body over until her left foot struck the ceiling. The light fitting there came tumbling down with a flicker, while Shizuka used her momentum to drive herself down and forward, shooting toward cancer-faced de Centina like a javelin.

She struck him sword-first in the chest. The sword pierced the armor weave of de Centina's uniform, and was followed by the full weight of Shizuka as she barreled into him, driving a vicious punch to his jaw.

De Centina went down, crashing to the floor in a heap while Shizuka leaped free of his falling body. Shizuka was on her feet in an instant, running at the other Pretor, the reanimated figure of Ruiz, whose pixie-short hair was losing its luster the longer she spent not breathing. As she ran, Shizuka set the second flash-bang she had been carrying when she entered, twisting its trigger so that it detonated the very second it left her hand.

For an instant, the whole corridor was bathed in brilliance, accompanied by a thunderous roar of noise.

Ruiz's blaster fired again during that moment, sending a burst of fire in Shizuka's direction as the samurai woman hurtled toward her. The bullets went wide, missing Shizuka by inches. And then Shizuka was on the dead woman, driving her katana through the dazzled Pretor's chest just below the breastbone, pushing upward to pierce lungs and heart.

Shizuka snapped back, drawing the sword from its sheath of flesh with a flourish. In its wake, Ruiz's body—already dead but reanimated by the mad mathematics of Ereshkigal—started to divide, two halves falling away from one another and revealing a gaping chest wound.

There was no time to celebrate. Shizuka was back through the door to the incident room, calling to Cáscara, her sword catching in the sparking light of the shattered overhead.

"We need to go," Shizuka stated breathlessly.

Cáscara pulled herself from the floor, wincing from her hip wound and rubbing at her eyes where she could still see spots. "Agreed," she said, making her way over to the computer terminal once more.

"What are you—" Shizuka asked.

Cáscara reached for the printer that was located beside the terminal, taking the single-sheet report she had printed earlier. "All done. Let's go," she said, snapping up the report.

A moment later, the two women were hurrying through the ruined squad room toward the sealed door that opened onto the staircase, Cáscara moving as fast as she could with the wound in her leg. Behind them, the sounds of moving bodies—dead but somehow alive—could be heard as four dead Pretors struggled to right the damage to their bodies and give chase to the beacons of life. Shizuka was determined that they would not get the chance.

THEY REGROUPED IN the stairwell, with Shizuka, Cáscara and Brigid hurrying back to street level as fast as their wounds would let them while Kane and Grant broke the door frame so that the door could not be easily opened again from within—it would provide a meager defense.

Downstairs, the lobby remained eerily empty, just dead bodies and shed blood, all color seemingly drained from the atmosphere.

"They must have come in as Pretors," Cáscara lamented, "known and trusted as they were, and committed a massacre before anyone realized what was happening."

Brigid looked at her with sympathy. "There was nothing that you or your partner could have done," she said. "If you'd been here you would have simply been caught up in it."

"I know," Cáscara said, nodding. "So much death, it's just hard to process."

Brigid agreed. She had seen a lot of death—too much, wherever the Cerberus warriors were called. This time they appeared to have lost a city.

Kane and Grant joined the women in the lobby, confirming that they had sealed the level. It was a temporary measure, Kane lamented, but so much of what they did where the Annunaki was concerned had proven to be just that.

"I think this thing, this Ereshkigal, came from the southwest," Cáscara said, "beyond the city."

"Any reason you think that?" Grant asked.

"I think she infiltrated through the south gate," Cáscara said. "I checked where the people in the squad room were posted. A patrol disappeared out there this morning. I suspect that it's all connected." She showed the others the map she had printed out, which showed the route of the Casillas patrol.

"So we follow the route?" Grant asked.

"And see what we find," Brigid said, nodding. "It makes sense." She turned away and fired up her Commtact, and a moment later she was requesting Cerberus headquarters provide some satellite surveillance of the route in question.

Kane looked over the map. "Looks like a whole lot of nothing to me," he said. "How do you propose we get out there?"

"Sandcat maybe," Cáscara said. Then she cursed, realization dawning. "The keys are up there, in the squad room."

"Your Wheelfox is still outside," Grant reminded her. "Keys are still in it, I guess."

Cáscara looked uncertain. For one thing, the vehicle had been badly damaged in its would-be death plunge. For another, her dead partner was still sitting in the driver's seat. Pros and cons, then. Something clicked into place in her mind and she nodded. "We're out of options," she said. "Let's go see whether she'll still run."

Chapter 31

Back at Cerberus headquarters, Donald Bry worked the satellite surveillance software, following Brigid's instructions. He set the Vela-class reconnaissance satellite to sweep the area to the south and west of Zaragoza, searching for anything out of the ordinary. It did not take long to find a likely target.

THE CERBERUS TEAM, Shizuka and Cáscara were inside the Wheelfox, bashed, battered and generally the worse for wear but still operational even after its drop from the high levels of the multistory parking garage. The vehicle had started on the first try, and now Cáscara was working the pedals, navigating her way through the dead streets of Zaragoza, her eyes fixed on the road through a gap in the cracked windshield. The chimes of the church bells had stopped, and the streets seemed too empty now, the husk of something that had once nurtured life.

The dead body of Cáscara's partner, Juan Corcel, had been sat up in one of the rear seats. Cáscara had refused to leave him behind; she said that the man deserved a proper burial.

Kane was up front with Cáscara as Donald Bry's message came through.

"I've found something approximately twenty-five miles south of the city walls," Bry stated. "Looks like a stream, but it's not marked on any maps. Furthermore, the stream is a rust color."

"Rust?" Kane questioned.

"Like…red," Bry elaborated. "The stream leads to a—well, I'm not sure what to call it—looks sort of like a flower, only it's big."

"How big, Donald?"

"Sense of scale is difficult to judge where it's surrounded by scrub," Bry admitted, "but it looks to be as big as a building."

"But you said it's a flower?"

"That's right, Kane," Bry confirmed. "At least, I think it is."

"That's one big-ass flower," Grant rumbled; he, too, shared the open frequency.

Cáscara passed through the south gate, still open from where Ereshkigal had entered with her demented retainers, before speeding out of the city. Beyond, the great dusty plains of northern Spain stretched in a gradually undulating landscape. "Your people find something?" she asked, glancing across to Kane where he sat beside her.

"Sounds like it," Kane said. "Bry, you want to give us some coordinates on this thing?"

AT HIS POST in the Cerberus ops room, Donald Bry brought up the telemetry for Kane's transponder and expanded the map on his screen until he could place him in relation to the flowerlike structure. "Keep heading south, follow the road you're on for two miles, then cut right at the pass. I'll guide you in."

KANE SHARED THE info with Cáscara as she navigated the slick ribbon of road.

"Do you have any idea what's waiting out there?" she asked.

"Trouble," Kane told her. "Trust me, it always is."

THE ROADS WERE EMPTY. Here and there, the dented Wheelfox passed a parked wag or a line of scrappy tents, but for the most part it was wasteland out here, the same way it had been for the past two hundred years since the radiation had leaked across the continent.

Donald Bry gave directions, following the Cerberus field team's progress in real time via satellite and biolink transponder. When they neared the mysterious flower, he instructed them to go off-road so that they could reach it. "That's all the assistance I can give you, guys," he said apologetically, "but I'll keep monitoring the situation, and if there's anything you need from me, let me know."

The Wheelfox bumped off-road and over the dusty terrain. The earth was a kind of washed-out golden color here, with scrubby lines of tenacious grass sprouting in scattered clumps across the landscape.

The Wheelfox bumped over a ridge and suddenly the colossal flower came into view. It stood poised silently amid the wastes, a narrow stream of red blood washing toward it. The stream was no wider than a man's spread legs, and along its edges a line of stakes had been forced into the ground, upon which hung the limp forms of people—some of them Pretors—their exquisitely cut bodies dripping blood into the stream to fill it. The flower's black petals folded together like a crocus, blue veins running up the center of each sloping petal and highlighting their rims. Each petal was as large as a house.

"What the hell is that?" Grant asked as the flower loomed before them, framed in the rectangle of the windshield.

"Organic technology," Brigid said, "an Annunaki specialty."

"I think we could have found this without the satellite," Kane muttered.

Cáscara eased off the accelerator, slowing the Wheelfox

and causing dirt to shift noisily beneath its drive wheel. "They've grown a flower to live in?" she asked, incredulous.

"The Annunaki pull a lot of incredible shit," Kane told her wearily.

Brigid elaborated, "They're masters of combining mechanical principles with a self-expanding system."

As they proceeded forward, something metal glinted in the sunlight to one side of the giant flower structure. The Wheelfox pulled to a halt with a whine of brakes as Cáscara recognized what it was. It was a Sandcat, marked in Pretor colors with the Zaragoza city shield on the side. The vehicle was empty, partially buried in the sand with its doors open. It would not have been left like that, Cáscara knew, unless something urgent had called its occupants away. Her heart sank at the thought—it was the missing patrol, Casillas and his team. Dead then, evidently.

"What now?" Cáscara asked. She was clearly struggling to process what she had seen and learned in the past thirty seconds.

Before anyone could answer, Ereshkigal appeared on the far rise, leading a group of at least thirty people, many of whom looked ragged and were scarred with dirt and blood. They followed the line of the artificial stream, and the people in the Wheelfox watched in horror as people willingly planted themselves on those upthrust stakes, pushing the old blood-letters aside and forcing the points into their bodies, cutting themselves so that they could add their blood to the river.

With her two assistants beside her, Ereshkigal disappeared into the flower, a dozen people in her mental thrall following while the rest assumed their places on the blood river.

"Time to finish this," Grant said. No one in the vehicle objected.

KANE, GRANT AND Shizuka exited the Wheelfox together
and made their way toward the sprawling structure down
the slope. Brigid and Cáscara waited behind, both of them
suffering from the wounds they had received and concerned that they might prove a burden.

"I'll stay in touch with Baptiste," Kane assured them
both, "let you know what's in there."

A flat plain of dirt led up to the flower itself, a tunnel-
like entryway visible where two of the mammoth leaves
met.

Kane paced ahead, his reloaded Sin Eater ready in his
hand while Grant and Shizuka followed, he with his Sin
Eater, she with her katana sword held tightly in her right
hand. Kane stopped before the entrance, peering into the
darkness and listening intently, trusting his fabled point-
man sense. He could hear uncertain noises like singing,
voices droning together in a slow dirge like a funeral
hymn. There was a smell emanating from within the tunnel like decomposing mulch. But nothing else, no hint of
guards or any other threat.

Before he entered, Kane glanced back at his companions and smiled grimly, running his index finger along the
side of his nose in the one-percent salute. The salute was
a superstition shared by Kane and Grant and dating back
to their days as Magistrates in Cobaltville. It referred to
the fact that no matter how much they might try to make
a situation safe, there was always that one percent margin
of error, where the unknown might come to surprise them.
It reminded both men to stay on their guard.

The entry was wide enough for two men and led into
a tall, narrow tunnel with sloping sides that reached up
toward an arch-like apex. Kane walked warily ahead,
his blaster held ready. It was dark within, the walls lit
by veins that glowed red. Kane described it in a whisper
over the Commtacts, and Brigid proposed that it might

be a type of luminescent lichen. It reminded Kane of something else, however—a period barely a year before when the Cerberus redoubt had been remodeled by an enemy who could control stone. The familiar walls of the redoubt had been charged with volcanic lava, casting the once-secure base in a hellish red hue. Disdainfully, Kane pushed the memory aside, the funereal dirge echoing faintly from up ahead, voices of men and women groaning out the unclear words.

Grant and Shizuka entered after Kane, moving slowly, their weapons ready.

The tunnel stretched twenty feet before opening out into a grand chamber, the light of a pool reflecting in silver flickers across the veined ceiling at the tunnel's end. Kane stopped at the mouth of the tunnel and peered out, seeing Ereshkigal's lair for the first time.

A line of steps wound ten feet down into a vast, cavern-like chamber dominated by a pool of blood. Twisted pillars held the petal roof upright, colored the dark blue of the evening sky, knotted and gnarled like tree trunks. Figures were placing themselves beside those pillars, kneeling in supplication before their mistress. The singing was louder here, forming a bed of sound to the cavernous chamber. The singing came from the kneeling figures by the pillars, Kane saw. Their eyes were screwed tightly closed while their voices were raised in what sounded like wails of pain, strangely musical as the voices blurred in harmony, agony and ecstasy, two sides of the same coin.

In the center of the room, Ereshkigal had her back to Kane as she strode into the pool of blood, feet and ankles already disappeared beneath the surface as she entered via a hidden ramp or steps. Her tail of feathers ruffled behind her in the breeze, and several fluttered away even as Kane watched. There was a whole trail of bloody feathers dotted across the floor already, like strange markers.

Kane stepped out into the cavern, leading with his right foot and bringing the pistol poised out before him. As he stepped onto the first of the springy, leafy steps, something struck him from behind, and suddenly Kane found himself falling, tumbling end over end down the steps.

He rolled as he reached the bottom, bringing the Sin Eater up as something leaped from the topmost stair. It was a man, dark-skinned and bare-chested—one of Ereshkigal's Terror Priests. But there was something else about him—his torso seemed freakishly long, his limbs stretching impossibly out at his sides like the wings of some dreaded bird of prey.

The man was throwing something. Kane saw it flash in the air even as he rolled.

Kane fired.

A razor-edged disc, three inches in diameter, sliced through the remaining sleeve of Kane's jacket, tugging at the shadow suit beneath before embedding in the floor.

The man landed on top of Kane feetfirst, dropping his arms back to ensure he struck with the force of a missile. Kane grunted, the breath going out of him as he tried to absorb the blow. He fired again, uncertain whether his first bullet had hit or not.

The second bullet skimmed across the man's torso, burning a line across his developed right pectoral before disappearing into the darkness.

Grant was at the top of the steps now, and he lined up his pistol, waiting for a shot. "Come on, Kane," he muttered, "get clear."

One of the Terror Priest's arms came sweeping down in a wide arc toward Kane, momentum driving the punch as he delivered a blow across Kane's jaw. There was something in that hand, another metal disc, held between middle fingers and grazing Kane's jaw as it struck. A line of blood spewed from the cut as Kane sank backward, splashing into the blood pool where Ereshkigal bathed ten feet away.

Kane groaned, then kicked out, shifting his weight beneath the assailant who was poised astride him. His attacker was thrown back, stumbling into the steps that led down into this cavern, the razor disc sailing from his hand with a clang.

On the topmost step, Grant fired, delivering a single 9 mm slug into the stumbling figure's head. The man crumpled to the floor in an instant.

Across the room, the entrancing figure of Ereshkigal was standing within the pool, her head and torso revealed as the blood lapped at her slender hips. There was a smile on her face as she fixed Kane with her stare. Her lips moved and she began to speak the words of the chant designed to deliver the equation to the human body—the equation that could kill a man. Around her, the tempo of the funereal dirge seemed to rise.

"Círculo alrededor del cuerpo," she began, *"Guarda silencio a moverse más..."*

Chapter 32

Nippur, Mesopotamia
Circa forty-fifth century BC

Nergal was a respected apothecary of the Annunaki. His work had moved into the realms of investigative medicine and he had begun to develop a strand of chemical devices which might be used to either treat or kill the apekin. Enlil had charged him to develop something that might replicate the effects of a pandemic, the kind of plague that could wipe out a whole race. Nergal had extrapolated the data from a number of earthbound diseases, including ones that only affected the settler Annunaki. Thus, he had been annoyed when a messenger from Enlil's palace had arrived at his workplace with an invitation to attend a royal banquet one day before trial.

"Damn Enlil and his paranoias," Nergal hissed, shoving past the Igigu messenger who had recited the invitation. Nergal was an Annunaki of tall stature, thin and skeletal with scales that shimmered between dark red and jet black, a spiny back-slanting crest of red atop his head. The skin of his face was stretched drum-tight over strong, high cheekbones and thick brows, lending to his skeletal appearance. His fierce eyes shone like drops of burnished brass, vertical slits bisecting them. His workplace was clinically clean and he employed six Igigi retainers to probe and test various subjects under his guidance, supported by over fifty of the local humans. The Igigi employees looked up at Nergal's outburst, then swiftly back to their work when they saw the fury in his red-gold eyes. "Always checking up, always suspicious of whom one associates with."

The Igigu messenger who had brought the invitation, a squat, lizard-like humanoid with lusterless green scales and a paunch, bowed his head respectfully. "Am I to convey that as your good sir's response, my lord?" he asked.

Nergal glared at the messenger, suspecting he was being mocked. The Igigi had become all too independent of late; perhaps it was time to cull their number in a show that reminded them that while they may be demigods to the local apekin they were nothing but slaves to the Annunaki.

"No," Nergal growled. "Please tell Lord Enlil that I am honored and overjoyed that he has seen fit to invite me, and that I shall be only too pleased to attend."

"So, that's a yes," the Igigu messenger said, glancing up and hiding his smirk—though not quite quickly enough that Nergal did not suspect what he had seen.

Nergal's work would have to wait temporarily while he prepared for this pointless exercise in massaging Enlil's ego. Perhaps as his next project he would work on a disease to afflict the Igigi.

ENLIL'S PALACE WAS draped in swathes of fine cloth and its floors were scattered with rose petals on the day of the banquet. All of the great Annunaki lords attended—Marduk, Zu, the Lady Lilitu, and many others. Nergal cursed having to attend this pointless waste of time, for his research was at a critical stage. But something occurred to him as he scanned the group of attending lords and ladies—Ereshkigal had not been invited.

Nergal raised the point with one of the Igigi retainers and was pointed to a young Annunaki called Namtar, whose scales were a bronze-brown hue. "Ereshkigal was too immersed in her work to attend," the retainer explained, "and so she sent her vizier in her place."

Nergal was horrified. "Her vizier?" Namtar looked to be about fourteen, still a child. He knew Namtar by hearsay only; rumor around the royal court was that he was one of Enlil's progeny, no doubt that was why Enlil had allowed the child to take the place of his mistress. After all, Enlil would trust his own offspring—wouldn't he? *Perhaps,* thought Nergal, *it is time to remind Enlil of the powers I wield, though they be not kingdoms or armies.*

The banquet was a way for Lord Enlil to keep tabs on his fellow Annunaki, to check that they were not plotting against him—inevitably, they were—or trying to obtain control of the life circuits of the wombship, *Tiamat.* Which also, inevitably, they were. But while Enlil delved into the plans and peccadilloes of his fellow Annunaki, silently observing who was most comfortable with whom, whose conversations seemed forced or veiled in secret words and phrases, Nergal became increasingly annoyed that he was unable to return to his research. He took out his frustrations on Namtar during the three-day meal, cornering him while the other gods enjoyed and plotted.

"You have no right to be here, child," he snapped, clicking the long claws of his fingers together in a clack to release the hidden chemical agent he had secreted there. He watched in grim satisfaction as the chemical agent sprayed droplets over the other's skin, seeping unnoticed into his pores. "Your mistress insults us all in sending you in her stead, an insult that will not be forgotten."

Young Namtar looked at Nergal with a mixture of confusion and innocence. "My mother was busy, my lord," he placated, unaware that Nergal had introduced a nasty little poison into his system. "Better that I attend than that her chair be left empty."

"'Mother?'" Nergal repeated uncertainly. "Ereshkigal is your…mother?"

"Yes, my lord," Namtar said with a bow. To Nergal's horrified eyes the child was already looking off-color, though he knew rationally that his little touch of plague would not work so quickly.

BEING AWAY FROM the sunlight for so long had driven Ereshkigal mad. She had worked so long on her logic experiments that her eyes had gone dark. When she emerged, she saw not Annunaki but equations, things to be manipulated and formatted and balanced until they became new things, extrapolated from the old.

Rumor had it she had killed several young, stolen from their eggs, tested to destruction.

She emerged because of what had happened to her son, Namtar. She had discovered that he had been poisoned at Enlil's banquet, and though the child had survived he was desperately ill, his once-lustrous skin patchy with the black sickness of plague.

When she emerged, her eyes were black orbs, and she held a skull-headed rattle that spoke of her purpose with more clarity than all the words of Babel—a death rattle. She came to Enlil's palace in Nippur, casting aside his servants and trained Nephilim warriors with vicious blows from her long-handled rattle.

"Who did this to my son?" Ereshkigal asked as she stormed into Enlil's throne room.

Lord Enlil was sitting in his throne being fed figs in syrup by a scantily clad human female. She appeared ugly to Ereshkigal's eyes, too thin, too smooth.

Enlil peered up from his delicacies, eyeing Ereshkigal warily. "Mathematician," he said, addressing her but somehow making it sound like an insult.

"Don't 'mathematician' me," Ereshkigal spit, swiping

at the apekin attendant with her rattle. The human woman went crashing to one side, skull caved in.

Enlil was standing then, his arms up to defend himself. "Ereshkigal, you are clearly upset—" he began.

Ereshkigal knocked him back with her death rattle, and Enlil found himself sitting once more in the throne amid a disarray of cushions. She held her hand out before her, chanting the words of the mathematical equation that could stop his heart, tapping out the rhythm on the rattle. Enlil felt it twinge, a jabbing pain in his chest as if he had been stabbed with a spear.

"My son," Ereshkigal hissed, standing over Enlil, "was poisoned at your banquet."

"Namtar?" Enlil looked surprised. The pain in his chest burned like lit oil.

"Yes!" Ereshkigal repeated. "My son."

"*Our* son," Enlil corrected. "But who—"

"Is this another of your wretched schemes, *my lord*?" Ereshkigal spit, delivering the epithet like a curse, the way he had called her mathematician. "Kill your child as you did to Ullikummis when he failed you?"

Enlil looked aggrieved, shaking his head heavily despite the agony in his chest. His heart would not beat. "No."

Ereshkigal stood over him with the death rattle raised, ready to rain down blows that would turn his haughty skull to pulp. But she stopped.

"Namtar posed no threat to me, Ereshkigal, no challenge," Enlil said, squeezing the words from breathless lungs. "I had…no cause…to hurt him. As…the child's… mother…you must…know that."

"Then why?" Ereshkigal snarled.

Enlil looked up at her through hooded eyes, the vertical slits of his irises narrowed to the finest of lines, like pencil marks on a plan. "You say that Namtar was poisoned?" he asked, checking the facts.

"Yes, his skin is ravaged with great black welts," Ereshkigal confirmed, "the scarabae sickness." Scarabae was a disease that only afflicted Annunaki, a kind of skin cancer that was fed by the direct rays of the sun.

"Nergal has been researching such things," Enlil explained, choosing not to reveal that he was doing so for him. "Why he would…do such a thing…I cannot say."

The fury in Ereshkigal's black eyes was like a raging inferno. "Look about you," she finally growled, muttering a few words under her breath. Enlil felt the pressure in his torso ease, felt his heart beat again at last, a great thud against his chest walls. "You see the brilliance of my mathematics. Control over everything—even the endless Annunaki."

She stormed from Enlil's chamber, seething with anger. A human retainer who was bringing water with which to wash Enlil's feet had the misfortune to step in Ereshkigal's way as she reached the twin, golden doors to the throne room. Ereshkigal said the other words then, the ones that triggered the hidden response in apekin's bodies, their minds. Enlil watched in awe as the human keeled over, heart stopped, brain ceasing to function.

Once Ereshkigal left the throne room, Enlil immediately left his throne and trotted across to join the fallen retainer, clutching at his own chest where his heart had been halted for over a minute. The human was dead. That Ereshkigal could do that to one of the apekin, could also now do it to an Annunaki—where would it end? The prospect filled Enlil—fearless Enlil—with trepidation.

THE WRATH OF gods is a horrifying thing to behold. In its aftermath, all fifty-seven apekin who had served Nergal lay dead, as did the six Igigi who had functioned as his researchers.

Nergal stood in his laboratory workplace struggling to control his breathing as Ereshkigal came for him, striding through the mounds of corpses, her skull-headed rattle sweeping before her to clear the bloody way.

"You killed them," Nergal stated with incredulity.

Ereshkigal stood in the lone doors to his laboratory, leaving him with nowhere to run. "Apothecary," she said, "heal thyself!"

And with that she threw the skull-topped staff. It sailed across the room, spinning over and over before slamming against Nergal even as he tried to get clear of its path. He dropped to the floor, whining with pain.

Ereshkigal stalked across the debris-strewn laboratory toward Nergal, kicking him hard in the guts over and over. Then she reached down for the fallen rattle-staff, plucking it up as the physician leaked blood on his once-clean floor. Ereshkigal picked up the rattle and raised it, ready to club Nergal over the head.

Nergal said something then, spit between desperate gasps. "I…didn't…know…he was…your son," he said.

"Does that matter?" Ereshkigal hissed. "He was my vizier, he was due your respect as representative in my place."

Nergal looked at her from where he was doubled over in pain on the floor. "They say…that…Enlil…is his father," he gasped. "I did it…because…of him. His…interference—" His words trailed off, the pain too much to work through.

Ereshkigal lowered her death rattle very slowly, her eyes scanning the mess that had once been a research laboratory. Enlil held her in his power. He owned the land where her own research facility was located. He took her as a mate when he wanted to, indulged her studies at his whim. To have an ally against him would prove useful.

"Can you fix the damage you have done to Namtar?" Ereshkigal asked.

"Can you…bring my…servants back…to life?" Nergal countered.

"Yes," Ereshkigal said, surprising and horrifying this master of plagues, "though you will not need them where we are going."

They left the laboratory together. To prove her fidelity, Ereshkigal raised Nergal's dead, though they lacked that essential spark that they had had in life. It was still an awesome demonstration of how much she had learned about death and its reversion.

In later years, Ereshkigal's words would become known as spells, but they were not that—they were just mathematical sums; sums that involved rhythms and logic that only one of the eternal race could comprehend.

Nergal joined Ereshkigal in her underworld kingdom beneath the banks of the Euphrates, developing his plagues for the day that they might utilize them. He knew better than to trust her, however, recognizing that strand of madness that lay within her. Her adherence to pure logic had corrupted her just as anything else might have when imbibed in vast quantities.

Chapter 33

The present, twenty-five miles south of Zaragoza

Ereshkigal was emerging from the pool in her temple, blood streaming from the curves of her body, piercing Kane with her dark, lizard slash eyes. All around, the voices of the beyond-dead choir were rising in their funereal dirge, unidentified words echoing from the walls.

"Círculo alrededor del cuerpo. Guarda silencio a moverse más," Ereshkigal chanted, the words echoing across the cavern-like space of the blood temple.

Kane stumbled at the words, dropping to one knee. He felt crushing doubt begin to take hold inside him, a weariness with life, with all he had seen, all he had done. So many faces flashed before his eyes—the faces of people who he had killed, lives he had cut short or negatively affected forever. So many hates built up, so much sadness he had left with his actions.

Distant now, a background bed of sound like the rushing sound of a river heard from several fields away, the voices of the choir of the dead droned on, embedding their dirge in Kane's thoughts the way the church bells had penetrated the minds of the people of Zaragoza, the way the death rattle had penetrated Enlil, focusing his mind on the words that Ereshkigal uttered.

The world will be better off without me, Kane realized as Ereshkigal's words droned on, echoing through the chamber.

And in death you shall know new joys, something seemed to answer, a voice inside him.

Ereshkigal was still striding toward Kane, her mouth continuing to form the eerie words of her chant.

"Gire vida lejos. Gire aliento. Abrazo fauces del inf—" she sang, the words trilling from the walls, the ceiling, the floor.

Kane's Commtact was translating Ereshkigal's words automatically, in fractured bursts ripped through with static as if it could not quite pluck her words from the air. It sounded like nonsense, and then the translation was cut short by Brigid's urgent words piping directly into Kane's ear.

"Kane, it's Cáscara—" Brigid cried. "I think she's—" The communication cut abruptly.

Ereshkigal was standing at the edge of the pool now, ripples of blood swishing around her calves and ankles, glaring at Kane in something that looked to be either anger, surprise or a mixture of both.

"Die," she said as the sounds of her grave-crossed choir rose and fell like the ocean waves. *"Matar a ti mismo!"*

"Sorry, babe, I don't speak Spanish!" Kane replied, lifting his blaster and firing. The doubts had left Kane the very moment that Brigid's words had been piped into his ear canal, and he had known, instinctively, that he needed to clear his head, stop this psychic attack the only way he knew how. With a shot.

A bullet came rocketing from the muzzle of Kane's blaster, crossing the cavern in a fraction of a second and drilling into Ereshkigal's left shoulder, just beneath her shoulder bone.

Ereshkigal was knocked back with the blow, shrieking in agony as she tumbled backward into her pool in a flurry of bloody feathers and awkward limbs. The choir's voices swelled.

Kane primed a flash-bang he had pulled from his pocket in that moment—his last—before letting it roll from his hand.

Ereshkigal's second Terror Priest, Namtar, emerged from behind a pillar at the same moment, charging at Kane with a staff in his hand. The staff was a re-creation of the long-handled death rattle that she had used millennia before, when Namtar had been a retainer for his mistress and mother Ereshkigal. It featured a skull atop its crest. Namtar swung the heavy staff-rattle at Kane even as the Cerberus warrior turned to face him. Kane took the blow badly across the shoulders, sinking to his knees again with a blurt of pain.

From the steps above, at the head of the stairs, Grant and Shizuka hurried to help Kane, shouting a warning that was lost in the cacophony of Ereshkigal's echoing splash in the pool of blood.

"You are dead, little man," Namtar growled in Spanish as he loomed over Kane, brandishing the staff, "and you'll never know the joy that you could have achieved."

At that moment the flash-bang exploded, filling the cavernous space with a sudden burst of light and sound.

With his head reeling dizzily and his eyes narrowed against the dazzling burst of light, Kane kicked, clipping Namtar across the ankles even as the servant to Ereshkigal brought the heavy rattle down at his head. The rattle missed Kane's forehead by less than an inch, crashing against the point where the side of his head met the floor with an echoing clang, clipping him hard as the choir wailed on. Kane dropped suddenly out of consciousness like a bullet train entering a tunnel.

Grant had reached the foot of the steps by then and he leaped for Namtar, reaching for him with his left hand even as he aimed his Sin Eater up to blast him. Namtar reeled back as the first bullet struck him in the center of his chest, dropping the razor disc he had secreted in his free hand with a clang of metal. Then Grant struck him, tackling him like a football player. Both men went crashing to the ground, six feet away from where Kane lay trying to gather his wits on the shores of the pool.

Shizuka followed Grant down the curving stairs, dropping a flash-bang in the face of Tsanti, the fallen Terror Priest whom Kane had met on the steps, as she hurried past his recovering form. Shizuka kept moving, leaving the flash-bang to erupt behind her in his face in a dazzling burst of light. Her attention was on the female figure who was just recovering from her fall into the pool of blood.

Ereshkigal emerged once more with blood pouring over her body, the tail of feathers turned red with the blood. She looked angry, her eyes now black-on-black lizard slits, her skin became the reptilian armor of the Annunaki. But there was a dark depression in the skin just beneath her shoulder blade where Kane's bullet had struck. The choir wailed on, their eyes screwed tight, their mouths taut in words that seemed to cause them pain to sing.

Ereshkigal had imbibed the genetic material from the pool through her own pores. Her transformation into Annunaki was almost complete, and now she was close to invincible—only the bullet wound marred her beautiful, rippling scales.

"Death to your world," she snarled in a tongue not spoken on Earth in over four thousand years.

Shizuka ran to meet her, swinging her sword from behind her in a long arc. As she reached the side of the pool, Shizuka's sword came around to slash Ereshkigal across the chest, cutting upward in a lethal strike.

Ereshkigal met the blade with her left arm, deflecting

it in a shower of sparks as the metal struck her armored flesh.

Shizuka grunted at the impact, twisting her body aside as Ereshkigal's right hand came darting up to grab her. Ereshkigal's hand snatched Shizuka's leg just below the knee as she tried to leap away. Shizuka suddenly found herself dropping face-first to the floor. She landed at the edge of the pool, blood lashing across her face and chest.

Ereshkigal still had hold of Shizuka's leg as the samurai warrior twisted, trying to strike a blow with her sword. The razor-keen katana whipped against Ereshkigal's leg, clanging as fire-forged metal met with alien skin as strong as it was. Shizuka groaned, feeling the blow resonate in her wrist as the blade met the unmoving limb.

Then Ereshkigal spoke again, chanting those eerie words in Spanish.

"Círculo alrededor del cuerpo,
Guarda silencio a moverse más.
Gire vida lejos,
Gire aliento.
Abrazo fauces del infierno."

Shizuka sank back to the ground, the pain of the physical attack too much. There was something in her mind, too, a kind of black cloud pressing against her thoughts. The black cloud had something within it, a deeper blackness, an absoluteness that was hard not to feel drawn to. Shizuka felt desire rise for that absolute darkness, craving it with all her heart. But no—she shook it away, forced it from her mind. That death would be dishonorable when there was a foe still to vanquish.

Ereshkigal kicked Shizuka across the jaw then, knocking her to the ground beside the pool. Shizuka drifted into blissful unconsciousness, the dark thoughts receding like the tide.

The choir around the pillars wailed once more, voices harmonizing in a kind of awful note like an animal in pain.

ACROSS THE DARK space of the temple, bullets and punches flew while razor discs cut the air. Grant emptied his Sin Eater's clip in Namtar's black-scarred chest before turning his prodigious strength on the Terror Priest. Namtar fought back, slashing Grant across the thigh with a blade.

With a cry of determination, Grant punched Namtar in the face again and again, watching in grim satisfaction as the reborn Annunaki servant sagged back against the ground, unconscious. Then he turned to face Ereshkigal as she strode toward him, her jagged crown of bones looming above her in some sick parody of a halo.

"Time to finish this, you snake-headed bitch," Grant muttered, raising the Sin Eater to target Ereshkigal as she strode toward him. But before he could pull the trigger he felt something strike him from behind, right between the shoulder blades. He sagged down to his knees with a cry of pain, spots flashing before his eyes as he sank into the pool of blood.

Pretor Emiliana Cáscara was standing at the top of the staircase leading down to the chamber, her Devorador de Pecados pistol held steady in her hand from where she had shot Grant in the back. "Wait!" Cáscara called, her voice echoing across the vast chamber.

Ereshkigal looked up at the sudden intrusion, bemused by what was occurring.

"You are Ereshkigal, are you not?" Cáscara asked.

Ereshkigal nodded once.

"It is said that you control death and the hereafter," Cáscara said, bowing her head and staring at her feet in humble servitude. "If that is true, then please, I beg you, bring my partner back to life. Let Juan Corcel live again." As she spoke these last words, Cáscara reached behind her and pulled Corcel's dead body from where she had dragged it into the temple and propped it against the tunnel wall. "Please. I will readily give my life in return." Wincing, Cáscara bowed down to her knees before the Annunaki goddess, holding her head down until it almost touched the floor that looked like leaves.

An alligator's smile crossed Ereshkigal's lips, predatory and inhuman. "You would give your life regardless," she said in whispered Spanish. "The bargain is worth nothing. Unless…"

Cáscara peered up through her drooping bangs, hope fluttering in her heart. "Unless, Your Eminence?"

"Do you know where there are more apekin?" Ereshkigal asked. "More…people?"

"I do," Cáscara replied.

"Can you bring them to me?"

"It…is possible." As a Pretor, Cáscara could enter the other walled cities of Spain and use her authority.

Ereshkigal's smile grew wider. Her formulas, her perfect mathematics needed testing, there was still so much she might learn, so many equations still waiting to be balanced. She could control death, yes, and the human body, too, commanding growth spurts that made limbs longer, stretched torsos beyond their natural limit with sufficient genetic input—sucking another's blood, for instance. But to have control of a world of apekin, to manipulate them with mathematics would take the one thing that Ereshkigal did not yet have—stability of body. When Papa Hurbon's agents had planted the seed that had formed her, Ereshkigal had emerged imperfect. Her body required a genetic infusion—blood plasma—to remain mobile, otherwise it would deteriorate and die. The other, the dead Pretor, could be revived to serve as one of Ereshkigal's Terror Priests, spreading the joy of the beyond-death. As for the woman…

"This shell is incomplete," Ereshkigal mused aloud as she stared into Cáscara's eyes with her hypnotic orbs. "It decomposes where it should hold intact, the formula is out of balance. I seek completion, balance.

"If you will offer yourself, give me the keys to that, then I shall grant what you ask."

"You'll make Juan live?" Cáscara asked, not comprehending—or thinking about—the other words that Eresh-kigal had said.

Ereshkigal just stared at the Pretor, waiting for her reply.

Cáscara nodded. "I accept."

And so are deals with devils made.

Chapter 34

Ereshkigal waved her hand toward where Cáscara was bowed, encouraging the woman to stand with a gesture. There was a patch of decaying blackness above her breasts where Kane's bullet had buried itself, the armored skin turning rotten like metal rusting away. Cáscara stood, then began to limp her way uncomfortably down the staircase to meet with Ereshkigal on the shores of the lake of blood. All around, the voices of the wailing choir rose and sank.

"What do you need from me?" Cáscara asked, gazing up at the taller woman whose dusky skin was ridged with the trace of lizard scales.

"All that you were," Ereshkigal said. Then she reached forward and pressed her hands against Cáscara's temples, gripping her so tightly that Cáscara grunted with pain. Ereshkigal's next words were in the ancient tongue of the Annunaki, pan-dimensional words only whose sibilance touched our plane of being, just as with her impossible formulas for death. The Annunaki were multidimensional, existing on many planes at once, beautiful when seen entire, like Julia Sets.

The next thing that Cáscara felt was a kind of warmth deep inside her, welling up from her core. The warmth turned to hot, to scalding. Her eye sockets hurt, her head began to pound and suddenly she cried out in pain.

"You may not fight it, apekin," Ereshkigal told her. "You must give willingly for the transfer to bond."

Ereshkigal continued speaking the words of hypermath, the high-end mathematics that bonded the universe and all its living things together. To Cáscara they sounded like a song, one barely remembered from childhood, the earliest memory of all. The song's words were lost on Cáscara but she knew the rhythm—it was the beat of her mother's heart when she was sleeping inside her womb.

Cáscara's body glowed with heat, shining like a star within the cavernous flower.

A single moment. A second; a day; a lifetime. The thing that had once been Emiliana Cáscara withered away and what was left was an empty shell, a body with no content, no mind to power it. Position vacant.

And then Ereshkigal took control of the empty shell, shunting her life into the woman's body, becoming Cáscara where Cáscara was departing, absorbing all she was. She would be doubled momentarily, a human suit to wear and to puppet.

WHEN GRANT HAD been shot in the back he had fallen into the pool of blood. He was still conscious, however. The shadow suit beneath his clothes had deflected four-fifths of the impact of that 9 mm slug, turning what should have been a devastating blow into just a glancing one. He would be left with an impressive bruise, but better that than a grave marker.

He was in the blood pool, lying on the shallow edge where the steps disappeared down beneath the surface. His head was tilted to one side and there was blood washing in his mouth. His body wanted to give up, to just take five minutes to relax, to shake off the effects of the battle but he knew there was no time.

Just a few feet away, he could see the radiance emanating from Cáscara's body where Ereshkigal stood before her, channeling her life essence through the other's body to absorb its genetic content, to reinforce her own body and make her whole, to bind the human to her. Ereshkigal was saying something. It sounded like a kind of chant. In the back of his mind, Grant knew that Brigid would have an explanation for all this—one that involved ancient myths and highfalutin physics—but just now he figured what he needed to do was stop Ereshkigal any way he could.

The radiance from Cáscara felt hot against Grant's side, even from feet away.

He reached out with his left hand, grabbed Ereshkigal by the ankle, and yanked her off her feet. She shrieked with surprise as she sank to the deck, landing at the pool's edge with a thud. As she crashed to the floor, her grip on Cáscara loosened and the glowing Pretor came tumbling past Grant and into the pool.

Grant pulled Ereshkigal closer, using his grip on her to drag himself out of the pool before drawing his right arm back. He still held his Sin Eater in his hand, thrust it against Ereshkigal's forehead and depressed the trigger.

Nothing happened. The gun sputtered weakly, blood running down its sides.

The blood in the pool, Grant realized. It must have gummed up the works. It would be a matter of minutes to dry it off, clean the gun, but they were minutes he did not have.

Beneath him, Ereshkigal shrieked again, leaning forward and beginning her wicked chant. It was the chant that could drive a man to suicide, that could shut down the human body in a matter of moments.

"Círculo alrededor del cuerpo,
Guarda silencio a moverse más—"

Grant grabbed one spoke of Ereshkigal's crown with his left hand, using it like a lever to push her face away from his, even as she grabbed for his wrist. Grant shoved as hard as he could, drawing on depths of strength he did not know he had.

"—*Gire vida lejos,*
Gire aliento—"

Grant shoved, driving Ereshkigal's head into the blood pool that lay beside them. The pool was getting hotter, had started bubbling where Cáscara's star-bright body had toppled into it. All around, blood was steaming in wisping vapor trails, casting a ferrous tang to the air.

"*Abra—*" Ereshkigal's words were cut off as her mouth went under the surface.

Ereshkigal struggled to get out, but Grant fought back, throwing a powerful haymaker that struck her jaw, even as he used the spike of her crown to force her under the pool again.

The pool was getting hotter. Grant could feel it against his knees where he knelt in the liquid, even through the protective weave of the shadow suit. The shadow suits were designed as environment suits and were able to regulate a wearer's body temperature, but even they had limits. Where his legs touched the pool, it seemed as if they were being lashed with a hot poker, burning right down to the marrow.

Ereshkigal emerged once again from the pool, her eyes black orbs. Her hands reached for Grant, grabbing at his collar. But Ereshkigal was no fighter—she was an academician, a student of mathematics and logic.

Grant grabbed her spiny crown with both hands and used it to force her under the surface again, holding her there as the red liquid boiled all around them and the choir wailed on. He held her for a long time as she struggled against him, ignoring the burn against his legs.

Grant kept Ereshkigal's face beneath the pool's surface while Cáscara's body decomposed in a burning pyre of whiteness. The pool of blood boiled, its surface bubbling like soup on the stove, and as it did so Ereshkigal's body was flayed alive. Grant's shadow suit gave him some protection—enough he hoped—while he held the Annunaki under the surface until she stopped fighting him. It took minutes, but they felt like hours.

Grant's muscles ached by the time he was done, he had been straining for so long. But when he finally stepped away, the thing that was Ereshkigal reborn was as dead as her own sick creations.

Chapter 35

When Grant finally looked up, Brigid was waiting at the top of the staircase leading into the chamber, standing beside the dead body of Juan Corcel. "What happened?" she asked, her eyes scanning the vast alien landscape and its occupants.

"It's over," Grant told her, trudging away from the pool of boiling blood.

He made his way across to Shizuka, whose unconscious body was sprawled against one of the walls, crouched down and spoke softly to her until she awoke.

"Grant-san? What…?" she began, confusion reigning on her pretty face.

"Kane took a nasty blow to the head," Grant told her. "I'm going to have to carry him."

BRIGID REMAINED AT the top of the steps, where Corcel's dead body had been left by Cáscara. Grant picked up Kane and, with Shizuka covering him, made his way up the staircase while the choir of the dead droned on. Brigid had her TP-9 ready to cover him, but it was unnecessary—nothing moved in the chamber apart from the ripples on the pool; everything else was dead. Even the choir was not a threat—presumably they would sing until they decomposed.

Outside, night was falling. The sky was beginning to darken and a crescent moon was already visible low to the horizon. The air felt markedly colder than it had just an hour before.

The Wheelfox waited twenty feet from the entrance to Ereshkigal's temple, its headlights on, enough to dazzle the newly dead. Its driver's door was wide-open. Brigid explained how Cáscara had knocked her out, using the butt of her gun to coldcock her. "I tried to warn Kane," Brigid said, glancing at his sleeping body where Grant carried him over one shoulder. "I figured that Cáscara planned to do something stupid from the way she was talking. I guess we didn't realize how attached she was to her partner."

"She's gone now," Grant said grimly. "Burned down to nothing."

Brigid shook her head in bewilderment. "I can't begin to imagine," she lamented.

"Ereshkigal was trying to say something when I held her under the...water? Blood? I don't know what it was," Grant explained.

"The music, the words," Shizuka mused. "It all meant something, didn't it? Like an instruction for everyone within earshot. An instruction to literally curl up and die."

Grant rested Kane's dozing form gently in the rear seats of the Wheelfox before turning back to Shizuka and Brigid. "Is such a thing possible, Brigid?" he asked.

"Hypnotic suggestion," Brigid said uncertainly, "is one way to make people behave in a manner wildly at odds with their personality, and it's the only thing I can think of."

"And if Ereshkigal was an Annunaki," Shizuka pointed out, "then what might such a hypnotic suggestion entail?"

"Good point," Brigid mused. "They fooled the whole world into believing that they were gods once—a kind of mass hypnosis by consensus. So I guess anything is within the realms of possibility."

"Anything," Grant repeated dourly.

Shizuka rubbed him gently across the shoulders. "And we'll be ready for it," she assured him. "Ready for anything."

ZARAGOZA HAD SURVIVED. There were pockets of resistance, people who were not susceptible to the mathematical spell that commanded men's bodies to destroy themselves. Some had been rounded up and killed by the followers of Ereshkigal, but many had hidden, barricading themselves inside the great monuments of the city—the Basilica of Our Lady of the Pillar cathedral and the Aljafería Palace—old structures that had survived world wars.

The revived dead lost purpose when the church bells stopped ringing, and after a few hours without sustenance they simply ceased to function, unable to draw any more energy from their rotting bodies to power tired limbs. In total, the city lost an estimated fifteen hundred people in a single hour, but given the circumstances it remained a triumph.

The Pretors had been decimated, however, and the strictures of law and order took a backseat to common sense and man's infinite capacity to share and to help his fellow man, to survive. The dark days of the Deathlands were long behind them, but people still remembered the lessons that dark period of history had taught them — that survival at any cost was not really survival at all.

Ereshkigal's temple was left untouched, for there was little that the Cerberus warriors could do without ground explosives or an air strike other than to warn people away. Cáscara's body burned itself out within the pool of collected blood, fizzling there like potassium in water for a very long time until it had simply disintegrated to nothing.

Ereshkigal's two retainers—or Terror Priests as they were known—Namtar and Tsanti—were rounded up by a Cerberus pickup squad led by Domi three hours after Kane's team had exited the temple. She found them still inside the temple, walking in aimless circles as they waited for instructions from their dead mistress. Domi's squad—CAT Beta—carefully captured them and brought them back to the Cerberus redoubt for incarceration, where they could be questioned and studied.

BACK AT CERBERUS, once everyone had had a chance to recover, the field team sat down to consider what had happened in Spain. Kane's head was bandaged where he had been struck with the staff, and Brigid's wounded ankle had been properly dressed, but everyone was getting back to normal. Shizuka joined the group known as CAT Alpha on the plain outside the redoubt's massive, rollback doors, accompanying Grant at this impromptu meeting spot as the sun rose over the valleys of the Bitterroots.

"Some vacation, huh?" Grant said as Kane, Brigid and Domi filed out from the dark recesses of the redoubt and onto the sandy plateau.

"One to remember," Shizuka replied pragmatically.

"Think it's one I'd prefer to forget," Grant said. He looked up as Brigid approached, catching the woman's emerald eyes. She was limping from her twisted ankle, but she looked less drawn. Painkillers working miracles, Grant guessed. "You figure out anything yet?" he asked.

Brigid shook her head. "Nothing much, just assumptions and guesswork really," she admitted. "That chant she was reciting—I translated it. It translates as something like this.

Circle around the body,
Be still to move no more.
Turn life away,
Turn breath away.
Embrace Hell's gaping maw."

"Embrace Hell's gaping maw," Kane repeated with disgust. "Cheery kind of poetry, huh?"

"I think it's a kind of instruction," Brigid said. "I spoke with Reba, while she was bandaging my foot—" Reba DeFore was the staff physician for the Cerberus redoubt "—and she agrees it's possible to use some kind of hypnotic suggestion to make people take their own lives."

"But why didn't it affect us when we heard it?" Shizuka wondered.

Brigid shook her head. "I...don't know," she admitted.

"Spanish," Kane said as he found a jutting rock on which to sit. "I don't speak it, nor does Grant. Shizuka?"

"No," Shizuka confirmed.

"See, we rely on our Commtacts to translate in these situations," Kane reminded everyone, "but—I never really thought about it until now—they wouldn't properly translate those words that Ereshkigal chanted. Like they were, I dunno, unable to affect to the translation software."

Brigid shook her head with uncertainty. "That's all well and good, but I can speak Spanish, Kane," she said. "So I could understand the words. I've just proven that."

Kane looked up at her thoughtfully. "Is translation the same as native tongue?" he asked.

A smile slowly crept across Brigid's face. "No, I guess there are differences," she admitted. "The act of translation involves an additional step in the brain, albeit a very swift one for someone fluent in a second language."

"But there is a step," Kane said, holding his hands out before him and widening the gap between them as if to demonstrate, "a jump that needs to be crossed mentally."

"I guess," Brigid agreed reluctantly. She hated it when Kane out-thought her.

Domi looked up from where she sat cross-legged, sharpening her knife, a broad smile appearing on her face. "Brigid, I think Kane just out-logicked you," she said.

"Maybe," Brigid said with a tight smile. "Hypnotic suggestion, if that's what it was, can also affect different people in different ways. Early reports from the mop-up crew suggest that not everyone in Zaragoza was affected."

"This went deeper, though," Grant said. "From what I saw, the bodies of those affected were just kind of turning on them. Some of them, anyhow."

"Maybe we'll never know," Shizuka admitted.

"One thing we do know," Kane reminded everyone, "is that the Annunaki *were* dead. Let's not forget that. So where did Ereshkigal come from?"

"I guess Hell's maw opened wide and eschewed her," Brigid proposed, "but maybe it didn't do so by itself."

The allies were solemn then as they considered Brigid's words. For a moment the atmosphere seemed very, very grim.

Shizuka stood after a moment, turning to face Grant. "You promised me dancing on our vacation, Grant-san," Shizuka reminded him.

"Yeah," Grant agreed. "I guess I did at that."

Shizuka stood with hands on hips, challenging him. "Well?"

From across the plateau, Domi clapped her hands and shouted encouragement, "Dance!"

Kane and Brigid took up the rhythm, clapping in time with Domi in a kind of fast polka.

"None of you are going to sing, right?" Grant checked. Then, reluctantly, he stood before Shizuka and executed a low, formal bow, taking her hand. Then, while Domi, Kane and Brigid clapped out a rhythm, he and Shizuka danced on the plateau outside the redoubt, beneath the rising sun of the new day. Whatever was out there could wait, at least until the dance was over.

Epilogue

Somewhere in the overgrown wilderness of Louisiana, in the *djévo* located underground within an abandoned military redoubt, Papa Hurbon was reading through the Zaragoza report. He read it twice before looking up at his comely companion. It had not been satisfactory. Over a thousand had died, yes, but the dragon's tooth seed had failed to take root, or to branch.

Hurbon frowned regretfully as he handed the report back to Nathalie so that she could file it for him. She had created the report from ground observation, two days after the occurrence itself.

"Much to consider here, Nathalie," Papa Hurbon said as he handed the report over.

"It did not go as planned, my beacon, my guide," Nathalie lamented.

"No," Hurbon agreed. "But these are early days, the first salvos of an advance. Considered purely as a proof-of-concept test, this worked admirably."

Nathalie's brow furrowed in confusion. "Ereshkigal died before she could complete her plan," she said.

"The seed planted, new life emerged," Hurbon corrected her.

Nathalie looked uncertainly at Papa Hurbon where he sat amid his totems in the imperfectly mirrored room beneath the earth. Hurbon glanced up, saw her expression and smiled his broad, toothy smile, reminded of an ancient refrain.

"A man who slits throats has time on his hands," Hurbon assured her.

* * * * *

COMING SOON FROM

GOLD EAGLE®

Available June 2, 2015

THE EXECUTIONER #439
BLOOD RITES – *Don Pendleton*

When rival gangs terrorize Miami, Mack Bolan is called in to clean up the city, but the mess in Florida is just the beginning. The drug trafficking business is flourishing in Jamaica…along with the practice of voodoo and human sacrifice.

STONY MAN® #137
CITADEL OF FEAR – *Don Pendleton*

Able Team discovers that Liberty City, an economic free zone in Grenada, is a haven for building homemade missiles. Phoenix Force arrives just in time to provide backup, but the missiles have already been shipped to a rogue group with their sights set on the California coast…

SUPERBOLAN® #174
DESERT FALCONS – *Don Pendleton*

In the Kingdom of Saudi Arabia, a secret group is plotting to oust the royal family. Their next move: kidnapping the prince from a desert warfare training session outside Las Vegas. Mack Bolan must keep the prince safe—but someone in the heir's inner circle is a traitor.

Available July 7, 2015

THE EXECUTIONER® #440

KILLPATH – *Don Pendleton*

After a DEA agent is tortured and killed by a powerful Colombian cartel, Bolan teams up with a former cocaine queen in Cali to obliterate the entire operation.

SUPERBOLAN® #175

NINJA ASSAULT – *Don Pendleton*

Ninjas attack an American casino, and Bolan follows the gangsters behind the crime back to Japan—where he intends to take them out on their home turf.

DEATHLANDS® #123

IRON RAGE – *James Axler*

Ryan and the companions are caught in a battle for survival against crocs, snakes and makeshift ironclads on the great Sippi river.

ROGUE ANGEL™ #55

BENEATH STILL WATERS – *Alex Archer*

Annja uncovers Nazi secrets—and treasure—in the wreckage of a submerged German bomber shot down at the end of WWII.

CNMGE0615

"I'd say it's just about ready to get serious," J.B. said, sounding more interested than alarmed.

Krysty looked back. The people who had gone on board the barge to fight the fire in the fabric bales were scrambling back across the thick hawser that connected the hulls. She was relieved and pleased to see Doc trotting right across, as spry as a kid goat, holding his arms out to his sides with his black coattails flapping. Despite his aged appearance, he was chronologically a few years younger than Ryan. The bizarre abuse and rigors the evil whitecoats of Operation Chronos had subjected him to had aged him prematurely, and damaged his fine, highly educated mind. But he could still muster the agility and energy of a man much younger than he appeared to be.

Ricky came last, straddling the thick woven hemp cable and inch-worming along. But he did so at speed.

Avery had vanished. "You and Mildred best head for cover," Ryan said.

"They'll only hit us by accident," Mildred said, "shooting oversize muskets at us."

"They're going to have a dozen or two shots at us next round," J.B. said. "That's a lot of chances to get lucky."

"Looks like some smaller fry are heading this way," Ryan reported. "Krysty, Mildred—*git!*"

"Come on." Krysty grabbed the other woman's wrist and began running for the cabin. Though Mildred was about as heavy as she was, Krysty barely slowed, towing Mildred as if she were a river barge. She was strong, motivated and full of adrenaline.

Krysty heard Ryan open fire. Given the range, the bobbing of the approaching lesser war craft, and the complex movement of the *Queen*—pitching fore and aft as well as heeling over to her right from the centrifugal force of the fastest left turn the vessel could manage, she doubted he'd be lucky enough to hit anything significant.

The women had almost reached the cabin when the next salvo hit, roaring like an angry dragon. Krysty saw stout planks suddenly spreading into fragments almost in her face.

And then the world vanished in a soundless white flash.

Don't miss
IRON RAGE by James Axler,
available July 2015 wherever
Gold Eagle® books and ebooks are sold.

GEDLEXP123